MW01488769

Praise for Denise Tompkins's
Legacy

"A perfect blend of humor, suspense, and nonstop action kept me glued to the pages of *Legacy*. The intricate plotting made it hard to detect the villain which made for a surprise ending. I hated for this book to end and for a debut book, that is saying a lot."

~ *Fresh Fiction*

"*Legacy* was a bundle of fun with the thrill of having the lead character be a paranormal-type Sherlock Holmes."

~ *Seeing Night Reviews*

"Strong dialogue and excellent character interaction engross the reader... The world created by the author feels real, and the mystery is intriguing. And lest I forget, the romance while not the main point of the novel is still scorching! This is Ms. Tompkins's debut novel and all I can say is brava!"

~ *Romance Reviews Today*

Look for these titles by
Denise Tompkins

Now Available:

The Niteclif Evolutions
Legacy
Wrath

Legacy

Denise Tompkins

SAMHAIN
PUBLISHING

Samhain Publishing, Ltd.
11821 Mason Montgomery Road, 4B
Cincinnati, OH 45249
www.samhainpublishing.com

Legacy
Copyright © 2012 by Denise Tompkins
Print ISBN: 978-1-60928-787-0
Digital ISBN: 978-1-60928-511-1

Cover by Kanaxa

This book is a work of fiction. The names, characters, places, and incidents are products of the writer's imagination or have been used fictitiously and are not to be construed as real. Any resemblance to persons, living or dead, actual events, locale or organizations is entirely coincidental.

All Rights Are Reserved. No part of this book may be used or reproduced in any manner whatsoever without written permission, except in the case of brief quotations embodied in critical articles and reviews.

First Samhain Publishing, Ltd. electronic publication: October 2011
First Samhain Publishing, Ltd. print publication: September 2012

Dedication

This dedication has to be shared between several important people in my life. First, my everlasting love and gratitude must go to my husband, Jay. Without your support and encouragement, I wouldn't have taken this first step.

A special thank you goes to my parents who, despite it all, have continued to love and support me throughout the years.

I want to thank the members of my writers' group—Betty, Lenny, Paulette, Paul, Sabrina—for their feedback and encouragement. Without each of you this book wouldn't have come to life like it did. Betty, I owe you extra thanks for going above and beyond.

Janna, thank you from the bottom of my heart for the long hours you put in. Your feedback and unwavering support have made me a better writer from the very beginning.

Prologue

I once heard someone say it's a good thing the world sucks or we'd all fall off. At the time, I laughed. Now I'm thinking of having it tattooed on my ass. Everything has changed for me in the last eleven months, and I'm so emotionally tired in the wake of the changes that I'm nearly dangerous to myself and others. My parents were killed in a train derailment. I had been an only child—now I'm an orphan. I no longer believe in a happily-ever-after that will last. Too many things, important and irreplaceable things, can be taken from you in the blink of an eye. In a moment of rash behavior I sold everything I owned, quit my stable, predictable job as a copy editor and decided to go to the United Kingdom for a solid month to try and rebalance my life. Total bug nut behavior if there ever was such a thing.

There's a strong pull to be there, in England. I don't understand it. It may have something to do with my dreams, dreams that are dark and disturbing. If nighttime is my enemy, sleep is my nemesis. There is a need to stand and commune with the past at the stone circle I see when I fall victim to sleep. There are aerial shadows that make me duck and run, skittering like a mouse from cover to cover, knowing I'm chased by something beloved yet deadly. There is something separate that moves among the forests of my mind like mist, never materializing enough to identify itself as ally or enemy. But it follows me, and in my dreams I shift away from it instinctively. Then there are the bodies. They weep the tears of the dead, holding out their hands to me in pleading supplication. They beg silently, mouths gaping, for help. I wake up screaming, terrified and full of a longing for the smell of London fog and the feel of Highland heather under my feet... Things

I've never known before, but that feel as familiar to me as breathing.

All I know for sure is that right now I need to be somewhere, anywhere, but here.

Chapter One

If sleep deprivation driving was an Olympic sport I'd be gold medaling tonight. Exhausted after so many sleepless nights, the effects of jet lag were a real concern. However I was determined that on my first day in England I would get to Stonehenge, damned roundabouts notwithstanding. There was no reason, valid or otherwise, that I *had* to see Stonehenge immediately. It was a draw, a pull, some inner-compass leading me there. Unfortunately that same compass didn't have a true north, so I was stuck wandering, chasing the famous megalith on a strange British map.

The sun had long since set, and the roads were inky paths bleeding black through the grassy hills and across the plains of Wiltshire. I hadn't passed another car in more than a half hour, and it was a lonely feeling. It was Mid-Summer's Eve, at least for a little while longer. According to the car rental clerk, a strange little man with violet eyes, it was a beautiful time to be here. We'd see about that when the sun rose, hopefully finding me having seen Stonehenge and finding my way back to my hotel in London. I thought it reasonable to assume I'd see it, satisfy this slightly obsessive inner draw, then come back later as a traditional, mentally stable tourist. I rounded a corner, lost in thoughts of feather-topped mattresses and 600-thread-count sheets, and I nearly missed it. I screeched to a halt and backed up, weaving like a drunk. I was gobsmacked at its size and beauty, by the subtle power implied by the huge stones set atop others like door lintels. Cloaked in moonlight and shadows, the stone circle appeared as it had in my dream and, though it seemed imposing, it still called to me like a siren's song. I parked the tiny car haphazardly on the edge of the small road, unfolded myself from the driver's seat and walked toward the stones.

A small, nagging pulse began to build at the base of my skull, worsening with every step I took closer to the standing stone circle. I shook my head, trying unsuccessfully to clear the fuzziness that descended. Pressure built until my ears needed to pop, and I worked my jaw to no avail. Still I moved forward. I stumbled when, in a moment of clarity, I remembered the stones been fenced off years ago to prevent just this sort of thing. *Perhaps something had changed*, I thought. *Perhaps.* My mind shifted to the dense shadows cast by the tall stones and my concern dissipated, a puff of breath in the cold air.

The night was silent save for the sound of the wind. It was clear and cool, bordering on cold, and my little windbreaker wasn't really jacket enough. I couldn't bring myself to leave, though, even to go back to the car for a heavier coat. I wandered among the stones, thinking about their history and mine, wondering what would be left of me after so long. Would I leave a mysterious legacy? Or would I crumble under the elements and disappear? The latter felt more likely.

I paced the circle and drew my fingertips over the weathered stones in no repeatable pattern as I walked this circle from my dreams. The intermittently clinging moss lent a random slickness that contrasted harshly with the weather-roughened stone. There was a sense of peace that came from standing within what I had come to think of as my circle. I trailed my fingertips around the largest of the standing stones and looked up. What an unbelievable night sky. The stars were so dense they made me dizzy. I stumbled to the altar stone and lay across it like the proverbial sacrifice. The alter stone was somehow smaller than I thought it would be, and, in turn, it made me feel smaller, insignificant. Tears slipped from my eyes unbidden, sliding passed my temples and into my hair, leaving cold tracks the breeze danced across. I felt broken, adrift. My parents had been my mentors and my very best friends. Losing them was a physical pain I wasn't sure I could withstand. Eleven months since the accident, and I still didn't know how I was going to live without them.

The night sky was so close it felt like I could touch the stars and pluck them one by one from the heavens. I picked one out of the infinity, a less brilliant one toward what I assumed was the south, and thought, *Starlight, star bright, first star I've chosen tonight...* Wouldn't it be cool if I could wish away my problems, my hurts, my reality? I could be someone else, here in this land of myth and mystery, and I could obliterate my past. I could be strong again, and quick-witted, with little fear of the unknown and a great sense for adventure. In three words— my old self. And what harm could wishing do, really? Urged on by memories of a sunny childhood and simpler days where nothing was impossible and I was loved unconditionally, I followed through and wished for just that—a changed reality. Love, unconditional or otherwise, would have to be a bonus the Fates would figure out because the loss of my parents had shattered my heart. With the smashing return of their memory my hope winked out. But my wish had been made. Things beyond my understanding were set into motion. I couldn't take it back.

Without any warning the stars spun, increasing in velocity, and the altar felt as if it tilted hard to my right. I dug my fingers uselessly into the stone, breaking fingernails down to the bloody quick. Bracing my feet against the end of the altar, I tried to hold on through this inexplicable rush of vertigo. I got incredibly nauseous and two spins from tossing my last American meal, the world stopped. I felt weightless for a moment and I heard the stones breathe, *"Adael i ddechrau."* *Let it begin.*

Why could I interpret that voice? I rolled off the altar and ran for the car like a drunk on a three-bottle bender.

I reached the little coupe and wrenched the door open, physically throwing myself inside. I slammed the door shut and locked it. Breathing hard through my mouth, I shook uncontrollably and felt like I couldn't get enough air.

I'm dreaming, sleepwalking. I have to be hallucinating—no other explanation than that.

The last sign I'd passed had promised me I was less than two hours from my hotel bed, and I decided I'd be damned if I wasn't going to make it back there. Surely a good night's sleep would cure my overactive imagination. I couldn't stop myself from glancing back over my shoulder at the standing stone circle as I turned the key and cranked the Mini's engine over. Standing near the altar, a shadow within a shadow, was a person. And that person was staring at me. I left a trail of burned rubber as I headed back to London.

The lights of the city danced over the car's shiny red paint as I drove past a handful of traditional tourist stops that were far from common—Kensington Palace, Parliament, Big Ben. I'd finally slowed when I reached the outskirts of the city. The farther I got from the standing stones the more likely I thought it that I had both suffered some sleep-deprived auditory and sensory delusions and imagined my shadowy observer. It was easier to convince myself of my temporary break with reality, too, since the shaking had stopped. I found my hotel and, after the night I'd had, chose to spring for valet parking. Being American, I was predestined to pull in through the wrong lane. The valet smiled indulgently, and I could tell he knew I was a foreigner. The Nikes, faded blue jeans and Abercrombie T-shirt probably labeled me an American just as much as my backwards driving did. Oh well.

"Good evenin', miss," he said, tipping his hat to me.

"Hi," I replied, smiling. I love how some British don't pronounce the Gs at the end of words. I handed him my keys and turned back to reach into the car and grab my laptop case out of the back seat. I noticed a folded up sheet of ivory-colored paper in the passenger seat. Huh. I didn't remember buying any paper like that. Maybe it was from the previous renter. I grabbed it, struck by its odd texture, and stuck it in my back pocket. I would inspect it when I was checked into my room and settled. I walked through the revolving front door and into the lobby, impressed that the travel website had actually been right about this place. It was lush. Done in white and gray Italian Carrera marble, the walls were washed in a soft gray with mahogany wainscoting all around. The ceilings had to be at least twenty feet high, and there was a small fountain littered with coins set in the middle of the lobby floor. The elevator doors were polished silver, not that tacky brass color that American hotels use. The furniture looked antique, though I would probably never be able to tell a reproduction from an original, even at gunpoint. The wood on the furniture matched the mahogany color of the wainscoting, but the velvet on the sofa was what arrested my attention. In deep, blood red velvet, it was the only primary color in the room.

I went to the long reception desk and presented my reservation.

The black-jacketed clerk looked everything over and took my credit card for incidentals.

"It's a non-smoking room, right?" I asked. All I needed after all this stress was an excuse to buy a hard-pack. I missed my cigarettes.

"Of course, unless you'd like to change?"

Oh cruel world, why do you mock me? Feeling more like a cocaine addict than a nicotine junky, I set my jaw and shook my head. "No, no change, thanks."

"Very well. Welcome to the UK, ma'am," he said with a smile, swiping the card and handing it back to me with an electronic room key imprinted with the Union Jack. "Enjoy your stay at the Pemberton. Just press star zero if there's anythin' we can do for you."

"Thank you," I said. I pulled out the travel handle on my laptop case and asked, "Will the bellhop bring my bags up tonight?"

"Of course," the clerk replied. "Do you need them immediately?"

"No. In the next half hour will be fine. Will you call up before delivery, though, in case I'm in the shower or something?" I requested, trying my best to not draw attention to my travel-ravaged hair or my wrinkled clothes.

"Of course," the clerk replied again, studiously avoiding looking at my bedraggled self. The guy gave great eye contact.

The manager, dressed in a fitted black suit, walked out of his office behind the desk and greeted me. "Hallo, Ms..." he paused, looking at my reservation, "...Niteclif. It's nice to have you with us. Wait. Niteclif? The American?" He looked at me expectantly, almost anxiously.

"Yes," I said, unsuccessfully stifling a yawn.

"There's a message for you." He disappeared back into his office. He returned quickly, carrying a message on ivory-colored paper. As I accepted it I realized it had the same look and feel as that that had been on the car's front seat. What were the odds?

"You must be mistaken." No one knew I was staying here.

"No, ma'am. I'm relatively certain this is correct as the gentleman who dropped it off earlier this evenin' was *quite* adamant that you receive his missive upon your arrival." He flushed, pulling at his collar. Either the guy had tipped the Manager well or he'd threatened him.

"Okay," I said. "I'll, uh, just take it to my room." I took the message and saw my name written on the front in an elegant black script—Madeleine D. Niteclif. The bellhop approached with my bags as I was about to comment on the red wax seal melted over the back flap and impressed with a serpent of some type. He tipped his cap at me in the same manner the valet had, friendly but formal. I decided that all of the ivory-papered messages in the world couldn't be as intriguing to me as the number of pillows on the bed. I was exhausted. So I thanked the desk clerk and manager again and, with the bellhop hot on my heels, headed to my non-smoking hotel room and a good, quiet night's sleep. Let's hear it for willpower.

Ten. That was the number of pillows on the heavenly bed in my room. Done in the same marble and mahogany as the lobby, with still-impressive twelve-foot coffered ceilings, the room was lovely. The walls were a complementing soft gray, with the floor-length curtains done in a dark smoke. But it was the bed that had stolen my heart. There were Celtic designs carved into the headboard and climbing vines carved into each of the four posts. The duvet was a white and gray striped silk, and there were solid white and gray throw pillows artfully arranged against the headboard. One blood red pillow was the sole splash of color in the room. On the wall, at the foot of the bed, was a plasma screen TV. There was a small writing secretary under the window, with an antique-looking chair sitting in front of it. I was in love with the whole room. I'm generally not a mystical-whimsy-and-throw-in-some-vines kind of girl, but the bed was so romantic, and I was in England and it all fit together of a piece. I'll admit, once, that I rolled around on the bed like a kid. Okay. Moving on.

I peeked into the bathroom, curious. If the bedroom screamed *I'm worth a fortune!* then this room quietly projected wealth; no screaming here. It was all Italian marble and polished chrome fixtures. Not modern, exactly, just elegant. The shower was a solid green-glass-walled enclosure with four fixtures and enough controls to launch a satellite into orbit. I would have to figure it out later. The bathtub was an old claw-foot tub made for soaking. There was even a telephone on the wall nearest the door.

The bellhop waited while I dug around in my backpack for my

wallet and I tipped him what I hoped was a decent amount. Then the bellhop surprised me by counting off a few notes and handing the rest back to me.

"This is more'n sufficient, miss. Wouldn' wanna cheacha or nuttin'," he said, bobbing his head. "Have a good evenin'." He gave me one last shy smile, and he was gone.

I clearly needed to learn my pounds from my silver or I was going to get screwed at some point. I'd have to worry about it tomorrow, though, because right now I needed a bath. I desperately wanted a shower but, like I said, the controls were going to take some non-sleep-deprived concentration. The tub? Simply run hot water. I could do that.

I made sure the security latch was thrown on the door, and I shed my clothes. Just being out of the grimy things made me feel better. I stood in the bathroom, waiting for the tub to fill up. The papers. I had forgotten all about the two pieces of paper—one from the car, one from the front desk—that I wanted to look at. But the tub was almost full.

They've waited all evening. They can wait a little longer.

I stepped into the hot water and sat slowly, leaning back and sinking almost to my chin. I could feel individual muscles begin to relax and I sighed, running my hands back and forth through the hot water, grateful for such a small pleasure. The water stung my broken nails a little, and I made a mental note to rub an antibacterial cream into the tips before bed. I could feel myself slipping off to sleep. As I didn't want to drown, I sat up and began scrubbing the travel grit off myself. I washed my hair, dunking it to rinse it out. I'd cut it pixie short before the trip so maintenance would be an easy task. Finishing the bath, I got out and toweled off. I reveled in my bare skin and, catching a glance of myself in the mirror, turned to analyze what I saw. I held my arms out parallel to the floor and looked at myself from all sides. I was tall for a woman at an even six feet. My waist was slightly indented above insignificant hips, which only served as a place to join my legs to my torso. My arms and legs were toned due to kick-boxing lessons, but they were still soft enough to be feminine. My breasts? All woman. I'm tall but not large, and thin but not runway model anorexic chic. My hair was naturally a dark brown bordering on black, my eyes a light green. I had always been easy going and generous with my smiles, with an open and accepting personality. I had even once been considered quick-witted by friends and co-workers. Of course, none of that mattered much anymore. Grief was my new moniker, and I wore it and bore its weight well. I sank slowly to the floor and watched as I disappeared from the sink's mirror. Disappeared. How appropriate. Curling my arms around my legs, I made myself as small and insignificant as I could there on the cold marble floor and I allowed myself to weep for my losses. Grief, rage, terror, longing, abandonment—they all poured out in an open cry of invocation to any deity who would hear me, but my spiritual phone didn't ring.

I pulled myself up off the floor, emotionally as well as physically thrashed. I treated my fingertips and crawled up into the highboy bed, yielding to the pull of sleep before my head hit the pillows. I began to dream.

Standing in an empty ballroom, I was wearing the most amazing gown. It was a sheath dress, which suited my tall figure well. Simple but stunning, it was done in a deep garnet color—a haltered number that highlighted my long arms and pale complexion. The slit on the side of the dress ran nearly to my hip and gave no question as to my length of leg or the fact that I was built like a woman. The lack of a true neckline combined with the plunging back made my neck appear longer, and left no doubt about my lack of a bra. I wasn't the type of woman who should, or really could, go without and I felt slightly self-conscious, even in sleep. My short, dark hair was tousled as if I'd just rolled out of bed. It was all sexy as hell, and I was talking about *me*. I've never thought of myself as beautiful, but in the dream I was. My only accessories were a large diamond pendant hung on a white gold chain and white gold wrist cuffs. I was barefoot.

I walked across the ballroom, the only person inside. Music played somewhere else, a waltz, and I wondered if I could learn to dance to it. I stopped and swayed for a moment then began to walk again, but this time my step was in time to the music.

"With only a little modification, my love, you've learned the steps," said a deep male voice behind me. I knew I was dreaming because I didn't spin around in fear. Instead I turned, focused on being graceful. Anyone who knew me would know that grace and I didn't have a long and happy history. Anyone who knew me...for one moment I thought of my parents and the ache in my heart was like a mortal wound, my shoulders hunching to protect my heart. Time froze for a moment, and then the pain loosed its grip, and I stood straight again under the heavy burden of my grief.

Oh the beauty of dreams. The owner of the voice stood close to me, clothed in a light blue silk shirt over faded out jeans. He, too, was barefoot. Odd, I'd never had a foot fetish before. But I did have a thing for tall guys, and this guy fit the bill. He was easily 6'7", with broad shoulders, lean but evidently well muscled as the shirt slithered across his shoulders and around his waist as he moved. It was almost like the shirt was a living thing, and my fingers twitched with the need to rub it between my forefinger and thumb. His hair was a dark brown, shot through with strands of gold and copper and it brushed the tops of his shoulders. He had a square jaw with firm, full lips, and gorgeous shaped eyebrows sitting on a perfectly proportioned face. But the eyes were what did me in. His eyes were an almost sapphire blue, dark with an even darker ring around the iris. How did I know? I'd drifted toward him as I took him in, almost as if he'd called me to him. I stopped. *Had* he called me?

"Only out of sleep, my love," he said, his voice hinting at the potential for a deep Scottish brogue. Oh sweet hell, I could fall for the voice alone.

I closed my eyes. "Say something else," I said in a cool, commanding voice.

He chuckled, an almost sinister sound that echoed in the ballroom. "Something else," he parroted.

My eyes snapped open. "Very funny." I glared at him. "This is *my* dream, so lose the pathetic humor and just stand there and look pretty."

"'Look pretty'?" he asked, incredulous. "Did you just tell me to look pretty?" His eyebrows rose, mocking my choice of words.

"I don't read romance novels, so I refuse to use the words burgeoning, smoldering, blazing, heroic, manly, or turgid in any of my conversations—even in my dreams. So yeah, look pretty. Besides, this is *my* dream. You shouldn't be provoking me."

"Is it your dream?" he asked, moving even closer to me. He

19

smelled like sunshine and night air combined right after a new rain. It was a mouthwatering smell. I leaned in to breathe him in since there are no codes of decorum in sleep.

He chuckled again.

"What?" I demanded.

"Already you're drawn to me," he said softly.

"Arrogant much?" I stepped back, agitated. He raised a hand to caress my cheek. In a move as natural as breathing, I laid my face in his hand and sighed, my irritation immediately forgotten.

The stranger's head snapped up, and he let out a low string of creative curses, dropping his hand. "I got here first," he growled, the sound reverberating in his chest.

"Ah, but the point is I *got* here." I turned toward him and gasped. The newest voice belonged to a prime male specimen. He wore a black suit, with a black silk shirt and cool European-style black shoes. He was the epitome of tall, dark and handsome, topping out somewhere around 6'3" and built like the statue David. His hair was black, a true black that I knew would have hints of blue in the sunlight. Pushed back from his face it hung past his jaw to his jacket collar and it was almost hard to see where the hair ended and his jacket began. His face was absolutely gorgeous, with sculpted cheekbones, dark brows and lashes that I would have considered literally killing him to get. His eyes were a bright light green, like new grass, and they were intense, focused on me and Mystery Guy #1.

"Did you think that a mere dream walk would keep me out, Bahlin?" asked the dark-haired man. "I am more powerful than that and, like you, I have a strongly vested interest in Madeleine's future."

"Maddy."

"Pardon?" tall, dark and yummy asked, turning his attention back to me.

"I go by Maddy. But if this is *my* dream, you should know that." I fisted my hands at my sides, the irritation returning as I recognized the sheer number of idiosyncrasies in my dream. It was like I didn't know myself very well at all, and it struck me that this whole dream sequence was, somehow, very wrong. "You know, I've never dreamed of two men arguing over me. That's ridiculous. Men, plain men, don't argue over me. You two Greek gods definitely wouldn't. Argue, that is."

"Greek gods?" Bahlin chuckled.

"But we're not Greek gods," said the other man. "We're—"

"No," roared Bahlin. "You will not reveal our true natures to her in a dream. Besides," he said, his voice cooling, "it's just a figure of speech. Right, Maddy?" With less than a thought he was standing at my side again, his chest nearly touching my right shoulder. I turned toward him slowly, like a flower turns toward the sun, because it must, when the other man approached me. He walked quickly but with the grace of a dancer. His approach stopped my turn to Bahlin, as I'm sure he intended.

"Then I shall introduce myself formally, at the very least." He moved lightly for such a large man. He bowed a very courtly bow in front of me and said, "I am Tarrek, First Prince of Faerie." He picked up my limp hand and kissed it, and the contact was electric, sending little jolts along my nervous system.

"Really? A faerie prince? That's odd. I can't figure out why I'd dream about the Tuatha de Dannan. I'm not into that supernatural, paranormal crap that seems to have taken over literature—okay, the world. Though I really do absolutely love Laurell K. Hamilton, and I did like Twilight, but..."

"Do you always talk this much?" asked Tarrek, curiosity evident in his voice, while still holding my hand.

"Hey! My dream, my altered reality." I took my hand back more forcefully than absolutely necessary. Something stuck in my head—*my altered reality.*

Bahlin chuckled from somewhere behind me and said, "At least you had a better response than being told to look pretty." He stalked around me with lethal, predatory grace and I was suddenly facing him too. He stood inches away from Tarrek and the tension between the two men nearly crackled, as if proximity made their dislike of each other even worse.

"Then I, too, shall formally introduce myself," he said. "I am Bahlin Drago, but you may simply call me Bahlin." He took my hand and bowed over it, but his bow was different, less deferential. "And the pleasure is all mine." He turned my hand over in his so that my palm

21

was facing up and he kissed it, lips slightly parted, slow and sensuous. A cool breeze blew through the room, ruffling the men's hair slightly. The wind carried the scent of Bahlin, and I was momentarily speechless.

"A pleasure for me, as well," I said, trying to recover some type of control over my behavior, but the harder I struggled to master myself, the less in control I felt. I began to shiver, disturbed even in sleep. I felt almost as if my thoughts were somehow being steered to influence me, though to what end I had no idea.

The three of us stood in silence, a tight living and breathing triangle. The tension between the two men continued to escalate until Tarrek said through clenched teeth, "We will not fight tonight."

"The choice may not be yours," Bahlin responded, fisting his hands at his sides.

"Stop," I cried, and I shot up out of sleep like a drowning woman coming up for air.

Disoriented, I looked around the bedroom and it took me a moment to remember where I was. I was drenched in sweat and the bed was destroyed. The duvet was on the floor, the silk sheets were pulled off the mattress, and the pillows looked as if I'd thrown them around the room in a fit of rage. Strange. I couldn't remember exactly what I'd been dreaming, but it didn't seem like it had been this disturbing. It definitely wasn't anything like the nightmares I'd been having prior to leaving home. Even the memories of those dark dreams made my stomach cramp with remembered fear.

Unable to sit still, I got up and began collecting pillows. I picked up the duvet and set the bed to rights. It took longer than I expected because the bed was so tall, but I got it done and crawled back in between the sheets. Seemingly impossible, yet true, I felt even more exhausted than when I'd first laid down. What had I been dreaming? The memory became more elusive the harder I chased it. It felt like it had been important. I slid back into sleep and for the first time in months it was, thankfully, dreamless.

Chapter Two

I awoke late that morning with a headache more indicative of the personal consumption of a bottle of Grey Goose instead of a simple late night bath and blurry dreams. I'm talking full-blown, head-pounding, wish-I-could-die-and-get-it-over-with pain. I stumbled into the bathroom, less impressed with its opulence now that my demise seemed imminent. I managed to dig out three ibuprofen from my travel case and dry swallow them. I was afraid even a sip of water would make me lose the meager remaining contents of my stomach. I longed for a cigarette, or even some second-hand smoke.

I made my way back into the bedroom and found myself grateful for the heavy gray curtains that were keeping the daylight at bay. I sat on the edge of the bed, waiting for the pills to take effect. When I became certain I wouldn't be sick, I lay down on my side and cradled my head on my arm. I again slept without dreaming.

The next thing I was aware of was someone knocking at my door. I slid off the bed, disconcerted, and slipped on the hotel's bathrobe, stumbling toward the door, running fingers through my bed-head. The headache had, thankfully, abated. I was curious but not alarmed about my visitor. Someone probably had the wrong room. I peeked through the fish eye and gasped, spinning around to press my back against the door, all vestiges of sleep gone in an instant. With a sudden rush my dream from early this morning came roaring back into my conscious memory.

My visitor knocked again, harder, and I jumped, making a disgusting *"Eep!"* sound that is generally restricted to startled women and stampeding sheep. I hate that. I took three large steps away from the door and spun to face it, more like I was dueling with the damn thing rather than contemplating my visitor on the other side. Maybe I was mistaken and this was another dream. I scrubbed my hands over my face, my heartbeat already beginning to slow. That only made sense. Now how had I woken myself up earlier? Something about—

"Maddy?" he called through the door, interrupting my train of thought. "I need you to open the door. There's much to do tonight."

How had he first invaded my dreams and, second, found me in person? And what did he mean tonight? I hadn't even been up for the day yet. I peered around the corner of the bathroom wall and looked at the clock on the bedside table. It read 7:07, but there was no a.m. or p.m. It was only logical that it was evening, though, since I'd woken up earlier today and been relieved the sunlight was blocked.

"Maddy? I know you're awake. Open the door, sweetheart."

"What do you want, Bahlin?" I asked, taking a strange leap of faith that I recognized him from that dream. Besides, I was curious and feeling brazenly safe on my side of the door.

Something that sounded like "Bleedin' faeries," came through the door.

"What?" I asked, confused. Clutching my robe to my chest, I crept closer to the door.

"Nothing. Look, open the door and we'll talk."

I stood there, undecided.

"It would be easier if you'd willingly open the door, sweetheart."

I kept the security bar on the door flipped closed and opened the door about two inches, my heart thundering in my chest, breaths shallow and fast. He was even bigger in the flesh. I began to hyperventilate and tried to slam the door shut. He shoved his giant sneaker-clad foot into the door and forced me to keep it marginally open.

"Don't make this difficult, love. Open the door so I can rightly introduce myself to you," he said, voice cajoling.

"Who. Are. You."

"You've already answered that, Maddy. I'm Bahlin, and you're about to be in over your head."

"Oh right. Get me to open the door by threatening me. Brilliant." I stepped away from the door, figuring that if I couldn't get his foot dislodged, the very least I could do was grab some clothes and lock myself into the bathroom while I dialed front desk security. I turned away from the door and heard it shut with a clear *snick*. My shoulders sagged a little bit. Thank heavens he was gone. Maybe I should call for security before—

The security latch flipped back with a *thunk* and the electronic lock hummed right before the door swung open. Bahlin stood in the doorway scowling, wearing the same outfit he'd been wearing in my dream, plus the shoes.

"What the he-hell—" I stuttered, eyes nearly bugging out of my head.

"I told yeh it would be easier all around if yeh'd open the door, woman," he interrupted, stepping inside the room and shutting the door. He shoved his hand through his hair, stalking into the room. "But no, yeh couldn't answer the door like normal folk. Just like yehr great-grandda yeh are..." He stopped at the small secretary, yanked out the chair and sat.

It was like my brain suddenly engaged and thoughts clicked into place: The dream? *Click.* The lock disengaging itself? *Click.* The door opening? *Click.* My great-granddad? I passed out cold.

I have no idea how long I was out. All I knew was that I came to with Bahlin leaning over me and pressing a cool cloth to my forehead.

"Gaaaa," I yelled, sitting up so fast I should have hit him in the face. He sat back on his heels, apparently anticipating my physical reaction to his nearness. My head was pounding again, but nothing like it had been before. I could live with this. Now, what exactly had happened? Oh, yeah, he opened the door from the outside and said something about my great-grandfather. In a rush of adrenaline, I crab walked backward, putting some distance between us and likely flashing my cookies in the process. He stayed squatted on the balls of his feet, watching me.

"Are you going to listen now?" he asked, voice much calmer, brogue much less pronounced now that he wasn't upset. What a shame. About the brogue, I mean.

25

"Listen to what? You confirm that you're a maniac? Got it in one, Bahlin." I crouched back against the bed, wedged into the side rails as if they could provide me with some type of protection. It was obvious, even to me, that I was thinking clearly.

"Did you not get my message then?" he asked, standing and walking over to the desk.

I cringed back even further, nearly shoving myself under the bed.

"I'll take that as a no." He sat in the chair and dropped his head in his hands.

"What note," I whispered, voice flat, eyes wide. I should have made for the front door, but in my panic to get away from him I'd put myself almost as far from it as I could have. Dumb, dumb, dumb. And then I remembered the two pieces of vellum-like paper that had come into my possession: one left in the car and one left here at the hotel.

As if reading my thoughts, he said, "I left a note for you at the front desk."

"I got it," I said quietly. "I just haven't opened it yet."

"What? Why the hell not?" His eyes flashed strangely in the lamplight as he shoved himself to standing and towered over me.

And it was then that I decided that if this lunatic was going to threaten me, I was going to give him a fight. I wasn't going to get killed my first day in a foreign country and become a statistic so easily. No, I was going to at least make him bleed. I shot up off the floor like I'd been launched from a catapult, and he took a fast step back. But not fast enough. My upper cut caught him on the chin, snapping his head back. The pain blossomed in my hand as if I'd hit a brick wall. I'd never hit anyone before and the satisfaction was gratifying in the face of my determination.

"Bloody hell, woman." He recovered before I could do more than turn to make a break for the door, and he grabbed me from behind. His arms were like steel bands wrapping around me and lifting me up off the floor. I'm no petite wallflower, so his strength was evident. I struggled, cursing him as actively, violently and creatively as I could. I kicked and struggled, but it was no use. He held me as if I were no more than a big load of laundry. It was humiliating.

"Stop," he commanded in a cajoling voice, and for a moment I felt like obeying him. Yeah, that passed pretty quickly.

"Up yours." I kicked some more, managing to wiggle an arm free, and I swung it down and back as hard as I could. Contact. He dropped me like a bag of grain, going to his knees and cupping his groin protectively, knocking the chair over as he went down. He bellowed with rage and was already getting up as I got away.

I sprinted across the room and went straight to the first open door I saw, the bathroom. I locked myself in and, breathing like a racehorse, I sank to the floor.

"Damn it all to hell, this is *not* happening," I said, gasping for breath. There was nothing in the bathroom to shove under the door handle, so I turned around and set my back against the door itself, bracing my feet against the marble floor. I grabbed the telephone and called down to the front desk.

"Guest services. How may I help you?" came a pleasant voice over the receiver.

"Call security. There's a strange man in my room and I'm afraid he's—"

"Open the damned door, Maddy. Now," Bahlin yelled.

"Ma'am? Do you require assistance?" asked the voice, now concerned, on the other end of the line.

"Screw you, Bahlin," I screamed at him, panting. "I'm calling for security."

He laughed, a dark and threatening sound. "Good luck with that, Maddy. Open the door, girl, or I'll be in there with you in a heartbeat."

"Ma'am? I'm sorry. I can't call security on Bahlin. I can only assure you that, unless provoked, he won't hurt you. Thank you for choosing the Pemberton. Have a nice evening." And the cultured front desk voice hung up on me.

What the freaking hell? What kind of hotel had I checked into?

I dialed back, and the same voice answered.

"Send security *now* you coward. You better get someone up here before I come down there and—" *Click.* He hung up on me.

I threw the phone across the bathroom only to have it careen back when the cord drew tight. Now *I* felt like the idiot. I sat there breathing hard and thought about what the front desk clerk had said. I wondered if punching Bahlin in the 'nads counted as provoking him? I was going to go out on a limb and say yes. And since I'd been advised he wouldn't hurt me unless provoked, and I had deduced he'd been provoked by my person, I was in deep shit.

"I'll ask yeh one last time, woman," Bahlin growled through the door. Uh oh. The heavy brogue was back.

Stalling, I called out, "What about the note? What's in it?"

The answer was an extended silence, and then I could hear him moving about the room.

"Where have you hidden the damned thing?" he muttered. It sounded like he was going through my things. "Ah ha. Here we are. What's this?" I heard him pull the chair back into its upright position. He groaned when he sat down. "I doubt I'll be able to function properly for a week." There was the rustling of heavy paper, then total quiet.

I sat with my back to the bathroom door, listening to him first mumble to himself and then sit in silence. How had this happened to me? First the recurring nightmares, then my delusional experiences at the stones, then the notes left in my car and at the desk, then the morning's strange dream, and now the evening's even stranger reality. It was all so farfetched it was unbelievable. But then, the notes were solid. I'd touched them. The dream was real. I'd recognized Bahlin and known his name. The man was real. I'd felt him. Using *modus ponens*, if this was tangible then it must be believable. Ergo, it was very believable. Wait. I was using logic to make sense of this? And where the hell had I come up with *modus ponens*? I began to shake. First the imaginary events at the stone circle and now this. I was losing my mind.

I heard footsteps approach the door.

"Maddy," Bahlin said softly, a complete change of character from only moments before. "Maddy, open the door. Please."

I didn't respond.

"Maddy, I *will* open this door, but I would prefer you do it yourself."

I stood, my muscles shaking from adrenaline overload and the fear of my apparent break with reality. I turned and put my hand on the bathroom door handle. If I believed what was happening, then I knew Bahlin could open this door. Even if he couldn't use telekinesis, he was strong enough to force his way in. I turned the door handle, pulling the door open and jumped back. He was leaning against the door jam, eyes closed, arms at his sides. I took a quick step backward, wondering how I would defend myself in such a small space. Hair gel to the eyes? Then I realized he was holding both pieces of vellum in one hand.

"You went through my *pants*?" I shrieked, realizing where he had to have found the papers.

"You weren't in them so don't screech at me," he answered, never opening his eyes.

I stood there, not sure whether to push past him and retrieve my clothes or stand in front of him, indefinitely, in my borrowed bathrobe. I chose clothes.

"Uh, excuse me for a moment."

He didn't move.

"Seriously, Bahlin, I want to put on some clothes before we talk about whatever was so important to you that you felt justified in breaking into my room, accosting me, and then digging through my pants." I turned to the side and squeezed past him; he moved back a small step. I retrieved the clothes I had intended to put on earlier—jeans, navy T-shirt, underwear, socks. I went back into the bathroom and started to shut the door.

"Leave it open," he said quietly.

"No," I answered, equally quietly. "I'm closing it. I won't lock it, because that appears to be a useless means of keeping you the hell out. But I won't leave the door open. Get your jollies somewhere else, asshat." I shut the door in his face, and he didn't stop me.

I dressed in record time standing wedged in the space between the edge of the bathtub and the hinges of the door. I'd chosen to leave my shoes out in the room because I figured if I took them, Bahlin would assume I was going to try to run. Good assumption. While I was in the bathroom I finger-combed my hair but skipped make-up. What was the point?

I walked back into the room and found Bahlin sitting in the desk chair again, leaning with his head back, eyes closed, hands folded across his stomach. He appeared relaxed if you didn't look too closely, but the tension radiating off of him killed the superficial impression. I sat on the edge of the bed farthest from him and closest to the front door. That he wasn't forcing the issue about me sitting closer to him was a good thing. It gave me a sense of control of the situation, however false it might be.

"I'm ready to read the notes," I said softly.

His eyes opened to slits and shifted to look at me. The rest of him stayed very, very still. "They're here on the desk." It was an open challenge to get near him again.

"Fold them back up and toss them over here." I wasn't about to get within an arm's reach of him without being forced, so he could toss the papers over.

"Afraid?" he asked, sitting up and looking at me in a predatory way.

"Cautious," I replied. "I don't know you, yet you've starred in a dream of mine, then you've shown up here and basically assaulted me. So yeah, consider me cautious."

"Why not try for the door then, sweetheart?" he asked in a snarky tone.

"I have a feeling you'd do some freaky telekinesis crap, and I'd be stuck anyway."

"Smart girl." He folded the papers up and, standing, leaned over a part of the bed. I stood and moved away from him, taking a couple of steps toward the door. But all he did was toss the papers toward me and sit back down.

I edged to the bed in small steps, watching him like a field mouse watches a predator circling the sky overhead. But he only sat and settled in the chair, waiting, it seemed, for me to open the two notes.

"Open mine first," he ordered, and I looked at him. "Please. It's the one with the wax seal."

I picked up the note, lifting it in unspoken question. He nodded and I broke the seal, opening the note. Written inside the heavy paper, in flowing script was the following message:

In the lobby
7:00 p.m.

I looked up at him and couldn't help but smile.

"You expected me to take this seriously? This is stalker material, and I haven't been here long enough to be stalked. Or to know anyone that would inspire me to respond by showing up." I snorted, dropping the note on the bed.

Bahlin stood up and growled, literally *growled*, from deep in his chest. "You do not get to mock me for trying to make this easier, nay *safer* for you. I made a promise, and I'll keep it."

"What promise, Bahlin? We don't know each other, you are completely unfamiliar to me, and no one knows me here, so there's no promise you could have kept."

"Read the other damned piece of paper and we'll discuss it." He dropped back into his chair with amazing, unnatural grace for a man of his size.

The hair on the back of my neck began to stand up and the skin underneath got hot. I suddenly didn't want to open the other piece of paper, but I've never been a coward (see above regarding the strange man with the aching balls in my room). I reached across to pick it up and open it. I must have been too tired yesterday to notice that my name was on the outside in small, neat print. I began to unfold the sheet of paper and time slowed to a crawl. I could see everything in slow motion, even Bahlin standing up from the chair as he moved minutely closer to me. Inside was a family tree, drawn carefully and in great detail, with the Niteclif name at the top. I looked at the tree, beginning with the bottom, but most of the names flashed by my eyes without meaning until I came to my name nearest the top, and all by itself, on a defined limb. *"Madeleine Dilys Niteclif"* was written in, with my date of birth and an open-ended date for death. I raised my eyes and looked at Bahlin, the question evident in my gaze.

"Look three generation down, and read carefully as you go," he said softly, almost with compassion. Strange.

I saw the names of my parents. Then I saw my grandparents' names, no surprise. Then I saw my great-grandparents' names. There was no surprise here, either, since my mom had been an amateur genealogist. Then I looked closely at my great-grandfather's name: Aloysius S. Niteclif, more famously known as... *What the hell?* Sherlock Holmes. Wait. Was he telling me my great-granddad was a famous 19th century fictional detective, not a real person? Why was he on my family tree? I knew Aloysius Niteclif as my great-grandfather, but no way was he some fictional icon. That was so far off the crazy scale that it had come back around to probable. No way was this even remotely—

Bahlin interrupted my internal ramblings, my thoughts scattering without pattern or reason. "Aloysius Niteclif was a great man, a great detective, in our world. But he became disillusioned with the constant battles, the killings, and he wanted out. So he met a mundane man that he liked and respected, and they struck a deal. This mundane man was an author, and he would write Aloysius's memoirs as if they were fictional tales with human characters and human mysteries. In return, Aloysius would give him a peek into the world of the supernatural. It worked well. Three men ended up immortalized, and Aloysius was able to purge his conscience without fear of recrimination." He paused to look at me. "Do you understand what this means?"

I was sitting there, the family tree hanging from my fingertips. *Did I understand?* Of course I did. Bahlin was a certifiable nut bunny. Oh good. How was I going to get out of here without—

"Maddy? Your middle name. What does it mean?" he asked, speaking slowly like he was trying to talk me off a ledge.

"I don't know," I muttered, looking at the family tree and seeing nothing but *that* name.

"In Welsh it means genuine and your last name, Niteclif, is a Welsh derivative of detective. It's a play on words. You are, quite literally, a genuine detective." He paused searching my face for reaction. "I'll ask again. Do you understand?"

"Understand?" I looked up at him. The family tree drifted from my fingers to the floor. *Let him down gently*, I thought to myself, but the words were out of my mouth before I could stop myself. "Understand what, Bahlin? That you're off your medications? That the men from your cinder block institution are looking for you? *That* I understand. This—" I waved my hand at the fallen family tree, "—this is nonsense. I cannot be related to a fictional character—"

"Whose stories were based on the real life of your great-grandfather."

I got up and began pacing the small area from the bed to the front door, nine strides forward and nine strides back. I never considered I could just leave once I reached the door. I was overwhelmed with this information, hungry for any sense of belonging now that my parents were dead. My parents... I spun to face Bahlin. "Did my mom and dad know?"

"Your father knew, as you're a direct descendant on his side. I spoke to him shortly before his death about disclosing your relation to Aloysius and its implications for your future. Your mother, as a genealogist, suspected something was off kilter in your history. But your father said they had never discussed it."

"There wasn't time," I whispered. No time before they died. My heart ached. I missed them so much. And I wanted to talk to my dad now, to find out if this unknown man's wild claims held even a grain of truth. I was so hungry for family that a small part of me hoped he was being truthful. He claimed he was a connection to a past I thought I had lost, someone who could share the sound of my father's voice with me.

Bahlin stood and walked slowly toward me, treating me like a skittish horse, hands out to show he was harmless, movements slow and precise, eye contact steady but non-threatening. I stopped, staring at him.

"Maddy?" he asked. "Are you okay?"

I held up a hand toward him, palm out and fingers pointed up in the universal sign for stop, and he did. "No, I'm not okay. This is cruel. You're not well, Bahlin—" I began, but he interrupted me. Again.

"Maddy, this is all true. I swear it."

"Stop. Interrupting. Me."

"I apologize. Go on with your previous thought," Bahlin said, shoving his hands in his front pockets. He looked contrite. Apparently he was going to let me work this out on my own. He sat on the edge of the bed nearest my current position, which was standing close to the bathroom door.

I rolled my shoulders, then returned my thoughts to the family tree. "If I'm a direct descendant of a fictional character—albeit one whose stories were based on fact—what does that make *me*?"

"Maddy, what have you done since you came here?" Bahlin's eyes burned with curiosity. He shifted on the bed, drawing one knee up so he could turn to face me.

"I've rented a car, driven to Stonehenge... Stonehenge. I made a wish, a wish that my reality would be altered..." Surely not. I mean, seriously, I made a *wish* as in star light, star bright, that kind of thing.

"You wished for an altered reality, sweetheart, and you got it." Bahlin looked almost sympathetic. He didn't move, but sat there watching me work out the details of what I'd done.

"So my wish, it changed everything?" I wracked my brain, thinking back to the stone circle and the compelling need to wish for a changed reality. I remembered the spinning night sky and the wind breathing a strange phrase through my mind. Could it mean...surely not.

"No, the wish didn't change everything," he said, standing and moving toward me.

I stood there, too overwhelmed with all of the information to move. He came close enough that he reached out and traced my jaw with his fingertip.

"Your wish made your old reality fade or, more accurately, become transparent, thereby revealing your direct relation to that most famous of detectives. In case the family history can't be passed on, it's the way of the Niteclifs. And historically there's always been a choice to be made." Bahlin scrubbed his hands over his face. "Your granddad and father both refused their legacy in order to raise their own families. But every third generation must accept by the age of thirty and pick up the mantle of service for a minimum of ten years. Certain skills are inherited to make this easier for each Niteclif. And now that there's only you, and you're also the third generation removed from your great-granddad. I'm afraid you've no choice in the matter." An unrecognizable look passed over his face. Sympathy? Compassion? Maybe it was pity. "But, Maddy, there's always a significant event that sets off the family tree when the verbal story can't be passed on. You've had two events. First, you lost your parents. Then you say you wished

34

upon a star, yes?"

I nodded.

"Do you remember which star it was?"

I arched one eyebrow at him and said, "Oh, sure, let me run out and point it out to you in the night sky. I don't have a freaking clue which one it was, Bahlin! I think it was in the southern sky, not too bright. That's all I know."

"And which stone circle were you at?" he asked, still standing right in front of me.

"I thought it was Stonehenge... How many are there?" Panic fed into my voice.

Bahlin reached out to stroke my face again, and I calmed a little bit. He drew his eyebrows together and stroked me again. "Dozens."

"Can I undo this if I get back to that stone circle?" I pulled away from his touch, desperation painting my voice. Maybe I didn't want to change my reality so much after all. I hadn't fit into my old life once my parents died; how was I going to fit into a new life here? Then I slowed down and thought about it. My parents were gone. No matter where I was, I was going to have to carve out a new spot for myself. There was no getting around that. Suddenly something Bahlin said earlier flashed through my mind, supernatural.

Bahlin, still stuck on my last question and not privy to the discursiveness of my mind, answered me. "I don't know that it can be undone without serving the ten years, Maddy. Maddy?" He had picked up on a change in my facial features, probably noticing they'd gone slack with confusion.

"Supernatural?" I asked.

"What? What are you talking about?" He looked confused, running both hands through his hair and pushing it off his face. And then understanding dawned on him. He turned and walked back to the desk, seeming to gather himself with every step. He sat in the chair, shifting it slightly so it faced me. "Let's work out the family tree issue first, yes?"

"Let's pretend I can make the stretch and believe that my great-granddad, Aloysius, is who you're claiming he was. Now go back to the supernatural statement. Explain it to me, please." My knees had begun to shake and the reality of one of the dream men showing up in person really hit me. I sat abruptly, jarring my spine as I hit the floor. Delayed reaction sucks.

Bahlin jumped up in a flash of movement, intent on coming to me, but I held up my hand again. He sank back to his seat with a small sigh and leaned forward, forearms on his knees, face tilted slightly to the side. "Do you believe in anything supernatural?"

I folded my knees to my chest and wrapped my arms around them tightly in an effort to keep myself from falling apart. I gave a rigid shrug.

"I'm serious, Maddy. Okay, do you believe in mythology?"

"I don't know," I said through clenched teeth. "I'm not sure which mythology you're referring to."

"Much of it in general." He had begun to look uncomfortable, his eyes finding anything to look at but me, and it was making me nervous. "For now, though, we'll focus on the Isles."

"The Isles?"

"The Emerald Isles—England, Scotland, Ireland, Wales. Because that's where you were pulled to, isn't it?" he asked as if he already knew the answer.

"I felt a need to be here, but I don't think it was supernatural. I think it was simply a need to get out of my old life." My death grip on my knees had rendered my hands numb, but I didn't let go. "But there were the dreams, the nightmares."

Bahlin's eyes flashed again, an otherworldly look passing through them that gave me pause.

"Nightmares?"

I shrugged and he let me have my privacy.

"Maddy, dreams or no dreams, you could have gone anywhere in the world but you chose to come here." He stared at me, and I shrugged stiffly again.

"So?" I asked a little belligerently.

"Back to the point. You must realize that much mythology is actually based in fact—"

"Right," I said, my voice quavering but the sarcasm still crystal clear.

"Do you think I'd lie to you?" He looked incredulous.

"I don't know you," I said through gritted teeth, and I pushed myself to standing, using the wall for support. I was thrown by all the what ifs in my life. What if I'd never come here? What if my reality had been changed with a wish? What if I was related to one of the greatest sleuths of all time? What if there was truth behind a lot of fictional tales? What if—

Bahlin interrupted my mental wanderings again. He was really good at the interrupting thing. "Maddy, I want you to sit on the bed. I'm going to prove a point."

"Uh, no. I don't think I'll get any closer to the bed, but thanks for the offer."

He rolled his eyes and stood.

"Don't take a step closer to me," I ordered, pushing away from the wall and fisting my hands at my sides and doing my best to ignore my watery knees.

"I won't have to touch you in order to prove my point," he said. His eyes flashed, pupils becoming elongated and the irises turning an icy blue nearly devoid of color.

There was a buzzing in my brain. *What the—?* I didn't manage to finish the thought.

The bones in his face seemed to shift and elongate, his head getting larger and his shoulders widening, his fingers curling into claws. Muscles moved in ways that no human body would allow. He grinned a huge grin, showing me sharp white teeth.

"Take a good look, Maddy," he said in a voice approaching a difficult-to-understand growl.

And I did, too...right before I passed out. Again. Crap.

Chapter Three

"I told you to sit on the bed," Bahlin muttered. My eyelids were fluttering, trying to grab hold of a good opportunity to open. "Bloody woman, crashing to floor with every shock. You'll never survive this…"

"Yes, I will," I whispered in an obstinate voice. "Don't tell me what I can and can't manage. You don't know me." I focused on his face, seeing the dark blue of his eyes once again.

He grinned down at me. It was then that I realized I was lying in his arms and across his lap. I started to make efforts to get up, but he held me down easily.

"Rest a moment, Maddy."

His skin was firm and hot, but not scaly like I would have expected following that little conversational sideshow. He was tanned, though, in a country where the sun only showed its face every fourth day. His eyes shown with a faint inner light that made me a little dizzy, and I wondered what he was trying to do.

"No mind games," I said, my voice sounding disturbingly far away.

"So you know a bit about dragons," he said, smiling. "Remind me to send Laurell K. Hamilton a thank-you note. Look, you've had a great many shocks in twenty-four hours, sweetheart. I can ease some of the stress if you'll only relax and let me in your mind." He stroked my forehead with two fingertips and my headache was almost instantly gone. Now that was a handy trick.

"Laurell K. doesn't write about dragons." I held up a hand weakly. "Question?"

He inclined his head, still grinning albeit less toothy than before my recent lights out episode.

"How can you be a dragon and a regular man?"

"Don't ever mistake me for a regular man," he said seriously. "I am a dragon first and always, but all dragons have an alternate human form."

"If you say so. What do you mean I need to relax my mind?" My breathing was still shallow, so I made a concerted effort to slow down and take deeper breaths. He hadn't hurt me yet. I was having such a hard time holding on to the thread of conversation, like more than one thought was too much to process. Maybe he was right and I *was* in shock. If so, at least it didn't hurt. And really, shock was about the only explanation for the fact that I hadn't become either wholly catatonic or completely hysterical at this point.

"You need to put down your natural barriers to my kind. It's a predetermined defense for Niteclifs, as it helps to keep a wide variety of supes from toying with your mind. But you can control it or you should be able to with some practice." He palmed the back of my head and turned it so I looked up into his face. "Right now, though, you're locked tight as a bank vault. It's how you've spanked me regarding telling you first to open the door and later to stop fighting. It's impressive in one so young into the Change." He grinned, gently squeezing my head. It felt good.

"Why does the Change sound so ominous?" I have to admit I enjoyed the eased headache. Maybe he would be handy to keep around for a while. He was better than ibuprofen. And think, if I locked my keys in my car, he could automatically unlock it for me. No need for Triple A. I giggled. A dragon public service.

"Maddy?" Bahlin looked down at me. "I don't believe you're going to have any choice but to let me help with the shock."

I guess my mental shields, or whatever it was keeping Bahlin out, were weakened by the night's revelations because he suddenly rolled over my mind like a wave coming into shore, crashing down and spreading through the sand. I had flashes of memories, both his and mine, and it was his memory of my great-grandfather that surprised me the most. I tried to hold on to it, but it was like trying to hold water in your hands—it slips away, and you're left with a memory. From him I got the impression of great affection and then it was gone. His darker memories, things that had nothing to do with me, moved away from my consciousness like mist and I couldn't hold on to them either. I had a vague impression of Bahlin meditating and coming into my dreams, and an image of my own where I was standing at the stones. It was all so strange.

I came to, if that's what you could call it, with Bahlin holding me close to his chest, his head bent over mine, foreheads touching. It was as intimate as a kiss, this sharing of memories.

"So." I cleared my throat to get his attention.

He lifted his head slowly and opened eyes that glowed a rich, icy blue. His breathing changed as if he were drawing in great lungs full of my scent.

I briefly wondered what he had seen in my pathetic life that had wound him up so badly. "So...can you please let me go?"

He stared at me for a moment and then seemed to shake from head to toe, like a dog exiting a body of water, bringing himself back into the moment. He stood effortlessly with me still in his arms and set me on the bed. His strength was amazing, and the fact that he made me feel petite was a total bonus. Not that I noticed too much.

"I apologize," he said.

"The trip through our minds thing, is that something you normally do for people...supes...whatever?" I asked.

"Ah, no, no it's not. It takes a lot out of me to sift through someone's mind and—"

"What do you mean by that? What did you see?" I demanded, hands involuntarily parking on my hips. I know it looked silly since I was sitting, but I couldn't figure out how else to express my indignance at his statement and if I stood it would put me too close to him.

"About the interrupting? It really is annoying. I'll quit if you do." He seemed a little bit unstable as he stood in front of me. He turned and stepped around the end of the bed, walking to the desk chair and eased himself, carefully, back down. "My stones are probably black and blue, you know. You pack a mighty punch." He grinned.

"Stop changing the subject, Bahlin. What did you see in my mind?"

He sighed, but he met my eyes with his own. "Grief. Your grief over the loss of your parents is profound. It's been a very long time since I've experienced such a raw emotion."

I stared at him, uncertain what to say. My grief was such a private thing that I felt like I'd been violated. At the same time, I wasn't sure how he could have taken a skip through my mental daisies without stepping in it at every stride. I knew my grief seemed to permeate every aspect of my life, so it only made sense that my thoughts weren't immune.

"I apologize if you feel I was out of line. I had no way of avoiding it." Sincerity poured off him, and I believed him but it still stung. Besides, I couldn't argue as I'd just thought the same thing.

"No problem," I said softly. "Just do me a favor and don't make a big deal out of it, please."

"Done." He shifted in his chair, trying to get comfortable. I must have really done some direct damage to make him so uncomfortable.

"I, ah, apologize for...well, smacking you in the..." I stumbled across the apology, and he smiled, showing a mouthful of sharp teeth. Or maybe that was my imagination.

"In the...?" he prompted, making me blush. "So that part was true, then." He seemed thrilled.

"What part?" I asked, hoping we had skipped over the apology. No such luck.

"Apologies first, sweetheart. You're sorry for smacking me in the what, Maddy?" he prompted, undeterred. He seemed to be getting his kicks out of this.

"The burgeoning manliness that your nether regions represent," I said, affecting a strong southern accent.

He laughed out loud, a full, rich sound that made me shiver. "I thought you said you didn't read romance novels."

"I had one forgettable adventure with that type of novel, and it was so generally bad that I had to put it down. Now I stick to the darker stuff. Or I did..." I fumbled the end of the speech, lost, and Bahlin looked almost sad at that little revelation.

I thought about what he'd told me so far and I wondered, *What would my life be like now? Who would I be now that I had all this information?* I fervently hoped bad romance novels wouldn't figure in anywhere. At the same time, I had read some Holmes novels and I was worried at the potential for violence and death as more than fiction. I didn't truly know what I wanted in that moment, so I tucked it away to examine later, in private.

"Now," I said, getting back to the conversation, "what part of what you saw are you glad is true and why did it make you so happy?" I'm nothing if not indefatigable.

"Did you expect me to follow that?" he asked incredulously.

"Come on, it's not that bad. Now give."

"It should be noted that it disturbs me that I understand you," he muttered. "Fine. The part of your mind that told me you're inexperienced with men, though not quite a virgin."

I blushed so hard I felt light-headed, and he laughed.

"Charming," he said softly, looking at me with hooded eyes.

"Get that idea right out of your head, Bahlin. I've had a couple of wholly forgettable experiences that...wait. Why in the world am I telling you this?" I threw my hands in the air and dropped them on top of my head, eyes closed as I regrouped. "Forget it. I want to talk about my great-granddad and this curse."

He sat up straight in his chair. "It's not a curse, Maddy." If I didn't know better, I'd think he was indignant. "It's an honor as well as an obligation."

My mind pinged all over the place. I couldn't seem to stick to any one topic, mentally or out loud, for any length of time. I was suddenly back to the statement he'd made about the obligation being a ten-year minimum commitment. How was I going to be able to keep up with my Visa payment if I couldn't get a job outside of this detective work? I had my inheritance, but that was my nest egg and it wouldn't last forever or, realistically, even ten years. And how was I going to be a detective, by default a fact-finder, when half the time I couldn't find my own car keys? A little voice in my head reminded me about my earlier use of *modus ponens* and the impressive fact that I had had any idea what that was. Twenty-four hours ago I probably wouldn't have been able to give you the definition much less put it into general practice. But now? It was something I'd have to live by if I wanted to make this work. And did I? Want to make this work, that is? I didn't know. I didn't even know if there was a choice to be made. But after my little mind swap with Bahlin, I somehow believed him.

"What skills did I inherit?" I asked.

"Pardon?" he said, all polite innocence now.

"You said earlier, before I hit the floor, that there were certain skills a Niteclif would inherit to make the job easier. What are they?"

"So you'll do it?" His eyes shone more than they should in the lamplight, that inner light sparkling like sunlight behind stained glass.

"Doesn't sound like I have a choice, does it, if every third generation has to pick up the mantle of service?" I felt slightly resentful that my life was about to be overrun. I also felt slightly giddy about the same thing. I wanted and had asked for something profoundly different, a change, an altered reality. Apparently that wish had been granted in spades. And I couldn't have excluded this as an option when I made the wish because I'd had no idea something like this was remotely possible.

"There's always a choice, Maddy. But if you refuse it, then the family history stops here."

His answer sounded ominous.

"What do you mean?"

He slid lower in his seat and laced his fingers together over his hard abs. "There are no other children, so you're it. No one else can pick up the mantle of servitude to the supernatural community. It means that chaos will reign and justice won't be meted out fairly."

"And what happens in between generations when no one takes responsibility for this job?" I asked, making little finger quotes.

He steepled his fingers together, putting his elbows on the chair's arms, and sighed. "The High Council hands down rulings and enforces sentences, but like your political systems, it's not without its own forms of influence and corruption."

I scooted on the bed so that my back was against the headboard, tucking my legs under me.

"So how do I change that?"

"Niteclif word is taken as general law. You are the ultimate voice for justice, and you are deferred to in all investigations. Your findings may be challenged by either the guilty party or any member of the High Council, but Niteclif logic has never failed."

"Ever?"

"Never, Maddy." Bahlin's eyes narrowed as he watched for my reaction.

My mouth was suddenly dry, and I couldn't generate enough spit to even swallow. No pressure. Then Bahlin looked at me, and that look from earlier passed over his face. There was something he wasn't telling me.

"Spill it, dragon," I said, getting a weird rush from calling out his species name.

"What?" he asked.

"Whatever you're withholding. You've made your plea for me to take the job. You've spelled out the most basic foundation in the history of job descriptions for me. But you've got tells. Your eyes get tight, giving your perfect visage little lines at the corner." I looked him over carefully and girded my mental loins. "Your eyes drift to the left, just over my shoulder, and you answer whatever I've asked without looking at me. You put your feet flat on the floor. You get preternaturally still in all other ways. Oh, and your head turns to the left, but only a bit." *Huh? Man, I was good, and I hadn't even tried. Maybe I could do this.*

He dropped his hands and, if a dragon could gape, he gaped. "Amazing," he muttered. "No one's called me on those points since Aloysius."

And then it dawned on me: Bahlin being here when I arrived at the hotel. Bahlin leaving a note for me. Bahlin invading my dream. Bahlin being relentless in his delivery of my family history. Bahlin's intimate knowledge of my great-granddad. It suddenly all made sense.

"You were his sidekick," I yelled. "You're Watson!"

"No need to yell," he said on a sigh. "Yes, I was. And yes, I am."

I stared at Bahlin, amazed at him. He was incredibly attractive, unarguably intelligent, and *way* older than I had estimated. Not early thirties by a long, long, *long* shot.

"I made a promise to Aloysius when he left his term that I would become the guardian of whoever took up the Niteclif service." Clearly resigned to his personal history having been outed, Bahlin wasn't remiss to speak. "By the way, you're the first person to make the connection between the fictional character and the man for either Aloysius or myself."

I wasn't so sure about the man comment. I didn't know enough about dragon mythology to know what they considered themselves. A different species? A sub-group? Humans with extra options, like a car with a sunroof and GPS?

I sat there looking at this creature in the chair opposite my seat on the bed, and I felt a strange empathy for him. He'd made a promise to someone he had obviously cared about, and he was bound and determined to keep it. But he'd given me an out, an opportunity to turn away from family history and obligation and he would honor my wishes. I don't know why, but this touched me. Was it his selflessness in the dereliction of a promised duty or the fact that he cared enough about the Niteclif name to want the legacy to continue? The word *honorable* whispered through my mind.

"How does it work if I accept the ten-year, uh, sentence?" I asked.

He never moved, never blinked, just stared straight at me, his mouth mostly hidden behind his resteepled fingers. It was like he was making a concerted effort to not reveal any of his thoughts now that I'd pointed out his little tells. I stared harder.

"Exactly how old are you?" he finally asked.

"Twenty-eight."

He sighed, dropping his arms to rest on the chair's arms. "The ten years generally begins when you turn thirty, but the catalyst of your family tree's revelation has already occurred. So, to be perfectly honest, I don't know when your ten-year sentence," he made little finger quotes, "would begin. Possibly upon acceptance, possibly when you turned thirty."

"I don't suppose there's enough empirical evidence to make an educated decision," I mumbled. I flinched, and knew then that I was wrong. The decision wasn't mine to make any more than it was to decline. I was already speaking in detective-ese. Fate had made me her bitch. Great.

Bahlin saw my flinch and leaned forward, dropping his forearms to his knees. He looked up at me as I was sitting on the tall bed, putting me a full head and shoulders above him. I could see his mind working, and it was evident he came to the same conclusion I did.

He stood, total grace in motion, and said, "Shall we go down to the lobby restaurant and get you something to eat or would you prefer to order something from room service?"

My stomach growled loudly at the promise of food. I hadn't eaten in more than thirty-six hours.

"About that," I began, then paused, unsure how to broach the tactless subject of money. I slid off the bed, the satin sheets sliding with me in a quiet hiss of noise. Bahlin deftly picked up the fallen bed linens and tossed them carelessly on the bed.

"Yes? You have a preference regarding your meal?"

"No, not really. It's just, this hotel was my one splurge. I'm here for a week, but I'm assuming I'll have to find somewhere to stay for the remaining three weeks while I work out how I'm going to fulfill whatever my duties are from the United States. Look, I don't know a delicate way to say this..."

"For the love of this country's Queen, woman. Spit it out."

"Can the attitude, Bahlin." I crossed my arms over my chest and leveled my best hard stare at him. "I can't afford to live large because you decide you want room service or whatever. I have limited funds, I've quit my job and I refuse to use my retirement account to fund this psychotic side trip."

He gaped at me, the second time in less than an hour. I was betting that this was a personal best for him because he didn't seem like the type to gape at all. "Maddy, there are things we need to discuss. I'd prefer to do them in public so that you don't crack my jaw again or render me a eunuch. So we'll do it in the dining room. Dinner's on me."

I was immediately defensive. "I don't do charity. I can swing dinner, surely, but you need to know where I'm coming from."

"Sweetheart, we'll talk about it over a nice red. Consider it a job perk."

"Stop calling me sweetheart," I muttered, moving past him and reaching for my sneakers. I slid my feet into the shoes and stood, finding myself face to face with him. I could smell his cologne again. It was the same as in the dream—both sunshine and moonlight, clean air after a rainstorm and something beneath it that was all Bahlin. No matter where in the world I ended up, the smell would always remind me of him. Wondering at my moroseness, I turned toward the door and he followed close behind. He reached around me and grabbed my room key before I could reach for it, his speed impressive.

"Show off."

He laughed and reached around me again to open the door. Stupid dragon hearing.

It was going to be a long night.

We rode the elevator down in silence and stepped out into the lobby. Tonight it was busier, with men in suits and women dressed from semi-formal to formal roaming about. I suddenly realized I was miserably underdressed and hunched my shoulders defensively, worried about standing out.

"What's the matter?" Bahlin asked. He put his hand on the small of my back and directed me with the slightest pressure toward the restaurant. I could feel his fingertips like a brand, and I fought the urge to rub against his hand like a cat. Instead I arched my back away from him.

"Oh, I don't know." My voice was caustic. "You've encouraged me to come to dinner in the Friday night equivalent of my jammies. Why would that bother me?"

He chuckled, dark and sexy. "I'm in jeans and sneakers. Not to worry." He winked at me. "I think they'll let us in." Bahlin approached the tuxedo-clad maitre d', and without a word the man picked up a pair of menus, pulled open the heavy doors and escorted us into the quiet hush of the restaurant. He led us straight to a private booth in the back without any verbal exchange, which I found odd given the foot traffic in the lobby. The booth was a high back, deep cognac leather and the table was the same mahogany color as the wood in the lobby. The walls were a gray so dark they seemed to absorb the light offered by the individual chandelier over our table and the candles held in the wall sconces. There were sliding brocade curtains to close off private booths intimately, lending a false air of privacy to the seating arrangement. It was romantic and slightly eerie at the same time. In fact, the vibe the place gave off left me with the uncomfortable sensation of being watched, and it took all my self-control not to rub the back of my neck in an attempt to dispel the feeling. I didn't like that the entire encounter with Bahlin left me jittery with nerves. Maybe food would help.

"I guess the hotel likes its color schemes universal," I said, settling into the booth. I tucked my feet on the bench to hide my battered shoes from the high-heeled crowd. The maitre d' casually laid a napkin across my lap first, Bahlin's second.

"Don't you care for it?" He settled in and stretched one arm across the back of his side of the booth.

"Sure. Who wouldn't?"

The maitre d' bowed and backed away. "Enjoy your meal, sir." He closed the curtains behind him as he left. Bahlin inclined his head in a very regal way, seemingly at ease in the environment. I was cowed, and disappointed in myself for it.

"So, let's get this out of the way. Money," he said, "is not a problem."

"Did you not hear me earlier? I don't do charity." I ground it out between my clenched teeth.

"Do you have a job?"

"No."

"Have you had a job before?"

Was he kidding? "You took a waltz through my mind. You tell me," I snapped.

"Having had a job before," he continued, as if I'd answered him politely, "you should recognize the characteristics of one. The primary being commitment. You're considering committing to being the Niteclif for the next ten to twelve years. What makes you think you wouldn't be paid for it?"

"I have no idea what the hell this job entails, Bahlin. You've been vague and ambiguous at every turn, answering my questions with your questions and giving me snapshots of weird shit that's supposed to make me feel better." I vibrated with energy. Fear? Anger? Frustration. Yes. "Why would I think it pays? And if it pays, I'm sure I'll be expected to..."

He arched a brow at me. "Stay here" went unsaid.

"Sure you will. How can you conduct inquiries into cases here in the Isles from across the pond?" He toyed with his knife, spinning it on point on the table. "So let's set this to rights. The High Council has always taken on the salary requirements of the Niteclif. What would you think to be a reasonable amount per annum?"

I mentally scrambled, then shot off a ridiculous salary six times greater than the job I'd left. Maybe I could get fired before I got started. Fired was better than dead, and it sounded like dead wasn't out of the question.

"Done."

Now I was the one gaping. "Plus housing," I added. Why not? "And a private car so I don't have to depend on anyone."

"Again, done. You'll live here at the hotel for the foreseeable future. Of course, you'll be moved into a more suitable room."

"Suitable how? And who are you to this place?" I asked recalling not only the maitre d's behavior but also the desk clerk's earlier refusal to call security.

"Why, I own it of course." He grinned wickedly, teeth flashing in the low light of the chandelier.

"Of course," I whispered. "Do they, the staff, know..." and I tapped my teeth first, then the corner of my eye.

The waiter appeared around the corner of the curtains and I jumped, but he was only there to present the bottle of wine. I looked at Bahlin, chagrined, and he laughed out loud. "The red, as promised."

I couldn't help but smile back. This was obviously going to take some getting used to. I ordered without looking at the menu assuming that, in a place like this, if they didn't have what I wanted listed, they'd come up with it. The waiter didn't even ask Bahlin if he wanted anything other than the wine.

"To answer your question, yes, the staff knows. More than half the staff are of the same general persuasion. Supernatural, or mythological, take your pick."

I stared at him, schooling my face into polite curiosity. Inside I was stunned and nervous as hell. "Dragons?" I clenched my hands together under the table hard enough that the bones ground together.

"A few," he said, smiling gently, "and a number of other flavors."
He leaned forward and reached for my hands under the table, tapping
them softly with his fingertips. "Relax. Nothing's going to happen to
you here."

I unclenched my fingers and made a show of setting them on the
tabletop.

"A few other flavors?" I asked in a voice barely above a whisper.
He nodded. "How many is a few?"

"That's an age old question, isn't it?" He settled into the corner of
the booth and cocked a knee up as if he didn't have a care in the
world. "Not many in the mundane world realize what we are. Humans,
or mundies, have a tendency to see only what they want to see and to
go about blind to the rest of their world. There are a few of them who
know about us, though I doubt anyone knows about *all* of us." He
poured us each a glass of wine, and I watched him swirl his in his
glass then sniff it.

"More on that later, okay? I need to process this and figure out
the details of the job." My voice sounded hushed in the elegant
atmosphere. I closed my eyes and prayed the fear was my secret, not to
be shared with the...dragon. I was back to being worried, my thoughts
and emotions ricocheting around at breakneck speeds.

Bahlin sipped his wine and looked at me, his eyes appearing
almost black in the dim light. "Let me sum it up for you very handily,
Maddy." He set his glass down and leaned forward, elbows on the
table. "There are a few things you'll have to know, and some we'll have
to figure out together because there's never been a female Niteclif."

I started to get indignant at the sexist comment, but he cut me off
with a wave of his hand. "There's no reason to argue—the past is
unchangeable. As for your job responsibilities and a few of the perks,
your job is to investigate crimes turned over to you by the High
Council. The Council is composed of representatives from five supe
groups in the Isles—vampires, shapeshifters, which dragons fall under,
witches and wizards, faeries and the smaller groups who lack
representation in any number." He paused to see if I'd react to the list
of supernatural creatures, but I managed—just barely—to maintain my
cool façade. "You will likely, on occasion, encounter unreported crimes
and you'll investigate those as well. You'll have to live here in London

during your tenure though you'll be paid, and handsomely, to do so. You will meet the High Council tomorrow night, so we'll have to go shopping to get you some more appropriate clothes, unless you've brought something besides jeans?"

I shook my head, mute with fear. *Five supe groups? I hadn't known about* one. *And how many were not represented in any large number?* Thinking of my college mythology class I felt a little light-headed. *No, you feel like passing the hell out again.*

Bahlin ignored the mental charades crossing my facial features. "Not all of the groups get along. In fact, none of us really like each other much. You'll have to learn some of the political maneuverings that have kept us well enough to keep from killing each other," he said, apparently attempting supernatural humor. It was too early in our relationship, and the bottle of wine, for me to even crack a smile. He sighed. "There's more, but I don't want to have to help you out of shock a second time tonight. I don't have the energy for it."

"Don't stop," I whispered. "I want to get the basics out of the way." Sort of. Not really. My stomach was clenched tight, nausea welling just below my surface of attention.

"Fine. You'll not age—"

"Say again," I commanded.

"You will not age," he said very slowly and with emphatic articulation. He arched a single eyebrow, silently challenging me to panic.

I was going to try not to give in to that fear and prove to him I could handle this.

"So I come out of this the same as I go in. Okay. Go—" I had to stop to clear my throat. "Go on. What about the skills you said I'd inherit, or that I may have already inherited?"

"It's hard to say, Maddy, but I can tell you what I've known of the last two Niteclifs. Your logic skills will improve dramatically, getting better with use, and this will sway how you look at everything. You must have balance there to keep yourself sane." He looked at me to make sure I was listening. I nodded, and he continued. "You will have a certain innate understanding of investigative procedures, as well as a general knowledge of crime scene protocol."

He paused, and I nodded again. "Okay. Sounds all right so far."

"You will find it easier to accept the supernatural world while shunning the human world, walking between both existences. You must work diligently to maintain your humanity and your reality. You can't afford to lose them or you may not find your way out of this dual existence. But you must be equally active in the world of myth and legend and at the same time always remember that you're not truly one of our world. It can be dangerous to forget that."

"Wait. Are you threatening me?" I demanded, setting my napkin on the table and making moves to stand.

He laughed, but it was bitter. "No, Maddy. Sit. But that brings up another point. There are consequences for both failure and success."

I emulated him by arching a brow.

"Fail to succeed and the High Council can order your execution. Succeed and your enemies can order your assassination."

I started to laugh and then realized he was serious. "Damned either way, huh?"

"Making it out alive will be the truest measure of success you can have."

I looked down, resetting my napkin in my lap. I didn't know what to say. It seemed that to say I was a condemned woman would not have conveyed heavily enough the situation. Bahlin mercifully continued, moving my thoughts on to the next point of consideration.

"You'll have a basic knowledge of fighting skills, and a sort of sixth sense about things, though you'll always end up backing that intuition with logic. Listen to your gut because, in my experience, it won't lead you wrong and your head will get there eventually." He grinned.

My head was spinning and I hadn't had enough wine to justify the dizziness yet. I intended to rectify that, especially if Bahlin could resolve a hangover as easily as he could a headache. But wine didn't seem a fast enough solution. Now a tall glass of whisky—that sounded more promising. I waved my hand in a circle indicating he should continue while I contemplated moving the curtain aside to look for our waiter.

"You'll be in contact with the High Council on a regular basis, which means—"

"That you should have invited me, old chap." The curtain parted and Tarrek, First Prince of Faerie, stepped through.

Chapter Four

He was even more luscious in person than he had been in my dream. Tarrek wore all black again, and his eyes gleamed an unnatural green in the low light. I realized the color was eating away at the pupil in his eyes as they filled with some sort of light, glowing softly with strong emotion.

Bahlin seemed unimpressed and looked back at me, essentially dismissing Tarrek. "I didn't know we needed a chaperone for our evening out, Maddy. My most sincere apologies."

Tarrek's eyebrows shot halfway up his brow. "Am I interrupting a date?"

"No," I said at the same time Bahlin said, "Yes." He glared at me. I glared back.

"We were discussing my role as the potential Niteclif," I said, assuming that if the guy really was the First Prince of Faerie he would know about my great-granddad.

"Ah, yes. There are some rules you'll need to know about from the fae side of things." He slid into the booth next to me, and I shifted so I could see him. He leaned over to kiss my cheek.

Bahlin growled, and Tarrek stared at him, a slight wind coming off of him and stirring the long hair of both men.

"Enough," I whispered harshly. Neither of them backed down. "E-nough," I snapped, and both men turned to look at me. I suddenly realized I was trapped up against the wall with two supernatural creatures facing off in front of me. How did I keep managing to get myself stuck in a literal corner around the monsters?

"One thing you need to know is that we are both High Council members," Tarrek said, turning back to stare at Bahlin. "Neither of us rule, though both of us attempt to lead."

"That makes no sense," I said, thinking through the little I knew of their behavior. "Is there not a leader for the Council?"

"Not per se," Bahlin answered vaguely, returning his gaze to me. "We are supposed to rule the supernatural world as what you would consider a non-partisan governing body. It's not a successful strategy. It's one of the reasons there are five of us. There's never a tied vote on anything. As we rarely agree on anything, some will vote against each other at times just for the sake of doing so. That's really all you need to know at this point, darling."

Tarrek looked at me and quirked an eyebrow at the easy endearment. I shrugged. It was just a word.

I thought back to what Bahlin said about my great-granddad—"he became disillusioned with the constant battles, the killings, and he wanted out." Suddenly it made more sense. I closed my eyes, wondering if the no-aging thing would matter if I got myself killed in the proverbial line of duty. The thought of my own death seriously disturbed me, and I realized that even in my darkest moments over the last few months, I had never been to the point where I was truly ready to die.

"Madeleine?" Tarrek asked. "Are you well?"

"Maddy, Tarrek. I just go by Maddy," I whispered. He reached out and touched my hair and the same chemistry flared between us that had occurred in my dream. He sucked in air and stroked my head, saying something in an unfamiliar language. For some reason I didn't feel compelled to pull away from him.

"What did you say?" I asked.

"I said that you are an angel in the mist, a flower's bloom on a starlit night, a gift from the goddess. I will trust you, my Niteclif." He slowly removed his hand, and I felt bereft at the loss of his touch. What was wrong with me?

I shifted slightly in my seat, uncomfortable.

Bahlin stared at Tarrek for a moment before speaking. "It's a bit early to be committing to the woman, don't you think?" He sounded hostile.

"No. I have touched her and felt her soul. She is an angel with a brilliant mind. I will trust her," he repeated, and it dawned on me the words might mean more than their face value.

"What does that mean, you'll trust me?" I asked Tarrek. For some reason he was easier to address than Bahlin.

"It means that I will defer to your word as law. I will accept your rulings to be fair and just." His eyes blazed at me for a moment, so fast I wasn't entirely sure I'd seen it.

And then time stood still just as it had at the stones. The hair on my body stood on end, and I gripped the edge of the booth with all my strength. There was no sense of past or present; there was no noise, ambient or otherwise. I felt suspended in motion. With a sigh reminiscent of the stone circle, I felt time begin again. With stunning clarity I recalled the phrase that the stones had whispered following the pause of time—*adael i ddechrau.*

"What just happened?" I asked through clenched teeth.

"Glory, Tarrek. Congratulations, my man," Bahlin hissed. Turning to me, eyes glowing icy blue, Bahlin said, "He's accepted you as the Niteclif. He's confirmed your place. It's begun, Maddy."

Oh shit. It was done. I hadn't completely resigned myself to the decision, regardless of the signs and—let's face it—the money, but apparently I'd been set into office by another's sworn oath of allegiance. Great.

Tarrek looked confused and then his face went completely blank with understanding. "Maddy, I'm sorry. I had no idea you hadn't already accepted. I assumed if you were sitting with Bahlin of your own free will, you were discussing the murders."

"Murders?" I asked weakly.

"For the love of your goddess, Tarrek, shut the hell up," Bahlin growled.

Tarrek whipped his head toward Bahlin, a snarl on his face. What had been handsome was immediately feral, the threat more than implied. "You do not rule here, dragon. Walk softly along this path lest it open beneath your feet and swallow you whole." His voice echoed, the candles on the table flared and Bahlin slid down in the seat, crossing his arms on his chest and appearing wholly unmoved.

"Gentlemen," I said softly, forcing them to turn and look at me instead of each other. "Let's not do this here. There may come a time and place where it's appropriate, but the mundanes in this room are pleasantly ignorant as to your dual existences. Let's keep it that way." The last was said with steel in my voice. I had no idea I had it in me, the ability to speak like that. Cool. "Now let's talk murder."

Bahlin had the kitchen plate my meal and send it up to room 2210, several floors above my original room. He also made arrangements as we passed the front desk to have all of my personal stuff moved up to that room too. I felt a little weird about people packing and unpacking for me, but he assured me it would be fine. He tossed my old room key across the front desk and ordered that a new key be delivered to my new room within the hour. We barely slowed down as we passed the desk, but his orders had staff scrambling to obey.

We were waiting for the elevator car to arrive when I remembered the phrase I'd heard. I turned first to Bahlin then to Tarrek and asked, "What does *adael i ddechrau* mean?" The phrase was fresh enough in my mind that I thought I had the pronunciation pretty close.

Bahlin, who had been watching the descending floor numbers on the elevator's display, turned to face me. A look of disbelief colored his face. "Where did you hear that, Maddy?"

I looked at Tarrek and found that he was watching me equally as close.

I shrugged. "I know it sounds crazy, but I heard it breathe through the stones the night I made my wish and then I heard it again tonight when Tarrek made his oath and affirmed me."

Tarrek looked away, apparently uncomfortable.

"Sodding hell," Bahlin sighed. "It's truly done then." He ran his hands through his hair again, and I realized this was something he did when he was frustrated and unsure of himself. "It's an Old World Welsh phrase that translates literally to 'let it begin.'" He turned in a tight circle and stepped around me, grabbing Tarrek by his suit lapels and slamming him into the elevator doors with a great thud. "Do you realize what you've done to her you damned faerie?"

I grabbed Bahlin's arm just as Tarrek muttered something below his breath and Bahlin's hands were literally thrown from Tarrek's arms. In the rush of what must have been magic, I was flung to the floor, sliding about fifteen feet before coming to a stop.

"Damn it all to hell," I muttered, trying to get my feet under me to stand up. "I'm already tired of this freaking weird shit."

Bahlin glanced at his palms.

Tarrek strode to my side. "I'm so sorry, Maddy. I had no idea you'd grab hold of him at that moment." Distress was evident in his every word. He reached out to help me up.

"Forget it, Tarrek." I watched Bahlin approaching Tarrek from behind. "In fact, both of you forget it. Now." I clasped Tarrek's hand and stood, realizing belatedly that we had a small audience of hotel and restaurant patrons. "Let's leave this alone, guys. We've garnered enough attention, don't you think?" I was flushed with embarrassment.

We all returned to the elevator door at the same time it dinged to let us know our car had arrived. We all studiously ignored the imprint Tarrek's body had left in the metal doors.

The elevator ride to the room was tense and uncomfortable. Both men were standing as far from each other as possible, with their bodies turned away from each other but heads tilted toward me. I was in the middle again, literally and figuratively. We exited the elevator and the first thing I noticed was that the doors on this floor were spaced out much farther apart than those on my original floor. We went to the end of the hall and stood outside the door of 2210. Bahlin looked at the door and I heard a familiar muffled *thunk* and then the door swung open.

Ah, a repeat breaking and entering performance. I'd seen this before.

Regardless, I was proud of myself for being able to walk into the room on solid legs, no shakiness here finally. I stopped inside the door in the foyer of the room. No, not a room, but rather a suite. It was huge. Not sure how to react to the opulence, I didn't. I followed the men into the room and stopped in front of one of the two sofas. One leather monstrosity faced a huge glass window that took in a view of

Big Ben and the Thames. French doors off the living room opened into a large bedroom with a king-size bed.

Totally uncomfortable, I slowly turned to Bahlin and whispered, "I can't stay here. This is too nice."

"Maddy," he said, walking to me and taking my hands, "you've got a lot to adjust to. The least the Council can do is provide this room, which is after all only a room, so that you're comfortable. Consider it yours as long as you'd like to stay. And room service is at your disposal, courtesy of the hotel." He looked at me, bending down to try and catch my gaze. I lifted my face toward his, and the concern I felt must have been evident. He brushed at the bangs hanging rag-tag along my forehead. I was touched by his small comforting gesture. He seemed genuinely concerned.

Tarrek cleared his throat. Stepping away from Bahlin, I turned to look at Tarrek. "You mentioned murder. I assume it wasn't for the conversational shock value."

Tarrek looked at me very directly then wandered to the sofa and sat, stretching out in apparent total comfort, one arm along the back and his right ankle propped on his left knee. He looked like a GQ cover model come to life.

"I thought you'd been affirmed, so I did broach the subject, yes," he said softly. "And again, I'm sorry for that. Would you like to wait until tomorrow to discuss this first case?"

I turned to look at Bahlin who had wandered to the wet bar and was pouring a Coke over ice. "For you." He grinned mischievously. "Since I didn't get my red and you're apparently going to need the caffeine."

I smiled back at Bahlin, and Tarrek frowned.

"Thanks, Bahlin," I said, clinking the ice in the glass as I tipped it gently toward him. "I think I'm ready to give this a shot." He smiled at me and went to sit on the sofa opposite Tarrek. Both men shifted, inviting me silently to sit with them. I stood there for a minute then sat on the arm of Bahlin's sofa, but at the opposite end so I was directly across from Tarrek. It was the best I could do in a pinch. I looked at Tarrek and said, "Let's hear it."

He smiled. "That easily? You'll move into a case without any further preparation?"

I shrugged. "I wouldn't know what to do to prepare," I said. I'm nothing if not honest. "This is going to be a fly-by-the-seat-of-my-pants experiment in which I either succeed or fail. The only thing I can ensure is that, with any action I take, one of the two outcomes is guaranteed."

Bahlin roared with laughter while Tarrek chuckled softly.

Tarrek smiled at me. "I suppose I can't ask for more than such frank honesty."

I shrugged.

"There have been two murders in the last nine days," he began. Apparently we were really going to get right to it. "First there was the *far darrig*, or a type of leprechaun, that was killed; his tongue and voice box were taken and the body left outside his small shanty in the Scottish Lowlands." I set my Coke down on the coffee table, feeling slightly ill. "We've also lost a *cù sith*, or giant Highland hound. His body was found in field of heather in the Highlands but his muzzle, in its entirety, was missing. A farmer found him while walking his fences." I felt bile rise in the back of my throat. I was swallowing repeatedly. I didn't know if I could do this after all. "We had to alter his memory to avoid the mundane police's involvement."

Bahlin looked over at me and was by my side in an instant. "Maddy? Sweetheart, put your head between your knees. Slow, deep breaths." He shot a malevolent look at Tarrek and growled, "Could yeh no' go easy on her this first night? Have yeh no wits?"

Tarrek looked at me, head tilted to one side like a giant dark bird of prey. "I thought you said you were ready to discuss the murders."

I shuddered, taking air in slowly as Bahlin had suggested. "I thought I was, Tarrek. I'm sorry. This is going to take some getting used to."

"Unfortunately, Maddy, there's no time." Bahlin made a low, disgusted noise in his throat. "There's not, Bahlin. Much as it pains me to see Maddy suffer, for her spirit calls to mine as if they have once known each other, there's no time to lose. While there are two dead so far, one of mine has gone missing."

"When?" Bahlin and I asked at the same time. I sat up despite

Bahlin's protests.

"Near as I might tell, he disappeared today. Jossel was patrolling the forest around the sithen, or our faerie mounds, and he never returned. You know we live underground?" he asked me.

I nodded, seeming to remember some of this from mythology. "Can you take me there?" I asked. "I'd like to see where he was last known to be."

"Of course, Maddy. I'd be honored if you'd accompany me now."

Bahlin was on his feet standing next to me before I could blink. "She'll not be going without me, mate," he said in a low, dangerous voice. Then he turned to me and put his hand on my shoulder. "Don't even think about it, sweetheart. I have to eat before we go anywhere. Our little shock recovery session drained me. It will have to wait until I'm able to accompany you."

Of course, once he commanded me not to, I had no other choice. "Really? 'Don't even think about it, *sweetheart*'?" I rose to my feet, shrugging off his hand. "Tarrek, do you have a jacket I might borrow?" My clothes hadn't been delivered yet, so it was borrow or go without.

He took his suit jacket off and stepped around the coffee table toward me. Bahlin made a movement as if to interfere and I spun toward him, slapping my hand on his hard chest. He didn't flinch, though he did stop mid motion.

"You will not be my keeper, do you hear me?" My voice was a dangerous indicator of my tolerance level. "I will not be fawned over and treated like an incompetent child, even if I have no idea what I'm doing. You will humor me, as I'm the Niteclif, and this is my responsibility." I blinked, shocked at my tone of voice, my expressed intent, myself. I had no idea where it had all come from.

Bahlin stared at me as if I'd grown another head. "So you think to run off and play detective your first night out, hmm?" he asked. His tone was superficially friendly, but even brief experience had taught me that I shouldn't take him at face value.

"And you, my fellow Council member, would do well to remember that I can protect her as well as you can from all things that she may be protected from." Tarrek's voice was suffused with a lethal calm. He finished stepping toward me and held out his jacket. I shrugged into it and rolled my shoulders. There was little to do about the general size. It was just too big.

Bahlin stood motionless next to me, staring at Tarrek. "I could grab a bite now, my fellow Council member."

"Do not threaten me you vile overgrown lizard," Tarrek snarled, clearly pissed off at being reduced to a part of the food chain. A slight wind was emanating from around him again, stirring the men's hair in the breeze.

Bahlin laughed, though it sounded bitter, lacking any sense of amusement. "Worried about sullying that pretty outfit, Tarrek?"

I hopped up onto the coffee table and was shocked that I didn't knock anything off, over, or out. "Let's stop posturing for a minute, guys. Bahlin, I have to go. You know that. Eat my dinner when it gets here since I didn't touch it. I'll see about grabbing a burger on the way. We all know the scene is degrading by the hour, so cut the crap. Tarrek, there's no reason to goad him. I'm taking your side in this. So both of you shut the hell up and let me do my job. A fae's life is at stake, and that's got to be more important than either your pride or his," I said, glancing first at Tarrek, then at Bahlin.

Both men looked at me, then each other and, finally, away.

"You shame me, Maddy," Tarrek said on a sigh. His voice was soft and held sorrow like the brush of a butterfly's wings—faint, soft, barely there. "Let's be off and see what there is to see."

"He's right, much as it galls me to admit it. You shame us both." Bahlin shook his head and pinched the bridge of his nose. "I've got to eat, and your dinner won't be nearly enough for me to refuel. And it's too near dawn for me to get to the sithen via the air without risking being seen. I'll have to get some food and then grab a ride out there. I'm remiss to let you go without me, but I've no choice, *sweetheart*." Bahlin's voice was full of both mockery and misery. He stepped close to me and ran a hand down the back of my hair to my neck and then straightened to his full height, like a marionette whose strings had been pulled, and he grinned wickedly.

"Stay with me, Maddy. I'll take you myself within the hour." I stared at him, and my surroundings seemed to soften. I realized I had leaned into him and I shook my head, stepping back so quickly I stumbled. His hand shot out in a move too quick to be seen, and he stopped my fall.

"Thanks for making it easier to leave, Bahlin." Disappointment laced my voice and lay heavy between us.

He smiled a very self-deprecating smile and shrugged. "I had to try. Be off with you then. I'll eat and meet you there as soon as I'm able." The last was said to me while he looked at Tarrek.

"Fine. Oh, um, what did my great-granddad do to keep notes for you?" I asked, shifting from foot to foot, uncomfortable at having to ask how this was going to work. After all, I'd just given him a warped version of the "kiss my ass I'm leaving" speech, and now I had to ask how to do part of the job.

"He had a photographic memory. Notes weren't necessary," Bahlin said.

Naturally, I thought, and I sighed. I was worried that someone else was about to die because of my ineptitude.

"Let's be off, Maddy," Tarrek said. His tone was as gentle as the hand he put under my elbow.

And I let him lead me away from Bahlin despite the blossoming dread in my chest.

Tarrek and I stepped out of the hotel lobby into the early morning air, he on his cell phone speaking softly and I taking in my surroundings. It was cool, and I was grateful for the protection of his jacket. The lights from London obscured the stars, giving the sky an eerie, artificial glow. Traffic moved by us intermittently, the tires making a whooshing sound on the wet pavement. Despite the open air, I felt somehow cocooned with Tarrek, isolated from the world.

Tarrek snapped his cell phone shut, stepped up to my side and said, "The car will be here in a moment. I've instructed our driver to have the heat on."

"That's kind of you, thanks." I looked over at him, and he appeared surreal in his black clothes with his black hair and ethereal complexion. In the short amount of time we'd been outside, small drops of the heavy mist had collected in his hair and the streetlights gave him the look of a fallen celestial being, an angel, come to walk among mankind.

"What is it?" he asked, reaching out to touch my cheek before thinking twice and dropping his hand.

"You're absolutely stunning." Realizing I'd answered his question with such base honesty embarrassed me, and I turned my head away. He smiled and before he could reply, a black Mercedes sedan pulled to the curb. He stepped to the rear door and opened it for me. He nodded, motioning for me to get in. I slid into the car. The black leather was buttery soft, and the car still held that new car smell. The privacy tint on the windows so effectively prevented light from entering the car that I couldn't see many of the interior details in the pre-dawn darkness. It reeked obviously of opulence and, less obviously, of menace.

"Impressive. Is this how you usually travel?"

Tarrek slid in after me and pulled the door shut behind him. "Only if I'm dealing with mundanes or, now, you. Faeries dislike being around so much metal. It inhibits our powers." He settled back into the seat. "We are creatures of nature and much of our magic is tied to it. This is why we are so particular about where we build our sithens. There are certain things we look for, and certain things we avoid."

Well that's cryptic enough, I thought. I made a mental note to pick up several books on Celtic and Norse mythologies when I had a little free time.

Tarrek looked out the window, and I could see his face reflected softly over his shoulder. "When we travel alone we use what you might consider teleportation. It's called waxing and waning. While it's not tied to the cycles of the moon it is very similar. It means to appear and disappear, yes?"

I nodded, all thoughts of book shopping forgotten.

"It's a matter of willing ourselves from one place to another."

"Is it magic?"

He turned back to me and smiled. "Not for us."

The car pulled away from the curb quickly, setting deeper into our seats. I buckled my seatbelt then turned to try and look out the darkly tinted windows as the driver sped through the city. It was impossible to see anything through the double darkness of night and tinted window so I turned back to look at Tarrek, and he smiled. He was so startlingly attractive it took my breath away for a minute. I stared openly, but his smile never faltered.

He shifted in his seat and put his hand over mine on the center console. That same electric spark seemed to jump between us yet again. It was more than a simple attraction, more than what I had thought of earlier as intangible chemistry.

"Why are you and Bahlin so interested in me?" I blurted out. I blushed and cursed my pale skin and big mouth for the hundred thousandth time in my life.

Tarrek tightened his hand on mine slightly, and I shifted my grip to hold his hand back. There was something about the contact that was as comforting as it was confusing. "You are beautiful," he said, stroking his thumb over the back of my hand repeatedly. "Surely you're used to the attention of men?"

"Um, not really to either thing—not beautiful or used to the attention." I turned to face him, completely flustered with this conversation. "I mean, compared to you two, I'm like a third wheel on the beauty bike. Totally out of place."

"Beauty bike?"

"It's just a phrase. It means that a bicycle by definition has two wheels and a third is seriously unnecessary. You two are the wheels, and I'm out of place between you."

"Oh." He continued rubbing my hand. "I disagree. It seems impossible that you would see yourself as unattractive..." The look of concentration on his face lent me to believe he was having trouble finding the right words to convey his feelings. He looked down at our hands, then up at my face. "I sense no false emotion from you, so—"

"You can sense my emotions?" I asked a little too loudly. I saw the driver's glance in the rearview mirror, and I gasped. His eyes were dark orange, and it wasn't a trick of the dash light reflection. They were dark orange, as in *navel*. The pupil was a pinprick of red. It was disconcerting as hell, and hell was exactly what he brought to mind.

"Maddy?" I turned my wide green eyes back to him. "I realize I've not prepared you for this morning's visit to the sithen, or at least the exterior mounds. Unless something goes terribly wrong, there will be no need to expose you to the dangers that lie within for a mortal. Regardless, there are undoubtedly things you're going to see that are

65

new to you and will cause you some...well, let's just say that you're likely to see things you've never seen before. I would encourage you strongly to avoid staring at those things that catch you off guard." He smiled gently again then turned and said something to the driver in that same flowing language he'd used earlier. The man nodded his head and sped up. Apparently we were in a greater hurry now that we were leaving the city. "You need to prepare yourself. Most Seelie love to be stared at—"

"Seelie?" I asked.

"There are two different types of fairies—Seelie and Unseelie. The Seelie are what people often think of when they think of fairies, beautiful and ethereal, though not small and winged. They are what light mythology is made of. The Unseelie are the less traditionally appealing side of faerie, the things from which dark mythology was born. But what you will find is that not all that is beautiful is soft, and not all that is visually unpleasing is harsh. It can be just as likely that the opposite holds true."

"So you're telling me not to take anyone, or anything, at face value." I gently extricated my hand from his. He looked at me, unblinking, and took his hand back from the middle of the seat.

"That's precisely what I'm telling you," he said, his voice sounding and feeling detached, emotionless. His eyes cooled perceptibly. "A contingent of my guard will meet us at the edge of the mound nearest where Jossel was last seen. I would encourage you to stay within my site, even with them near us."

"I meant no offense." I looked down at his hand in his lap and then back to his eyes. "I'm only trying to find where I fit." I wished fervently that Bahlin had come with us.

"No offense taken." His eyes and voice both softened. "I forget myself. It must be difficult for you, with all of the changes to your life in the last day and a half."

I ignored that. "You never did finish explaining why you and Bahlin are so interested in me," I said. "Not that I want to push, but it might help me understand."

"Ah. You are persistent." He leaned his head back on the headrest and closed his eyes. "You might have noticed that Bahlin and I don't get along too well."

"Nope, hadn't observed that at all."

He rolled his head toward me, staring without smiling before he responded. "Sarcasm? Very well. So you've noticed. Bahlin and I have a long history of discord between us, though it has escalated to violence several times in the last several years. We had both been forewarned that the time of the next Niteclif was near—"

Interrupting him, I asked, "By whom?"

"If you'll give me a chance, I'll explain. There is a wizard on the High Council who foretold of your coming, and we both have access to Seers within our individual races. The three voices all foretold the same future. The time of the Niteclif was near, you would appear through the stones, and you would be a young woman. What neither of us expected, what *I* didn't expect, was that you would be so desirable."

I snorted and crossed my arms under my breasts. Just *having* breasts prevented me from truly crossing my arms over my chest, but I did the best I could.

"I am sincere, Madeleine. You'll find no falsehood in my words. When Bahlin entered your dream yesterday morning, I felt the contact because I'd been preparing to do the same." Tarrek shifted toward me, putting his arm across the back of the seat and tugging at the end of my hair. "So when I followed his magic trail into your dream and I saw you, I was stunned."

I thought about what he'd said about the Seelie fairies. "But you see beauty all the time. There's nothing special about me, Tarrek."

He reached out and pulled my hair, hard.

"Ow!" I leaned my head away from him and turned on my hip to face him, the movement partially restricted by the seatbelt.

"I'll tolerate no disparaging remarks about your person, Maddy, not even from you."

"Fine. Go on," I snarled.

"You were beautiful, and I was incensed that he had made it to you before I had."

"So I'm what? A competition between the two of you?" The words were ground out between clenched teeth. "Nice."

"No, not...really. You are the Niteclif, and you deserve respect. But you are also a woman, and we are men, and we have both found ourselves interested in you as more than our kinds' detective. Does this make sense?"

The answer was yes and no. Yes, I understood that they both were interested in me because I was the Niteclif, and I was the first female Niteclif at that. And no, I didn't understand how they could both be interested in me in a personal capacity when either of them could have had any female on the planet. I cleaned up okay, but I wasn't in their league. I'm average-plus on a great day and only average on every other. So as usual when it came to men, and especially these two, I was already conflicted. Even my newly developed skills of logic wouldn't help me out with this one because lust shuns rational thought. I answered as honestly as I could—I stayed quiet.

Tarrek stared at me as if trying to divine a response. Finally he said, "I am better for you than he, Maddy. I am able to offer you more than Bahlin can even dream of. Dragons are selfish and manipulative, and they care little for anything beyond that which brings them pleasure in the moment. At most you will have his passing affection. Consider that before you do anything rash."

I was quiet for a while before I turned toward him again, curiosity once more getting the best of me. "You act as if you're sure I'll choose one of you as a partner, lover, whatever. Why does it matter so much, Tarrek?"

"Your decision matters more than you can imagine." He reached for me, but I shifted slightly so that I kept some distance between us. Tarrek sighed, removing his arm from the back of the seat. We rode in silence for a while, the shifting rev of the engine, the hum from the tires on the road and the sounds of our breathing the only noises.

Tarrek turned toward me as if to say something but the car began to slow and he paused, sitting up straighter. "We're almost there."

Chapter Five

The faerie mounds were out in the middle of a large field. We turned off a paved two-lane country road and followed the single dirt and grass lane until it came to a dead end directly in front of the mounds. Lacking the disruption of the city's lights, the stars shone brightly in the pre-dawn sky. The mounds were equivalent to gently rolling hills placed very close together in an otherwise flat expanse of pasture. Sheep grazed nearby. There were no distinguishing markers that announced we were near any supernatural location other than four copses of trees, one at each point of the compass, at the farthest edges of the mounds in each direction. Tarrek got out of the car at the same time the driver opened my door. The driver was much shorter than I'd expected. I took in his appearance and, belatedly remembering Tarrek's directive not to stare, hastily looked away. What I'd gathered in my initial glance was that he was around five feet tall and dressed in very odd leather clothing, with decorative stitching at the cuffs and a large, rusty knife hanging awkwardly from his waste on his left side and strapped to his thigh. He wore a gun, holstered, on his right. As previously noted, his eyes were orange and his nose was slightly bulbous. He had grinned at me before I looked away, and his teeth looked rather sharp.

Tarrek was suddenly at my side, and I jumped. He put his arm around my shoulders and turned me toward the north, where his contingent of guards had appeared. They were all brutally attractive men, though there was something in them that I recognized as distinctly inhuman. One of them, apparently the leader, stepped forward and Tarrek walked to meet him. The guard offered Tarrek a lump of something dark. He accepted it and said something in Fae and then turned back to me and held out a new jacket. It looked like it was about my size. I shrugged out of the borrowed suit jacket and he nodded, stepping toward me. I slipped my arms into the sleeves, and it drew a sigh out of me. It was some type of leather, but it was softer than anything I'd ever touched. It fit like a glove, without being tight, and hung to my knees. Because it came from Tarrek it was black. I instantly loved it.

"Thank you," I said. "I appreciate the use of it."

"It's a gift. Our seer gave the head seamstress general dimensions and the information that you would visit us on a cold morning. I couldn't have you getting cold on your first visit to my home." Dimples decorated his cheeks when he smiled like this, and they made him even more appealing.

I couldn't help but smile back. "Then thank you even more," I said, and stood up on tiptoe to kiss his cheek where the dimple lay.

He looked very pleased and, as he bent at the waist to bring his face nearer, he turned into the kiss and made it a gentle contact between our lips.

I started, pulling back and blushing like mad. I was liable to pass out given the number of times I'd blushed in the last twelve hours. Embarrassing.

"Do I apologize?" he asked, grinning again but looking mischievous this time.

I rubbed my lips with cold fingertips and shook my head. "No. No, I don't think so. But in order to keep my head clear, can we go on to the site of the disappearance?" Something bothered me, but I couldn't quite put it together. I looked around at the guards and they were all armed even better than the driver had been. Maybe I was just uncomfortable with all the weapons. The only thing I had available to stop an attack was my mind, and it wasn't bullet proof.

"Of course." He held out his arm to me, and I took it. He turned me toward the northern copse of trees, and we began the walk through the field, our merry contingent hot on our heels.

The area where Jossel had allegedly disappeared was

unimpressive. It was located in the northern stand of the ancient oak trees. That was it. There was nothing remarkable about it, no flashing arrow pointing to a single clue. I began looking around the area with Tarrek trailing right behind me. I came across two sets of boot prints in the soft dirt, one large and the other, within the first, smaller. The smaller prints moved from tree to tree so that it appeared as if someone was stalking Jossel, or herding him in a particular direction. I held up my hand for everyone to stop. I got on my hands and knee to look for clues but also to say a quick prayer that I didn't make a total ass of myself. The guards all watched me carefully, aware of who I was but, more importantly, *what* I was—a woman. Being a descendant of the Father of Who-Done-It was a blessing and a curse. It occurred to me as I ran my fingers through the sparse grass that these men likely knew my great-granddad. I sighed. Again, no pressure.

"Tarrek?" I called out.

"Here," he responded, and I suddenly saw a pair of Italian shoes in my peripheral vision. "What may I do, Maddy?"

"I need a digital camera. Preferably a professional grade one. How possible would it be to get one out here this morning?"

"Give me a moment. Do you have a brand you prefer?" Before I could answer he turned and beckoned to one of the guards before turning back to me. I looked up at his face, which was all business.

"Uh, Canon is my personal favorite."

"It will be handled. Give me a moment." He stepped away and spoke to the guard, who nodded and disappeared. Literally. The guy was there one second, gone the next. I gasped. Tarrek walked quickly back to me and squatted down, forearms resting on his knees. "Remember what I told you about the ease of our traditional transportation? Earlier, in the car?" He touched nothing that was potential evidence. Or me.

"Waxing and waning," I whispered.

"Very good." He beamed. "You just saw Klayn wane. It's common for us, so you'll need to become used to it, okay?"

He talked about it as if it were that simple a concept. It was like saying, "We prefer tea over coffee, so be prepared to drink tea." I sat on the ground, hard, and hoped I hadn't squashed any evidence. Tarrek stayed squatted next to me while I thought through the strangeness that was now my life. Before I could come up with any profound explanation for the question *Why me?* Klayn appeared, or waxed, about ten feet in front of me. I made that horrible girly *eep* noise and the guards' collective chuckles rang through the morning mist that was developing. I scowled at them. Great. Now I was amusing.

Stepping up to me Klayn said in a surprisingly deep baritone, "I apologize, Niteclif." There was a small smile playing around his lips. In his hand was the camera. I didn't ask where it had come from or how he'd obtained it in a matter of minutes, but instead took the camera when he offered it to me. I looked it over and began adjusting settings. *This* I knew how to do, and I was comforted by the familiar.

"You know this piece of machinery?" Klayn asked.

"Sure. I have one of my own and was an amateur photographer before…before all of this." I waved my arm about, generally encompassing everyone I could see. "Nice to see modern equipment being mostly plastic works for your normal mode of transportation. Thanks for picking it up for me."

"You're welcome. Call out if you need anything else." He retreated to stand with the other guards.

With Tarrek right on my heels, I began walking around the scene of the disappearance and taking pictures of the footprints, using my sneaker-clad foot as a reference point to size. Some of the footprints were very clear, as were some of the prints-within-prints, while others were nothing more than a mess of disturbed earth. I followed the prints, making mental notes about the size and space of the stalker and stalked footprints and apparent strides. Jossel's footprints, which were easy to discern due to the direct pattern of his path, had been the larger of the two. Or was it three? A new set seemed to appear from nowhere. Taking more pictures, I walked on and came to a point where there had obviously been a fight. The boot prints were a mess, turning up dirt and grass, and there was a trail of rusty colored earth, likely where blood had been spilled, at the farthest edge of the struggle. But whose blood I didn't know. And then I made my first mistake, one I have promised myself I will never make again. I failed to look up. Tarrek's attention was focused on my progress, and as I turned to ask him about the possibility of typing the blood, I saw strange markings carved into the trees, spaced in a rough circle about seven feet up each trunk. Recognizing the symbols, I stood quickly and turned to ask Tarrek's opinion regarding their origin.

"Tarrek," I began, my voice sounding hollow to my ears, "look at—" Something huge punched me in the left shoulder. It spun me like a top, and I began to fall. The last thing I remember was Tarrek's bellowing rage, the rushing of the guards and the breaking of dawn. It was a beautiful sunrise.

I woke up sweating, covered in piles of blankets. It was so odd. My shoulder didn't hurt. Much. Okay, a little but it wasn't nearly as bad as I thought it would be. Because I was relatively certain I had been shot, though with what I wasn't positive. The only thing I was sure of was that someone had been aiming for my heart and had to have intended my death. And I was sure I knew who that someone was. I wanted to talk to Tarrek before outing the guy because this was going to affect him directly.

The door opened, and the devil himself came through. Tarrek had changed into cream leather trews, a long white poet's-style shirt and black knee-high boots. Sort of a roguish pirate look. Slap his image on a romance novel, and it was bound to become a best seller. Yum. He even had the short sword strapped to his hip. And I was willing to bet he had other weapons tucked away on his person.

"How are you?" he asked in a soft voice, as if I would crack from the sound.

"I'm fine," I rasped. "I could use some water, though."

He reached for a cup and poured something electric blue into it.

"What's that?" I asked, taking the cup from him and looking inside before I took a sip and made a face.

"It's a sleeping draught offered by our physician," he said, reaching over to stroke my hair. The air he disturbed with his movement swept over me and I inhaled deeply. He smelled and looked delicious. It was sort of a combination of oranges and cinnamon. Manly potpourri. What was going on?

"Are you wearing cologne?" I asked, my voice sharper than I intended it to be. He smiled, and I can only describe the look on his face as bashful.

"You can smell that?" He looked both embarrassed and pleased.

"Smell *what* exactly?"

He fidgeted, adjusting his boot tops, then his belt. I raised an eyebrow at him, and he said, "It's just me, myself. In the sithen the smell becomes intensified."

"Why?"

He shrugged. "It's my home, and it's my magic."

"But what is it?" I pressed.

"It's the smell fairies release to attract partners." He saw the look on my face and said, "I'm not doing it to gain your affections, Maddy. I can't help it. It's an involuntary response when a male faerie finds someone he wants. And each male's smell is different. It's sexual in nature, nothing more." He looked at me so intensely and said it all so calmly that I was even more flustered.

"I don't get you guys," I muttered. I had a moment of sudden comprehension, and I shrieked, "I'm in the sithen? How the hell did that happen? How long have I been here? Someone tell me what's happened! Did I really get *shot?*" I gasped the last, a full memory slamming into me nearly as hard as the projectile had.

Tarrek winced, no doubt at the decibel of my voice. "Maddy, relax—"

"*Relax?* How the hell am I supposed to relax when I've been *shot* by your driver."

"Maddox? No, Maddy, he wouldn't have done this. He's served the royal family for generations. You're mistaken."

I forced myself to sit up, doing my best to breathe through the pain in my shoulder that movement brought. "Find him, Tarrek, and find him *now.*"

"Maddy, you're wrong. Maddox wouldn't do this."

"I'm *not* wrong, Tarrek, and I'll tell you why once I've interviewed Maddox."

He got up and went to what appeared to be a mirror. He cast his hand across its face, and a mist filled it. Then there were images and Tarrek tapped the side of the mirror to change the images, apparently the faerie equivalent of channel surfing. His brows began to draw together, especially when he surveyed the exterior, because Bahlin was standing there and even *I* could tell he was pissed.

"Oh for the love of the goddess," Tarrek muttered. "I'm not letting him in. He'll have to stand out there and continue to wait." He bent and drew a dagger from the inside of his boot, spinning it in his hands in agitation and silent threat.

I began shifting covers off of me, my movements fitful.

Hearing the rustle of cloth, Tarrek turned. "Maddy, stay down. You're not supposed to get up for another day at the very least." He abandoned the mirror and rushed over to me.

"Screw that," I said through gritted teeth. "I need to see both of you, and you just indicated that he'd have to wait outside, so that's where I'm going. We'll talk there." I was sweating bullets, no pun intended, the pain in my shoulder much more pronounced.

"You'll be the death of me, and that's something." He took small, halting steps away from me and then back, like he couldn't decide whether to leave or make sure I didn't get out of bed. "Fine. Fine. I'll go get him." He threw the dagger down with a thump on the small dresser. "So I don't kill him," he muttered, and he stomped off.

I slumped back into bed. This gave me some time to look around the room. It was well lit and bright in the same way the morning sun brightens a lightly curtained room, soft and glowing. This may not sound noteworthy but there were no windows and no lamps. The room seemed to generate its own light. The room appeared carved from the earth, with floors that were natural gray stone and the walls whitewashed. The furniture was all extremely large, but it fit the space perfectly. The bed was another high bed, requiring a stepstool to get into it. The headboard was maple, with a darker burl all through the wood. Everything in the room had an organic feel. Steps from the bed was a doorway that led into the bathroom. From the little I could see, it looked as opulent and modern as the one at the hotel. I realized then how grimy I felt and wondered how I might get a quick shower.

I heard muted voices and realized they were coming from the mirror. I looked over and saw that Tarrek and Bahlin were yelling at each other, gesticulating wildly and aggressively. I stared, fascinated. It was like a car wreck—you know you're going to see carnage, but you can't look away. Bahlin suddenly punched Tarrek in the face, rocking the other man's head back far enough I instantly worried for his neck. Bahlin's movements were so fast they were only a blur. Tarrek recovered and charged Bahlin, catching him around the ribs and taking him to the ground hard and fast, landing at least two solid blows to the ribs. The men pounded on each other as guards poured from the sithen through unseen doorways in the ground. Guards broke up what would have been an ugly fight and both men stood, straightening their clothing—Tarrek in his fine clothes and Bahlin in jeans and a T-shirt. More words, calm words, were exchanged and both men headed inside the sithen. Oh boy.

It was about a half-hour later that the door opened, and Tarrek and Bahlin came through. Tarrek's mouth was already healing, and he'd changed clothes. Bahlin's split knuckles had healed, but he was still covered with the flotsam of the fight-grass, grass stains, a little blood. I smiled at them both. I couldn't help it.

"Maddy," Bahlin breathed, rushing toward the bed in a burst of speed. "Sweetheart." His eyes roamed over me, and I realized I was dressed in a very small tank top and my underwear; nothing else. Awkward. I pulled the covers up a little higher.

"I'm okay, Bahlin. It's kind of you to worry, but don't. Nothing can be changed about what's happened, okay? Tarrek?" He was standing near the door. I turned toward him. "Where do the lights come from?"

"Lights?"

"In the room. There aren't any windows or lamps."

He grinned, though there was a shadow behind his eyes that bothered me. "It's enchanted."

"I'm not buying that story," I said, shaking my head then wincing at the movement.

"It's true. It's enchanted lighting. There are words you can say in the old language to brighten or darken a room." He said something that sounded like *contarpay* and the lights dimmed to a mood-light setting. Then he said something that sounded like *pletenda* and the lights came back up. I laughed out loud. There's nothing like finding out that fairies do exist and then getting to stay in a magical sithen to lift a girl's spirits. Speaking of...

"Uh, thanks for taking care of me, Tarrek." The words were soft, my gratitude sincere. Bahlin let out the lowest of growls, raising the hair on the back of my neck in a primal evolutionary response. "Stop," I told him. "He saved me."

"How?" Bahlin demanded. "He let you get shot." His voice rose with each word.

"Don't yell," I scolded him. "No, he didn't *let* me get shot. I was shot. Period." This had to be part of the Niteclif heritage speaking, because in my mind I hadn't stopped shrieking yet. "Tarrek, come over here. I want to tell this once. First, did you see Maddox anywhere in the sithen when you went out to get Bahlin?"

"No, but I ordered the guards to look for him and deliver him here at once. The sithen is enormous, so he could be anywhere." He sounded defensive, and the tension around his eyes told me he was still convinced I was wrong.

"Thank you. When he can't be found, you'll be ready to believe this. Maddox was the shooter." Tarrek shook his head, and Bahlin looked interested.

"How do you know?" Bahlin asked. "From what I heard you went down pretty quickly." His face grew dark, and his brows drew together. A dark, heady spice was coming from him, but his smell was different than Tarrek's. Like the previous times I'd smelled his scent, he reminded me of fresh air and rain showers. They both smelled wonderful, though there was one my nose preferred. Regardless, it was apparent that Tarrek smelled it, too, because he glared at Bahlin. Oh good. At least I'd proven one thing successfully—testosterone has a smell. I'd always wondered.

"Listen, I began to realize something was off when I got out of the car, but I was too slow to figure it out in time. Maddox is right handed. His handgun was in his holster on that side. But his sword was on his left leg, and it had been put in backwards, meaning he'd had it out to use it and struggled to get it re-sheathed correctly, probably because he was in a hurry." I shifted, trying to get comfortable. "I also noticed the scroll work on his clothing. It wasn't decorative. It matched some of the symbols in the clearing where Jossel's blood was found. Those symbols were carved into the trees. The symbols must have provided some type of warding or protection, which means that whoever put them there intended to facilitate Maddox's errand, either as the killer or the killer's proxy when he shot me. His boots were the same style as the footprints within Jossel's larger footprints, and Maddox was the only one who hung back when we proceeded into the woods. No doubt it was to find a better spot from which to shoot me." My shoulder gave a harsh ache, and I sighed. Being shot at sucked. Being shot at and *hit* sucked more. "I'm betting he disappeared from the faerie mounds in all the chaos after I was shot, and I bet that whoever he's working for is not happy with him right now for missing me."

"But he didn't miss you, Maddy," said Bahlin. Tarrek looked pale and disbelieving.

"Yes, Bahlin, he did. He meant to kill me. He was aiming for my heart, but I turned at the same moment he pulled the trigger. I was going to tell Tarrek what I'd discerned." I looked at the other man, and he was stricken. "I'm sorry," I whispered to him. I held out my hand and he shook his head at me, getting up and walking out of the room. I dropped my hand and watched him go. He shut the door softly behind him, the sharp click of the latch making me jump in the echoing silence.

"I've met Maddox before. He's been with the family for hundreds of years and I know he helped raise Tarrek, so this will be hard to accept." Bahlin's voice was empathetic but firm. "However, as we discussed, Niteclif word is law, so he's done for."

The weight of accountability was the heaviest of yokes. I didn't know if I wanted this, the responsibility of being judge and jury burdening me like the weight of a thousand potentially wrong choices. Could I do this? Could I deprive some supernatural creature the length of life it had expected? What if I was wrong?

"How long do faeries live?" I asked in a subdued voice.

Bahlin smiled gently at me and shrugged, leaning his hip against the edge of the bed. "Easily three thousand years. That's the oldest I've known personally. Beyond that, I don't know. They're a fairly secretive race."

I thought about that and couldn't help but wonder how old Tarrek was.

When Bahlin told me I'd been in the sithen, unconscious, for three days, I lost it again. I demanded he get me some pants and get me up and walking. I couldn't stay in bed another minute, especially knowing the hurt my revelation had caused Tarrek and, I was sure by default, his family. Plus Jossel and Maddox were still missing. The shirt I wore was borrowed, from whom I had no idea. My pants had been declared ruined due to the bloodstains and were subsequently discarded. There were no other pants to be found. So Bahlin pulled his T-shirt off and let me borrow it so that I had a shirt that hung well passed my hips at least. He went bare-chested, and thank the merciful heavens for that. The man had a six-pack that made me long to trace the swells and valleys of muscle with my tongue. I could imagine running my lips all over that. Man I needed a cigarette.

He helped me get upright and supported me on my good shoulder, letting me walk around the room and look at the amazing floor, and the way the walls and floor seemed to meet seamlessly. I went into the bathroom and had to wonder about plumbing. Who did they call if they needed something snaked? And did they tie in to the public water system? If not where did the water come from? All these questions that I wanted literal answers for when, truthfully, there were probably no answers beyond *it's magic.*

I came back out of the bathroom under my own power, but it only took a couple of turns around the room for me to realize that I didn't feel well at all. Bahlin got me back into bed. My shoulder felt hot and stiff and I was getting light-headed.

"Maddy, I want to lift the bandages off so I can see the wound, okay?" He wiped the sweat from my forehead with a rag that seemed to have appeared in his hand.

"Fine, but don't look at my goods." I tried to smile, but the look on Bahlin's face said that whatever the smile had actually translated to was scary.

"Sweetheart, you're in no shape for me to check out your goods." He looked me over from head to toe and then said, "But the time will come when that's all we have to do, for hours upon hours."

"Pretty sure of yourself, Bahlin," I whispered, feeling the pull of sleep.

"Of course I'm sure of myself. Who could resist this?" He smiled

79

with forced cheer, making a sweeping pass across his chest and abs with his hand.

I laughed a little, and that seemed to make him feel better. "Of course you'd think so," I replied and I settled back into the pillows more thoroughly. "But that gives me the personal challenge to resist, and you know I don't deal with so well with those, personal challenges, these days."

"Point taken, and statement struck from the conversation," he said, his smile revealing a single dimple.

He bent over me, lifting the shirt over my stomach and off my left shoulder, gently beginning to peel back the tape and gauze from the wound. I looked down and realized his eyes had changed color. I slapped my good hand over my left breast and glared at him.

"Bahlin, tell me that your kind doesn't eat people, because you've got this weird look on your face..."

"Maddy, I'm old enough that I can resist the draw of meat which, incidentally, is what you are."

I stiffened and glared at him, daring him to say it again.

"Don't take offense, love. Dragons *have* eaten people in the past, so it's only natural that my physiology recognizes the potential." His smile softened at my obvious concern. "I'll not ravage your wound or attack your person. I promise, though, that last will cost me in personal comfort."

I skipped the sexual innuendo. "Have *you* ever eaten people?" I felt a little foolish asking, but where had I ever had any kind of experience with dragons?

Bahlin ignored me and continued to peel the tape away and I felt the tape pull against my skin in a tight, uncomfortable way. When the air hit the wound I gasped, shocked at how painful it was.

"This isn't good, Maddy," Bahlin muttered, shaking his head and leaning in close to the torn flesh. He sniffed me like he was some sort of preternatural bloodhound. "It doesn't smell right. It should be healing but it's getting infected somehow. Maddy?"

"Hmm?" I was so drowsy. I wished Bahlin would get closer to me so I could smell him again.

"Maddy, something's wrong. I need to heal this wound quickly. Do you understand?"

"Understand what? I don't heal like you guys do. I don't—"

"No, but I can temporarily give you some of my ability to heal the wound. Maddy." He snapped his fingers in front of my face.

"Fine, fine, fine. Whatever." My head rolled around on my shoulders like a broken doll's. "That's right. You were a doctor. Makes sense now." The room swam in and out of focus, the light seeming both too bright and too dim to see by.

I rolled my head toward Bahlin and saw him bend toward my shoulder. He snaked his tongue out and my eyes struggled to focus. His tongue was forked. I made a feeble effort to pull away from him, alarmed at how quickly I'd deteriorated after my short stroll around the room.

Bahlin took a deep breath and said in a rumbling voice, "This is going to hurt like a son of a bitch, Maddy. Apologies, love." Then he struck, shoving his tongue into the wound and breathing heat into it.

"Oh what the hell," I yelled, snapping out of my stupor with the pain of the dragon's strike. It felt like the wound was being burned from the inside out and I screamed, unable to bear the agony with any measure of stoicism. Bahlin bore down with clawed fingertips, holding me as steady as he could while I renewed my efforts to fight him off, thrashing about on the bed. It was useless. I was consumed by fire in his embrace.

Time became irrelevant, with seconds feeling like hours, minutes like days. The heat from his mouth became incrementally cooler by comparative day number seven, and I began to feel as if I'd survive after all. Several more minutes passed and Bahlin lifted his head, sweating and weaving a bit, retracting his claws from where they had pierced my skin. I watched as those same claws shimmered and returned to a man's hands, Bahlin's hands.

"Well done, sweetheart, well done." His voice was lazy, his eyes unfocused. Apparently whatever had poisoned my bloodstream had rendered him slightly drunk. Fan-damn-tastic.

"Bahlin? Bahlin?" I returned the favor, snapping my fingers under his nose. He looked at me and smiled with such innocence, and I was hit with a wave of his scent. He leaned in and moved as if to kiss me when I remembered his forked tongue. I turned my head, and he made contact with my cheek.

"Be a love and give us a kiss." His voice was lazy and seductive, deeper than normal.

Something low in my belly clenched, and it pissed me off. I wasn't kissing the *us* to whom he referred. *Did his dragon think like a second, individual person?* I wondered. Ultimately it was irrelevant. Angry without understanding exactly why, I said, "This should sound familiar—bugger off."

"You kiss blokes with that mouth?"

"You kiss the girls with that forked tongue?"

He reacted as if I'd slapped him. His eyes became clearer, and he took a sloppy step backward. "Beautiful," he snapped, "just bloody beautiful. You're welcome."

I cringed and rolled away from him, embarrassed to have behaved so ungratefully. But I couldn't seem to find it in myself to apologize. He'd crossed some invisible line I hadn't know I had. I'd begun to see him as a man, a very desirable man, and he had ruined that fantasy for me. Now the monster seemed to overlay the whole of him, and I couldn't see around it.

"You'd best get up and get a shower if yeh're wantin' one," Bahlin said in a hard, brogued voice. "Tarrek will be back soon with clothes, I'm sure."

I bit my cheek, turning back toward him to apologize when I saw my shoulder. There was a pucker of pink scar tissue and the area around it was bruised and looked like I had a huge hickey. But the shoulder appeared fine, if a little stiff. My eyes sought his as my finger gently poked at the healed wound, and he stared at me without blinking.

"You did this? With just your breath?"

He gave a sardonic grin. "Oh no, fair lady. No' *joost* me breath but me bloody forked tongue, a bit o' saliva and a little controlled fire, as weel." His tone was so acidic it could have blistered the paint off a car.

"Look, cut me some slack, o-oh shit." I flipped the covers off my legs and slid to the floor, my knees only slightly wobbly. "Oh, man." I yanked Bahlin's shirt back on with unsteady hands.

"What?" he asked, striding toward me, gripping my shoulder and spinning me to face him. I cringed, and he dropped his hand. "Do yeh think I'd *strike* ye? By the gods, woman! I've no' hit a woman since the Dragons' Conquest of 1712, and that was war." He threw his hands in the air and spun on his heel, stomping toward the bedroom door.

"Stop," I cried, and he froze. "Please, don't leave, Bahlin," I said. "I think I was poisoned."

"Shot and then poisoned? Yeh're the unluckiest of people." His brogue softened a syllable at a time until it dissolved. He turned back to face me. "Wait. Are you serious?" He walked toward me slowly.

"I'm dead—ha—serious." I took a couple of steps toward him so we met in the middle of the room.

"Tell me."

"Tarrek was in the room when I woke up. I asked for something to drink, and he gave me some blue stuff that the healer left for me and then the whole thing happened about finding Maddox and then you showed up."

"I didn't just show up, Maddy. I've been here the three days you've been knocked out."

"You waited for me? Why?"

He shrugged, looking uncomfortable.

"Oh yeah," I said, "the promise to Aloysius." *Why make more of it than it is, right?*

"Sure. That's it," he whispered, stepping closer to me. "Go on."

I pulled my fingers through my hair, tugging on the ends trying to stimulate my still sluggish brain. "Um, Tarrek went to get you, you guys came back and then...then... Where *is* Tarrek?"

Tarrek came back into the room more than two hours later. It had given Bahlin and I a chance to talk and for me to take a short nap. Regardless of Bahlin's contribution to my healing process, I was still human and incredibly tired.

"A death warrant has been issued for Maddox." Tarrek's eyes were drawn and grief etched hard lines around his mouth and eyes. "He'll be killed on sight."

I felt so sorry for him, but I was afraid to extend my sympathy lest he remember it was sort of my doing. So I stuck to the case. "I take it he hasn't been found then."

"The sithen has been searched. He's not here." Tarrek sat in a chair closest to the bed and looked at me, his hand absently reaching for the dirk. He took a deep breath as if to say something and he froze mid-motion, his eyes suddenly sharpened. "What have you been doing this afternoon, Maddy?"

Aw, crap. Looked like I'd get to smell that yummy testosterone smell again after all. "I've been healing, thanks. Bahlin made a small contribution to me healing the wound and it's better. See?" I flapped my arm as I had earlier. He stared at me.

"Do you understand what you've done? How you've potentially tied yourself to him?" he demanded, rising from the chair and approaching the bed.

"Take it down a notch, Tarrek. Why are you so upset?"

"Yes, Tarrek," Bahlin said, standing from the room's other chair near the door, "what's got you so upset, mate?" He looked lethal in his jeans and sneakers. And where Tarrek has stormed toward me, Bahlin moved like a large, lethal predator as he came toward us. Tarrek didn't give ground.

"You know what you can do by exchanging resources with the Niteclif," Tarrek said, his voice going deeper than I'd ever heard it.

"Mind yourself, Tarrek. Nothing's happened. There was no exchange, only a very minor contribution on my part." Bahlin turned his back on Tarrek and walked back to the chair he'd been sitting in.

"What can happen?" I asked, suddenly worried. Had I done something irrevocable? I sat up in bed, tugging the covers more securely around my hips and finger-combing my hair yet again. "Seriously, what's going to happen?"

Bahlin scowled at Tarrek and said, "Nothing, love. There's been no exchange to speak of. It can happen that if a Niteclif and an immortal exchange power that the two become bound."

"Bound how?" I demanded.

Tarrek sighed and Bahlin addressed him. "Why don't you go on and explain it to her now that you've got her disturbed?"

"I'm sorry, Maddy, I didn't mean to upset you." Tarrek pushed his hands into his pants pockets and rocked back on his heels. "Sometimes the two, the supernatural being and the Niteclif, can become bound to each other. The supe either becomes mortal or the Niteclif become immortal. It has happened twice before, with one of each result. But it's rare, you understand."

I refused to deal with this right now, no matter how relevant it was to my future. I was so close to unraveling, my mind began to compartmentalize—cope with this, ignore that.

Still wearing Bahlin's shirt, I swung my legs out of the bed and slid to the floor. "I need some pants and a better shirt. Is there any chance I could get set up?" I asked Tarrek.

"Sure, Maddy. I apologize for not seeing to you earlier. It's been a trying afternoon." And just like that, his grief was back.

I padded over to him, barefoot on the marble, which was surprisingly neither cool nor warm, like lukewarm water is neither hot nor cold. I laid my hand on his arm and said, "I'm so sorry, Tarrek. I didn't mean to cause you or your family any heartache."

He laid his other hand over mine. His eyes glowed a little and I realized that strong emotion would do that, make them blaze like two gems set into his face. "You did your job, Maddy, and it appears you've made your choice. Both were impressive to see, if hard to accept." With that he swept out of the room, not speaking to Bahlin again.

Tarrek was gone for a while, returning having changed into more formal clothes of his own and carrying a gown for me. It wasn't what I would have chosen. He brought me a lovely dress that was more appropriate for a Celtic festival than it was for fighting crime. But I didn't initially complain too loudly. Beggars and choosers and that whole lot.

Tarrek looked reserved yet shy as he handed me the green dress. "Bahlin was allowed to dress you in his dream walk. I'd dress you, even just once, in reality."

"Okay." I didn't know what else to say. He handed me the garment, and it was softer than anything I'd ever touched except the jacket he'd given me. The fabric was fluid like Tencel but even lighter without being see-through. The dress had an empire waist and buttoned down the back, though with luck I'd be able to simply pull it on over my head. The scooped neck would show my cleavage to great advantage but probably leave the fabric tight enough to bounce a quarter off of since it didn't seem to stretch. The length of the dress left it brushing the tops of my feet when I held it up to me. The shoes he handed me were soft, doe-colored ballet slippers but they were leather all around, no real soles. I accepted the clothes and was grateful to head into the bathroom and shut the door.

Both of these men were freaking gorgeous, but neither of them was attached. Problem number one—why didn't they already have women in their lives?

Both had maneuvered themselves close to me from the beginning. Problem number two—what did they hope to gain by being close to me and to this investigation?

Both of them had stuck around after I'd been wounded. Problem number three—who were they trying to protect me from and why hadn't they owned up to the truth about it?

And finally, neither had answered the biggest question I wanted to know but was afraid to ask. Problem number four—had either of them been the man at the stone circle four nights ago who had watched me drive away?

I turned on the shower and adjusted the water temperature to hot and just this side of scalding. I felt grungy from not having bathed since that first night at the hotel. The shower was divine, and I scrubbed until my skin was pink and glowing. I stepped out of the shower and toweled off, running the problems through my head over and over, then tried combining the problems I had with the men with the limited facts I had from the case. No clear picture emerged on either front. I left it alone for the moment. Compartmentalization at its best.

I dressed, did the best I could with my hair, then stepped out into the bedroom. Both men stared at me like I had something on my face. I ran my hands down the front of the dress and their gazes followed my hands. I stopped. So did their collective gazes. The back of my neck felt hot, and I wondered what the hell they were staring at.

"You, Maddy, we're staring at you," Bahlin said.

"How did you know what I was thinking?" I shifted from foot to foot, suddenly uncomfortable.

"I didn't. Your discomfort is all over your face. It isn't hard to put the pieces together." He stood up and backed away from me, side-stepping down the wall toward the door in the face of my unfolding temper. He apparently remembered my right hook.

Tarrek had walked up behind me. He laid a hand on my shoulder and I jumped, turning to face him. "Why have you dressed me like a doll? I need work clothes, not a party dress," I whispered in a hard voice. I was tugging at my hair again, agitated.

He dropped his hand and eyed me coolly. "You'll meet both my parents, who are king and queen, as well as the High Council tonight. The Council has been summoned to the sithen as a whole for the first time in recorded history in an effort to make your life a little easier. You need to dress the part of the Niteclif for formal events, which this is. You can't meet the Council in jeans and a T-shirt." His voice rose slightly as if he were having a hard time not yelling.

"I have *already* met some of you in jeans and a T-shirt," I snarled. Then I thought about what he said. This was a formal event. I needed to look the part.

I took a deep breath, and they apparently thought I was going to argue because Bahlin sighed and said, "For the love, Maddy, shut your trap before you dig a deeper hole for yourself."

I stood there gaping at him, then burst out laughing. No one had ever said that to me before. In fact, no one had ever spoken to me as harshly as he just had. Of course, I didn't think I'd ever behaved so ungratefully before so it hadn't ever been necessary. I walked up to Bahlin and tugged his hand downward. He bent slightly, not sure whether to trust me or prepare to defend himself. And he was a dragon. Ha. I kissed his cheek. Then I turned and did the same to Tarrek. Apologies were hard when you were on the delivery side of things, but I was ashamed of my behavior.

"I'm sorry, honestly." How could I explain my fear and insecurities to two supernatural creatures without appearing weak? They looked at me expectantly and I caved, sticking to the apology and holding my worries hostage in my mind. "I've been a little nutso since all this started after I left the stone circle. It's made me a bit, well. A bit something. Unpleasant? Seems some of what I've inherited as the

Niteclif is a wicked temper and a sharp tongue. I'll try to be better."

"It's only been four days, Madeleine...*Maddy*," Tarrek said, correcting himself and surprising me. "You're doing remarkably well. I think we're all a bit on edge, or nutso as you so delicately put it."

Bahlin hung back a bit, not trusting my radical mood swings or, apparently, my apology. While I was sincere, I couldn't blame him.

"Look, Bahlin, I'm sorry. Really, I am. It's only that it's all so new and I'm not handling it entirely well, especially internally, despite how things appear." I smiled up at Tarrek. "The voices in my head have yet to quit screaming and for the love of Pete, I was *shot* then *poisoned*. Can't a girl catch a break?"

"Who's Pete?" Tarrek asked.

I burst out laughing and suddenly Bahlin joined me.

"Faerie, you've made my day. Let's go greet the High Council." He turned toward me and held out his arm in a courtly manner. "Fair lady?"

I walked toward him, working very hard to appear graceful. I took his arm and he smiled down at me. All appeared to be forgiven, if not forgotten.

"Tarrek?" Bahlin asked. "You'll need to lead us to the others. We're not familiar with where we're going in your catacombs."

"The sithen is not a catacomb any more than it is a place for the unwelcome visitor, Bahlin. You will do well to remember that." Tarrek stalked forward and offered me his arm on my available side. To keep the peace, and because I couldn't help but wallow in a little female satisfaction at being put between two such unearthly, stunning creatures, I took his arm. Oh, there was some fear there, don't be mistaken. But I was the Niteclif, and we don't cop to fear too easily...out loud, anyway.

We walked out of the room with Tarrek still muttering, "I still don't understand. Who is Pete?" and Bahlin and I trying our best not to goad the faerie with our suppressed laughter.

The two men led me out of the room, with Tarrek slightly in front as we went through the doorway. The minute we stepped out of the bedroom Tarrek's guard fell in around us, three to the front, three to the back, and one next to Tarrek. Bahlin's side was left unprotected. The hallways were more than wide enough to accommodate the four of us as we walked toward our destination. The same lighting seemed to be present throughout the sithen, as if there were another sun that shone solely for the benefit of Faerie. With every step down the hallway, my stomach seemed to get tighter and tighter. I might be the Niteclif but I was human, and I had a feeling that nothing else I would meet tonight would be.

The guards seemed to know where we were going without any need for direction, so it felt as if we were swept along in the tide of leather and weapons as we moved toward our destination. Bahlin's arm tensed under my hand and I felt his anxiety. Maybe some of his stress compounded mine? I don't know, I only know I felt it through every fiber and nerve ending in my body. *Hold it together,* I thought to myself. *Now's not the time to make your insecurities public. Deep breaths, straight back, one foot in front of the other, Niteclif.*

"Maddy?" Tarrek looked at me. "There's nothing to fear tonight."

"How do you know I'm afraid?"

"You're going to draw blood with what's left of your fingernails if you don't relax your grip on my arm at least a little." He was compassionate in his words, but I could tell he meant it. I looked down and realized he was right.

"Sorry," I said, and attempted to draw my hand away from his forearm.

"I didn't ask you to let go of me, only to relax your grip." He looked over my head at Bahlin, who stared back.

"Of course," I muttered. I wondered what the guards thought of my miraculous recovery. I was shot, now not. A human up out of bed so quickly would bring questions, and there were only so many answers that were logical.

"Uh, Tarrek? What will we tell people who ask about my speed in healing?" I whispered.

"Not to worry, Maddy." Tarrek squeezed my hand then looked around at his guards. "My closest men are trustworthy and discreet. They'll have a good idea how the healing occurred, but none will share the speculation with anyone outside my contingent."

I wondered about that, because he'd had absolute faith in Maddox too. And that hadn't turned out so well for me.

Bahlin snorted, apparently as concerned as I was at Tarrek's blind trust of his people. I squeezed his arm, hard, and he looked down at me. His eyes glittered in the muted light and it was disconcerting. There shouldn't have been enough light for that type of reflection. He continued to stare at me, and I stared back until Tarrek cleared his throat.

"We've arrived," Tarrek said. And the guards drew open the huge wooden doors. Showtime.

The room we were led into was cavernous. Carved out of the subterranean stone and floored with the continuing theme of marble, the room was structured like a Roman amphitheater. Hopefully the entertainment venue wouldn't be the same. Seats and tables went up three sides, the seats filled with what I could only assume were the residents of the sithen. I was surprised at the number of fae, which I estimated to be around two thousand. Who knew? As Bahlin walked in I heard the murmur, "Dragon!" and "Niteclif!" over and over so that it sounded like wind speaking through the dry leaves of a tree: soft, whispering, persistent. Bahlin never visibly faltered, and I did my best to follow his lead.

Deep breaths, I reminded myself.

Straight across from the great doors was a huge dais, and on it were two thrones made of giant carved tree trunks polished to a glass-like shine. Jewels were set in recess into the wood and the value of each had to be enough that it could have provided Greece's financial bailout several times over. The thrones were empty. Across the floor of the amphitheater and in front of the thrones, a large table had been set up and covered with a diaphanous cloth. Refreshments sat scattered across the table, but I couldn't have told you what was on the menu. I was too absorbed with the beings sitting behind the table to notice.

Sitting at the center of the table was one of the most imposing men I'd ever seen. It was hard to tell how tall he was because he was seated, but his upper half was impressive. He was well muscled like a Mac truck is large, and his skin was very lightly tanned as if he worked in a garden regularly. His hair hung down to the middle of his back

90

and was that blond that's graced with darker and lighter colors. His eyes were pitch black, like his pupils had eaten the iris and left nothing behind. It was scary as hell. The power radiating off of him made me stop in my tracks, causing the others around me to stop awkwardly. There was a shift somewhere inside me and I felt like my soul reached out to him, as if we'd somehow known each other before, yet this had to be our first meeting. I would have remembered him, if not for the fact that his eyes scared me then surely because I inexplicably yearned for him from somewhere deep inside.

"Hellion, that's enough," said a soft, rich voice, thus breaking the spell. My eyes shifted over to the left, and I was suddenly looking at one of the most striking women I'd ever seen. I could tell that she was petite even though she was sitting, but she was no wallflower. Her hair was as dark as Hellion's was light, her eyes equally dark, and she had the same mild tan he had. Her power was immense. It felt like a weight pressing against my whole body. I could tell she was holding it in check, almost as if she was waiting to see how I would respond to Hellion. I relaxed a bit, and felt the fingers of invasion in my mind. I thought, "*No.*" Just like that the mental door was shut. She smiled a genuine smile and revealed perfect white teeth. I wondered what these two were to each other. I looked up at Bahlin and raised my eyebrows in question.

"Mates," Bahlin whispered. I didn't think he was talking about them being best buddies, either.

"Who's on the council?"

He squeezed my hand in warning and said, "Hellion is our Council member. He requested special permission to bring Gretta for this single meeting." His implication was clear. She was a guest, and her crap wouldn't be tolerated. Oh good.

"So it's true," she said. "We have a new Niteclif. And a woman, at that. Very good."

Hellion looked at me with his soulless eyes and said, "You and Bahlin seem unnaturally close for such a short acquaintance. Is there anything you wish to disclose?" And with the word disclose I felt compelled to tell him everything that had happened. Before I could speak, I noticed that Gretta and Hellion had taken each others' hands, presumably in an affectionate gesture unless you were attuned to the increase in metaphysical pressure in my head. I blindly reached for Bahlin's hand and, just as I was about to spill all my secret suspicions right down to my guess at his shoe size, the pressure was relieved.

"Hellion, Gretta, that's rude," said Bahlin in an almost casual manner. His hand had tightened on mine to a point just this side of pain, and the pain seemed to have helped me think more clearly.

"She should be able to stop me, mentally, if she's truly the Niteclif."

That pissed me off. I had taken so much on faith in the last few days, been dragged into a world of make-believe without much explanation, been shot and then poisoned and here he was questioning *me*?

"I would think that my initial efforts would have counted toward convincing everyone. Apparently I'm wrong." I dropped Bahlin's hand and stepped forward, but he stopped my progress by dropping a heavy hand on my shoulder. "It only seems fair that if you're going to increase the game by siphoning power off each other that I should be able to use what defenses are available to me. Or do you two not play fair?"

Black Beauty arched her eyebrow at me but set her hands on top of the table. Hellion gave a lopsided grin, shrugging.

Tarrek laid a hand on my other shoulder and said, "Gretta, Hellion, this is Madeleine Niteclif, though she strongly prefers to go by Maddy." No one else was bringing up my quick healing, so I left it alone. I wouldn't have to answer questions that were never asked. Profound, that.

Gretta inclined her head toward me, ceding this round, I supposed. I caught a movement out of the corner of my eye and turned to look at the woman sitting to Hellion's left. She smiled, and I noticed her canines were sharper than normal. Her skin was as pale as milk, and her hair was as dark as Tarrek's. But her eyes were her most startling feature. Her eyes were the color of the Caribbean sea. I gasped, guessing immediately what flavor of the supernatural she was. Vampire. She was sitting at the table in a leather dress that left little to the imagination, looking more like fetish-wear and uncomfortable at that. She stood to offer me a hand, and I realized the dress was slit up to her waist on each side. I was instantly embarrassed, and Gretta and

Hellion chuckled.

"You'll have to get used to Imeena," Hellion said, his voice deep and melodious. "She has her own sense of fashion, and it often involves as few pieces of clothing as possible."

"It will likely take her as much time to get used to me as I'm remiss to express my fashion sense beyond jeans and a T-shirt." I smiled.

Imeena smiled back. "You are kind to make no more of my aversion to boring clothing than it is, Niteclif."

"So you believe in me?"

She let her head fall back, and her laughter sounded like sex and dark nights and mystery. "Oh, I do at that, precious girl," she said. "I feel your heritage in my heart, for I knew your great-grandfather well. Therefore I will defer to your word as law. I will accept your rulings to be fair and just." She inclined her head slightly at the last word, and I felt a shockwave ripple through me. Those were the same words that Tarrek had said at the restaurant four days ago when he affirmed me.

"And that is enough then, isn't it? Because our two fair brethren have already made up their minds."

I looked at Bahlin, and he sighed. "I've yet to affirm her." He turned and looked at me. "If I say the words, Maddy, it's done. There's no going back because it will be a High Council majority. What would you have me do?"

"Aren't we missing someone?" I asked, counting through them again. *Bahlin, Tarrek, Hellion, Imeena—yep, four.*

"Sarenia is not here, but we have enough for a majority."

I thought about it. I had already begun to sense a difference in my thought process, more logical and less influenced by the ordinary. I knew, deep down, that my genealogy was true and that I was a descendant of the greatest sleuth of all time. The biggest shift was realizing he'd been real, not fiction. But I had to accept it. I'd gone from a mild-mannered, out of work copyeditor to a shot-up detective in a matter of days. Nothing like this happened to "normal" people, or mundies. I realized that there really was no backing out at this point.

"It's okay, Bahlin. I don't know if I believe this is my legacy, but it's where I'm at and I'm responsible for it. It began five nights ago with my own wish, and I think it has too much momentum to stop it now. Affirm me so we can get on with this." I felt a hand run down the back of my hair, and I turned my face toward Tarrek. He was like the night amid all this white stone and marble, though I knew he was a creature of light and life. But he looked so sad.

"I'm sorry, Madeleine. I would go back and stop this from being set in motion if I could."

"No, Tarrek. No apologies, okay? My dad used to always say that you ended up where you were supposed to be. So I'm here. And it's all right." I bumped his shoulder with my forehead. "Besides, I'll fake it 'til I make it, right?"

"Or until you are killed," said Gretta.

Oh good. An optimist. I looked at her and said, "No need to be threatened by a mundane like me, Gretta. Not if you're the real deal."

She scowled. "The real deal? What do you think I am?"

"A witch." Ah, so many connotations came to mind, but I actually meant the literal translation, even if I did say it with a little forcefulness.

Gretta's smile was just as snarky as my response in that it held worlds unsaid. "Very good, little Niteclif. Very good. I suppose how we proceed depends on Bahlin, then."

All eyes turned to him, and we waited. His gaze shifted to me and me alone. The amphitheater may as well have been empty.

In a voice resonating with leashed power, Bahlin's voice rang out over the silent amphitheater. "I will defer to your word as law. I will accept your rulings to be fair and just."

It was done.

Chapter Six

The room erupted in cheers, and I jumped like someone had stuck a cattle prod to my bare skin. Two people emerged from the crowd and began walking toward us. Male and female, they were tall, almost equally so. He was fair-skinned with hair to his waist, a slim yet muscular build and intelligent eyes. She was like the sun, hair of spun gold that hung to her knees, bronzed skin and tall, with few curves evident beneath her clothing. If not for her hair and her delicate features she could have been described as androgynous. The difference in their expressions, hers wary and his curious, was plain for everyone to see.

"Son," said the man, "introduce us to the Niteclif."

Tarrek inclined his head and then turned to me. "Madeleine Niteclif, allow me to present to you my father, Kelten, King of Faerie. And this is my mother, Gaitha, Queen of Faerie. Father, Mother, this is Madeleine."

I didn't know whether to shake hands, bow or curtsy, so I made a mixed attempt at a bow and curtsy and probably looked like I was having a mild seizure. But the introductions were made. *So much for being cool,* I thought, silently grinning at the absurdity of it all.

Kelten, his eyes on me, addressed the crowd in a strong voice. "Madeleine Niteclif has been affirmed. The High Council will meet here and discuss the murders. Maddox has been disavowed and will be killed on site for his involvement in the attempted murder of the Niteclif." The room fell so silent you could have heard the proverbial pin drop. "The queen and I will remain for the High Council meeting and will share what information we may regarding Jossel's disappearance and the murders to date. Return to your activities." The room's residents began to move quietly, with no more than a rustle of fabric as they made their way out the doors.

The king and queen took seats at the table. Tarrek and Bahlin both approached me to escort me to the table, which was flattering and frustrating. I looked from one to the other and said, "Look, if we have to work out a system for taking turns, we will. But for now, let's all sit, okay?" I moved passed them and sat next to Gaitha, directly across from Hellion. The two men stood staring at me, then took seats at the head and foot of the table, though it was beyond me as to which was which. I think if they'd been able to discern the head from the foot they would have fought over who sat where if it hadn't been for the king's glare at Tarrek.

Kelten turned to look at me, leaning past his wife so that he could make eye contact. "Madeleine—"

"Just Maddy, please, sir."

He quirked an eyebrow and in that instant I saw Tarrek in his face—the same eyes, the same jaw, the same mannerisms. It dawned on me that Tarrek was truly royalty. I bit my bottom lip and glanced at Tarrek. I'm ashamed to say it changed the way I thought of him, if even for a moment. Not that it made me any more or less attracted to him, but maybe that I was more aware he was royalty.

"Maddy," said Kelten, drawing my attention back to him. "I want to extend Faerie's deepest regret that one of our own, nearly a member of the royal family, caused you harm." I looked up in time to see Hellion and Gretta clasp hands and Imeena look down and away. What was with the avoidance? These creatures came from a world that was apparently more used to violence than humans, and definitely more than I had ever been exposed to short of CNN. So why look uncomfortable?

Kelten interrupted my thoughts, continuing his speech. "I would ask that you involve both me and the queen in the investigation's update as we've lost Maddox to the tragedy, and we will likely lose Jossel." I was struck by two things. First, that the king spoke of Maddox as if he were dead. Second, that he spoke of Jossel as if his death was imminent and unavoidable. I looked at the king hard, and he maintained eye contact. What was I looking for? Anything, I suppose, that would tell me why he was behaving this way.

"I think that it's all right if you sit in on this meeting, but after that I'll leave it up to the Council to vote on whether or not you can participate." The king looked shocked that I would deny his request. The queen looked like she was still grieving. "Ma'am?" I said, looking at her.

"Maddox was my uncle," she said, a bright sheen of tears showing in her eyes. "I have lost a member of my family, so forgive me if I am not thrilled to be a part of this discussion. Though I will not have you think that I am not sorry you were shot. I am. But I am grievously sorry you are sure that Maddox is the culprit." Tears spilled over her bottom lashes, and she swiped at them angrily, turning to glare at her husband.

Apparently no one had shared with these folks that I'd been poisoned.

"Gaitha?" She spun on me, the festering rage in her eyes not schooled to misery yet. "I'm sorry, Queen Gaitha?"

She inclined her head at me, never breaking eye contact.

"I'm sorry for your loss, truly. If this meeting will be too hard for you, I'd encourage you to leave. There's no reason to scrape at a pain that's so fresh."

"So you believe that I can disregard my duties as queen because it's too hard?" she said in a tone that was very close to mocking me.

"Nooooo," I said. "I just think it's not humane."

"And I am not human, Niteclif."

She was right, and I was a fool to forget it sitting at a table surrounded by the surreal as I was.

We discussed the particulars of the case, as few as they were, though I was hesitant to offer my speculation as to why Maddox shot me. Since once again Bahlin didn't bring up the poisoning, I said nothing. Discussion was loud and, at times, heated. Everyone seemed to think that political maneuvering was the foremost reason for the murders until I interrupted.

"Then why was I shot? Because all of this started before I even got here. To England, I mean." Everyone looked at me like I'd grown a second head.

"Pardon us," Imeena said. "We don't presume to have a more thorough knowledge than the Niteclif of investigative procedures."

"But—" I began.

Bahlin silenced everyone. "No, Maddy. Imeena's right. We won't know as much as you will about finding this killer."

I was confused. Bahlin had worked with the last two Niteclifs, so he should be as adept as anyone. "But Bahlin, you—"

"No, Maddy. I mean it." He looked at me pointedly. And I realized in that instant that his efforts, his identity, had all been concealed behind the fictional character of Watson. It was then that I remembered what he had said to me, *"You're the first person to put it all together."* No one knew who he was.

I nodded slightly and said, "Okay. Then I suggest that we save our individual speculations until I've had a chance to do some fieldwork. We can meet again, preferably in a neutral location, and discuss what I've found. Acceptable? Besides, I could use some rest." And it was true. I was wearing down fast.

"Agreed," said Tarrek.

Bahlin nodded back to me, looking relieved. We'd have to talk about trust if this was going to go on, us working together and putting our lives in each others' hands. Because while I was undeniably attracted to him, I didn't trust him. Or Tarrek. Or anyone in this room. I had a murderer to find, and no one was excluded from being suspect as of yet. No one.

Tarrek rose, helping his mother to her feet. She stared at me for a long minute then turned and walked out of the amphitheater. We all followed her lead.

Bahlin, Tarrek and I returned to the room I had called home for the last three unconscious days.

"What are the chances I could get some working clothes, Tarrek?" I asked, rolling my shoulders at the weight of the gown. I felt stifled and fraudulent. It just wasn't my style.

"Of course, Maddy. I'll go get something from one of the women and return shortly." He took my hand and kissed it softly. I retrieved it as fast as I could without being bitchy. Behind him Bahlin rolled his eyes.

"Okay, Bay, tell me how likely it is that what you did earlier will cause any lasting effects with us."

Bahlin sauntered over to the chair by the door and sat, leaning back and crossing his feet at the ankles, arms over his chest. "Would it be so bad?"

"I don't know how to answer that since I don't know what it might mean that we've shared whatever it is we've shared." I crawled up on the edge of the bed, the cumbersome skirts slowing my progress. Turning to face him, I continued with my thought. "Do I even have power to share?"

"You will, have power, that is. The longer you do this and hone your skills, the more power you'll accumulate. You've already learned that you can sense when someone is trying to use magic to manipulate you."

"I did?"

Bahlin sighed and said, "Maddy, you shut Hellion and Gretta down when they tried to compel you with magic to answer their questions. Right?"

"Yeah. How did you understand that?"

"I'm a dragon, love. We're magical creatures in our own right."

"I want to know more about dragons."

A soft knock sounded at the door. Bahlin held his finger to his lips to silence me and motioned for me to get all the way back in bed. I climbed further in, pulling the covers up around my hips. He took three short, light steps to the door and peered out, exchanging soft words with the visitor before letting her pass. She was petite, blond and ethereal, seemingly ageless though she walked with the aid of a walking stick. I wouldn't have cared if she was, literally, a hag, because she was carrying what looked like pants and a shirt. Bahlin followed her closely as she made her way into the room, keeping no more than a couple of lengths from her.

Moving with more glide than walk, she made her way to the side of the bed, depositing the clothes next to me gently. "Madeline Niteclif, I am Pirsen, the Seelie's primary healer. I've been attending you since your arrival. I'd like to look at your shoulder."

"Just Maddy." I nodded, unreasonable fear flooding my veins. The blue tonic was what we assumed had poisoned me since it was the only thing I'd ingested after waking and I couldn't help but worry that she was the responsible party. I watched her as carefully as a rabbit watches a coyote. She turned to the bedside table and picked up the blue sleeping concoction that had been left for me.

"I see you didn't drink much of the draught," she said. "Did you sleep freely then?"

I shook my head. "I took a bit and it made me—"

"She hasn't needed it," Bahlin interrupted, the underlying malice in his voice leaving no room for argument. "I used some of my skill as a healer to help move the natural process along." He looked at me, his mouth settling into a harsh line. If he wasn't telling her, either, of our suspicion that I'd been poisoned, I was pretty sure there was a good reason. He moved in behind the healer and cocked a hip up on the edge of the bed, the mattress depressing and rolling me toward him. I pushed myself back closer to the middle of the enormous bed with a grunt. Bahlin nodded his head so slightly that I wondered if I had imagined it. Then I understood. He wanted me further back from the healer in the event there was any conflict. We were both so much larger than her that the idea of us fighting with her was ridiculous.

Voice nearly devoid of inflection, Pirsen kept her back to us and said, "How much did she drink, dragon?"

"So you were the one to leave the sleeping dram? I suspected as much when you were the one to return to the room instead of Tarrek," he said conversationally. "So where did you stash the lad?"

Confused, I looked between the two and then it dawned on me. Tarrek had gone out for clothes and not returned. He wouldn't have sent Pirsen in without sending word. He'd been too involved in overseeing my care and recovery to suddenly abandon his watch over me.

Pirsen sighed and her hair began to darken, lengthening from her shoulder to her hips in seconds and ending as a deep black. She curled in on herself and when she stood, her power flowed through the room sending a feeling like biting ants up and down my bare skin. Her walking stick glinted metallic and before she could turn around, Bahlin yelled, "Run, Maddy." Then, instead of giving me a chance to respond, he grabbed the covers and flipped me off the opposite edge of the bed. I landed in a tangle of limbs, skirt and sheet on the floor, striking my hip hard enough to send pins and needles down one leg. If I survived this, I'd end up with a nasty bruise. There was a tremendous crash and a masculine grunt of pain followed by the sounds of flesh striking flesh. I crab-walked backwards trying to get my back against a wall and scanned the room for some type of weapon. The only thing I could see was the dagger Tarrek had taken off when he went to meet with Bahlin earlier. I scrambled to the dresser, grabbed the dagger and turned toward the fight.

The woman held a short sword and had split Bahlin's arm from elbow to wrist and I could see the red of meat and muscle laid open to the room. That arm hung ineffectually at his side, but he was fighting well one-handed. My movement had distracted the woman, and he grabbed her by the hair and yanked, propelling her past him and knocking her off balance. Unfortunately Bahlin's back was to me, and he inadvertently threw her in my direction. Bahlin spun around and the look of shock on his face had him pausing. I didn't have that luxury.

With a shriek of rage, the woman gained her balance and launched herself at me, walking-stick-turned-sword raised over her head as she prepared to cleave my head from my shoulders. A primal survival instinct took me like a firestorm, and I lunged forward to meet her charge.

"No," Bahlin roared.

I dropped to one knee and blindly struck out and up over my head, the dagger gripped in my fisted hands. The feel of the knife entering my attacker's body was a shock. It wasn't anything like the movies portray it, where the knife slips into flesh like it's little more than butter. Instead there was brief resistance before my dagger pierced her flesh and grated across her rib cage. Her momentum carried the knife well into her chest cavity and, I would later learn, shredded her heart. At the time I didn't care. It was her or me, and I was intent on it being me. She sagged on my blade, her sword falling back behind her head before her fingers relaxed in the first throes of shock and then death, and she dropped the sword to the floor with a metallic clatter. Her weight, combined with my position, left me with trembling arms that quickly gave out and her limp body fell on top of me.

Her breath rattled in her chest, and her glazed eyes sought mine. "I am only one spoke in this wheel, Madeleine Niteclif. My death changes nothing." Blood trickled from her mouth and ran down her chin as she fought for air. "We won't fail." Her face went slack, and the last remaining tension in her body dissolved. She was gone, and I'd never been able to ask her what she meant.

Bahlin took several large steps toward me and yanked her body off me like it weighed no more than a bag of grain and tossed her haphazardly to the side, falling to his knees at my side. I lay on the floor, arms and legs akimbo like a crash test dummy. The receding adrenaline rush paired with shock, and I began to shake. He snatched me up to his chest, holding me so tight it was difficult to breathe.

Was he shaking too? I wondered. Because I felt like I was coming apart at the seams, and he was the only thing holding the pieces of my body and soul together. I had killed a woman and my mind was rejecting this new reality, trying to deny that I was capable of taking life. He was murmuring to me in Gaelic and rocking me gently. Through the haze of fear, I realized my stomach was wet.

"Bahlin? Bahlin," I said in a reedy voice. "Bay, I'm okay...I think. We need to get up because I'm having a *Fatal Attraction* moment where I'm waiting for her to surge up and try to strangle one of us from behind and we never see her coming and it scares the shit out of me and I think my heart would stop beating if she twitched and—"

"Hush, *muirnin*," he crooned, "hush. She'll no be gettin' up again, I promise ye."

"But—"

"Hush, I say. Let's make sure yeh're okay." Without releasing me completely he leaned my body back in one arm and concern creased his brow. He plucked at the bloodied dress and ripped open the bodice without pretense. Modesty be damned. I was too scared to look, afraid she may have snuck in a slice before I killed her, because I knew with certainty what my mind rejected. She was dead. The spreading pool of blood under her body was unquestionably unforgiving.

"Yeh're fine, *a stór*. Yeh're fine." The relief in his voice was palpable. He folded the fabric back across my bared torso then gripped my shoulder and gave me a harsh shake. Apparently the compassionate portion of my recuperation was over. "I told ye to run ye fool. I'd ha' taken her in a moment more."

I had a flashback to the color of her eyes and a wave of nausea rolled up my spine and out my mouth in a heated rush before I could do anything about it beyond turn my head. He pulled me tight to his chest once the sickness passed. When I closed my eyes in relief, I remembered seeing parts of Bahlin's arm that no human eye should ever see. I scrambled out of his arms and knelt in the heat of her slowly advancing blood and at the edge of my vomit and grabbed his wrists. He yanked one arm away while the other twitched in my hand.

"Let me see," I ordered him. With a long-suffering sigh he acquiesced. His forearm was still cut deeply, but the wound had begun to heal. Not as quickly as the aftermath of his fight with Tarrek, but it *was* healing. Blood only seeped from the tissue. It seemed that if I stared at it without blinking I could see the muscle reknitting itself as we sat there. I touched the clean edge of the gash, and he hissed.

"It may heal quick like, but it burns like a bugger while it's doin' it." He glanced at me and then looked around the room, not quite ever making it back to my face. "And I seared the tissue."

I looked at him questioningly, and he grinned a huge grin.

"I'm a dragon, Maddy. And speakin' o', I'm goin' to have to get fuel soon. At this rate I'll need a side o' beef or a sheep. But there's no way in bluidy hell I'm eatin' anythin' from this forsaken catacomb." Pushing himself to standing, he reached for me with his good arm and helped me up.

I made it to standing and locked my knees, taking a partial page from Bahlin's figurative book on coping and looked anywhere but at the body. "Is that who I think it is?" I asked, following Bahlin with wide eyes.

He moved around the room, picking up the short sword first and laying it on the bed. I looked away from him as he approached the body. I heard a squelching sound and assumed he'd retrieved the dagger from her chest. He looked back at me and nodded. "It's Gretta, Hellion's mate."

"Hellion?" *Not Hellion,* I thought. *Don't let me hurt him.*

"Remember? He's the large bloke from the High Council. The wizard." He picked up the discarded pile of clothes and shook them out a piece at a time. There was a pair of black leather pants and a white tunic. He laid each piece of clothing out on the bed and turned toward me.

I stood there staring at him in disbelief. How could he be so calm? I'd killed a mate of one of the High Council. After getting shot. And poisoned. And condemning a faerie to death. And losing Tarrek. Not bad in the way that an atomic bomb is considered an explosion.

"Was she mortal?" I asked.

"Yes. You'd have had a tougher time with her if she'd been immortal. She moved slow for all that she is, or was, magical." He held out a hand and beckoned me forward, holding out the dagger to me. I shook my head and he stalked toward me, took my hand and curled my fingers around the hilt. "I'm going to say this once, and I expect you to heed me, no arguments. You defended yourself. Now go into the bathroom and take the fastest shower of your life."

I must have looked confused because he turned me toward the bathroom and gave me a little push. I took an unsure step forward, worried about being away from him. He smiled at my obvious hesitation.

"We have to get out of here immediately, pet. Shower, get out, get dressed and wait for me to come to you. I'll only come in provided I'm alone in this room. If anyone else comes in the door, and it's not Tarrek, and they make a grab for you, slit your throat. It will be a kinder, faster end than what they'd have planned for you. Once I come for you, we're getting the hell out of here." He gave me a very gentle second push toward the bathroom door. "And Maddy? Leave the door open, at least partially."

This time I didn't argue with him.

I was only in the shower long enough to rinse the blood out of my hair and off my body. Shampoo and soap would come later when I had the luxury of time. Oh, and the luxury of distance from the sithen. I dried off with a linen bath sheet and hopped into the leather pants, literally. It took hopping to get into them. Whoever they had been made for didn't have hips or thighs. *A man, maybe?* I wondered. *And a small, damnably skinny man at that. Figures.* The pants laced up the front, and laces located anywhere on, near or around the pelvis are *not* user friendly. The white tunic slipped on over my head and was slightly sheer, giving me pause. I was entirely commando. I'm modest by nature, and the thought that there wasn't even an *option* for panty lines and the fact my nipples showed through in even the slightest way was embarrassing. But if I had to give up an inch of modesty to gain a literal mile, or more, of distance from this hellhole, I was going to do it. Besides, there was the whole beggars and choosers and that lot...again.

I listened carefully, and no noise came from the bedroom. Following Bahlin's instructions, I stood and waited on him, dagger clenched in my sweaty hand. I hoped that I would be brave enough to end myself if need be, because I knew I wasn't strong enough to endure any type of serious torture. But I was the Niteclif, and we don't cop to fear too easily...out loud, anyway. My conscience jumped in, reminding me that this wasn't the first time I'd had that particular thought. I mentally threw it half a peace sign, and I waited.

The door creaked and I tensed, lifting the dagger despite my initial queasiness. It was Bahlin. He again held his finger to his lips and motioned for me to follow him. Heart thundering in my throat, I padded along behind him barefoot. We passed through the bedroom, and he held up a hand for me to stop while he checked the hallway. He was gone for only a few moments before he came back and took my hand, tugging me forward. I was so terrified my bowels felt loose.

Bahlin looked back over his shoulder and, with more breath than voice, said, "There's a doorway at the end of this hall. Last I checked, it opened into a large foyer with three doors inside it. I'll go through and check each door until I find the exit. The sithen has been known to move things about to trap the non-fae inside, so wait for my all-clear signal."

My eyes must have widened perceptibly because Bahlin just shook his head, took my shaking hand and led me forward. As promised, there was a large wooden door banded with metal and sporting a huge metal locking mechanism at the end of the light-suffused hallway. Physically setting me to the side of the door, thus leaving me partially hidden once the door was opened, he peered into the foyer beyond. I breathed in shallow pants, afraid to draw any attention to myself, continuing to grip the dagger in my right hand and fisting my left. I was ready to defend myself as well as I might should trouble find us, and I knew without a doubt that it was actively looking.

Bahlin returned to me in minutes, deftly reaching around the edge of the door and grabbing my wrist above the hand that held the knife. Wise man, er, dragon. I squeaked involuntarily and then mentally flagellated myself for my lack of bravery. *Fake it 'til you make it, Niteclif,* I chastised myself. Bahlin seemed to hear my thoughts because he rolled his eyes and shook his head, dragging me forward. He stopped in the doorway and looked at me closely. "Take a deep breath."

My heart jumped. "Why?"

"I can feel your pulse, and it's making *me* nervous."

"Sorry," I said, and attempted to draw my hand away from his forearm.

"I didn't ask you to let go of me, only to control your breathing."

I shifted my hand to grip him with my fingertips, though I still clenched his arm.

"Here," he said, and took my hand, lacing his fingers through mine. He squeezed my fingers in reassurance. "Better?"

I took a deep breath and nodded. We moved forward.

There was no sign of anyone in the foyer and only one door was open. Darkness shown beyond the doorway like a savior's beacon and we streaked across the foyer like twin wraiths, emerging into the night like we'd been belched from the earth. The night air felt as if it breathed through the open doorway like it was the nose of a sleeping giant. I could feel the fresh air move past my cheek, back and forth, back and forth.

Once we were outside, the door slammed shut behind us with an echoing bang making us both jump, and then I had both feet on the ground at the same time. My body was suddenly lifted up by an unseen force and thrown backward toward the now grassy hillside, no door in existence. I was slammed down with something as resonant as a sonic boom. My body felt as if the reverberations had dislodged major organs, and my heart hurt for a moment. I lay there, stunned, staring at the night sky and relearning how to breathe.

"What in great glory's name," I wheezed, "just happened?"

"So much for stealth," Bahlin said, grinning. "I forgot to tell you that, as a mortal, you would immediately gather all the time you'd spent inside the sithen. Inside, your lifespan is increased a thousand fold. Outside, well, you catch up with whatever time you lost. Since you're not aging while you're the Niteclif, it just hurts like hell. Your body is shocked but not affected."

I pushed myself to sit with a grunt. "And it never dawned on either of you to tell me this before I left, huh?"

"It's not like we had a great opportunity, Maddy," Bahlin said softly. "We were, *I* was, more worried about keeping you alive."

"Sorry." *Again. Man I was turning into a bitch.* "And that was only four days?" Reaching for my hand, Bahlin helped me up, holding it for an extra moment when he had me vertical. He looked at me, and I felt the color rise in my cheeks. He squeezed and let go, stepping back.

"The longer you're in there, the worse leaving will be. Ah well. It's done now. I suppose we had better depart with all haste." He began unbuttoning his pants, and I spun away from him.

"How the *hell* is getting naked going to help us get away from this damnable place?" I hissed. "I understand the whole near-death-reaffirming-life sex thing but this isn't the time or place to—"

His deep, breathy laughter was my only answer. Something hit me in the back and I flinched, looking down as whatever it was slithered down my back. His jeans. I bent and picked them up without turning around, preparing to toss them back over my shoulder at him with some witty comment when I felt the air move. It wasn't wind, but rather a disturbance of the molecules themselves. Static was everywhere, and my shirt crackled with it as I pulled his jeans into my arms. I was suddenly aware that something very large was behind me, and I froze, unable to even blink for a moment.

"Bay?" I asked in a soft voice, the kind you used to call out for your parents when you were a child scared of the night.

A deep snort sounded behind me, like a horse blowing out after a run, and I turned in slow motion and looked up, and up some more.

Denise Tompkins

He had shifted.

Bahlin's dragon form was breathtaking and terrifying and beautiful all at the same time. He was enormous, standing roughly eight feet tall at the withers. In the pre-dawn darkness it was impossible to discern the color of his scales, but they were inky, so dense he seemed carved out of the shadows of night itself. He crouched in front of me on four legs, with two great muscular rear legs and two sinewy forelegs that were more like arms. Each foot held five claws as large as my forearm. His tail was long and barbed, and it swished back and forth with implied impatience. His eyes were the same icy blue I had experienced before, set into a massive head adorned with a horned crown at the end of a long neck. His face was shaped like a horse's though his nose was slightly beaked and he had a sparse beard of spikes along his jaw. And his teeth. His teeth were massive and filled his mouth like daggers.

But it was his wings that stole my heart. Set into his shoulders where his arms met his body, they were iridescent and partially translucent, enough so I could see stars through the membrane of the wing. With a structure like that of a bat, the wings were like secondary arms. He had a small hooked claw at the upper bed of the wing and structural boning throughout to build support. The lightest of veining could be seen in the translucence. I stepped up close to him and reached out a hand tentatively to stroke his graceful neck and gasped with surprise at the texture of his scales. They were smooth and tight to his body. He really did feel like a lizard, but he was clearly warm-blooded. And while his scales must provide some type of protection, they were so supple they felt like saddle leather. I smiled and stroked the juncture of wing and body and he snorted and gave a grumbling growl, turning his head back to nose me closer. I couldn't figure out what he was after until he bellied down to the ground and continued pushing me toward his back.

"You're kidding," I choked out. "I am *not* getting on your back."

He snorted and looked back in the general direction of the door as if to say, *"Don't be stupid. Of course you are."*

I studied his back skeptically before I realized it really was feasible. If I sat just in front of the wings and hooked my knees carefully... I'd decided to give it a try when I heard the shout of pursuit

108

behind me. Decision made.

   With studied carefulness balanced with haste, Bahlin pushed me to his shoulder, stuck his nose under my butt and lifted me up. I scrambled ungracefully onto his back and with a great surge of power he unfurled his wings and pushed off with his hind legs, nearly unseating me. I leaned down and wrapped my arms as far around his neck as I could and we were off, bulleting into the night sky, the sithen erupting with activity below us as his jeans drifted slowly back to earth.

Chapter Seven

The pre-dawn air was cold, and my nipples puckered painfully in response. Tears streamed over my cheeks, brought on by the racing wind in my face and the near constant fear of the last five days. In fairness, I knew it wasn't his fault, but he was the closest target for my rage. I balled up a fist and punched him in the shoulder. He didn't flinch.

Bahlin moved through the night sky in near silence, the only sound the disturbance of his wings cutting through the air and the occasional huff of breath. I could feel his lungs expand and contract between my knees and it was oddly sexual, though I didn't examine that feeling too closely. He raced parallel to the breaking dawn. It wasn't long before I began shivering with true cold. I couldn't feel my feet at all. Bahlin dipped lower over the open expanse of farmland, the ground getting closer and closer, the only break in the landscape the fencing and small herds of sheep and cows that scattered instinctively as the predator raced passed them. I realized Bahlin was beginning to breathe harder, his movements less graceful. He banked to the right and dove toward a small cottage that seemed to grow out of the hillside, setting down in the front yard. I was shaking in earnest now, my skin tinged blue from the cold, my joints frozen in macabre positions. Bahlin bellied down to the ground again, but I couldn't move. He turned his enormous head back to look at me.

Teeth chattering so hard I worried they'd crack I stuttered, "I-I-I c-c-c-can't-t-t-t..."

He rolled his shoulder to the ground and reached behind him, so incredibly gentle with his clawed hands, and pulled me into his arms. I tried to struggle, but I couldn't gain any semblance of control over my traitorous muscles. He held me close to his chest and began to hum. The sound seemed to generate deep in his chest, rumbling out, sounding like a monk's liturgy. In a moment of hysteria I laughed. Should I offer to insert a quarter or pray? When I realized he was warming physically, I knew what he was doing. He was generating body heat to warm me up. I rolled into his embrace and cuddled with him and he sighed, a content sound. I laughed out loud again, though this time the sound was less harsh. I was snuggling with a dragon. We sat that way until the sun rose over the horizon, and we were casting a soft shadow. I looked up and gasped. His scales were a matte midnight blue, nearly black. He was like the night sky incarnate, touchable and tangible. Suddenly I stiffened. What if we were seen? What if the cottage occupant caught us on the doorstep? How do you explain the unexplainable?

"Put me down," I hissed, struggling in his arms.

Bahlin set me on the ground where I promptly collapsed. I was still cold enough that I couldn't command my feet or legs to obey. He looked at me and then looked at the door, nosing me toward it. The only thing he accomplished was disturbing the grass and royally pissing me off.

"You are insane if you think I'm going in there," I said in a harsh whisper. I swear he cocked an eyebrow at me. "No. No, I am *not*," I said in the same low voice.

He turned and looked toward the sky, unfurled his wings and pushed off the ground, gaining height more slowly and laboriously this time. He left me sitting there in the yard, gaping at his retreating form, alone.

I lay there for a minute, flexing my muscles and trying to get them to warm up. I finally stood, albeit unsteadily, and turned back toward the cottage. I screamed, jumping back and falling on my ass yet again.

"I'm sorry. I didn't mean to startle you," said the woman who had been standing at my back. Without asking or straining, she bent and lifted me to my feet, setting me down gently. Then she stepped back. "I assumed if Bahlin dropped you off here, you knew of me." Her brow furrowed, and she looked at me with some concern. She was as tall as me, and it was a novelty to look a woman eye to eye. Her hair was a

111

deep mahogany and fell to her diminutive waist. Her eyes were a shade or two lighter than Bahlin's intense blue, and her skin was lightly tanned but completely unlined. Her voice was like rich cream, soft and decadent, and it held the softest hint of Scotland. She was ethereal, and I think I hated her a little bit for it.

"You, uh, *know* about Bay, uh, Bahlin?" I stuttered, trying to reign in my galloping heart and wheezing breath.

"'Bay'? I like that. To answer you, yes I know very well about Bahlin."

My hackles rose, and I found myself jealous of this unknown woman. Who was she to him? And why did he leave me with her? Before my brain could stop my mouth I said, "So you know him well. *How* well?"

She chuckled and said, "I think you may want to come inside. He has probably gone to feed and, in that case, he'll be gone a while. Would you like a cup of tea?" She turned and walked back into the house, all grace and perfect form, her skirt swirling about her ankles, as if dragons coming and going and depositing strangers in the yard were simple everyday things.

Unsure what to do, I followed her. I had dropped my dagger sometime during the flight, likely after the shaking had taken over. So I was unarmed and alone. I didn't like it. But if Bahlin thought this was a safe place, I had to trust him. After all, I had no one else. He and I were definitely going to have to talk about this.

The thatch-roofed house was much larger than it appeared from the outside. The front door opened directly into a large living room with an attached, open, eat-in kitchen. The stone hearth was huge, with a baking oven built in above the firebox. I looked around, appreciating the simple decor and the hand-scraped wood floors, the plush furniture and soft-colored walls. It was all so charming with a cohesiveness I'd never be able to achieve without hiring a decorator. I think I hated the house a little at that moment too.

My hostess walked down a long hallway and returned with an enormous sweatshirt. Handing it to me, she smiled and said, "It's Bahlin's. I'm sure he won't mind if you borrow it." Her manner was proprietary, and it made me even more uncomfortable. She grinned, her eyes flashing that icy blue then back to sapphire. Had it been the light? I accepted the sweatshirt and pulled it on slowly, enjoying the smell of Bahlin so close.

Realizing I didn't even know the woman's name I stuck out my hand.

"I'm Maddy."

"I know." She looked me over very carefully, her eyes cooling as I cuddled the sweatshirt a little. "You're the Niteclif."

"How did you—"

"Know? I knew well before you did." She arched a brow at me and crossed her arms over her small, *I really do hate her*, chest.

"I'm sorry. Have I pissed you off somehow? Because I'm pretty sure I don't know you well enough for you to be so catty." I stared at her hard, my own eyes growing cold, as I rolled the sleeves up on the sweatshirt just in case this conversation came to blows. With the way my last few days had been, it wouldn't come as a surprise.

"Oh no, I'm not pissed as you Americans say. I'm fine. But I have a strongly vested interest in Bahlin's well-being, and I won't have you come in here and..."

"And what?" I demanded, stepping closer to her.

"If he's not told you, I don't believe I will."

"But—"

"Leave it," came a deep voice from behind me. I spun around, finding Bahlin coming through the front door wearing a pair of ratty sweats and nothing more. His torso was lean but well muscled with cobblestone abs included, the only hair a line from his belly button to his waistband.

"What the hell is it with everyone sneaking up on me around here?" I exclaimed, frustration lacing every word.

Bahlin laughed and walked to me with a hip-rolling swagger. He wrapped me in his arms and said, "I borrowed Aiden's sweats from his gym bag, Brylanna. Tell him he needs to wash the damned things on occasion." He looked down at me. "Has my Brylanna been kind, Maddy?"

"Define kind," I said, standing stiff in his arms. What did he mean *his* Brylanna? He chuckled in my ear, his breath playing through my hair and down my neck and giving me goose bumps. I wiggled my hands up to his smooth, muscled chest and pushed back from him, needing space to think. "Why are dragons so keen on avoiding questions?"

"Ah, so she told you she's a dragon, then?"

"Nope, you just did."

He laughed again, but softly this time. "What gave it away?"

"The eyes flashed that weird blue color. Then she said she knew I was the Niteclif. Only the supernatural world knows about my existence, so logic says she must be one of your world. Then you came here in dragon form, without concern of being seen, so she had to know about you. Simple deduction."

"Well done, Maddy. Ah, the eyes. She must have lost her temper then. Brylanna?"

"She provoked me," the woman said, sounding sulky.

"And you know better than to be provoked," Bahlin said, sounding reproving. "Maddy, Brylanna is my sister and yes, she's a dragon, as well."

Ah, sister. I hated that I felt relieved, so I took the offensive, though it was more curiosity than anger in my voice. "Explain the whole she-knew-before-I-knew thing." I walked to the small dining table and sat.

"Make yourself comfortable," Brylanna said in a sickly sweet voice.

"Brylanna. She is my guest. Respect her as such." Bahlin's voice brooked no room for argument.

"My apologies, Niteclif," she said, looking honestly chagrined.

"Maddy, Brylanna. Please call me Maddy." Deciding to be the bigger person, I stood and walked to her, sticking out my hand again. "I'd like to start over with you. It seems that we've somehow taken off on the wrong foot."

She tilted her head to one side and considered, then stuck out her hand. She grasped my hand and bent her head over the joined digits, humming in a way similar to Bahlin's heat-generating sound. I tried to take my hand back, and she tightened her grip to just this side of pain.

Beginning to feel trapped, I looked at Bahlin and realized his eyes had changed to icy blue. I tugged harder. Brylanna's head snapped up, and her eyes matched Bahlin's in their other-worldliness.

"Your path has changed, Maddy," she said in a resonating voice. "You've lost someone from your inner circle, and it is unclear whether he will be returned to you."

"Tarrek," I whispered and her hand squeezed mine tighter. Panic fluttered in my chest.

"Brylanna's a Seer," Bahlin said softly, having come up behind me. He laid his hand on my shoulder.

"Bahlin, remove your hand. It clouds my Site," she said in that timbered voice. She bowed her head deeper over our joined hands. Suddenly she was grinding the bones of my hand together. I grunted in pain and she fell to her knees in front of me, hissing.

"Brylanna," Bahlin shouted.

"Oh, goddess, she's dark, Bahlin. I cannot see beyond—"

"Leave it," he ordered again, grasping our hands and wrenching them apart.

Her head snapped up, and she growled at him. "It's not for you to divine now is it, *brother?*" she asked cryptically. He held out a hand and helped her to her feet. She accepted then flung herself free of him, turning away from us and wrapping her arms around her middle. I stood shaking, unsure what had just happened, clutching my bruised hand to my chest.

"What did you see?" I asked.

Taking a deep breath she turned back to us, her eyes no longer that icy blue. She looked first to Bahlin and then to me. "Part of it I will not tell you because he,—" she inclined her head toward her brother, "—doesn't want you to know. But as for the other, you should be prepared. You are hunted by something dark, soulless. It comes for you in stealth, though you know who it is already. And you are ill prepared to defend yourself. Bahlin will come to your aid, but it may not be soon enough. If it is not, you will both perish. Bahlin," her voice cracking, "the shadow—it's after your stone."

In a moment of hysteria, I burst into tear-inducing laughter. Both dragons turned to look at me, astonished.

"It wants his *stone?*" I gasped for breath and wiped my wind-chapped cheeks. "Isn't that rather personal?"

"Oh for the love, Maddy," Bahlin said, rolling his eyes. "Get your mind out of the gutter, chick. My stone, not my stones." Suddenly he was chuckling and we paused, looking at each other.

"Fine. Laugh if you will, but this may be the death of you and *I cannot see.*" Brylanna stormed toward the front door. "Do what you know you will. I'll be back tonight—after." She grinned at Bahlin and left the house. Moments later I heard a car start and drive away, the sound of the engine fading until there was only silence, the sounds of our breathing and the little sounds of the house settling around us.

Hiccupping, I said, "What's your stone?"

"Every dragon has what is uncreatively called a Dragon's Stone. It's located in the center of the brain and contains a wealth of information. It's said that each infant dragon retains some of the knowledge of the parents, and it's how dragon magic is passed from parent to child. To hold the stone is to own the knowledge and skills, or magic, that the dragon possesses."

"Dragon magic?" I asked. I'm nothing if not skeptical, even in the face of a mythological creature. Go figure.

"Yes, magic." He stared at me hard as if trying to decide how much to tell me. "Each dragon has a set of gifts. Brylanna's include divination. She can see the future, though not always clearly as you'll have noted. One of my gifts is healing, which is how I helped you at the sithen."

"What other gifts do you guys have?"

"Ah, I think I'll save that for later. For now, let's get you cleaned up."

He headed down the short hallway that Brylanna had been down earlier, and I followed him. There were two bedrooms in the house, one on either side of the hallway. He stopped at a closet and took out towels, then grabbed my hand and pulled me through the doorway on the right. The room was large, with the biggest bed I'd ever seen. I glanced at him from under my lashes, confused and embarrassed. Was this his room? The soft, earthy colors couldn't compete with the dark blue silk sheets and comforter of the rumpled platform bed.

Easily interpreting the look on my face he said, "I know it's a bit of a contradiction, but I've learned from living in London that I'm a creature who values comfort versus style in his living space. When possible I'll elect both and stay at my hotel, but Brylanna's more a country soul. This bed is her one concession to me and she'd be rid of it if I didn't need a hideaway on occasion." He walked into the bathroom and came back out.

"It's fine," I said, not sure if he cared for my opinion, but offering it anyway. "Uh, the bathroom?"

"Through this door. I'll use Brylanna's. I'll leave some of her clothes on the bed for you to borrow. I'm sure she won't mind."

I looked at him.

He laughed. "Okay, she'll mind, but she'll get over it." And he walked away leaving me with a view of his wonderfully taut ass.

The bathroom was sparse but fully functional. Soap, hot water and time were what I really needed, and this offered all three. I ran a bath, needing to soak my aching muscles and, likewise, warm them up. I still felt chilled. I peeled the leather pants off and swore to do my best to avoid them in the future. Remembering I didn't have any underwear available made me curse and hope that Bahlin delivered a non-sheer shirt for me to borrow.

The water was borderline too hot as I stuck first a toe then a foot into it, slowly adjusting to the temperature. I stepped in and sank down, reminiscing about my first night in England. I'd ended it in a bathtub, too, though it felt like it was both yesterday and years ago, and I was ending this day with the sunrise. Still, I followed tradition and washed my hair, dunking it to rinse the shampoo out of it. I drained the water and refilled the tub and crawled back in to soak, drifting on the edge of sleep until a soft knock sounded at the door.

"Maddy?" Bahlin's voice was soft but concerned. "It's been nearly an hour. Are you okay?"

I sat up and held my hands out in front of my face. Yep, prunes. I was finished.

"I'll be out in a minute, Bay," I said, pushing myself up to standing and reaching for a towel. I stepped out onto the tile floor and briskly dried myself off, wrapping the towel around my torso. It was a near thing, but it went all the way around. I'd be okay if I didn't move too much. I finger-combed my hair and went to the door, peaking out. Bahlin sat on the edge of the bed in a pair of boxer shorts. He looked up at me and smiled, and it was such a winsome look that I smiled back.

"You're beautiful when you smile like that," he whispered, standing and moving toward me. I noticed the slight tenting of his boxers and whipped my gaze back to his eyes. Gently he said, "I believe that, to quote you, it was something like 'sex and the whole near-death-reaffirming-life thing,' wasn't it?"

I continued to stare at him, unsure what to do. I had had two lovers in my lifetime, both results of relationships affectionately referred to as monogamous monotony by my girlfriends. Neither relationship had left me with a wild, passionate view of sex. One ex-boyfriend had even accused me of being an ice princess, unreachable, unpleasurable. Such stellar reviews of my past performance definitely tainted the developing fantasy I had about the man standing in front of me. So did I give in to the raging primal instinct to reaffirm life, or did I stick to my basic moral code and lock myself in the bathroom and wish him luck with himself? Of course, in all my mental ramblings I'd forgotten to take into consideration one thing: the man himself.

Bahlin approached me slowly, his boxers twitching from their internal assault. He reached me and, instead of pulling me up into a wild embrace, he ran a finger down my bare arm leaving a trail of goose flesh in its wake. I looked up into his eyes and they were the deep, dark sapphire color that had stolen my breath in my first night's dream. He sank his head toward me and brushed his lips over mine, breathing out the words, "*A stór*," as he nibbled his way to my jaw. I was barely breathing, scared to encourage him and equally scared he'd stop his exploration of my neck, then my shoulders. He began working his way back up to my ears, his breath hot.

"Ah, my love, you're such a temptation," he whispered.

"You don't love me," I whispered back.

He lifted his head, drawing his attention from my ear to my eyes. "You don't know that," he said in a gentle voice.

"I do," I said. "You've not known me long enough for me to drive you crazy. The only people who loved me unconditionally are dead." Tears blurred my vision and I looked down, giving them permission to

118

slip down my cheeks.

"Ah, your parents." He lifted his hand from my shoulder to chin and pushed up gently, forcing me to meet his gaze. "They are gone but never forgotten, *mo muirnin*. Never doubt that." He stroked a finger down my neck, and I shivered. "And, with all respect due you, I don't believe you're qualified to tell me how I do or don't feel."

I nodded my head too fast, pushing yet more tears over the dam of my lower lashes. He bent his head even closer to mine and kissed the tears away.

"We are fated, you and I," he said.

"Fated? Is that what I'm not supposed to know?"

"Ah, no." He took a deep breath and stepped back from me. But he didn't elaborate.

I felt adrift in the large room without him to serve as my anchor. I reached out for him, and he stepped into me with the passion I had expected with his first approach. He wrapped his arms around me and crushed me to his chest so tightly I let out an *oompf* and he laughed, squatting down and picking me up by wrapping his arms around my upper thighs before spinning me around. I locked my hands behind his neck and bent my forehead to his.

"Do you want me as much as I want you, *mo chrid*?" he asked, sliding me slowly down the front of his body. His erection, trapped behind the thin cotton of his underwear, was blazing hot against my lower belly as he gripped my hips and held me close to him.

I let my head fall back and he feasted on my neck, kissing and nipping from jaw to shoulder with more intent than moments before. He quickly dipped his head and licked his way along the top of my left breast over my heart, slipping his tongue under the edge of the towel.

"Holy crap," I gasped, as the heat of his tongue went straight to my womb. I had never been so aroused in all my life and this man had taken me there in minutes.

He pressed his lips firmly to my heart, bending low and running his hands up my outer thighs, under the towel until he could grip my ass hard.

"Maddy? Say the word and I'll stop, but if you don't stop me now, I'm going to throw you down on that bed and have my way with you."

119

I couldn't get his words through my head. All I wanted was the heat, the passion, not conversation, and definitely not responsibility. For once I wanted breathless recklessness.

But Bahlin wasn't programmed for recklessness when it came to me, apparently. "Maddy? Look at me and tell me you want this." He softened his grip on my ass, running his hands in small circles over the branded skin.

I looked at him, *really* looked at him. I wanted him so badly, but Tarrek was out there somewhere. I couldn't do this, not now, not with obligation weighing down on me.

"Bay..." I didn't know how to say this. Looking at me, he recognized the hesitation in my face and he released me, stepping back. "I'm so sorry." *Damn it.*

"No apologies, Maddy. You feel as you feel. It only means I'll have to wait you out, and I reckon I'm one of the most patient blokes in the world. I've waited over...let's just say I've waited a very long time for you," he said light-heartedly.

"Give me some time, Bay. It's been too much, too fast. All of it." I sighed heavily and stepped back, putting some distance between us. And then I smiled. "How old *are* you, anyway?"

Holding his finger over my lips he said, "First, no apologies. I meant that. And I'm much older than you." He turned, walked to the bed and straightened the bedding, folding it back to some sort of order. "I'm going to suggest we sleep together—"

"We discussed that," I said snarkily. "And how much older?"

"Ah, but we weren't discussing *sleep*, my love." He waggled his eyebrows and I laughed, the tension broken just like that. "I think it's safer if, from this point on, we're not separated. You're going to be hunted by the High Council for the murder of Gretta. And apparently whoever is murdering different beings is after my stone. Do you agree that we should stick together?"

I nodded. I was reeling from his shift from sex to murder, and I felt like I had a tenuous grip on reality, at best. I was going to need him to walk me through this and, according to his sister, save my ass.

There was only one answer: "I agree."

"Then let's put all this aside," he said, waving a hand between the two of us, "and focus on finding a murderer and saving our own skins." He crawled into bed and rolled onto his side, opening his arms to me.

"And Tarrek, Bay," I said. "We need to focus on finding Tarrek. And, uh, I still need clothes."

He sighed and closed his eyes for a moment. "Dreams never fade," he said, reopening his eyes and looking at me very directly, "though I never imagined taking you to bed with the faerie between us, even figuratively." He ran his hand back and forth over the silk sheets, the hiss of skin on the fabric seeming to thunder through my ears. "The clothes are sitting on the bed in the other bedroom. Hurry and change before I do my best to change your mind, Maddy."

For the second time in less than twelve hours, I hurried.

Bahlin had set out a pair of sweats and a black V-neck T-shirt. I pulled the clothes on, grateful for the solid shirt even if I didn't have what I now thought of as the luxury of underwear. I padded back across the hallway to his bedroom, and he opened his arms to me again.

"Just sleep, right?"

He smiled, his eyes flashing color to ice blue and back. "Of course. It's what we negotiated."

"Negotiated?"

"Never forget, Maddy, that I'm a dragon at heart. When you're dealing with mythological creatures, and particularly dragons, vampires and the fae, you will need to negotiate everything. We are selfish creatures as a general rule, though we can be ruled by our hearts on rare occasions."

I thought about that. Had he stopped his seduction because he was following his heart or because I had somehow negotiated it without meaning to? Questions for another time. I was exhausted. I walked to the bed and sat on the edge, pulling one knee up to my chin and looking over at Bahlin.

"I'm too tired to go through negotiations, especially since I didn't know I needed to, so here are my terms: sleep. Only sleep. No nasty, not now, not ever."

"Not acceptable."

"Come again?" Oh shit, not what I meant. "I mean—"

Bahlin roared with laughter, rolling onto his back and tucking his hands behind his head. "No sex, not now, and I'll agree to not seduce you while you're in this bed *this time*. All bets are off when you leave the bed, though."

"No nasty, no *attempt* at the nasty, until we get back to London and get a bead on Tarrek."

"Son of a bitch, Maddy. That could be weeks." He exploded into a sitting position, throwing the covers back to reveal his still impressive erection.

"Take it or leave it, Bay," I said softly. "Because I'm sure Tarrek would find the terms acceptable if your positions were reversed."

"Don't bloody bet on it, love," he said darkly. He seemed to truly think things over before he answered. "Fine. I agree."

I crawled into bed and lay down on my side, resting my head on the pillow closest to me. He reached out and snagged me around the waist, pulling me close as he spooned me, and nestled himself between my ass cheeks. I began to struggle, and he laughed darkly.

"You didn't negotiate no cuddling, love. Sweet dreams."

Damned dragons, was the last thought I had before sleep claimed me. This time I dreamed.

Chapter Eight

I was walking through the forest wearing a medieval-looking gown that felt familiar to me. It was more appropriate for a Renaissance fair than a nature hike. Where had I seen it before? The night was moonless, and there wasn't a star in the sky. It wasn't the gentle dark that comes with sweet dreams, but the cold and calculating dark of nightmares. I shivered from the bones out.

"Run," hissed a deep voice that was neither male nor female. "Run as fast and as far as you dare, you American whore," said the voice.

Almost involuntarily my legs began to pump, faster and faster still, until I was tearing through the forest blindly, not watching where my feet went. I put my hands up as if to ward off the unseen blows of limbs slapping at my face. My mind echoed with the words, and it gave me pause.

I'm no whore, I thought timidly and then more firmly. "I'm no whore," I yelled. "Who the hell are you to be throwing down the verbal gauntlet?" I taunted, leaning back and forcing my legs to either slow or allow me to fall. They slowed. Then I stopped, spinning in a circle and I screamed out, "Coward."

The blow landed on my shoulders and made me face-plant into the dead leaves and moss of the forest floor. I choked on the detritus in my mouth, spitting it out. Warmth spilled down my face, and I realized I'd bit my bottom lip when I hit the ground and I'd split my forehead open at my hairline. It didn't hurt, which meant it was either nothing much or something serious. I pushed up to my knees and took a well-placed kick to the ribs. Grunting, I went back down. That was going to leave a mark.

The asexual voice seemed to come from all around me when it said, "Do you challenge me?" It sounded amused.

I couldn't breathe to answer.

"I didn't think so," it chuckled. "Now let me spell this out—"

An iron fist gripped my shoulder, and I wheezed in fear.

"Get up."

I struggled to my hands and knees and pushed myself to kneeling, wavering slightly and holding my side. A light shown in the darkness, and I turned my face to it just as the voice bellowed.

"No. *I* rule this night. You've no leave to be here."

And I was yanked from the forest floor, airborne with a dragon for the second time in less than a day.

"Maddy?" came Bahlin's voice.

I was confused. He sounded worried. My eyes fluttered, and I smiled up at him. "Why did you glow?"

"Huh? Sweetheart, I didn't. I felt you twitching and then you grunted and began bleeding, the wounds and bruises appearing as I watched." Bahlin gathered me up in his arms and cradled me close to his chest with amazing tenderness for such a large man. He bent to bury his face in my hair. "Meditating to dream walk with you again was the hardest damned thing I've done in more than two centuries. I didn't know if I'd be able to relax while I watched you fight some unseen battle."

"Ow." I cringed as I tried to twist to a more comfortable position in his arms. "I think calling it a nightmare walk would be more accurate. I got my ass kicked in record time."

He held me away from him and looked into my face, wiping the blood from my brow. "No jokes, Madeline." He kissed my lips gently. "Why did you ask if I glowed?"

"I saw you coming for me, and you were glowing and you told me to get up. I turned to face you right as you snatched me...up. You snatched me up. You came from above."

He looked concerned. "Of course I did, Maddy. I sent my dragon form into your dream this time because I could tell something violent was happening. I wanted his power available to you. I plucked you from above because I was flying when I hit the dream."

I pushed myself to sitting in his lap, finding it ironic that I found myself repeating the same events of our first night together. "You came from above—"

"So I think we've established, Maddy."

"Stop it. Someone was coming through the forest..."

"Do you have a concussion?" Bahlin asked, feeling around on my head for any major knots, then gripping my chin and looking at my eyes.

"Stop it. I'm serious. I think it was Tarrek."

"I'm being serious. It wouldn't be unreasonable except we don't know if he's..." Bahlin looked away, clearly uncomfortable.

"He's not dead," I said vehemently. "I'm not too late."

"Who was this voice?" Bahlin set me down on the bed and walked into the bathroom, calling over his shoulder, "I'm listening, go ahead."

"Uh, I don't know exactly."

"Male or female?" he called back.

"Both?" I said, knowing it sounded impossible. "Didn't you see anyone when you snatched me up?"

He walked back out of the bathroom, still in his boxers, and carrying a small basket of first aid supplies and a handful of damp washrags. "Forgive me, darling, but you were my priority," he said wryly.

"Sure, and don't get me wrong, I'm *very* glad you showed up when you did. But I need to know who the voice was, and how Tarrek was able to dream walk into my sleep." I winced as Bahlin sat on the edge of the bed, and my abs tightened involuntarily to keep me sitting upright.

"Sorry," he said quietly. "This is going to sting a little." And faster than thought he slapped a rag on my forehead.

"Son of a bitch!" I jerked my head back so hard it bounced off the wall. Whatever was in the rag burned nearly as bad as his dragon fire had. "What *is* that stuff?"

"Uh, some type of antibacterial stuff Brylanna had in the wash cabinet. I know it burns. She's used it on me before."

He didn't look nearly contrite enough for me, and I reached up to yank his hand away. He relented, and I glared at him. "Next time just do that dragon magic stuff. It hurts about the same," I groused.

"'That dragon magic stuff?'" he said, amused. He set down the rag and began digging through the basket, coming up with butterfly bandages and liquid stitches.

"Whatever. But no more of that crap."

He leaned over me and treated the split in my forehead, holding the edges of the wound together. "It's only about an inch wide," he said, answering the unasked question that must have been written on my face. "I don't think it will scar." He added a couple of butterfly bandages then kept his hand cupping my head. The simple touch was my undoing.

Suddenly the fear from the dream came crashing back down on me, and I shuddered.

"Maddy?" Bahlin dropped his hand.

I launched myself at him, both of us grunting as I slammed into his upper body. His arms automatically caught me, wrapping me up in a strong embrace. I wrapped my arms around his neck and lifted my chin up. We were suddenly face to face. My legs snaked around his waist, and I clung to him like he was my lifeline. His lips caressed mine in a butterfly's kiss, and I shuddered for a new reason. This validation of life was as good an excuse as any, but if I was honest with myself, Bahlin chased away the fear and raised in me a sense of passion that I'd never before experienced. I pulled his head down to me and kissed him, expressing that passion with a deep, hard kiss. Our tongues touched tentatively at first, growing bolder with each pass. Suddenly he was exploring my mouth as if he were on a mapping expedition. I moaned into him, breathing harder by the second. He gripped the back of my head and fisted my hair as much as he was able, holding me firmly to his mouth. Bahlin's erection jutted out from his boxers, tenuously contained by the small button on the fly.

Wrapping his arms tighter, he lifted me up and laid me back on the mattress, fitting his body over mine. Bahlin continued to kiss me, and I felt like I was going up in flames. No man had *ever* kissed me like this. It was insane the feelings it produced. My core throbbed and ached with wanting him. I ground my hips into his instinctively, and he lifted his mouth off mine with an unsteady gasp.

"By the goddess, Maddy," he said, breathing hard through his nose. "You'll kill me before we get to the good part if you don't quit." He flashed a grin and dove back for my mouth. The split lip had ceased to ache under the onslaught, and I hadn't even noticed. I wondered fleetingly if he'd healed me again. Curious but definitely a question for later...much later.

I twisted my head to the side and pushed at Bahlin's chest and he gave way, falling onto his back though not without protest.

"Don't tell me you want to stop, Maddy, or you'll see a grown man cry, I swear it." His face was serious while his eyes were full of mischief.

"Oh no, dragon boy, I'm not stopping. I only want you in a better position," I whispered, dropping my lips to his bare chest. I rained kisses over his collarbones and down between his pectorals. I made it to his chocolaty nipple and latched on, forcing a gasp from him as he arched his back. I sucked harder, running a hand down to caress him and he groaned.

"Maddy," he rasped, one hand reaching for my hair and the other fisting in the sheets.

"So you like that?"

"Too much talking," he growled and, grabbing my shoulders, flipped me onto my back.

I squeaked with alarm and then he was ripping my clothes from my body with enough force to lift me off the bed. Without the semi-protection of underwear, I was suddenly naked before him. What had been a pup tent was suddenly a circus tent at the front of his boxers, and I worried for the barest moment. *Would he be built like other men?*

With one smooth move he dropped his shorts and answered my question. While he was physically built like a human man, his proportion was outrageous, even to my limited experience. His erection pushed his navel with every heartbeat, and I worried about us making this work physically.

He must have seen the look of worry on my face because he said, with a combination of pride and sympathy, "It will take some doing, but we'll go slow." And then he lowered himself on top of me. I braced for invasion but he only began kissing me again. I squirmed underneath him as I started to reheat, my need rising faster with each stroke of his hand on my bare skin. He worked his way down my front, paying attention to nearly every square inch of my body until he reached my center. I gasped as he breathed hot air on my lower lips, and groaned when he nuzzled my inner thigh.

"Bay, please," I begged, arching my back as he gently bit the tendon at the inner crease of my hip and thigh.

"Please what?" he teased.

"Less talking," I repeated on a hissed breath as his mouth brushed across my mons.

With a sigh, he settled in and began laving me, rasping his tongue across that centralized nerve bundle again and again. I felt the orgasm building almost immediately and I strained for it, amazed that he could bring my body to pleasure so quickly.

Pausing he lifted his head and said, "Relax, Maddy."

I whimpered and pushed at his head, trying to force it down. He chuckled darkly and set to pleasuring me with a zealous fervor, kissing, stroking, sucking. The orgasm built, layer upon layer, as he massaged my hips with his hands. In one minute it was building, and the next it was wracking my body and overwhelming me with its intensity. I screamed out my pleasure, arching my back and digging my heels into the bed. Bahlin didn't relent but pushed me harder, drawing out my climax until I was physically spent, my body limp.

Before I could completely come down from the high, Bahlin crawled up my body. Without a word he lifted one thigh up, hooking it over his elbow and placing his hand flat on the bed beside me. The other hand he used to guide his erection to my entrance. With gentle but unrelenting pressure he began pushing his way inside me.

"Holy shit, Maddy, you're tight," he groaned, pausing to allow me to adjust to his girth.

I gasped at the feeling of him, only partially inside me, stretching me almost too tight. The feeling was borderline painful.

"Don't stop, Bahlin, please don't stop."

"I don't...think...I can," he grunted and pushed forward some more, pausing with every inch. I must have winced because he began to ease out.

"No," I said, wrapping my free leg as far around his hips as I could. I pushed my hips up off the bed and reclaimed the ground, and then some that we'd lost when he retreated. I hissed in discomfort at the reclamation. His head fell back, and he breathed hard through his nose.

"Maddy, I won't last long, sweet."

Turning my face toward his arm I breathed, "Finish it, Bay."

He surged forward, seating himself all the way to my womb and I cried out. He held still for a few moments, giving me precious time to adjust to his girth and length, before he began to move. I whimpered at the feeling of being stretched to the point where pain and pleasure converged and were indiscernible from each other. Hearing and recognizing the sound, Bahlin stopped being gentle and began to pound into me in earnest, forcing me into the mattress with every downward stroke. In no time at all I was meeting his thrusts with my own and grunting as the head of his penis hit my cervix over and over again. Without warning, the orgasm crashed over me and I tightened around Bahlin's cock, gripping his shoulders hard enough to dig my fingernails into his flesh and draw blood.

I yelled his name to the heavens, pleading for more and he gave it, drawing out my orgasm. With a shout he joined me, and I could feel his ejaculate pulsing into me with hot urgency.

He held there for a moment longer before he collapsed on his side, breathing heavily, a look of sheer awe on his face. He drew me closer, kissing me more gently now, and running his hand up and down my back slowly.

"I had no idea it could be like that," he said softly, lifting a heavy limb to caress my face.

I turned my head into the caress and whispered, "Me either."

"You were amazing, love. I'm not sure I've ever been quite so swift in reaching the finish line." His smile was self-deprecating.

"Not a cold fish?" I asked, old insecurities rising to the surface and I resented the hell out of their presence in this bed.

"A cold fish?" he asked incredulously. "Whoever told you that was lying to cover his own inadequacies, *mo chrid*. You are wildly passionate and incredibly responsive. Why, I thought you'd milk my cock to—"

"Okay." I laughed, blushing like mad. "Okay. Thank you for that, I think." We lay there looking at each other, the silence unexplainably comfortable. "What happens since you broke your word after my good faith negotiations earlier?"

He laughed out loud, pulling me tighter into his arms. I went willingly, pressing flesh to flesh and finding comfort in his touch.

"My love, you are a wicked woman. *I* didn't seduce *you*, rather *you* seduced *me*, so no promise I made was broken."

"Well, shit."

I laid my head on his shoulder and it fit well. He massaged my head with deft fingertips, and I was asleep in moments.

A car door slammed, and I jerked awake. Bahlin's side of the bed was warm but empty. Why had he left me alone? I looked around the room for clothes but the only thing remaining was in shreds, evidence of our lovemaking. I heard the rumble of his voice and an answer too soft to make out, though I thought it was Brylanna. Foregoing politeness, I dug through Bahlin's dresser and grabbed a long T-shirt that covered the important parts. I sidetracked to the bathroom and cleaned up, then snuck down the hallway toward the voices. They paused when I got near.

"You might as well come out, Maddy," said Bahlin. "I can see we'll need to work on your stealth skills."

Harrumphing, I walked into the living room and saw that I had been right. Brylanna had returned. I walked over to Bahlin and, before I could protest, he pulled me into his lap. He was wearing the same boxers he'd had on earlier.

"I see I was right," Brylanna said coolly, looking me up and down.

"Brylanna, you *will* be courteous at the very least," Bahlin said, his voice warming with anger. "I've warned you about this before."

"So you have," she said. She tipped her head toward me in apology. I shrugged.

"Right about what?" I asked.

Bahlin's chest rumbled with a deep growl.

"I foretold that he would screw—"

"No need to be crass," I interrupted her, a flush climbing my cheeks. "I'm fully aware of what we've done, and don't need to know you can pull a play by play from the stars, or however you do it, because that's just seriously wrong. Do me a favor?"

She looked at me intently, then nodded.

"Stay the hell out of my love life," I commanded in a tone leaving no room for argument. "I don't care if you see a ménage a trois in my future. It's none of your business, so don't go looking for it. And especially when it comes to your brother. That's just squicky. Who looks in on their brother's love life anyway?"

She looked astounded that I'd speak to her that way. Little did she realize that I was only pausing for breath.

"And furthermore—"

Bahlin interrupted me by gently covering my mouth with his hand. "Enough, Maddy. Your point is made. And we'll likely need her in the future so there's no need to alienate her, right?"

I didn't answer him.

"Maddy," he warned.

I nodded, and he removed his hand.

He bent me backward and looked at me, quirking his eyebrow.

"Right," I groused. "You're right."

He sat me back up, hugged me tighter and pressed a kiss to the back of my neck.

Brylanna watched our exchange with interest and then sat across the table from us. "I've come with a warning. The weyr has met and is prepared to offer you its protection, Maddy."

"The weyr?"

Bahlin stroked my back and said, "A group of dragons is called a weyr. Our weyr is very powerful, so to have their support is a good thing." To Brylanna he said, "They must not believe she killed Gretta without cause."

Brylanna looked at him for a quiet minute and as I was getting ready to break the tension when she said, "I told them what I had seen regarding the fight. Combined with your account of things, it will be enough for them for now. The King and Queen of Faerie are imploring us for help in find Tarrek before it is too—"

"Can you see him?" I asked, interrupting.

"Tarrek? No. All I can tell is that he's bound and is in a dark place, but nothing more comes to me."

"Maddy," said Bahlin, "we need to get back to London. How soon can you be ready?"

"Um, I need to borrow some clothes."

"Brylanna? Take her to your room and get her outfitted. I'll put together a few supplies, and we'll be off."

Without a word Brylanna stalked down the hallway. I followed after her keeping a cautious distance.

Chapter Nine

The sun was setting as we finished our preparation to return to London. The overcast sky diffused the light and lent everything a softened look. Stone walls became romantic, dirt roads endless and grass greener. Because we didn't have a car, Brylanna had agreed to drive us back. We were in the countryside near Swindon, about two hours from London, and the idea of being trapped in a car with her wasn't my first option for a good time. But we needed her if we weren't going to utilize Bahlin as alternate transportation. I snickered, and he looked at me. I shook my head, and he finished loading a small bag in the car. He'd packed some basic first aid supplies, which concerned me but seemed reasonable given the last few days, and he'd packed a change of clothes, sans underwear, for me. I couldn't attest to his underwear status, though I'll admit to being curious. He was wearing a pair of faded jeans and an age-softened navy rugby shirt. I had been dressed by Brylanna and wore a pair of black leggings and a large gray sweatshirt that was too tight across my chest. I bitched. Bahlin said he didn't mind. I'd stuffed one of his extra sweatshirts in the backseat of the BMW in case I couldn't stand the trip in the tight shirt.

The windows on the car were darkly tinted and, when we crawled into the backseat to let Brylanna drive, I couldn't help the flashback to getting in the car with Tarrek only days ago. I felt like I had neglected him today, though I'd needed the actual sleep, and it left me feeling guilty.

We settled into the backseat without a word, Bahlin pulling me under his shoulder protectively. I snuggled into his side as we bumped down the country lane toward the highway. Snapshots from my earlier dream and ass kicking kept coming back to me, and I couldn't help but try to focus on specifics.

First, I knew the forest was dense and old. The decaying vegetation on the forest floor was seasons worth, and there was little undergrowth except a few shade-loving plants. No solution to the mystery there.

Second, I knew that the attacker had been cautious about attacking me from the front. I thought about my fight with Gretta. Women tend to attack other women from the front. We're programmed that way, typically because we throw taunts first. Verbal creatures, we. But instances of assault prove that men will often attack a woman from behind. So that led me to believe my attacker was male.

Assuming my second assumption was accurate, then he had, thirdly, disguised his voice. Between the attack from behind and the disguised voice, I deduced that I must have seen him before at some point and would, thereby, recognize him. Brylanna's foretelling that I had seen him before only reaffirmed my suspicions.

And fourth, and most importantly, I knew Tarrek was the light in the forest because he'd dressed me in almost the same dress he'd brought me in the sithen. He'd reached out to me in my dream, tried to give me answers, and had been stopped by the owner of the voice. He, the voice, had to have some pretty serious mojo to leave me with the creepy crawlies so long after waking.

The car bumped and shifted from the dirt lane to the paved highway and suddenly our travel was quieter, the purr of the engine more intent now than during the careful traversing of the earlier rutted road leading from the house. I sighed and leaned into Bahlin's shoulder more. I was sore and tired.

"Rest, *a stór*, and I'll wake you before we get to the hotel," Bahlin said gently, seemingly reading my mind. He stroked my head with those talented fingers, and I found myself waning to sleep.

"Not for a while yet." I looked out the window and watched the scenery go by, content but contradictorily tense. I didn't want any of this to be happening, but I was so happy, at that very moment, where I was.

Something caught my eye out the window and I shouted, "Stop the car!"

Seatbelts tightened, brake pads ground and people grunted as the car came to a radical stop, swaying back on its shocks. I fumbled with the locked backdoor and finally got it open. Jumping out of the car, my exhaustion forgotten, I raced across the empty highway and scrambled over the fence, never taking my eyes off the prize—the stone circle. Stumbling into the center of the circle I fell to my knees, though I felt nothing beyond the bitter taste of desperation. I got up and walked the perimeter, tracing my fingers over the stones, my mind racing in random patterns trying to figure out what I had done that night that made the stones come to life for me. I turned to find that the altar stone was not there. I stared, slack-jawed, at the empty center circle.

"Maddy?" Bahlin asked quietly. "What is it?"

"I thought... See, I thought..." I stumbled.

"Ah, you thought this was the same stone circle you were at previously, right?" His voice came from behind me.

"Yeah, I thought this was it. But it's not, is it?"

"No, Maddy, it's not. You'll remember I told you there are many stone circles about Europe. This one is only a partial circle, thereby its magic is disrupted. It couldn't have compelled your change." A heavy hand came to rest gently on my shoulder. "Do you wish so badly to unmake your decision, then?" His voice was carefully devoid of emotion.

"I don't know what I want. I thought..."

"Come back to the car. We've got to make it to London as early as possible so Brylanna can make her drive home."

He slid his hand from my shoulder to hand and directed me back to the car. He held my door open for me and I slid in, then he went to his side and took his seat. Brylanna glared at me in the rearview mirror, and I looked away. She stepped on the gas hard enough for the engine to roar and force me back in my seat before my seatbelt was fully buckled. Once I was settled, I began to get pissed, so I glared back at her. What the hell was her problem anyway? It wasn't her life on the line here. Bahlin was suspiciously quiet. I looked at him with my peripheral vision and found him staring at me.

"What?" I asked, self-conscious of him for the first time since we'd had sex.

135

"Nothing," he said softly. "I suppose it's nothing." He turned to look at the window, laying his head back against the seat, eyes unfocused.

"Bay?" Something was wrong.

He rolled his head toward me, and his eyes flashed icy blue. We looked at each other quietly, the tension mounting to the point it had texture on the air. Still he said nothing. When he spoke it was in a voice tinged with sorrow, like a sky with the first hint of snow: penitent, mournful, cold. "Do you regret us so soon, Maddy?"

I stared at him. "Regret you as in you, in particular, or this situation?"

"That's what I was afraid of," he said. "You're going to second-guess yourself back into celibacy." He closed his eyes and turned away. "You're being foolish."

"Bay..." I wasn't sure what to say. I didn't regret my time with him, but I wasn't keen on the whole shot and poisoned and now hunted thing.

"No need to express your regrets out loud," he whispered. "I'll live."

And then I knew he was speaking specifically of our time together. Had I been able to wish away this existence while at the stones, I may have done it without thinking of the consequences. Specifically, I wouldn't have thought of the loss of Bahlin. The thoughts roiled in my mind like hard-boiling water.

"Bahlin, look—"

At his name, he opened his eyes, dark blue once again, and said, "No, Maddy. No excuses. It is what it is. You'd go back to your old life if you could. That much is evident."

"Bahlin, listen to me, please. *Please.* I miss aspects of my old life, particularly not being shot, poisoned or hunted." I reached for him then withdrew my hand, unsure whether my touch would be welcome or not. "The idea that I could go back to boring appeals to me greatly. But what we had this afternoon—well, that gives me something else to think about. I don't want to go back to boring in that department."

A very unlady-like snort sounded from the front seat, and the radio volume went up so that Pink's voice carried over the quiet conversation.

"Later," he said with finality and turned to the window again.

It was a long ride back to London.

We arrived sometime around seven o'clock that evening. Surprisingly, Bahlin had directed us back to the hotel again. Following my stunted conversation with Bahlin after the stone circle, neither he nor Brylanna had said a word to me as we rode through the settling twilight. It had been a silence filled with tension and angry rock music, leaving my nerves on edge and a song stuck in my head. I involuntarily hummed "Don't Let Me Get Me" thinking I really was a hazard to myself, as the lyrics suggested. I snorted at the irony, and Bahlin looked at me. I shrugged, and we walked through the lobby. He gestured me toward the elevators, but he headed to the reception desk to speak with one of his managers on duty. Everything looked the same, but my senses were on red alert. Something was off. Bahlin came back toward me looking grim.

"Hellion has been here already. It's not safe to stay here without endangering innocent people. I've sent a bellhop to your room for your bags. Stay here." He walked behind the desk and into the manager's office and shut the door with a hard shove only a breath shy of a slam.

I wandered over to the blood-red sofas and took a seat. Despite their harsh appearance, the sofas were incredibly comfortable. I had just curled up and settled my head against the back when a voice said, "You look relaxed."

I jolted upright and looked at the woman now sitting across from me. I gasped, unsure what she was but knowing she was less human than I. She smiled, and I noticed her teeth were a little sharper than normal. But that was nothing compared to her hair. It was shades of deep, dark blue with light green highlights. It sounds odd, but it was gorgeous on her. Her eyes were the color of green glass marbles, clear and bright, and her skin was pale with almost a green tint. She was wearing a gossamer dress, and I could vaguely make out her breasts through the front of the material. I was instantly embarrassed. What was it with the see-through clothes floating around Western Europe?

"I am Sarenia," the woman said, her voice rich and melodious. "I am here to see Bahlin, though I'm honored to meet the new Niteclif as well."

"So you believe in me?" I asked. "Just like that?"

"Oh, I do at that, precious girl," she said. "I feel your heritage in my heart, for I knew your great-grandfather well. You've the look of him, you know. I hope you'll serve us as well as he did."

There was that no pressure thing again. Just fabulous. I continued to stare at her and unbidden the word *mermaid* breathed voiceless through my mind. I wondered if recognizing supernatural creatures was one of my skills that Bahlin had referenced. I thought I'd test the envelope since I was as alone with this woman as one could be in a crowded hotel lobby.

"What are you?" I asked more bluntly than I intended. I winced, hoping I hadn't offended her.

She chuckled and her voice sounded of sea gulls calling out over the waves, and I knew I was right. I smiled, and she smiled back.

"You may refer to me as a mermaid, as the sailors' legends do. But to be accurate, I am an Atlantean and a member of the High Council, representing the smaller groups who lack significant numbers."

I stared at her, confused.

Interpreting my look, her smile gentled as much as it could on her severe face and she said, "Atlanteans come from Atlantis, child."

My mouth formed a silent O, and I couldn't quite catch my breath. "Okay. If you're a member of the High Council, where were you yesterday?"

"I had an emergency that held me away. I understand you were fully affirmed, though I will offer you the oath myself. But right now,—" she inclined her head toward the front desk and Bahlin's approach, "—it will have to wait."

"Sarenia," came his voice over my shoulder. "It's good to see you here. I've received your message. What may I do for you?" asked Bahlin.

"We've found a body," she said, sorrow lacing her voice. "She was a limnade, and—"

"Pardon me," I said quietly, "but what's a lemonade?"

"No, Maddy. Limnade. It's a water sprite that lives in a lake. Water sprites have the gift of foresight, and sometimes the ability to make prophecies. It was a sprite that first told of your coming." She looked at Bahlin, and he looked irritated. "You have not told her of this?"

He hunched his shoulders defensively and said, "She knew she was prophesied."

"Hellion took the prophecy offered by the same sprite that was just killed and delivered it to the Council in her stead. She came later and repeated it to ensure we knew when you would arrive."

"So you *all* knew I was coming?" A dreadful thought was developing.

"We did, Niteclif. We knew the day and time, even the event, that would trigger your heritage Change."

"And only the Council knew?" The feeling was getting worse.

"We agreed we would not share the information lest an unnaturally large gathering of people showed up in the middle of the night at the circle to watch your indoctrination event." She cocked her head to the side, looking at me intently, her eyes darkening the slightest bit. "Did you see anyone at the circle?"

She was too observant by half. Maybe *she* should take over the Niteclif role. I was ready to give it to her. And now I was in a position to have to disclose that I'd been watched that night. I didn't want to do this.

"Maddy?" Bahlin asked, steel lacing his voice, his back ramrod straight.

"You knew?" I turned toward Bahlin. "So you knew the stone circle that I'd come to, even before I was affirmed?"

"I did. But Tarrek affirmed you so fast that there was little time to do aught but move forward with your Change. Once he said the words, Maddy, it was irrevocable."

I stared at him, the tenuous trust we'd built shattering into a million tiny pieces. I couldn't trust what he said to me now that I had a small inkling that this could have been stopped, that *he* could have stopped this. Probably, anyway. Or maybe. Hell, I had no idea, but I felt like he'd lied to me regarding a major life event so that I would choose the path he thought was best, and then I went and had sex with him. As illogical as it was, and heritage be damned as this had nothing to do with logic, I felt betrayed. I glared at him and he glared back, his eyes flashing to that eerie white, ice blue. The hair on the back of my neck stood up, recognizing the threat. I looked away first, uncomfortable with the intimacy of his gaze, no matter how harsh it was.

"There was a man," I began, and I told them everything.

Letting out a low string of curses, Bahlin got up and walked away, getting in the first available elevator and going up. I turned and followed his retreat, staring after him, confused at his reaction. *I* was the injured party, not him. If anyone was going to be storming off, it should have been me. I continued to stare at the elevator, watching the light indicate stops and starts at each floor. I thought I knew who the man was now, though with all of the other supes who had foretold of the event, it was impossible to be positive. Not without confronting him, which I lacked the courage to do. Yet. I had a dragon's ass to kick first. Great way to hone my fighting skills, I guess.

"Why is he so upset?" I asked, though I didn't direct the question to Sarenia or anyone else. It was merely a verbalization of thought. "I'm the one who's been wronged here."

"Likely he's upset because he wants you to trust him," Sarenia answered. "And I suggest you strongly think about your second statement."

I looked over my shoulder at her. "What? Why?"

"As to the first, he's worked with the Council for the last three hundred years, offering guidance to Niteclifs ever since his election as representative of the shape-shifting and were-factions.

"And regarding the second, to your statement you've been wronged? How, child? An honorable man falls in love with you, and you seem to think you got the short end of the stick? It doesn't follow any form of logic I'm familiar with."

I didn't correct her calling me a child. Hell, she had seen and done things that were so old the history books had omitted them as no longer relevant. Freaking *Atlantis*. I was little more than embryonic when compared to her. What was disturbing was that such ancient creatures would entrust justice to me, but there it was.

And as for logic? I covered that already.

"How has he offered guidance?" I asked, working hard to school the emotion from my voice. Jealousy had no place in my queries.

Sarenia, though, wasn't fooled. "He has counseled them throughout their ten year term, in both their activities and their investigations. He is a wise man, Maddy, and you will do well working with him."

Jumping from topic to topic I replied, "And there's no way to definitively qualify whether or not he loves me in such a short time. I wouldn't even trust probability statistics to that problem."

Sarenia leaned back on the sofa, closing her eyes and rubbing her temples. Great. I was giving an ancient a stress headache.

"Love is not a probability statistic, girl, and logic has little to do with it, if anything. It is what it is, no more, no less. And the only who can legitimately qualify those feelings would be the owner thereof." I began to open my mouth to comment that she'd called love both logical and illogical and she said in a reverberating voice that drew stares, "No arguments, Madeleine Dylis Niteclif. None."

I hunched my shoulders and thought about what she'd said. She was right, and I hate being wrong—hate it enough that I fought against the urge to apologize. "Trust has to come into play. Unfortunately, that's something Bahlin and I need to work on in every aspect of our professional relationship."

"And personally?"

"Let's not go there yet, okay? I may have just sent us down in a blaze of glory, setting a new worldwide record for the decimation of a relationship in less than twelve hours. I'll get back to you." I paused, thinking about Sarenia's role, the mythology of the Atlantean people and their alleged braniac status, and I wondered if she knew about Bahlin's service to the Niteclif family. She had answered so many of my other questions with insight, but she hadn't answered what I wanted to know. Did she know who he was to history's records? I couldn't work off an assumption that she was aware of Bahlin's activities.

"Does the whole Council know that he's provided, um, guidance to the Niteclifs?"

"No, I'm sure they don't. Most are not as attuned to each other as I am. But the years will do that..." she trailed off, introspective, and I wondered how old she was. When had Atlantis allegedly disappeared?

Something like 9600 BC.

Before I could stop myself I asked, "How long have you known Bahlin?"

Sarenia stared at me, her eyes darkening to the color of the deep sea. She seemed to look right through me, and it flat gave me the creeps. Right before I told her to forget it, she said, "If you'd like to know how old he is, you should ask him child."

I glanced at the elevators quickly before returning my full attention to the Atlantean. Obviously Bahlin wasn't coming back any time soon. "You're right. I should be more direct. But he's avoided any direct conversation regarding his age," I admitted truthfully.

"Then I suggest you negotiate with him," she said with a sharp smile.

I grinned, appreciating her innate female darkness. Obviously she assumed that I had something with which to bargain and, in this instance, she was right.

"Oh good idea," I said, smiling even wider.

She stood, offering me her hand. I took it and followed her up and, without releasing my hand, she led me to the dining area. She smiled at me over her shoulder and looked almost chagrined.

"I know it's probably dreadfully predictable, but I love sushi and Bahlin's restaurant has the best in the area."

I smiled, still following her by the hand. "They have great steak, too, so I'm cool. Eat anything that you want but the guests."

She gave me a sharp look, tightening her grip on my hand for a brief moment, and I cringed. Maybe that hadn't been a couth menu suggestion. But her shoulders relaxed, her grip following suit.

"I gave up the murder of humans a very long time ago," she said softly, her eyes boring directly into mine. I felt the weight of her words as if she'd laid them in my hands like a counterweight on the scales of justice.

"I apologize for my poor attempt at humor," I said in a quiet voice. "I'm not familiar enough with you to make such personal jokes."

"As your people say, no foul, no harm," she said with a small smile.

I smiled in return. "Close enough." I was relieved to have both feet firmly out of my mouth and on the floor as the waiter led us to a prime corner booth that faced the entire room.

"Leave the privacy curtain open," I instructed the waiter. He bowed and did as I asked before walking away.

"Smart girl." Sarenia looked pleased with my directive.

"Not really. It's only that I don't want anyone sneaking up on us or listening in to our conversation. So," I said, adjusting the napkin in my lap and taking a sip of water before continuing, "tell me about the murder of the limnade."

"A limnade is a water sprite, as I told you, though they are sometimes call nixies. Females are much more common than males. Limnades have the ability to live outside in the fresh air or to build their homes under water and live as true underwater creatures. They are very versatile in this sense though they are few in number. Their prophesies are never wrong, though sometimes they are vague enough to be open to interpretation." Her voice had taken on sorrow enough I could have carved my name in it with the butter knife. "If you catch a limnade, you can have your future told, and they never lie though they can be obscure, intentionally or otherwise. The dead limnade is the one who foretold of your coming when Hellion caught her on the bank of her lake. Her body was left, though her lungs and her corposis were taken."

"What's a corposis?" I felt so out of my element.

"It's a small organ at the base of a limnade's brain that is their prophecy center. There is much speculation as to how it works, but no one knows for sure. It's a biological and astrological interpretation of some sort." She sighed. "There's so much I don't know, and this murder is especially hard." Her eyes shown with a sheen of tears before she ducked her head, and her hair fell to cover her face.

I reached a hand out to her and gently touched her hair. The texture felt a lot like seaweed, even though it looked like hair.

"Sarenia?"

She looked up, and the tears coursed down her cheeks. "This limnade's name was Meyla, and she was my only daughter."

I wasn't sure how to comfort someone on the loss of a child, but I could relate to the grief of losing someone to violent death. I gripped her hand hard and let her silently cry, saying nothing to her. Because honestly, there are no words that will make you feel better when you've lost a piece of your heart to death.

A quarter hour passed and she finally looked up at me, and her eyes were the color of storm-tossed seas. "Niteclif, I want the killer brought to me for justice. An eye for an eye. I will have his lungs mounted on Atlantis's gateway as a testament of your findings. I will find no mercy for when the time comes." Her voice resonated like a speaker under water, the words muffled but dense, echoing through my body and making my stomach vibrate. It was a sickening feeling. And this was coupled with the familiar yoke of justice that my life now carried, and the weight was harsh.

I looked at Sarenia, unsure how to console her, knowing the truth would not ever be enough. "I will do my best to find your daughter's killer and leave it to the High Council to mete out justice. I cannot turn the killer directly over to you without a Council vote, Sarenia. I just can't. It goes against all that I am to condemn a man to violent death, so I'll leave it to the Council to decide. If they give the killer to you, I will walk away from the case satisfied and wish you well of each other. But until that time, I will not be influenced in my decision. Justice is more important than vengeance." My voice had taken on that unfamiliar steely tone and I froze with the utterance of the last word, worried that I was about to get myself killed. Cause of death? Brazenness.

"I agree with you," Sarenia said, her voice haunted with grief. "You are the Niteclif. Justice will rule the case. I knew better than to ask for other than this from you." She set her napkin on the table and stood. "You'll pardon my departure, Madeleine Niteclif. I am not the slightest bit hungry."

"Sarenia?" I stopped her from standing all the way by grabbing her forearm. "How many people know of Meyla's death?"

"Only the people of Atlantis." She gently, but without compromise, extracted her arm from my grip.

"Would you please consider keeping it confined to only the people who know already? I don't want anyone else to know yet, and that includes the High Council."

She arched a dark brow at me but gave one sharp nod of her head agreement, bending to kiss my cheek and I allowed it. Sarenia smiled at me, though it never reached her eyes, then she stroked my head and walked away.

The waiter chose that moment to return with our orders so I sat across from a plate of sushi and an empty seat, and I began to eat my steak alone.

Bahlin showed up two bites into my fabulous meal, his face drawn and eyes tight. He sat in Sarenia's seat without a word, watching me eat. The food turned to lead in my stomach, and I put my fork down.

"Get everything done upstairs that you wanted to do?" I asked. I was astounded at how calm my voice sounded in the wake of my tumultuous emotions.

"Where's Sarenia?" he asked, his aggressive tone setting me back in my chair.

"She came to see you, but when you left so abruptly she decided to leave as well."

He looked at first my plate, then the sushi. "So this is all yours, I assume?"

"You said both room service and dining were on the house. Reneging?" I goaded.

He growled at me, soft and low. "Fine, avoid the question. Our rooms were tipped, so I ordered housekeeping to gather what was salvageable and pack it in luggage to be picked up tomorrow."

I stared at him. "What were they looking for?" I asked. "What did I have that could be of any value?"

"The family tree, for one, as it proves you're the Niteclif."

"And? I've been affirmed so that shouldn't matter."

"Ah, but it does. Your date of death was open-ended, Maddy. That tree will tell the owner if decisions he or she makes will likely lead to your death. It can influence what decisions are made regarding you, Niteclif." His voice was hard, his eyes flat.

"Holy hell. So this will tell them whether or not their plans will lead to my *death*?" I hissed, tossing my napkin on the table.

145

"That's what I said."

"Then tell me why we left without taking it earlier? Why did no one tell me about the significance when the tree was discovered?" And then I remembered. Bahlin was the only one to have seen the tree. Bahlin was the only one to have been in the room with me. Bahlin had ordered my bags packed. Bahlin's sister was a Seer.

"Was it you at the circle? Was it you who took the tree?" I asked, standing up to create room for maneuverability if I needed it. "Was. It. You."

"Don't be ridiculous," he snorted, leaning back in his chair. I was learning that this was his piss off look. He glared at me, then said, "I could have taken it and run a number of times the first night I met you."

"But that would have been obvious," I said. "No intrigue there, huh Bahlin?"

"Maddy, you've gone off your meds, sweetheart, if you think—"

"Don't you dare call me sweetheart, Bahlin," I growled. "I need a safe house, and I need it now. Do you provide it or do I need to go to someone else on the Council to get that taken care of?"

He was dumbfounded, staring at me with his mouth hanging open in either shock or surprise. I wasn't sure which.

"Shut your pie hole, Bahlin. All you'll catch with it is flies," I snarked.

He snapped his mouth shut and sat up, looking up at me slightly since I was standing over him. "I'll take you to the safe house I had arranged. We'll discuss this further when we get there."

No we won't, I thought sadly. *No we won't.* Because I was going to figure out a way to get away from him.

Chapter Ten

With a great sense of *dèjá vu*, I exited the hotel lobby on a dark evening with a gorgeous supernatural creature by my side. The rain misted and gathered glittering dewdrops in his hair. It looked like he wore a dusting of diamonds. Cars swept past us with a subdued swooshing sound, though more frequent in number than the first night I'd stood at the curb waiting for a car. Streetlights offered bright nimbi of light at regular intervals, creating an artificial halo of color that the overcast sky offered back to us in purples and grays as we waited on Bahlin's car to be delivered via valet. We didn't speak.

Only moments later the valet driver pulled up to the overhang in the Mini I'd rented days ago.

"Yehr car, sir, is going tehr need some repairs."

"Repairs?" Bahlin asked.

"Yes, sir. The windows are smashed and the tires slashed. And it looks like someone took a heavy object to the hood and bashed it but good," said the valet.

Bahlin sighed. "But Ms. Niteclif's car was left alone?" Bahlin stalked around the car and looked for signs of damage, going so far as to check the undercarriage. Finding none, he opened the driver's door.

"Apparently whoever's messin' with ye either didn't know about Ms. Niteclif's car or didn't recognize it since it's such a regular little ride." The valet jogged around to open the passenger side door for me, and I balked.

"My car, I drive."

"Just get in the car, Maddy," Bahlin said quietly, climbing in behind the wheel.

"My car, I dr—"

Bahlin shut the driver's door and started to pull away from the curb. I threw myself in the open passenger's door, and he sped away before I had the door firmly latched. "Holy underpants, you sadistic, power-hungry, conscienceless son of a bitch. What is your problem?" I fumbled with my seatbelt, relaxing a little when I heard it click. "Maybe it's *you* behind the attempts on my life."

For the second time in less than six hours, my seatbelt locked up when the car was ground to a halt hard enough that the air bags should probably have deployed.

"What did you just accuse me of? Because I'm no' sure I heard yeh right," he said in a dangerously soft voice. His eyes were dragon blue and the cat-slit pupils were narrow in the bright lights of the city. Cars honked, driving around us. Bahlin didn't even flinch.

"I was trying to get your attention, and it worked."

"So does me bloody name. For the love of the goddess, Maddy, yer pushing just to push and yeh need to quit. We're in trouble here, and yehr distractions and fight picking may get us killed. So can the attitude and give a little help or so help me I'll tan your ass when we get to the safe house!" Bahlin roared, beginning to end. Nostrils flaring, he stared at me hard, vibrating with an otherworldly energy that left the same biting sensation from earlier marching across my skin. He grabbed his hair and pulled hard, making the muscles in his forearms flex. "Nothin' to say now? Well, if yeh've shut up for hurt feelin's, I'm sorry for it. The truth is a wicked bitch of a mistress, Maddy, but I'll use her well if it keeps us alive. I'll no' lie to yeh, no' now, no' ever, though I reserve the right to lie to others if I think there's a specific reason that might keep us unharmed. And then I'll be sure to apologize for it later. But yeh've got to trust me. If yeh canna give me that one confidence, then we're dead already."

He turned back to the road, breathing hard. Gathering his wits about himself, he shoved the car into gear and drove on. We were headed toward the northern side of London to the trendy neighborhood of Battersea. I rode in silence, not once answering any of his rant with one of my own. Truth? I didn't have much to say after the discussions first with Sarenia and then with Bahlin. I was feeling pretty much like an incompetent ass. The turning point in all of it had to be when I found out that Meyla, the dead limnade, was Sarenia's daughter. I'd found my common ground in this world where I didn't belong, death. More specifically, the death of someone so beloved that your whole world is changed with her loss. That's what the loss of Meyla did to Sarenia. It changed her permanently, and I knew that if I could stop this from continuing to happen, I would.

Bahlin pulled into an underground parking garage and parked in a numbered slot. Still silent, he got out of the car and went to the back, retrieving small travel bags I hadn't seen. Apparently at least some of our personal stuff had been retrieved and returned to us to get us by. I'd have to find a couth way to thank the hotel staff personally for my underwear.

Climbing out of the little car, I followed Bahlin to the elevator where we rode up to the penthouse floor in strained silence. It required an elevator key to access it and, once there, it was the only residence door in the elevator's little foyer. We got out and the elevator hissed shut, automatically descending. Bahlin stood there, staring at the front door. Then I heard the locks turning, and the door swung open.

Before I could ask, Bahlin said, "The door is magically warded. It takes dragon magic to get inside. Not even Hellion will be able to snatch you from here. Unless, of course, he's hired a dragon to retrieve you. But let's not borrow trouble. The flat's got two bedrooms, so you won't be forced to endure my presence too much. Nice, hmm? Oh, and don't touch the door or it will burn you—badly." He walked inside leaving me to drag my bag along and do my best to get inside the door before it swung shut. Nightmares were made of things like this.

The apartment, or flat, was a rectangular shape with a small foyer that was part of the dining room. Passing through, I found the bedrooms, one on each side of the living room. Bahlin came out of the room on the left and said, "This one's mine. You're welcome to the other or to the couch."

I flinched, and he said, "It's a product of your own making, Maddy. I won't feel guilty about what happened between us, I will not let you trivialize my feelings for you, and I will not take the blame for the way your life has turned out. Sort it out, and fast, because we have work to do. If you want to take a rest, I'll stay awake in case you dream." And with that he turned on the television, sank to the couch and started watching a rugby match.

I wandered back into the bedroom that he'd said was mine. It was efficient, with a single window over the bureau, the double bed shoved up against the wall near the door, and the utility bathroom was through a door across from the bed. Nothing like the opulence the hotel provided, the whole thing was trendy and modern. My stomach growled, and I realized I hadn't eaten in forever. Two bites of steak just didn't count. I decided I'd grab a shower and change into my own clothes before foraging for something to eat.

The shower was a single-person tiled stall almost claustrophobic in size. It was like standing in a plumbed coffin. I cleaned up as fast as I could and went out to my bedroom to put on some clothes. The TV was turned off, and I wondered where Bahlin had gone. I dug through my sparse bag of clothes and pulled out—hallelujah!—underwear, a pair of jeans and a non-see-through long-sleeved T-shirt. Digging further I found socks and a pair of Nikes. I dressed quickly and went to find Bahlin and see about something to eat. He was stretched out on the sofa, hands crossed over his stomach, the remote on the floor. It looked like he was sleeping until I got closer to him and realized there were dark shadows beneath his eyes and a sallowness to his skin that hadn't been there before. All I could think of was poison and I literally threw myself at him, terrified. He gasped for air as I landed on him, his arms and legs coming up around me automatically to bind the movement of his attacker. He snugged me down close and hard to his body and I couldn't breathe and I didn't care. For a minute, for just a minute, I'd had the sheer terror of irretrievable loss again. I didn't want to look too closely at the emotions behind the feelings I was experiencing, so I laid my head on his chest, listening to his heart thump in adrenaline-induced double-time.

"Maddy?" he asked. Then, realizing there could be danger, he flipped me over and put himself on top, shielding my body with his. His eyes switched color and he scanned the room, looking for danger. He scented and found nothing, and it was only then that he began to relax. He pushed himself off of me slightly and he asked, "Maddy? What's happened? Did you dream again? How long was I out?"

Tears were coursing down my cheeks. I shook my head and

struggled to get my arms free. He let them loose, and I threw them around his waist and pulled him down to me. As angry as he was with me, his body had still offered a primal response to the threat. His erection pressed against my stomach, and I smiled a little where he couldn't see me. Men. I hugged him hard, hiccupping a little, ashamed to have fallen apart because, for the love of his goddess, he'd been *napping*. I didn't want to tell him the truth, but I couldn't lie, either.

"Maddy?" he asked again, and this time the impatience was palpable in his voice.

"I came out to speak to you and you were sleeping," I began. "You looked horrible—dark circles under your eyes, sallow skin, short breaths, no movement, and I thought..." I tilted my chin up to look at him and he looked down, his eyes still dragon blue. Maintaining eye contact was difficult, but I considered it a sort of penance for our fight. "I thought you were sick or dying, and I had a flashback to the terror I felt when I lost my parents and it just gutted me, Bay. I don't think I could stand to lose you, not now."

He smiled at me, his eyes flashing back to midnight blue. "You've not lost me, *mo chrid*. I'm angry with you, but you have a right to be angry with me too. I haven't been totally forthcoming with you about what I knew about your Change. I probably could have influenced you more to try to stop the Change, but I didn't want to." He paused, rolling us to our side on the little sofa so that it was cling to each other or fall off. He rubbed his hand up and down my spine gently, laying soft kisses on my forehead. He sighed and rolled to the floor before standing up, leaving me alone on the sofa. "This isn't going to work."

I couldn't school my face fast enough to hide the heartbreak I felt at his words.

"The sofa, my love, the sofa is what's not going to work. Come with me to my bedroom."

"Bay—"

"Cuddle time," he said, grabbing my hand and relieving me of the responsibility of thinking through the implications of getting back into bed with him. I didn't even want to negotiate. I wanted the solid firmness of his reality shielding me. Just for a moment I didn't want to hunt or be hunted.

Hand in hand, we walked into his bedroom. Bahlin pushed me

gently toward the bed and I went, sitting on the edge. His room was a mirror image of mine, though the bed was larger and took up more of the floor space. I missed his bed at Brylanna's house. He moved through the room, picking up candles and holding them to his face, humming then breathing on them gently to light them. When he got to the window, he closed the shades and the curtains, dropping the room into flickering darkness. With his back to me, he pulled his shirt off over his head and I held my breath for a split second.

"Bay, I'm not ready to—"

"Sex has no part of this. We're reconnecting, my love. Sometimes a little skin-to-skin contact is good for that, don't you think?"

I shrugged. "I don't know."

"Haven't you ever fought with a lover before?"

I blushed and my heart hurt a little. I'd not had a lover passionate enough to fight with—ever. And it hurt that he had obvious experience in this type of thing.

"No, Bahlin, I've never had a lover I fought with." I looked down, afraid to meet his eyes. A pair of bare feet made their way into my field of view. I couldn't look up. He reached out and pulled me close.

"No wonder our argument affected you so, Madeleine. Hush now," he said, and I realized I was crying again. Stupid girl hormones, they raise their damnable heads at the most inopportune times and make you feel like a wimp. I sniffed and laid my head on his chest.

"Hush," he said again. "I'm sorry I was angry with you. You have a knack for infuriating me, and I'm scared for you and that only makes it worse because I can't always express my fear so it bubbles over as unnecessary anger sometimes. And now I'm rambling. Truth?" he asked.

"Always." He looked skeptical. I snaked a hand to his face and grabbed his chin, pulling his face down toward mine. "Always," I growled, "no matter how badly it might hurt. I don't know how to trust you otherwise." I shook my head, and released his face. "And I don't know how to reconcile these feelings I have for you, either. Truth. Always."

He took a deep breath and exhaled sharply over my head. "Okay. I don't like how I feel about you." I flinched. "You said truth, so here it is, Madeleine. My feelings for you are new and raw and I want to protect you from all comers, but I can't. I can't, and still let you do your job. It gutted me that you would consider giving up whatever is building between us to go back to your old life without a backwards glance or thought for me." He sighed, more softly this time, and stepped away from me. "And the murders keep coming and I feel like we're not getting anywhere on them and it concerns me." He laid his cheek on my head, and I wrapped my arms around him.

"Truth?" I asked him.

"Always."

"Stop calling me Madeleine."

He laughed out loud and crushed me to him in a bear, er, dragon hug.

We cuddled together in silence for about an hour before my stomach revolted and began to growl in earnest.

"Is there any food here?" I asked.

"Probably a little, though I wouldn't eat anything in the fridge. In fact, don't even open it. I'm not sure what's in there but whatever it is has likely spoiled. It's been a while since I was here last."

I got up and straightened my clothes and walked to the kitchen. I swear I'd heard him tell me not to open the fridge, but out of sheer force of habit it was the first place I went. I pulled it open, gasped, and slammed it shut.

"Bahlin?" I squeaked out. I turned around and slid down the face of the fridge, landing on my butt.

"I told you not to open the fridge," he called from the bedroom, where I could hear him rustling about. "It's probably got goddess knows what in there, and it's too likely rank."

I giggled, a high, unnatural sound for me. "Bay?" I breathed out.

He padded out of the bedroom, still barefoot, got one look at me and froze. I know the grin I was sporting was Hannibal Lecter-ish, but it was appropriate.

"What is it, Maddy?" He didn't move closer to me. He closed his eyes and took a deep breath. "Death."

"There's a head in your refrigerator, Bahlin."

Chapter Eleven

I sat with my back against the refrigerator and tried desperately not to lose myself to hysterical laughter. If I started I didn't think I'd stop for a long, long time. Bahlin had been right when he told me not to open the refrigerator door. What was inside was definitely rank. I watched him move back and away from the refrigerator and, closing his eyes, take a deep breath.

"Clever. Now that the refrigerator has been opened, I can't smell anything but the stench of death in the air. Whoever was in the apartment must have intended it that way." He sat on a barstool and looked at me. "Are you ready to get up yet?"

I shrugged. I was pretty sure my legs would work. What I wasn't sure about was whether they would take me from the room at a dead run or let me stand and be rational about my find. Taking a chance, I stood.

"Good girl. This will get easier."

"That's partly what I'm afraid of." I didn't want death to get easier. I didn't *want* this to become commonplace—where I was afraid to open a cupboard or appliance or drawer for fear of what might pop out at me. My mind and heart were racing, and I took a deep breath in an attempt to slow things down. I needed to approach this logically.

"Why don't I smell anything?" I asked.

"The fridge kept it cold. You wouldn't smell it unless it was taken out and warmed up, giving decomposition a chance to begin."

"Sure. Okay." I swallowed down the bile that was trying to rise up the back of my throat. "Did you recognize the, uh, I guess we'll call it the head?"

"I'm willing to bet it's Jossel."

"And I'm betting you're wrong." I knew whose head it was with absolute certainty. Because I'd seen him once before and tried very hard not to stare. Death had cooled the color of his eyes, but the nose was absolutely the same.

Bahlin crossed his arms over his chest. "Okay, super sleuth, tell me who it is, then."

I glared at him, irritated at his supposed superiority. "Bulbous nose, black hair, sharp teeth and eyes a little less vibrant but still orange. It's Maddox."

"Well damn, you're right." Bahlin pushed off the stool and stalked toward me. "Move over, luv. Let's get him out of there."

I didn't need to see the head to be sure. I'd tried so hard not to stare at him the one time I'd seen him alive that I knew who I'd seen. But I followed Bahlin's directive and stepped aside. I turned to watch him and found myself looking through the dining room to the front door.

"Bay, how did the killer get inside?" I asked.

"What? Oh sodding hell, the front door wards." He froze, his hand momentarily suspended in front of the handle to the refrigerator door.

"Didn't you say only another dragon could get inside?"

"I did. I set the wards myself." Clenching his fists, he turned slowly to face me. Eyes blazing with fury and taller than a normal man, he looked like an avenging angel.

"I haven't met another dragon, have I?" I did a mental file flip, trying to remember everyone I'd been formally introduced to.

"You've met several. The valet, for instance, is a green dragon though he's still a youth," he said, voice tight with anger. "You're not suggesting I set this up, I'm sure."

"Never crossed my mind." And it hadn't. "Where was I when I met the other dragon, or dragons? And why didn't I know it?"

"You've not come into your full strength. We've talked about this." Bahlin spun on his heel and went for the front door, moving with the contained fury of the righteously pissed. "Several of the staff of the hotel are dragons. Though I'd swear none knew of this apartment until I left tonight and gave the address for delivery of our clothing. Even then, it would have been left with the doorman. It takes a bit of time to find out which apartment belongs to a person, particularly in a building this size. Besides that, it's been my personal hideout several times over the years, and it has never been breached before."

Bahlin reached the door and ran a hand swiftly across the back of it, barely above the surface. I gasped in surprise. Faint runes showed in glowing acidic green against the black color of the door. I didn't have any idea what the runes meant, but they were complex in nature. I could tell that much simply by the intricate design of each one and the delicate way they were connected in forming the pattern I saw. Bahlin made a rough swiping motion over the door, and the images disappeared.

"I can't get anything from the wards since I was the last one to open the door. It was foolish of me to not even check before we entered the apartment. Nay, not foolish but arrogant. I won't be making that mistake again."

I quirked an eyebrow. I might not have known Bahlin well, but I already knew enough to know that arrogance was simply a part of his persona. I would bet my life on it. But I let it go, deciding it was best not to poke the angry dragon.

I took a deep breath and said, "Let's open the fridge and get this over with." I could immediately taste my pulse in my throat.

Bahlin walked back into the kitchen and put an arm around me in camaraderie. "Agreed. Let's get it over with. Take a deep breath, sweetheart, the first time's always the worst." He grinned a lecherous grin and waggled his eyebrows at me, and I laughed. Having accomplished what he set out to do, he opened the door and we faced the head together.

Just as I'd thought, it was Maddox.

"I suppose he was killed because..." I paused, unsure what to say. I wasn't fishing for a response from Bahlin, but I got one anyway.

"There could be a number of reasons, pet," he said. He set the head directly on the counter and I made a mental note to never, ever use the counter for anything food related. Hell, I doubted I'd use that little stretch of counter *ever*.

Maddox's head had been severed right below the jaw line in a clean cut. Due to the temperature of the refrigerator there was very little blood beyond what had pooled on the shelf the head had occupied.

"How long has he been here do you think?"

"Depends on a number of factors," Bahlin said.

"Check the temperature setting on the refrigerator," I suggested. "If it's been set lower, we'll know he's been better preserved. In fact, let me get that. You look at the head first. I'll get there in a minute." I'd buy as much time as I could before having to get close to the noggin.

Bahlin turned the head on the side, resting it on the ear, and I spun around to the refrigerator. No need to throw up on my first violent crime scene. I opened the door to the refrigerator and saw all the congealed blood and the smears through it where Bahlin had removed the head. I had the briefest moment to think, *Too bad I'm not gonna make it*, and I threw up all over the inside of the fridge, right on top of the evidence.

"You're lucky I'm not a sympathetic vomiter," Bahlin said, chuckling. "Grab a look at the temperature on the fridge and then go rinse your mouth in the sink."

"I'm so sorry," I mumbled, wiping my mouth with the hem of my shirt. I glanced at the setting on the temperature gauge and shut the door on the mess. "I think I'd suggest you just buy a new fridge. In fact, take it out of my first paycheck." Because however rude it was, I knew I wasn't going to be cleaning up *that* mess.

"No worries, Maddy. Now rinse your mouth and let's go over Maddox here."

"No. Let's not give the head a name. It's too personal. Call him it, or thing, or head, but not..." I couldn't even bring myself to say his name. Even though he'd shot me, I was somehow remorseful to see him dead, especially by violence. Because I was betting the murderer hadn't put him down humanely and *then* cut his head off.

Bahlin grinned at me over his shoulder. "Sure. Then rinse your mouth, and we'll go over *it*." He laughed and went back to the head on the counter, bending to look at the underside of the jaw.

I went to the sink and washed my mouth out. Realizing I had

vomit detritus on the bottom of my shirt from where I'd wiped my mouth, I told Bahlin I'd be right back and went into the bedroom to change. I didn't want any of the sickness on me. The smell was burned into my nose and I almost couldn't stand that much of a reminder that I'd tossed my supper. Bahlin had said sympathetic vomiter as a joke. I was the real deal, even if it was just residual. *Could one be sympathetic to one's self?* I wondered, snorting out loud. This wasn't the time to be engaging in my own philosophical internal dialogue, even as a means of escapism. I had work to do. I dug out a clean T-shirt and dragged it on over my head, dropping the dirty shirt in the corner of the room as I walked back to the kitchen.

Bahlin stood aside, motioning me forward with a sweep of the hand. "You've got to get close to it eventually, Maddy. Might as well jump in now that you've emptied your stomach."

"Never, ever refer to this moment again, Bahlin," I growled at him. "Never. Do you understand me? It is not to ever be repeated. It is not to ever be mentioned. It is not to ever be recounted in any form."

"Ah, I can't make that promise, Maddy, for fear I'd be lying to you, which I already promised not to do. I will, however, promise not to make jests today."

I shrugged, figuring it was probably the best I could do at the moment. I walked over to the head and looked at it. The skin was gray, probably from loss of blood but also from Maddox's natural color when he'd been alive. I was loath to touch it but I did, doing my best not to recoil from the firm, rubbery texture. Looking at it analytically, there were several factors I had to take into consideration. I needed to see the head from several angles to form a hypothesis. But first I had to wash my hands to get the death cooties off. Yes, I know they don't exist but after touching the body I was creeped out. I washed my hands thoroughly with water as hot as I could stand it and dried them on my clean shirt.

Turning to Bahlin I said, "Bay, would you handle the head for me? I'm not quite there yet."

"Sure. Want me to roll it around?" His eyes sparkled with mischief.

"Did you act this way with Aloysius?" I grumped.

"Absolutely I did. He threw up at his first body, too, you know.

Though no one wants to talk about that in the memoirs. But it's true."

I smiled up at him, nearly ignoring the fact I'd bent closer to the head. "Thanks for that. But remember, we're not discussing it. It never happened."

"Ah, see, I apologize. I didn't mean to lie earlier."

"No problem. Would you tip that head this way, then let me see the bottom side?"

Bahlin rolled the head around slowly, letting me get a good look at it from different angles. As I suspected, the cut was clean, the separation of the spinal cord surgical. After several more minutes of careful review, I asked him to set it down. I walked into the living room and sat on the sofa, but Bahlin stayed in the kitchen.

"Come in here with me after you've thoroughly washed your hands."

Rolling his eyes, Bahlin went to the sink and washed his hands. "You realize we've got to get out of here, right? Now that we've looked the head over, there's not much time to be sitting on the couch and discussing things."

I was embarrassed to admit that I hadn't, in fact, thought that far ahead. I shrugged and said, "So, do we need to leave now?" I glanced out the window in the living room. The surreal events of the evening had screwed up my perception of time. "What time is it?"

"It's about eleven," he said, glancing at the stove clock. "We really should leave..." he trailed off, looking concerned. I think we were both a bit out of sorts, I because of the severed head, and he out of concern of me and my reactions.

"Remember, truth. What's bugging you, Bay?"

"I'm going to have to get us out of here, and I'll need to phase, or change forms, to do it. We're leaving your car because I'm concerned the killer will recognize it now that we've been here, and so has he...or, in fairness, she. What do you think about leaving via dragon flight?" He smiled but it was a half-hearted effort, and I could see the concern etched in the little lines beside his eyes and around his mouth.

"I've seen the show, Bahlin. It's fine."

"That's what you think," he muttered. "Let's grab some stuff and get out of here."

"Where are we headed?" I asked, pushing up from the low, narrow sofa and heading into my room. I froze, groaning at my unintentional slip of the tongue. Bahlin snorted and rolled his eyes again.

"Bad joke. And as to where we're going, I would really rather not answer that, luv. Who knows who could be listening, right?" he called out from his own room.

Shit. I hadn't thought of that. An even better reason not to discuss the head until we were far away. Seemed like I ended up running from everywhere I ended up. What was that quote— everywhere you go there you are? I seemed to end up running, and I wasn't sure it wasn't, at least partially, from myself.

We were on the rooftop deck less than fifteen minutes later. We'd combined a couple of changes of clothing each into one soft messenger-style bag and we stood, side by side, looking into the night as if we could foretell the dangers.

"So what now?" I asked.

"Goddess help me, you're impatient. I've got to work up the nerve to scare the shit out of you. Do you mind?"

"All right, crank, get on with it."

"Brave fool," he muttered. He pulled his shirt off over his head and tossed it at me. "Put it, and the jeans, in the bag." He was still barefoot, which seemed to be a personal preference, so no shoes to worry about. Besides, I didn't think another set of size sixteens would fit in the bag. His feet were huge.

He peeled his jeans off and I was more than a little thrilled and happily scandalized to realize he went commando. I shoved his clothes in the bag, trying unsuccessfully not to stare at him. He was gorgeous, and standing here in the night he seemed to rule it with confidence. Glancing at me one last time, his eyes flashed first, changing to that inhuman blue. He crouched down, hands and feet on the ground and the air began to shimmer around him. Bones and muscles began to move under his skin in an unnatural way, the sound thick and wet. He began to shape shift, his hands digging into the decking as if he were in pain. A tail jutted out from between his buttocks, making me gasp as it slithered along the ground behind him. He seemed to fold in on himself and then grow larger by leaps and bounds. His wings folded out from his shoulder blades as if they'd simply been hidden there all along, hiding. Stretching out from his shoulders, his neck elongated and I recognized the small, soft spikes that grew out from his spinal cord. With a dark, silent flash, his skin was suddenly scaled and the transformation was complete. I was stunned into immobility. His form took up the entire top deck, though he was dark enough I wasn't entirely worried about being seen by the neighbors. He huffed out a breath, and I walked toward him with small, unsure steps.

"Bay?" I asked quietly.

He huffed again, and I knew he understood me.

I laid a tentative hand on his shoulder. It was hard to reconcile the monster to the man, but I knew he was in there. I rubbed his shoulder in small circles, as much to comfort myself as anything.

"How do you want to do this?" I asked.

He pushed up with his front legs so he was squatting and, reaching down with his forearms, he scooped me up and held me close to his body. He turned his head to the side to eye me carefully and I nodded, not quite trusting my voice. Bahlin sighed deeply.

The night air seemed to grow denser around us and I realized that images were not quite so clear. It was like trying to look through dark smoke. I began to struggle to get down but he only held me tighter. With a giant push from his hind legs and a cracking sound behind us, he launched us up into the night sky, unfurling his wings so they propelled us away.

Every muscle in my body vibrated in fear at being carried this way. One small fumble on his part, and I'd be free-falling to the ground below. As the sights of everyday life grew smaller and smaller, I became more and more frightened, scared to move even the slightest for fear of distracting my dragon.

We flew for at least an hour before I realize that the stars were clear again and the haze we'd left London in was gone. Shivering less than on my original flight, I was grateful for the jacket I was wearing and for being tucked up close to Bahlin's warm body.

I smelled the ocean before I saw it. It was fresh and crisp, and the pounding of the surf was interrupted only by the flap of Bahlin's wings and the occasional puffing of his breath. Taking in a great lungful of air and holding me tighter, Bahlin trumpeted in a joyful voice, spinning once as we hurtled toward the ground. I squeezed my eyes shut and began contemplating anew my miserable mortality among the immortal, or nearly immortal, monsters. The air dampened as we got closer to the ground. Rocky, uninhabited cliffs formed through the fog. Bahlin set down gently, with a great backwash of air from his wings, and set me on my feet so he could balance on all four legs. He stared at me quietly, breathing deep lungs full of the fresh air and then he bellied to the ground again, nudging me toward his back.

"You want me to get on again? Are you insane? I'm too damned glad to be on solid ground again." Skepticism laced every word.

He hummed in response and butted me none too gently toward his shoulder with his forehead.

"Pushy bastard," I muttered, but I did as he wordlessly asked and clambered onto his back, once again sitting just in front of his wings.

I wrapped my arms as far around his neck as they would go and held on tight, unsure what to expect. Nothing could have prepared me for Bahlin launching us over the edge of the cliffs. We were in free-fall for a moment before he flapped his wings hard and veered off to the left, taking us nearer the cliff face than I was comfortable. I shouted in alarm and I could feel him rumble between my legs, though I wouldn't have bet my own money on whether he was bemoaning my lack of courage or laughing at me.

Suddenly we were cloaked in the heavy, smoky miasma of London again and Bahlin flew straight at the cliff, pulling up short of the rocks. Reaching out with his forearms he pulled us to the cliff face and began climbing diagonally across the rocks toward a black fissure that I hadn't seen before. He scrambled like a goat, sure-footed and quick, his claws securing footholds in the shale. We were through the cave's opening in a moment. Bahlin scrambled further and further into the tunnel, the light disappearing behind us. The cave was completely devoid of any light, and my eyes strained to pick out even the smallest details in the encroaching darkness. Bahlin took a deep breath, and the void ,was split by a burst of flame emanating from my lover's mouth. Shocked, I gasped and sat up, cracking my head against the cave's ceiling. The bright bursts of color the flame had burned into my corneas were all I could see. When it finally receded I realized he'd been lighting torches along the wall. Very barbarian chic, I suppose.

Bahlin turned and nosed me to the ground. The messenger bag slid from my aching shoulders, and I stumbled when I touched the floor before getting my feet under me. With a shimmer of air, his dragon form seemed to rend itself in half and the man emerged, gloriously naked. He knelt on the floor, limbs trembling slightly, hair dampened with sweat, obviously exhausted.

"You all right, pet?" he asked, his voice rough.

"Sure. You?"

"Truth? I'm completely knackered. Cloaking is one of my skills, but it wears me thin to extend it to another creature and to carry that creature for so long in my arms when I've not eaten properly. It's not so bad when you ride."

"Where are we?" I asked, looking around him and into the room beyond. The cavern wasn't huge, but there were visible natural tunnels leading away from that main room that gave the impression of extended size and depth. The sound of trickling water indicated a small underground stream somewhere nearby.

"This is what's referred to in mythology as a dragon's den, or lair. All dragons of a certain rank have them. It's our most closely guarded secret. You're the first person I've brought here since Aloysius." He looked around for the bag I'd dropped when I stumbled from his back.

"What are you doing?"

"Getting dressed. I was under the impression that your sensibilities preferred me with clothes." He ran his hands through his hair, arching his back, his eyes never leaving my face. He was beautiful in the firelight, like a gilded Renaissance nude, and I wanted to reach out and touch him.

"Go ahead," I said huskily.

"Go ahead and what?" he whispered.

"Clothes would be a good thing. No need to reaffirm life for Maddox's death."

Bahlin laughed and bent to dig through the bag, pulling out a pair of jeans and a long-sleeved charcoal shirt. After slipping into the clothes he stuffed his feet into sneakers, impressing me.

"Not going barefoot?"

"Even my feet get torn up on this rock when I'm in human form," he answered. "Come inside and we'll have a seat."

We walked further into the cavern, and I realized there were what I considered basic necessities. There was a sofa and several chairs, a bed in one corner, and a number of weapons—swords, knives and handguns. The room was not large itself. In truth, it would have been nearly impossible for Bahlin to enter in his dragon form and do much more than turn around.

He walked to a small larder and pulled out a round of cheese and some bread, and a large packet of what looked like beef jerky.

"I need to eat again," he said. "It takes a lot out of me to change because my form is so large, so I have to eat regularly and protein's a must."

He gestured me over to one of the chairs, and I sat. He pulled a small knife out and carved a piece of cheese off the wheel for me and then gave me a chunk of bread. We ate in companionable silence.

When we were done, and Bahlin was only snacking on the jerky, he said, "I suppose we'd better talk about the head."

I looked at Bahlin and took a deep breath. "I think I know who did it."

Chapter Twelve

Bahlin choked a bit and looked up at me, surprised. "Go on, then. Tell me what you've got."

"I'm going to be an adult about this and call it, him, Maddox." I shuddered. Sure I was. "He's been missing for four days. We know that the only ones to know the case specifics were the High Council and the king and queen of the fae. Right?"

Bahlin nodded, crossing his feet at the ankles, one hand behind his head. He looked relaxed but his entire attention was focused on me.

I held up my pointer finger. "First is Sarenia. She wasn't at the meeting, so she didn't have specifics of the crime. As an Atlantean, Sarenia wouldn't have had a reason to hire Maddox, assuming he was the killer's proxy. She could have dragged me down to her sunken city and simply drowned me. No need to hire a shooter. She's also over eleven thousand years old, as much as it boggles the mind. She's had plenty of time to come up with better ways to commit murder than the obvious. Finally, I don't believe she would have had her only child murdered, not for power, not for anything."

Bahlin's face went slack, and he looked confused. "Meyla is dead?"

I nodded, not considering he might have known her. *Way to go, Niteclif. Nothing shows compassion like blurting out, "Hey your buddy's dead."* I shook my head and opened my mouth to apologize—again.

"No. Go on."

I hesitated, my mouth opening and closing like a guppy's. "You're sure?"

Denise Tompkins

His answer was absolute silence and a hard stare that made me feel guilty.

"Right." I cleared my throat and held up a second finger. "Imeena is a vampire. They are highly attracted to faerie blood, so she wouldn't have wasted any of it if she'd killed Maddox. She would have ripped his throat out, yes, but she wouldn't have discarded such a treat. Nor would she have left Maddox in the fridge. As a vampire she's capable and willing of killing on her own without a proxy. She has all the tools she needs to kill me without hiring someone to shoot me." Remembering her canines, I shuddered. "And she would have had access to me at night, when she could have really reached out to touch me, as a High Council member. Hell, she's my employer. I would have come to her whenever she called. And I can't reconcile her motive to kill these creatures." I paused to catch my breath.

Bahlin's eyes narrowed and he had developed a tic in his jaw. "Go on, luv, you're obviously on to something."

Third finger. "The king and queen of the fae may have asked Maddox to kill me. But if they'd had Maddox kill me it would have been an act of loyalty. He wouldn't have run. He's been with them for generations and was considered a member of the family. They wouldn't have killed him but instead would have hidden him away from the Council's reach inside the sithen. It would have been easy since the Council has to be granted access to enter. Say no and no one gets inside, so hide him there and he's out of harm's way. The only thing I can't figure is where Tarrek's disappearance fits in for them.

"Tarrek was abducted, so he couldn't have done it." I didn't even hold up a finger for this one. I glared at Bahlin, daring him to argue with me.

"If you're sure. But what about me?" he challenged me, forcing me to look closely at another suspect I didn't want to consider.

"I'm sure. You didn't do it either."

"Why not?"

"You've had too many opportunities to kill me. And when you had the family tree in your hands, the date of death didn't appear. From what I understand, if you were the killer and your intent was to off me, the date of death would have shown up. Right?"

166

"Depending on the probability of success, yes." He leaned forward, sensing the rising tension in my voice. "So who did it?"

"Who's left?" I whispered.

Bahlin took a deep breath, held it, then let it out on a long sigh. "Gretta and Hellion."

"Gretta's dead. I killed her," I said softly, my pulse so hard in my throat I was sure Bahlin could see it jumping beneath my skin. "I killed her," I repeated, "after Hellion ordered her to kill me. They were mates, and she was never supposed to die, Bahlin. He didn't intend for it to happen. But Maddox had failed them. Remember, Gretta came after me with a sword, but it was too large for her to handle properly. She would have killed me if she'd been able to heft it over her head like she tried to do. But she couldn't, and I stabbed her with the dirk when the sword fell behind her head and shoulders." I closed my eyes momentarily and swallowed the bile that threatened. "Hellion now had an open reason to come after me, as well as a scapegoat for his crimes. He could kill me while claiming to avenge the murder of his mate and blame Gretta for killing the other beings, at least until he found a way to continue his efforts.

"And if together we figured out he killed Maddox and took his head, then it was all well and good because Maddox had been issued a death warrant by me just before we met. The king decreed it after Maddox was sentenced."

Bahlin pushed himself up off the couch and stretched, my hormonal body, mind, and spirit admiring and coveting his body as he did. Hands locked behind his head, he walked to the pantry and retrieved two bottles of water before returning to sink down on the couch. He cracked the lid off his drink and tilted it toward me in salute. "How do you know for sure Hellion killed Maddox?"

"The sword marks on Maddox's neck. The sword skidded off his chin with enough force to continue along the jaw and sever the head all the way to the spine. The spinal column was cut through surgically, ensuring that there were no bone pieces or meaty bits to get stuck to the killer's clothes or hands. It was very clean. That has to take strength and skill with a blade. Next to you, Hellion is the largest, and likely strongest, man on the Council. Gretta couldn't wield the sword against me. She didn't have the strength to cut Maddox's head off that cleanly, even if he held still and showed her where to swing and strike. That means it was a larger person's sword, and if Hellion sent her to kill me, it's only logical deduction that he's our killer."

"So Hellion is killing the other creatures?" Bahlin asked, his eyes sparking in the flames of the torches lit about the room.

"Yes, he is." I didn't want to say this. Not out loud. Because once I said it, it was real. And another man was going to be sentenced to death, though I thought he likely deserved it. But I was afraid that the man across from me would be the one to dole the sentence out, and I didn't want to put him in harm's way. But I didn't know what else to do. He'd reached the conclusion with me. It was too late to stop justice's forward momentum.

"Why, Maddy? Why is Hellion doing this?" he pressed, forcing me to say out loud what I had suspected of the killer since Gretta had come to my room to try to poison me then stab me.

"He's stealing the strongest pieces of each immortal creature so he can morph them into himself. He wants to be immortal."

Bahlin surged to his feet, pacing the small room. He seemed more raw here in the cave, more animalistic. "So that's why you don't think Tarrek is doing it? Because he's immortal?"

"At the least you said he'd live for thousands of years, Bahlin. Possibly thousands upon thousands. What good is immortality if you already nearly have it? And power? He's got it in spades." I reached out and grabbed Bahlin's arm as he stormed passed me for the fourth time. "I didn't realize it until I met his parents and fully understood that he's fae royalty. He will eventually command the light and dark sides of faerie. He can make his own magic in the sithen, really. What more does he need with others' magic?"

Bahlin sank back into the sofa, resting his head in his hands. "Finish the thought, Maddy. Tell me why Hellion wants the collective power of the creatures he's killed."

I was about to drop the final brick for Hellion's tomb. "As a wizard, he isn't immortal. But he will be when he pushes all this power together, immortal creatures forced into a mortal man. How can he not be? And once he's achieved that kind of power, he wants to take over the Council, which is why he needs me dead. You said it yourself, there's no leader and without a Niteclif, chaos will reign unless the

Council leads. Hellion is aiming to change that and become your leader."

Time was immeasurable without the sun as a point of reference. Instead of walking to the front of the cave we sat together on the sofa, listening to the sounds of the earth around us: running water, the muted cry of gulls, the distant and subdued boom of surf. Bahlin was physically exhausted and when he pointed out how tired *he* was it was like someone threw a switch in me. I just crumbled. The sofa was a futon-style piece, but even open and laying across it diagonally it wasn't long enough for me. No way would it fit Bahlin. After several minutes arguing with me, he convinced me to come to bed with him for the third time in roughly twenty-four hours. Protesting too loudly was silly, really, since we'd already done far more than simply sleep together. But I insisted on keeping my T-shirt and underwear on. Prudery, thy name is Niteclif.

Bahlin dug through a small bureau next to the bed and pulled out a pair of lounge pants when I flatly refused to sleep with him in the nude. He hadn't packed any boxers, whether by oversight or planned seduction. It didn't matter. No clothes, no sleep companion, no negotiation.

I made one major mistake in my calculations, though, and you'd think I'd have learned because I was a repeat offender in this area. I didn't negotiate no cuddling. So the minute he crawled under the blankets he wrapped me up in his arms and spooned me close. I was about to drift off to sleep to the sounds of the shore when Bahlin tucked his head into my neck, picking up a thread of the earlier conversation I had hoped he'd leave alone. Because for all my pushing over the last few days, I suddenly didn't want the answers I'd so seriously thought I needed.

"And me, Maddy? How long do you think I'll live?" he asked quietly. "Is there any last reason you can find to not trust me. Truth, remember?"

I rolled over to face him and propped myself up on my arm, looking down at him. His hair was spread over the pillow like burnished foam in the light of the one torch I'd insisted he leave burning. I stared at him, the vestiges of sleep held off for a moment longer.

"I've asked you plenty of times how old you were, but you've never seen fit to answer me. I can only imagine you have some valid reason for not wanting me to know. But it does cast a shadow of doubt on you, Bahlin. Why not be honest with me about your age, or your longevity? Or even try to be more forthcoming about your species. And it bugs me how your sister is always referring to something she's seen regarding me that you don't want me to know. What is it? Do I end up with Tarrek after all this?" I half joked. He didn't answer, and I swallowed hard. "Bahlin? What has Brylanna seen?"

He draped an arm over his eyes, refusing to remove it when I tugged. "I won't answer what Brylanna has seen. Her visions are subjective. And I don't answer your questions about me as a dragon, Maddy, because I'm afraid it will be one more reason for you to step away from me. Besides, it's a bit insulting. Have you realized that you never ask me questions about me as a man?"

My mouth hung slightly open, and I knew he was right. I was more focused on the dragon than the man who constantly mastered him.

Bahlin continued without pausing for my internal revelation. "You've been looking for reasons not to come back to my bed, and you've already contemplated turning away from the Niteclif oath to get away from all things mythological. And this was all accomplished within a short day's time. Why would I add to your resolution?" He rolled into me and wrapped his free arm around my waist, pressing his chin to the crown of my head. "I don't want to risk you running, Maddy. I felt that if I could make Tarrek a bit more monstrous than I was then I'd stand a better chance with you myself."

I gently pulled away from him and sat on the edge of the bed, but that wasn't enough distance for me to think. I slipped my feet into my Nikes and walked slowly to one of the dark tunnels leading off the cavern. I didn't know what to say. He was right. His little metamorphosis earlier had been a great act of trust on his behalf, but it had put him even further into the monster column for me, no matter what I tried to tell myself. I hugged my arms around my middle and shivered. How much was too much monster?

I got cold quickly, so I quietly returned to the bed. I crawled under the covers and pushed at his shoulder to make him roll over flat on his back. I laid my head on his chest without a word, and he wrapped his arms around me gently. Breathing deeply, I smiled. *Bahlin*, I thought to myself. There were so many positive attributes I could tie to that one name: loyal, trustworthy, charming, sexy as hell, amazing lover, protector, friend. But could I call him a man? No, I couldn't. He'd warned me himself that he was, first and foremost, a dragon. And I wasn't sure if that one word was more important than all the positive attributes I could assign to him in one lifetime. I fell asleep with my head on his chest and the sound of his heartbeat in my ear. It kept the dreams at bay.

For the second time, I'd gone to bed with Bahlin only to awake and find him gone. I sat up and saw him sitting at the cave's entrance tunnel. He had his knees bent and his forearms resting on them, and he was flipping what looked like a gold coin. He paused and turned to look over his shoulder at me. I ran my fingers through my bed-head and settled the covers around my hips.

"I've been thinking about our next step," he said.

"How long have you been up?"

"A couple of hours." He grinned and turned back toward the entrance. "You're a cover hog."

I had no idea if he was joking or not, but I *was* cocooned comfortably in the blankets.

"So what's the next step?" I asked. Bahlin quirked a brow at me and didn't answer me so I said, "Er, maybe I should ask instead if you have any suggestions."

He turned so he was facing me and propped himself on his elbows, stretching his legs out in front of him. Still wearing nothing more than his lounge pants, his abdominal muscles collectively tightened and knotted, emphasizing his cobblestone abs and hard physique. I tried, unsuccessfully, not to drool.

"Want me to come back over there?" he asked, standing up and brushing the dirt and rocks from his hands, his muscles bunching and releasing as he moved, captivating me like a snake does a small bird. I wanted to feel him move under my hands. I wanted to knead those muscles when they were tense. I wanted to get a grip on my hormones before this got out of control again.

"I, uh, okay." Very suave, that's me.

He walked toward me, predatory grace in motion. "You know what I want, Maddy?"

"Breakfast?" Hells bells he made me nervous. I wasn't some simpering virgin, but he made me feel like it.

"Not so much, unless you're on the menu, love." He'd reached the edge of the bed. He grinned wickedly and stripped his pants off before getting back into bed.

"Hey. Put the drawers back on, buddy." I scooted to the opposite edge of the bed. "We've got to plan our next move."

Bahlin stretched, hands clasped, arms arched behind his back, and his back arched. It was a good stretch. "I've got it covered. But we've got hours to kill before we can leave the cave. I can only cloak myself with darkness, daylight won't work." He reached over to stroke a hand down my neck and across my breastbone, stopping just above my heart. "Do you remember what I told you?"

I trembled at the memory, locking my elbows at my sides to keep from wrapping my arms around myself in comfort. A fine bead of sweat popped up on my upper lip and my scalp prickled, and all from his earlier promise. "You said that one day we'd have hours uninterrupted to spend together in bed."

"That day's come earlier than I thought, Maddy."

I scooted farther away from him, close enough to the edge of the mattress I was in real danger of falling off. "I don't know, Bahlin. I've always been so cautious with, well, with sex. And you make me feel reckless and out of control, and I...I don't know, Bahlin." My heart almost needed life support just thinking about the possibilities. I knew what he was capable of, and a screaming orgasm delivered as a wake-up call didn't sound like a bad idea. But my prudery was a stubborn beast and I couldn't give in without at least some semblance of a fight, no matter how badly I wanted to. This way I couldn't hold myself entirely responsible for it if things went south. Irresponsible, yes. But at least the only one I was attempting to fool was me. I was sure that to everyone else my idiocy was as transparent as plastic cling-wrap and probably equally as dicey to handle without ending up with a wadded up mess.

Bahlin rolled toward me and pulled me into his arms, sliding his hands over my ass, under my T-shirt and up my bare back. His fingers kneaded my tense muscles and I allowed myself to relax when he didn't press any further than that.

"I think that's the nicest thing you've said to me yet. Take off your shirt, *mo chrid*," he whispered, leaning in to kiss me. His lips were hot to the touch. He slanted his mouth over mine and rubbed gently, licking my lower lip and nibbling on it as an effective means of coercion. I leaned in to the kiss, responding and opening to him and our tongues touched, gently at first. He took the kiss deeper, pulling me into his chest, gripping my thigh and drawing it up over his hip. I gasped into his mouth and he smiled, undulating his hips against me. His erection was enormous, searing my skin through my underwear. I jerked at the contact and he grunted, rubbing even more firmly against me. I wondered if it was possible to spontaneously combust during early foreplay.

Bahlin reached down between us and grabbed the hem of my T-shirt. "Maddy, please, take it off. I want to touch your skin. I want to suckle your breasts and feast on your shoulders. I want to nibble your belly button..." His voice was muffled against my skin, his tongue licking out to touch between the words as he worked his way from my ear to my collarbone and back, ending by laying little kisses all over my neck and jaw. I clung to him, terrified to truly let go. My internal man vs. monster debate wasn't nearly settled, but I wanted him nearly as badly as the pleasure I knew he could give me. *To hell with it*, I thought. *I deserve whatever happiness I can carve out of this life.* I'll pick up the debate later, after I sweep up the remnants of my shredded morals.

I grabbed the bottom of my T-shirt and pulled it up over my head, quickly laying back down in Bahlin's arms.

"Love me, Bay," I whispered into the hollow of his neck. "Make love to me."

Bahlin sighed deeply and said, "With pleasure, my love. With pleasure." He kissed his way down the front of my body, his lips soft but insistent in their exploration. He gently suckled my breast,

173

plucking at the beaded nipple with his teeth. He sucked hard, garroting the skin behind the nipple and biting down, dancing on the border of pleasure and pain. I arched my back and moaned, begging with my actions for what my mind couldn't articulate. Pain hadn't ever held any fascination for me, even in my limited experience. But what Bahlin did to me made me cry out for more, begging with my body for his attention. He repeated the same pleasure with the other breast, leaving the swollen and distended nipples a deep, dusky red. Then he kissed his way down my ribs, licking and sucking at my belly button, making me laugh. When he reached the band of my underwear he ran his tongue under the edge, licking my hipbones and tickling my lower belly. I whimpered and grabbed his head, pushing him lower. I *needed* him.

"Patience," he admonished, hooking his thumbs under the edge of my panties and tugging at the satin. I lifted my hips to help him, and it seemed that my participation was the trigger he'd been waiting for me to pull. He pushed my legs apart and dove for my center, his sole focus loving me with joyful abandon. His skill was alarming, pushing me with force toward a fast, hard peak. I threw myself back against the bed and cried out. Bahlin immediately stopped, leaving me right on the precipice of release.

"Bahlin," I panted, "you son of a bitch. Finish me." I didn't even recognize my deep, throaty voice.

"I want to be inside you when you reach your pinnacle, Maddy." He kissed and bit his way back to my mouth and, grabbing me around the waste, pulled me on top of him. I straddled his bare hips, rubbing my cleft along the ridge of his penis. He was like molten silk, and I groaned. Bahlin hissed, involuntarily jerking his hips up to meet me in motion. I devoured his mouth, and he ate at mine, the kisses bruising. But neither of us took the final step of consummation, instead drawing the pleasure out to dance precariously with pain, the ache evolving to burning need, primal and base. We tormented each other endlessly with Bahlin pushing my boundaries and experiences beyond simple definition.

Bahlin rolled me back over and bit my neck, rolling my pounding pulse around his tongue.

"I can't wait any longer," he panted, and he drove into me in one

174

long, hard thrust.

I screamed, scoring his back with my nails and lifting my hips to meet his relentless invasion. He stretched me to the point I felt I'd split in two and I groaned, only his thorough prep work saving it from hurting like hell. Beyond the physical connection it felt so good, so *right*, to be loved by this man. He reached between us and rubbed my clit in hard little circles, never relenting in his aggressive lovemaking, his balls slapping my ass as he rammed his way through my tight channel. The sound was so incredibly erotic. I moaned, feeling the orgasm just beyond my reach, coming closer with each thrust and every manipulation.

"Maddy, I'm close, I'm close," he said, the muscles and tendons in his neck standing out in relief as he strained to prolong the pleasure. He pinched the hood of my clit hard and it was all I needed. I went over the edge of the abyss, yelling his name into the void of the cavern. He fell over seconds later, the echoes of his shouts mingling with mine until we were one voice.

I lay there beneath him, sweating and panting, finally understanding why the French called orgasm the little death. I couldn't move. Nothing was responding to my commands to get out from under Bahlin. So I laid there, relearning how to breathe. His heart began to resume a normal pace and he rolled to the side, cuddling me up to him.

"Don't say anything, Maddy," he said softly. "I don't want you to say anything."

"About what?" I asked sleepily. I couldn't figure out why people wanted a cigarette after sex. This was way the hell better than any nicotine buzz I'd ever had. In fact, if Bahlin could keep up his success rate at doling out climaxes, I could probably swear off cigarettes for life.

"*Tha gaol agam ort*," he whispered.

I slipped back to the surface of thought, unsure what to say or do. "What did you say?" I asked softly.

"It's Gaelic." He shrugged, burying his face in my hair.

"Say it again." He did, and I repeated it to him. "Did I say it right?"

His voice was harsh with emotion. "You said it perfectly, my love."

"What does it mean?"

"I love you."

I stiffened, and he held me tighter. I started to pull away and he said, "I meant it. Don't say anything that might ruin this moment. I want to remember the first time I told you I loved you with affection, not frustration."

"Do I annoy you so badly?" I asked, refusing to turn to look at him, refusing to address his surety that I would love him back.

"No, not annoy. But you have tried to tell me how I feel and don't feel. You need to simply accept that my love is what it is, Madeleine Dylis Niteclif. I love you. I've never felt this way about anyone in my long life, and I've never given the words to anyone, freely or otherwise." He tightened his arms around me.

"Bay, I wasn't sure what I was saying..."

"Shut up, Maddy." Bahlin sighed, and I smiled. I didn't want to ruin this, either.

"I want the words from you one day, *mo chrid*, but I want them freely. I'm willing to wait out your indecision until you see reason and understand we're meant to be together." He ran his hand up and down my front in lazy strokes and I felt myself begin to respond. My nipples pebbled, and my belly tightened under his touch. "This is only a part of what I want from you, Maddy."

"Well," I said, "you promised me hours upon hours in bed. Better put your money where your mouth is."

He rolled over, pulling me around to face him. "Oh, pet, you have sealed your fate."

Let's just say the man didn't make idle threats.

Chapter Thirteen

We spent the morning making love. Sometimes it was passionate, other times poignant, but any way you looked at it, it was always good. The dragon was talented and...creative.

After a solid nap, Bahlin pulled on a pair of jeans and his Nikes and got out of bed, walking to the larder. He took out a large, white bowl and said he'd be right back. He took off down one of the side passages leaving me to stare at the natural entrance to the cave and wondered about our next step. While Bahlin had indicated a plan of action, he hadn't shared his thoughts with me yet, as usual. It was an annoying habit, one he'd have to modify if we were going to work together at the very least. I knew we'd have to meet with the Council at some point, if for no other reason than for me to confirm the facts surrounding Gretta's death but I intended to take it a step further. I was going to question them about the Meyla's death.

A burst of light down the tunnel Bahlin had taken caught my attention. I watched, and Bahlin emerged moments later with the same white bowl but it was full of gently steaming water.

"I know it's not as good as a bath, but the water's warm," he grinned sheepishly.

I watched him bring the basin closer and asked, "So you, hm, blew *fire* on the basin to heat up the water? Or is my assumption too Hollywood?"

He looked at me with such a serious look before answering. "I fetched the water from the stream you can hear and yes, I 'blew fire' on it to warm it up. Does that bother you?"

A little bit, I admitted to myself. To Bahlin I only said, "No, I'm only happy to be able to take a warm sponge bath, so thanks. A little privacy, though? Please?"

Bahlin tossed me a rag and said he'd go to the front of the cave while I cleaned up.

Considerate of him, I thought, wincing as the rag ran across a particularly tender spot. Bedding a man as endowed as Bahlin was more pleasurable than painful, but it left its marks too. I'd have to refrain from jumping him again for a couple of days. *Slut,* I mentally chastised myself, grinning at the absurdity of the turns my life was taking at speeds far faster than was prudent. I'd never been free with my body. He didn't give me the choice to be anything but. It was incredibly out of character for me.

Bahlin called out down the tunnel to see if I was finished, and I shouted in response that he could come back. I was pulling my clean T-shirt over my head when he rounded the last corner. I sat on the edge of the bed to put on my shoes and he grabbed our meager remaining food supply, carving up the last chunks of cheese and bread and bringing the diminishing bag of beef jerky to the sofa. We snacked in companionable silence once again, hesitant to interrupt our surreal time together yet both knowing our obligations grew heavier with each passing hour.

"I think we've got to go back to London and call a Council meeting," Bahlin said, breaking the silence. He looked at me from the corner of his eye, gauging my response.

I gripped my hands together so hard my knuckles stood out in white relief. "I don't think I'm ready to face Hellion yet, Bay, but I know it has to be done."

Bahlin slid over to sit hip to hip with me, wrapping a long arm around my shoulders and pulling me in close. I sighed and leaned my head against his still bare chest.

"Do I simply make the accusation that I think he's the killer?" I asked, albeit sarcastically. "Because I'm sure that will go over like a ton of fresh shit."

"Lovely mouth there, sweet," he said. "No, I don't think there's enough concrete evidence to support such a charge."

"But you agreed with me yesterday." I pushed away from him and stood. My breath came short, and my hands fisted involuntarily at my sides as I faced him.

"I did, and I still agree with your initial logic. But the facts really aren't concrete enough, Maddy. You can't condemn a man to certain death based on preliminary facts alone." He rose and laid his heavy hands on my shoulders then bent down in a sincere effort to capture my eyes, but I continued to look over his shoulder as he spoke. "You're still new at this and a bit naive, sweetheart, for all that your logic is good. There must be *irrefutable* facts, without conjecture, that draw a case together before you issue judgment."

"If that's true, then tell me please what I did that was so different with Maddox?" I asked as I relaxed slightly with his explanation, trying not to take his observations as criticism. "Why did you agree with me so easily then?" Sarenia had counseled me to make the best use of Bahlin's experience as I could. This was my first step in taking her advice...and maybe burning up the label of naiveté Bahlin had stuck me with.

"Your facts were concrete. The bloody sword, the gun, the boot prints, his positioning, his dominant hand and the matching runes all played a part in helping your conviction hold water with me and, later, the Council."

"And if I'd pushed? Tried to make my findings stick without such support?"

"Your word is law, but that doesn't make it right, Maddy," he said reprovingly.

"Give me a little credit, Bay. I was only curious. I'm honestly trying to accept this, but to go from pleasantly oblivious of my family legacy one day to dumped into a world where mythology is actual history the next? It's tough." I stepped into him and I relaxed a little, wrapping my arms around his waist and he hugged me back with spine-cracking zeal.

"You're doing exceptionally well, Maddy. Don't doubt that." More gently now, Bahlin disentangled himself from my grip and walked to the entrance tunnel, bending over and picking up the gold coin he'd been tossing earlier. Handling it seemed to relax him. He began tossing it again.

"Is that really gold?" I asked, unable to help myself. I was curious.

Bahlin looked at me, several thoughts openly crossing his face before he spoke. He walked back to the sofa and sat, turning on one hip so he faced me. "Yes, it's gold." He tossed it to me and I snatched it out of the air, surprised at how heavy it was. "You wanted to know more about my species? Here are a couple of quick facts. The myth of our obsession with gold is one place where fiction took its thread straight from fact. The rumors of dragon hoarding are true. We're treasure junkies, and gold is like a drug to us. Just handling this coin soothes me. Ironically, the need to have more doesn't soothe me in the least. *That* drives me a bit nuts." He shrugged and smiled self-deprecatingly. "And we come by it through, ah, alternate means. Dragons don't subscribe to the same rules as humans. Anyone who found my lair could raid it. I'd have to defend it to keep my treasures. It's one of the reasons we're a bit fanatical about keeping the location of our lair so private."

"When you say defend it, do you mean fight? Like to the death?"

He grinned, rubbing the end of his nose to try and hide the smile. "You've watched too much telly, Maddy. No, it's generally not to the death. But it can be a very violent fight depending on the sect, or weyr, that the raiding dragon is from. Black dragons are the most violent of our kind and green's the most docile. The rest of us fall somewhere in between.

"My lair's never been found, though, so it's all irrelevant."

The thought of Bahlin locked in a violent fight made my right eye twitch. And the thought of him seeking out a fight made the left eye join in.

"Have you ever found someone else's lair?" I asked, pressing my fingers over my eyelids. I was disturbed about the depth of feelings Bahlin was dragging from me.

"Of course," he replied nonchalantly, stretching for all the world like a large cat. "Young dragons get a small coming-of-age deposit from their father. After that, we tend to keep an eye out for treasures small and large to build our holdings. The older we get and the more we've accumulated, the more seriously we take the protection of our precious." He said the last in the creepy voice of Gollum from the *Lord of the Rings* trilogy and I did the obligatory eye-roll. He chuckled, and I handed the gold doubloon back to him. He began flipping it through

180

Legacy

the air, scarcely looking at it.

I changed the subject. "Bay, what will happen when we meet with Hellion?" I couldn't keep a modicum of fear out of my voice. I needed to be prepared.

"He can't do anything to you for defending yourself, but he may ask for a recounting of what happened. I will bear witness for you since I saw the whole thing. It has to be done, you know, and soon. The longer it's put off, the worse it will be."

I stared at the entrance to the cave. It felt like that short tunnel was the barrier between safety and threat, being either the hunter or the hunted. I closed my eyes, wishing I could stay here and forgo my new responsibilities. But I knew that wasn't an option.

"Okay. So how do we call a Council meeting?"

Bahlin had me pack the meager belongings we'd brought with us. I stuffed everything back into the messenger back, somehow fitting his lounge pants in there, too...just in case. I couldn't do anything about Captain Commando and his lack of underwear, but sleep gear I could influence, especially if he wanted me under the covers with him. I might allow, or even encourage, my own seduction, but I'd put a pretty bow around its neck to make myself feel better if that was what was necessary to keep my morals from choking to death on my lust.

Bahlin walked back into the cavern. "I made the call to Brylanna. She's acted as Seer for the Council in the past. I've asked her to call all the Council members together to meet at Manderson's Pub tonight at midnight, so we'll have to hurry to get there."

"We're meeting at a pub?" I asked. "Isn't that a little public for a discussion like this?"

"It normally would be, but Manderson is a pech, sort of like a gnome but with strength that defies description, and he's a back room we can use that's made for private meetings." He smiled and roughed up my hair. "Fix your hair or no one will wonder what you've been about in all this time away with me."

"Nice, Bay," I grumbled, running my fingers through my hair, trying to pull it into some form of submission. No luck. "You've got to stop saying things like that, you know it?" I bitched, pushing myself to

181

standing and stomping away from him.

"Why on earth would I stop teasing you, Maddy?" he asked, incredulous. He smiled hugely, batting his eyes and clasping his hands to his chest in mock sincerity.

"Because you make me feel cheap when you say stuff so casually." I blushed and looked down, spinning to face away from him. He was quiet for a moment, then I saw his feet move into my field of view. I refused to face him, embarrassed at the brutal feelings behind my outburst and, worse, worried they were true.

"My heart, look at me. *Look at me!*" he commanded and I started, looking up instinctively. His voice was hard and non-compromising, his jaw set so tightly I could see the muscles ticking under the skin.

"I am sincerely sorry my teasing led you to believe I thought of what we have as cheap. It slays me that you would think so, my love. You are the purpose in my life, and I love you," he said, grasping my chin.

I flinched at the last and he cursed, releasing my chin albeit gently.

"I told you I'd wait for you to come around and I will. But I won't be patient about it indefinitely, Maddy, no matter what anyone says."

That confused me. "What do you mean? No one has said anything to me."

"Forget it," he muttered, turning away with jerky movements that were totally out of character. He had been thrown off balance by this last exchange as much as I had. "Let's get to the pub so we arrive early enough to not have to watch our backs. While there's no violence allowed at Council meetings, there's always the arrival and departure of which to be wary." He had slung the messenger bag over his shoulder and headed for the mouth of the cave before I could demand he answer me.

I took the time to look around the cavern one last time and I fell behind. I walked down the dark tunnel with my hands forecasting my path along the wall while I took small, shuffling baby steps in the darkness to ensure I didn't trip. I called out for Bahlin but I didn't get an answer. I wondered if I had somehow taken the wrong tunnel when I kicked something soft and forgiving: the messenger bag. Bay had definitely been this way. I picked it up and continued on. It was still dark but there was a slight lightening of the tunnel up ahead, so I forged my way on toward the light. I sincerely hoped my moving toward the light wasn't foreshadowing of my decision to confront Hellion. I giggled in panic, and then I froze. Something was behind me. I turned slowly and there he was, my dragon. His eyes shown in the darkness like twin beacons of light, bright enough to draw a ship to shore. How had I moved by him without seeing him? He took up nearly the whole passage. I swear he grinned at me. All I gave him in return was a bland smile. I had to stop copping to fear. It was giving me a poor reputation with myself.

"So how do you want to do this?" I asked, all professional and cool. Riiight.

Bahlin backed up a few steps and bellied to the ground. I moaned at the thought of riding him back to London. Honestly, I was a little sore to be sitting astride anything more difficult to ride than a couch cushion. Bahlin huffed out his command, showing me his teeth.

I threw the messenger bag down and got in his face. He was scary as hell, but I knew he still heard me and I was absolutely sure he still understood me. "You expect me to believe you'll wait for me to fall in love with you when you can't even give me a couple of minutes to work up to setting my aching body on your back? You're a real riot, Bay," I snarked. I turned my back on him as I scooped up the discarded bag, doing my best to appear nonchalant with a monster at my back.

He closed his eyes and laid his head on the ground at my feet. He took a breath so deep his folded wings brushed the cave tunnel's top. I swear I read remorse in his eyes when he opened them. It was startling, the depth of emotion displayed. I looked away and, for something to do, slung the bag over my shoulder then inspected the strap—anything to keep from looking him in the eye.

"I'm ready." My voice was barely audible over the sounds of the wind and the waves. "Belly down a little farther and be gentle helping me up." Bahlin did as I asked and I scrambled onto his back without any hesitation this time.

Keeping low to the ground Bahlin slithered out toward the night sky. The smell of surf was tangy with salt and the more pungent smells that hinted at the ocean's living inhabitants and dead victims, large and small. Bahlin seemed to pull in on himself and once again we were wrapped in night's invisibility. He gathered himself on the edge of the tunnel ledge and threw himself out into the night air. I gripped his neck as hard as I could, my eyes wide open. The moonlight reflected on the relentless surf as it crashed into the rocks and I laughed out loud at the thrill of falling, for the first time confident in my dragon. It was a heady thing and I threw my head back and screamed with joy at the freedom of newfound faith. Bahlin trumpeted in response. At the last possible moment Bahlin spread his wings and pushed at the air, shooting us out parallel to the water and close enough that I felt the spray dampen my jeans. I leaned over his neck and hugged him, feeling more secure initiating affection when he couldn't see me. Sad, that, but true. But for the first time since the death of my parents eleven months ago, I held a tenuous thread of hope that love might exist for me on some level.

We soared higher, the temperature cooling predictably as we gained altitude. We crossed fields and wooded glens, racing the clouds to catch glimpses of the moon's laughing face. It was heady, this freedom, even if I knew it was short-lived.

I began to suspect where we were headed when Bahlin moved lower to the ground and circled counterclockwise around a small hillside. I recognized Brylanna's cottage and cringed, wondering if she'd been peeking in on our extra-curricular activities. Again I say, squicky. Bahlin set down in the front yard and before I could clamber down, the front door flew open. Brylanna moved like lightning, racing to Bahlin's side and throwing her arms around his neck.

"*Mo bhrathar!*" she exclaimed, "*ciamar a tha sibh?*"

I thought I knew what she'd said but still I said, "In English, please, Brylanna. That way I know if I need to defend myself or not." I slid from Bahlin's back. My knees, stiff from the cool wind, buckled slightly as I hit the ground and I stumbled into Bahlin's side.

He turned from Brylanna and caught me up in his forearms and effectively gave her his back. She stiffened.

"Of course, Niteclif. I simply said 'my brother how are you.' Nothing derogatory, I assure you." Her manner unyielding, she turned and walked stiffly back to the house, calling out over her shoulder,

184

"Dinner's on the table and we've only a short time to eat it before we have to leave, so don't dawdle...or shag on the front lawn." She slammed the door on us before I could come up with a suitably witty response.

Bahlin's dragon form shimmered and folded away, leaving the naked man crouched on all fours in the grass. I knelt next to him and dug out a pair of jeans and his long-sleeved rugby shirt. I struggled to keep my composure, trying desperately not to laugh at the absurdity of the situation. My lips twitched, and I looked up at Bahlin only to recognize his were doing the same thing.

"She knows what we've been up to then?" I asked, pinching my nose and trying to keep control of the situation.

"Without a doubt. Serves her right for checking in on us, even if it was done with the purest of intentions." Bahlin's eyes twinkled merrily, and he lost the battle not to smile. His grin made me feel so alive, like freefalling from the cave all over again. I smiled back and then, realizing he was still kneeling naked in front of me, I blushed so hard it made me light-headed.

"Here," I nearly shouted, shoving his clothes in his hands and turning my back on him. I still knelt on the grass beside him as I spun away, probably staining the knees of my jeans green in the process. Great.

He reached over and tugged my windblown hair, leaning in close enough that his breath slid down my bared neck like warm caramel over the skin of an apple. His lips touched behind my ear, gently, and he slid his hands around my waist. It might not be politically correct to admit it, but I loved how small and protected he made me feel as he bent his body over mine.

"Do you need help?" I whispered, running my hands over his arms and leaning back into his bare skin. *Please say no...or yes. No. Say no.*

"No, *mo chrid.*" *Well damn.* "We've not had a proper meal in days and I'm flat starved. I know if you help me I'll end up hauling you out to the barn and having my way with you in the hayloft. So come inside with me before you distract me for certain." He moved away from me and I heard the rustle of clothing as he dressed behind me. There is something seriously sexy about the sound of a zipper, whether it's going up or down, in the dark. Suddenly Bahlin was in front of me and

185

holding out his hand to help me to my feet. Despite the temptation to stare, I'd kept my eyes turned away from him while he got dressed, and he had to step well around me before I would look up at him. He laughed. "You've seen the goods, handled the package and helped me make the delivery, Maddy. Don't you think the time for shyness has passed?" He chucked me gently under the chin. "Never mind. I forgot for a moment who I was speaking to." Grabbing the bag, he walked into the house and waved me along with his free hand.

I got up and followed him into the cottage, feeling like it had been eons since we'd last been here when in reality it had been less than forty-eight hours. *How the mighty has fallen—flat on her back.* I sighed mentally. I paused in the doorway, unsure what to do. There were a number of creatures gathered around the table, all of whom looked human but collectively they gave out waves of power that made my skin want to crawl off the muscle. Of course, had any of them meant me harm they would have had all the time in the world to act on it because I just stood there, the fight-or-flight instinct equally entrenched in my conscious mind as the two warred internally for superiority. I'd have to lose the logic and internal monologues in critical situations or I was going to end up dead, and probably sooner rather than later.

"Maddy," Bahlin said, drawing me forward with a reach of his hand, "come meet some of my friends and family."

His family? *Oh shit.* Brylanna had been bad enough. I didn't need to meet any more people she could influence, or had *already* influenced, to dislike me. I shook my head in the smallest motion I could, staring at him.

"No, Bay," I breathed quietly. "I'll just, um, I'll wait outside while you catch up with everyone, okay?" I asked, assuming we'd be going to London via car again. I began backing up slowly, a reverse death march, the tension radiating off me as our arms pulled tight against one another.

Bahlin tightened his hand and gave a gentle yank forward to make me quit pulling. "Stop," he said, soft enough to be personal but loud enough that it wasn't private. "I want you to meet my ma and da, as well as my younger brother Aiden. There are several members of our wyvern here too. Let me introduce you?"

He scored major points for asking instead of demanding that I concede. I nodded as slightly as I had moments before declined, and he grinned again. He shifted his hand so our fingers laced together without a conscious thought on my part and he pulled me gently to his side, walking me back into the room. Introductions were made all around before I finally came face to face with his immediate family. Brylanna stood there, proud and tall, smirking at me as if she was in on some dirty little secret that I wasn't going to like. Next to her was a younger man who, with the exception of the dark blue eyes and his brother's extra height, was clearly the spitting image of the woman seated in front of him. This had to be Aiden. Which meant the woman in front of him was his mother, *Bahlin's* mother. She stood and I was shocked to see she was a petite little thing with light brown hair and dark brown eyes. She was nothing in size like the gargantuan children she'd given birth to. She smiled at Bahlin and wrapped him in a hug as only a mother could, clearly adoring him and embarrassing him in one economical movement. The man seated next to her at the head of the table was a behemoth of a man. Bahlin looked exactly like him in every way—dark blue eyes, burnished hair, high cheekbones, full mouth, broad shoulders, roughly the size of a small country.

"Maddy, allow me to introduce my da, Leith, and my ma, Adelle. The young lizard behind them is my little brother, Aiden. My da is the ruling Glaaca, or head of the wyvern."

Bahlin's parents took turns shaking my hand, and his mother encouraged me to fix myself a quick meal while she busied herself loading a up a small trough for Bahlin. Leith looked me over very thoroughly, giving nothing away.

"Da?" Bahlin asked, his tone cool and careful.

"So she's our new Niteclif?" Leith asked in an insolent tone.

"She is," Bahlin answered, his voice hardening just a bit. If I hadn't seen his mother's hand jerk as she lifted a spoon of mashed potatoes from the sideboard I wouldn't have realized anything was wrong. Thankfully I had that small bit of warning, otherwise I would have likely fallen over at Leith's next comment.

"So you've taken to sporting with her already, son? Awfully quick, even for you." His tone was cold. Adelle looked from one man to another, clearly shocked at her husband's rudeness but unsure what to do with herself. She finally pulled out a chair at the table and dropped her head in her hands, not in a defeated manner but more a frustrated one. Behind Leith, Brylanna paled a bit.

"Maddy, I'm going to ask you to step outside for a moment," Bahlin said, his tone so cold I drew my hand from his instinctively. He turned to look at Brylanna and said, "Why, *piuthar?*"

Brylanna lifted her chin and said, "You know why and she should too. You *have* been sporting with her, but have you been honest with her, Bahlin?"

I'm not sure what the final straw was, whether it was Leith's rudeness or Brylanna's, but between the fae, the dragons and the murder-minded magicians, I'd had enough with the cloak and dagger shit. I rounded on Brylanna and said, "All right already. You've hinted again and again that there's something I need to know. Here's your opportunity. Give it your best shot, you fire-breathing, scale-sporting, knobby-spined bitch."

She stared at me for a split second and then laughed with wicked glee as if I hadn't spoken. "So you've truly not told her then?" The look of pale fear on Bahlin's face was her answer. "Fine. I will. Madeleine Dylis Niteclif, I had a vision about you before you arrived. You would be a woman fair of face, sharp of mind, with fresh grief your heaviest burden. You would be vulnerable to empathy, despise sympathy and be so hungry for a sense of belonging that you would be willing to accept your lot as Niteclif with only limited explanation and minor manipulation. Better yet, you were predestined to fall in love with a male member of the High Council and forsake yourself for the opportunity to be loved. That member of the High Council would gain in power and influence for being in your bed and would end up being the first individual ever to lead the Council. This meant there would be a competition to get you on your back. And the man that first won the right to rut with you would break your heart." Brylanna's grin faltered as she watched my face, stepping back from me as I processed her prediction.

"Who knew this?" I asked. No one answered me and I yelled, "Who knew?"

"The High Council and our wyvern," Brylanna answered with new trepidation, obviously afraid of the crazed woman I had morphed into as I stood there and digested her little newscast.

"Looks like you win the prize for biggest bitch I've ever met, Brylanna."

It was so quiet that the tick of the water heater seemed to boom and echo in the room. I turned on my heel and walked slowly to the front door, but not before I looked at Bahlin with bitter eyes.

"Maddy, wait," Bahlin said, grabbing my arm.

I looked down at his hand and said in a deliberately soft voice, "Get your damned hand off of me you pustulant ball sack. You've lost the right to touch me, Bahlin. Don't you dare speak to me. Not when you've lied to me and manipulated me from the beginning. Don't. You. *Dare.*" He dropped his hand, and I walked out the front door without another word.

Chapter Fourteen

The sound of raised voices exploded as the door shut and latched behind me with a distinct *click*. I could hear snippets of the developing argument as I walked down the lane leading from the house. Male voices were raised in anger, interjected now and then with a softer voice—likely Bahlin's mother. Brylanna's voice was suspiciously absent.

I had no idea where I was going to go, but I knew I had to get away from here. I picked up the pace, breaking into a slow jog. What had been a lovely night had, appropriately, turned misty and cold. I shivered in my jacket, though whether it was from the chilly night air or my frozen soul was beyond me. I felt like such a fool. I'd done everything Bahlin had told me to do from the moment he'd shown up in my dream. He'd dictated my acceptance of my heritage by manipulating my emotions. He'd set the pace of the investigation by using what he learned of me to influence my decision-making. And he'd coerced me into his bed and wormed his way into my heart by playing on my need to be loved. Worst of all was that I'd fallen for every single bit.

I tripped over an unseen rock and went to my knees. I stayed there for a moment, unable to move, the tears dripping off the end of my nose. *When had I started crying?* I heard a car start and I scrambled to my feet, brushing my hands off on my jeans. I took a few running steps and realized I'd never make it far enough down the single lane road to pick up another ride before the driver of the car caught up to me. Looking over my shoulder I saw headlights swing away from the garage, twin shafts of light slicing through the night as the car started down the long, desolate drive. I hopped over the low stone fence into the bordering pasture and lay on my stomach, face-down on the ground so that the majority of my pale skin was covered by either clothing or my dark hair. The sound of the car's engine got closer and closer, finally roaring passed me. I'd made it farther from the house than I'd originally thought. I was relatively certain that Bahlin was driving. If it *was* him, he was unquestionably looking for me. Fine. Let him look. I lay there on the cold, wet ground and rubbed furiously at my eyes. I didn't feel I had any room available for new grief in my heart when I hadn't yet fully processed the grief of losing my parents. Bahlin didn't deserve to share space with them. Instead, he'd have to settle for being a nasty little black piece of my mind, or a kernel of hate in my gut, or something cold and calculating in my soul. Because my heart was not his. Period.

The car came roaring back down the lane, and I stayed hidden behind the stone fence. I heard gravel scatter as the car ground to a halt in the dooryard of the house, and the driver's door slammed seconds later. Shouting renewed inside the house, but I was up and moving as soon as I knew the lights of the car were extinguished. I figured if I could get to the road I could either hitch a ride back to the city or find my way into a town where I could rent a car. I jogged slowly away from the house, startling a hare from the feverfew that dotted the field. Cows lowed nearby and in the distance a dog barked, universal country sounds made ominous by the night. This was particularly true considering the *cú sìth* that had been killed, the shapeshifters and vampires I now knew existed, the wizard I knew was hunting me, and the dragon wyvern that was arguing somewhere behind me. I jogged a little faster.

The general quiet made it impossible to ignore the hurt careening through my mind. I'd never felt so betrayed in all my life. The entire High Council had known I'd fall for one of the men, and both Bahlin and Tarrek had tried to influence me into choosing them. Hellion had left me alone, though Gretta had probably had something to do with that. *Who would I have chosen had Tarrek been around?* I wondered. Because his absence had made Bahlin's job a great deal easier. I stumbled to a stop. Tarrek's absence... What if Bahlin had done away with Tarrek? What if Bahlin had set everything up to make it appear he

191

was innocent when in reality he wasn't? What if he'd had something to do with the murders? It had been all too easy to not look too closely at him when I was in his bed. But now that that was resolved, I probably needed to think about what he stood to gain. Truthfully I couldn't get my mind in the game at the moment, so I vowed to consider him carefully after a solid night's sleep and some emotional distance. Of course, that might mean I didn't get around to him for months. Speaking of the High Council, though, I was never going to make the meeting. Too bad. They'd just have to understand. I choked a bit, picking up the pace. They'd all been in on the joke. *I'm sure they'll understand just fine when they get a new seer to announce that I've been used as predicted,* I thought, continuing to berate myself for my stupidity as I jogged on.

I rounded a small hill and saw an overhang of rock as the sky transitioned from spitting a heavy mist to dropping a light rain. Grateful that something had gone right tonight, I sprinted for cover. I bent at the waist, flicking water from my hair and shaking out my jacket before I curled up in a small ball, thankful I wasn't any more wet that I was. Depression rolled around me like a riptide and pulled me under, forcing me into sleep. And without Bahlin's heartbeat to soothe me, I dreamed.

"Maddy," said a soft voice behind me. "Maddy, can you hear me?"

I turned, taking in my surroundings as I sought the familiar voice. I was in the small living area of a crofter's cottage, and it was dark outside. I could hear the rain pattering on the thatched roof, and it was a comforting, homey sound. The room was warm. I was grateful for the heat emanating from the fireplace. Small wooden furniture dotted the room, and a large quilt-covered bed stood in the corner. I was so tired. I took an involuntary step toward the bed before I remembered the voice. I looked at the table and there he was.

"Tarrek!" I took three large steps toward him.

"Stop," he commanded, and I froze, my momentum so impeded that I took a stumbling step forward before I could right myself, throwing out my arms to regain my balance.

"What is it?" I asked in an alarmed voice, looking around the room again.

"I must ask you—is Bahlin with you?" Something was off. He seemed different, almost gaunt, and his eyes darted around the room like a cornered animal's.

"No, he's not here. Why?" I asked.

"The High Council is no longer safe, Maddy. I must insist you keep our conversation private. I am in Scotland somewhere near Castle Duncan. You must come for me before the new moon rises or all is lost. I do not know..." He looked around me and asked, "If Bahlin is not here, where is he?"

I shrugged, uncomfortable. "We've had a bit of a parting of ways." I looked out the pitch-dark windows. It felt like the night was outside looking in. I shivered despite the heat from the fire.

"What happened?" he asked in a deadly voice. "Tell me." He slapped his hands on the wooden table hard enough to make the jug on the tabletop skip off the doily.

I jumped. Even in the short time I'd known Tarrek I knew this wasn't like him. "What's happened to you?"

The wind picked up suddenly, howling about the cottage, rattling the door and windows. I gasped, feeling the hair on the back of my neck stand up.

"Tarrek? What's going on?" Chills that had nothing to do with the temperature danced up and down my spine as cold sweat collected in my armpits. I stared at the faerie and wondered if he was really who he seemed to be. Was it possible someone was making me think I was seeing Tarrek when I wasn't? Who was that powerful? Only one name came to mind—Hellion.

"Answer me, woman," said the figment of my dream. "What has happened between you and Bahlin?"

The wind howled louder.

"We became involved, but he lied to me. Nothing more." I shrugged, uncomfortable with the turn in the conversation. "Tell me who has taken you and—"

The glass shattered, imploding and skittering in shards across the floor. Tarrek yelled as I screamed. I shot out of sleep as if I'd been catapulted.

I sat up and gasped for air, feeling the residual fear crawling around my gut. My muscles twitched involuntarily, the urge to run primal. Flight was winning over fight, and it felt like it would be a landslide victory. I looked around my shelter, assuring myself that I was indeed still alone. Suddenly there was a great backwash of wind into the little depression, and I screamed again as Bahlin's dragon head peered under the rock ledge.

"Mother*fucker!*" I reared back and punched him on the soft part of the nose. He hissed and drew back, undoubtedly startled but not even mildly injured. I clutched my throbbing hand, the irony not lost on me that this was the second time I'd punched Bahlin within four conscious days of knowing him.

Bahlin's dragon form folded away and he was suddenly standing there, gloriously naked in the rain.

"Maddy. Are you all right, love? I heard you shout," he said, glaring about as if daring even the shadows to threaten me.

"Go to hell, Bahlin," I growled as I pushed passed him and walked into the encompassing night.

"Maddy—" Bahlin started again, reaching out to lay a hand on my arm.

"Don't touch me, Bahlin. I meant it earlier. I don't want anything to do with you, not now, not ever. You've lost that right." I jerked my arm out from under his hand and kept walking.

"Maddy, stop," Bahlin commanded in a resonating voice. My feet actually faltered, and I swung around to face him.

"If you ever, *ever*, attempt to command me to do anything again, I will cut your prized possession off and shove it down the gullet of the nearest carnivore, Bahlin, and I'll make sure he *chews*. Does that make my feelings clear enough for you? Because obviously you didn't get it when I said it before."

He actually paused, squinting at me as the rain ran into his eyes. "Are you going to give me a chance to apologize?" he asked uncomfortably, shifting back and forth in the obvious cold.

I snickered, for once keeping my eyes off his prize without trouble or embarrassment. "Right. You give new meaning to speaking with a forked tongue. Get lost, asshat." I kept walking across the field, and he followed about ten paces behind. I didn't acknowledge him until I reached the blacktop. I looked over my shoulder and said, "You might want to phase back and fly your happy ass back to the house, or London, or the third circle of hell for all I care. Just get some clothes on before anyone gets the wrong idea about the two of us."

I crawled over the fence and a blast of air in the back let me know that Bahlin had taken my advice. He was gone.

I walked for nearly an hour before the lights of an approaching car slowed, the driver's side window rolling down. A brown-haired man stuck his head out.

"Need a ride?" Aiden asked.

"Yep, but not from you." I kept walking, ignoring him as he eased along beside me.

"Come on, Maddy. Bahlin feels horrible," he pushed.

"And you know this after how long in his glorious presence this evening?" As juvenile as it was, I walked faster. I knew I wasn't actually going to outpace the damn car, but it made me feel better. At this point I'd settle for whatever salve I could find for my wounded pride.

Aiden sped up incrementally until he pulled ahead of me and cut me off. He jumped out and placed himself in front of me before I could get around the bumper of his beat-up little coupe.

"Listen, Maddy. He's still back at the house rowing with Brylanna and Da. Ma's taken his side, saying that Da and Brylanna were awful to yeh and this after hearing Bahlin loves yeh, so yeh've divided the family whether yeh want to or no. The least yeh can do is afford me a moment of yehr time, right?"

Cheeky little brat had his brother's habit of speaking in a heavier brogue when he was upset. One thing Brylanna hadn't touched on in her let's-make-Maddy-look-like-a-chump speech was how well guilt worked on me.

"You've got ninety seconds, junior. Starting now." I stuck my numb hands in my pants pockets and refused to admit to either of us how much I'd rather have had this conversation in his car with the heater on full blast.

Calming visibly now that he had my attention, Aiden said, "Bahlin is crazy about you, Maddy. He might not have gone about this the right way, but he's a good man. He's bucked the Council for you. He admitted he's taken you to his lair, which is nearly as serious as the wedding vows between dragons, and he's said he'll take your side in the case of some murder you've committed. And have I mentioned he seriously loves you?" the teen said. "Can you not cut him a little slack for where he *is* and not hold it against him how he *got there*?"

Cheeky. Brat. I glared at him, my eyelid twitching again. I slapped my hand over my eye. *Great poker face, Niteclif. Why don't you just take out a billboard that says "Hello, I'm frustrated."* Geeze. But all the internal dialogue in the world couldn't change what Aiden said. How did a young guy get so smart? It irked me that he had some valid points. Unfortunately my pride was as wounded as my heart, and I wasn't going to roll over on this. I'd already tried the rolling over, under and around with Bahlin, and it had gotten me nothing but screwed in every sense of the word.

"Look, Aiden, I know you're trying to look out for Bahlin, and I respect that sense of loyalty. *I do*," I said when he just looked at me blandly. "And you don't know me so you'll have to trust that what I'm about to tell you is the truth. Bahlin has pulled some serious offenses in my book. I've ended long-term relationships for far less than what he's done to me in a week. He had the opportunity to be honest from the outset, and he chose not to. He *chose*, Aiden," I said, taking a step closer to him, eye-level with his chin. The kid was going to be as big as his brother.

Aiden's eyes flashed to light blue, and he slammed his eyelids closed trying to mask his emotion. But it was too late. I'd seen the switch. It dawned on me that I didn't know him well enough to know whether or not he'd cause me harm. After all, dragons were monsters and Aiden was a dragon, ergo he was a monster. Loose logic, but there you have it. Right now I had zero faith in the monsters.

"Look, just leave me alone, okay?" I said, stepping around him cautiously. I walked down the road, looking back over my shoulder every few paces.

He leaned back on the hood of his little car and stared at me. "So you won't forgive him?" he called after me. His voice suddenly sounded so young and unsure, like whatever answer I gave now would help him develop his view of one part of the world. I didn't want that kind of responsibility. My burdens were heavy enough without it.

I slowed, hating myself a little more, and turned back toward him. I wasn't going to lie to him. If I'd learned anything in all of this it was that honesty sucks but it was better to just get it out and over with, and that being soft will get you taken advantage of because it was often considered being weak. Being a truthful hard-ass would bruise him now but it would hurt him less in the long run.

"Will I forgive Bahlin? Not yet," I said softly, "and maybe not ever."

Another set of headlights topped the hill, and I stepped to the edge of the road and held out a hand. An older woman pulled up next to me and, thankfully, she was a complete stranger.

"Going to town?" she asked cheerfully, taking in the sight of me and Aiden and probably drawing the wrong conclusions. I didn't care. If she'd get me out of here, she could think whatever she wanted about me.

"I'm going as far as you'll take me," I said, conscious not to give my final destination directly within earshot of Aiden. With one last look at Bahlin's brother I got into the woman's truck and yanked the door shut. I buckled my seatbelt and stuck my hands in my jacket pockets. My right hand bumped into a heavy object. Wrapping my fingers around the smooth edges, I drew my hand slowly out of the pocket. The gold doubloon glinted merrily in the light from the dashboard.

The woman was going to Uxbridge on the outer West End of London. I rode along in silence, answering her questions early in the ride and feigning sleep later. She clucked over my disheveled state, skillfully asking what had happened without asking what had happened. When I finally said I was exhausted she let the conversation drift, turning on the radio for company and allowing me to rest. She roused me from my false slumber when we reached the center of the borough. I thanked her for her kindness, and she dismissed my thanks with a heartfelt wish for good fortune to me. Thinking on this, I asked her if she would trade me a few pounds for the gold doubloon and she nearly fell out of the truck in her haste to take me up on my offer. I took her money and left the coin without a second thought. After all, no amount of money was worth the painful reminder.

I caught the train into the West End of London and switched routes three times to get back to the Pemberton. I knew I'd have to check out of the hotel or face Bahlin, so checking out it was. I made my way into the hotel with a large group of tourists and hoped that I'd maintained my anonymity. I reached Room 2210 and keyed myself in, grateful I'd managed to snag the key card from the messenger bag as I'd packed up in the cave. Foresight or dumb damn luck? Who cared? I moved quickly about the room, deciding to forgo taking my clothes since everything could be replaced when I got home. I grabbed my purse out of the room safe and headed back down to the front of the hotel. I knew the front desk staff saw me when the three of them gathered together to watch me leave the lobby and one of them snatched the phone up, dialing madly. Tattle tales.

The doorman hailed a cab for me and it had hardly stopped when I crawled in and sat back, content to rest and enjoy the ride to Heathrow. If I could just get out of this forsaken country...

The cabby shook me awake and said, "That'll be eighteen quid even, miss."

Disoriented, I dug through my wallet and gave him the fare plus a healthy tip and rushed into the airport. The next flight leaving for New York was in forty-five minutes, so I dashed to the counter, bought the ticket by leaving an arm, a leg and my credit card number, and I ran for the gate. I made it onto the plane with only moments to spare. I walked to my seat, equally grateful and heartbroken. *Chaos can reign for all I care. I just need to get back home and start over. I'll pretend this never happened*, repeated through my mind. I was so tired I had a hard time keeping my eyes open for take-off and once we were in the air. I vaguely remember hearing the pilot welcome everyone aboard before sleep took me under with no apologies.

Chapter Fifteen

The attendant shook me and asked me to return my chair to its upright position and I complied, feeling the plane begin its descent. Disoriented due to the heavy, dreamless sleep of the last eight hours I rubbed my eyes and reached over to raise the window shade. Dawn had long ago broken over the horizon, and the sky was bright but overcast.

The pilot's voice came over the intercom and said, "Thank you for flying with us today, ladies and gentlemen. We're beginning our final descent into London's Heathrow airport now. Local time is 10:53 a.m. and the temperature—"

I didn't hear anything else after that. I reached up and punched the attendants' button frantically, looking over the seat-tops for the woman who had told me to raise my seat back. She came down the aisle with brisk, teetering steps, frustrated at my repeated buzzing.

"Yes?" she asked in her best professional tone, reaching across me and firmly turning the call button off.

"Why are we landing at Heathrow?" I demanded, my voice pitched high and slightly crazed. "Why? I bought a ticket to New York!"

"Ma'am, calm down. This is the flight from New York to London. Seems you slept harder than you thought." She smiled brightly, no doubt placating the loon.

"No. No, no, no. I left Heathrow last night," I insisted, leaning toward her.

"Is there a problem, Kay?" asked another attendant, this one male. He did his best to look threateningly over Kay's shoulder, but it was difficult in his little blue vest and jaunty red necktie.

"No. This young lady just slept harder than she thought and got confused about her destination."

I shut up, trying to figure out what to do. I *knew* I'd left London last night. I *knew* I had. Wait. What if I'd been dreaming? What if this whole thing was a nightmare? No, I'd fallen for that when I'd met Bahlin, thinking he wasn't real. I wasn't going to do this again. I waited until we'd landed and taxied to the gate before I jumped up and opened the overhead bin. If I'd only been dreaming and this was my first trip to London, I'd have carry-on luggage because my first trip had been luggage-heavy. If I *hadn't* been dreaming, there would be nothing there. I opened the cover and looked inside. My heart fell: the bin was empty. I sat back down, watching passengers disembark.

When the plane was empty Kay approached me again, a concerned look on her face. "Do you need help, miss?"

Yes, I needed help, but it wasn't the kind she could provide. Regardless of her intent, her chipper kindness made me feel violent, and I knew I needed to get off the plane without any trouble. I shook my head, grabbed my purse and got up, walking slowly up the aisle to the gangway and out through the airport. Reaching Heathrow's cab queue, I grabbed a taxi and asked the driver to take me to any mid-range hotel, his choice. He looked at me like I'd lost my mind, and I knew he was only about five minutes away from the truth. I was about to lose it. The cabbie tried to make conversation for the first few minutes of the trip and then gave up when he realized I was nearly catatonic. Instead he turned the radio up and sang along to some type of Indie music with a grating beat.

Twenty minutes later I was standing in the quiet and graceful lobby of the Hardley, though I couldn't have cared less what it looked like. Checking into a single room, I moved like an automaton and the clerk watched me from the corner of her eye. I suspected I looked frightening but, again, didn't give a crap.

I made it to my room and walked in, glancing around woodenly. The room was nice but sterile, with none of the charm and elegance of the Pemberton. I turned the air conditioner down to its lowest setting and stripped off my clothes. The bed was sufficient and that was all I cared about as I folded the covers back and slid under. I huddled with my head under the comforter, my breath heating up the small, enclosed space quickly so it became humid and stifling. Still I was cold. Rolling onto my side, I curled into the fetal position. *So this is what rock bottom feels like. I'm much more lucid than I'd hoped for. Oh well.* Sleep claimed me without apology, and I slid into its dark embrace with a sense of giddy relief.

"You've really bunged this up, child," said a deep voice.

I suspected I was dreaming when I sat up in bed and found a strange man in my room. I looked around and saw the owner of the voice was of medium height with a pipe and a British accent.

"Who are you?" I asked, rubbing my eyes and yawning. "My dreams—hell, my realities—haven't had much normalcy to them lately, so you're a pleasant surprise. Unless... You're not anything supernatural, are you?"

The man chuckled and pushed up from the chair he was occupying at the small two-seater Formica table. The sweet scent of his tobacco wafted over me and I inhaled, thinking of my father. He'd smoked a pipe similar to the one the stranger held between his teeth. The man wore a charming three-pieced suit sans jacket, with shirtsleeves rolled up his forearms and the top button of his shirt undone. His shoes were well made but worn. His face was gently lined from laughter, his hair graying slightly at the temples.

"I'm not familiar to you? I took this form simply to try to be recognizable but it appears I've failed. What do you see when you look at me?"

I hesitated. *What the hell. It's a dream.* So I told him what I saw.

"Very good, though superficial. Now tell me what you *see*." He stood very still, almost as if posing for a painting.

"Your hair is well-cut but in need of a trim, so you haven't had time to see a barber. You shave yourself because there's a small knick on your chin that indicates a horizontal swipe of the razor, barbers go top to bottom. Your facial hair is as dark as your head hair and graying in too random a pattern to be died, so I know it's your natural color." I took a deep breath and looked even closer. "Your nails are trim, clean and buffed, so you don't do heavy work with your hands though you're lean and lightly muscled, so you're not totally idle, either. Your clothes are well tailored, so you have some form of funds. The pipe you're gripping between your teeth is well worn, and you speak clearly around it so it's familiar enough that I believe you smoke it without apology. Your shoes are clean of mud and dirt, so you're not from the country nor have you walked far in London. Finally, you've got the look of a scholar that's only further enhanced by the wire-rimmed glasses poking out of your vest pocket." *Crap. The Niteclif legacy was alive and well.*

He smiled, puffing away. "Sound familiar?"

I just stared at him. "If you're telling me you're Aloysius, you can just jump right out that window, mister. A three floor drop will hurt but you can't die twice. I don't need to be haunted on top of everything else."

"But it's still a long way to the ground and, as you indicated, it could hurt." He smiled more widely, his eyes twinkling with mischief. "Besides, how's that for a way to greet your great-granddad, Maddy?"

If I hadn't been sleeping I would have pulled a repeat fainting performance, but since I was already out cold, I had nowhere else to go. So I got mad. Throwing the covers off I stalked around the room like a caged lion, staying just out of reach of the man himself. "What the hell? Are you serious? If it's true and you're really him, why haven't you manifested or whatever before now? I could seriously have used you before now, you know. I have been beaten, shot, poisoned, stalked, forced to commit murder, ridden a dragon and had my heart broken in less than a week! You *suck* as a granddad, Aloysius."

My visitor sighed and sat back down in the same chair. His eyes dulled a bit, and he looked tired. "There were lessons you had to learn that were best learned the hard way." He looked away and whispered, "Except for the heart... For that, I'm sorry."

"You *saw* all of that? Please tell me you and Brylanna are the only peeping Tom's out there. I can't take much more of people looking in on my love life, Pops," I said sarcastically. I threw myself down on the bed and gasped, rolling myself up in the cover. I was still nude. "You sick bastard. Why didn't you remind me I was naked," I shrieked.

"Maddy, I'm only taking the form of Aloysius because it was supposed to be familiar—"

"Then who in the sweet hell *are* you?" I yelled, my anger boiling over into rage.

His form shifted and shimmered and a giant of a man, easily taller than Tarrek, stood in front of me. He wore a thigh-length forest green tunic with rough black pants underneath and a wide leather belt around his waist. His hair was white-blond and shoulder length with a slight wave to it. Over his shoulder he wore a back scabbard in which a sword large enough to be considered a claymore was sheathed. "I'm the first Niteclif, my dear. You may call me Tyr."

"As in the Norse god of wisdom, war and justice?" I asked. *Why did I know who the hell he was?*

"One and the same," he said, looking pleased. "I was the first Niteclif, and I am thus charged with helping new Niteclifs transition into their roles with as little heartache as possible."

"Yeah, well, you freaking suck at your job." I huddled in the comforter and stared at him. I wasn't sure how much more I could take before I completely lost my tenuous grip on what was left of reality.

Ignoring my snark, he said, "As you are the first female Niteclif, we'll learn together how best to suit each other's individualities. Agreed?"

"Whatever. I'm tired." I flopped back on the bed, fully intent on ignoring the crazy apparition in my dream.

"Do not mock me, Niteclif!" he boomed in an earthquake-inducing voice.

I jumped and, holding the comforter, stood. "Fine. Then I need your actual help. No more hanging out to see what happens. No more letting the Fates have their way with me, regardless of their Greek affiliations. No more neglect. Your tender mercies are as humane as Bahlin's." I shoved a finger in his face. "And let me tell you, I don't need *any* more of that shit."

"Sit you down, girl," he growled. Involuntarily my body complied. "Here are the things you'll need to know at this point. One, I can only come to you in sleep or deep meditation. With your temper I wish you the best of luck with the latter. Two, you will inherit certain gifts from your lineage—language skills, enhanced self-defense, weaponry knowledge, superior logic skills and natural immunity to the sway of the supernatural. You will need a tutor for self-defense and weaponry.

Use Bahlin." I blanched, but he didn't even pause. "Other skills may develop, but I will not discuss those until they manifest. This way you're not disappointed or misled in any way. Three, I will help you through the beginning of your tenure and will be available to you at any time during your service as Niteclif. It is my lot. Four, I will not answer questions for you regarding the creation or end of the world, love, investment tips or the manner of your pre-determined death. Period." He stared at me hard, and I nodded. A Norse god was the icing on Hell's cake as far as I was concerned, but my impertinence didn't slow him down. "Five, I *may* answer other questions for you but never, under any circumstance, will I do your job for you. It's against the rules, and Odin looks unfavorably on that. Six, I needed you to learn that you have a lot to learn. The path you've just navigated was the most circumspect. Are we clear, child?" His voice softened at the last and he looked me over, head to toe.

Jaw clenched to keep from gaping, I nodded.

"Good. Then let's discuss your first case. But Maddy?"

I sat staring at him. *A real Norse god. Huh.* "Yeah?"

"Put some clothes on."

I came out of the bathroom after grabbing a quick shower. He was immortal. He could wait. My hair was still wet, and I continued to dry it off with a hand towel as I sat across the table from my infinitely great-grandfather, Tyr. I smiled slightly at the thought that I trumped Tarrek's royalty with my own deity.

"I know what you know so far, so ask away," he said, forgoing niceties in lieu of directness. I could play that way, especially as raw as I was over Bahlin.

"Why a Norse god instead of a Celt?" I asked, meeting his eyes with unspoken challenge, daring him to lie to me.

"The Celts are descended from the Norse. Their gods are the infants of ours."

"Oh. Why can't I leave England?"

"You can, but only to move about the British Isles."

That explained why I ended up coming back here on the Hitchcock flight. What a waste of money. Hopefully my Niteclif salary kicked in soon.

"What happens at the end of my ten years?" I asked.

"You'll serve twelve years given the nature and timing of the Change." He held up a hand when I started to argue, stopping me before I could even get a good, deep breath. "It's unchangeable, so bear it with grace.

"You must see through the veil that most humans do not, recognizing that the paranormal and the mythological walk among your kind on the same plane of existence. The purpose of the Niteclif's evolution is to lift the veil for one person—you—and render justice for the veil's other side."

Tyr paused, almost as if unsure how to go on. I rolled my hand at him, indicating he should just continue. He sighed, clearly annoyed with my impatience. "You must keep one foot on either side of the veil without falling victim to the gray in between. Should you fail, you will lose yourself at the end of your time and you will become a fictional character whose exploits and adventures are immortalized in literature. You will physically cease to exist."

I gasped and a small, panicked giggle broke free. Tyr arched an eyebrow at me, but I just shook my head and motioned him on again.

"In truth, this is what happened to Aloysius though it is not common knowledge. Even Bahlin is unaware. He lived his life well, but was absorbed by the mythological element of his existence. We wrote him a happy ending. One of our kind remembered him on paper out of respect. The same fate awaits you should you fail. Your author has been preordained. The end of your time of service will not be discussed yet, so do not ask me the outcome."

I sat there, feeling almost anesthetized with shock. If I failed, I would essentially die but be immortalized on paper for my efforts, like a consolation prize. If I died literally, as in fell victim to death by murder, I'd just be dead. The options for survival were down to one: I couldn't fail. Anxiety gripped my chest like an iron band, and I struggled for a moment to catch my breath.

Typical me, I coped by avoidance as I thought about my next question. I couldn't ask if Bahlin loved me, but I could ask questions surrounding that. "Is it within the rules to ask what Bahlin is to me?"

Tyr's eyes lit up as he realized what I was doing. He stared at me as he formulated his answer. "It is. Bahlin will be your physical familiar."

I just arched an eyebrow and looked at him. He wasn't amused at the turnabout.

Answering my unasked question he said, "No, you are not a witch. But he will serve much the same purpose, offering *sincere* support, knowledge, protection, affection and advice. Use him well." Tyr paused before continuing, leaning forward slightly and cocking his head to the side as if deciding how much to tell me. "Forgive him." Thunder rumbled within the room, and Tyr smiled.

Ignoring the last of his answer I asked, "Why am I accepting this is true and not checking myself in for lithium treatments?" I was scared of the answer, but I needed to know.

Tyr looked at me pointedly and said, "One of your gifts is that you are able to accept what is irrefutable fact, Madeleine, and discern fact from falsehood with logical methodology. What does not fall to logic must be analyzed and appropriate risks taken. Think on it and do not avoid out of anger what I am trying to tell you."

"Just call me Maddy, please. This whole Madeleine thing is pissing me off," I grumped. I thought about what Tyr said. If I could accept what I saw when I detected the truth, then I should be able to tell whether or not Bahlin was sincere when he said he loved me. It was worth thinking on, but it would have to be later. First things first. I needed to find and rescue Tarrek.

"Do you know where Tarrek is, Tyr?"

"Yes, but you have to deduce the location and get there yourself."

"Was it Tarrek in my earlier dream?" I asked, looking up at Tyr through my lashes. I was growing uncomfortable under his direct, unblinking stare, self-conscious of the fact that I was stumbling about without Bahlin's guidance, and frustrated I'd not made it any farther in the case than I had.

"Tarrek did come to you in a dream, yes. Look at the clues you have in front of you and tell me what you know for sure."

"I suppose that's as good a place to start as any." I leaned the chair back on two legs and rocked backward and forward, my fingers nervously tapping out a rhythm on the tabletop.

Tyr reached over and firmly put his hand over mine. "Relax."

"Sure." I slammed the chair forward and leaned my elbows on the table, fingers laced together tight enough to pull the skin against my knuckles and turn them white. "The murderer is collecting supernatural creatures. This means that the killer is not immortal because otherwise he, or she, wouldn't have a need for the stolen powers. Right?"

Tyr cocked his head to one side, thinking. He said, "What if the killer just wants the powers the other supernatural creatures possess, and it's not immortality he, or she, is after?"

Possible, I thought. "Why kill them?"

"That's for you to discern, Maddy."

"Okay. Let me put all my cards down. The killer wants the supes' powers. To get them, he, or *she*, has to kill to obtain them. The killer is compiling these powers in order to take over the High Council and make himself the ultimate leader. How am I doing?" I asked, chewing on my bottom lip.

"Go on," he said without answering.

"Tarrek has been taken for his ability to generate magic with few restrictions. I believe that the *cù sith* was taken for its ability to smell the truth, which any person in power would value. The *far darrig* was taken for his ability to generate luck at will, making the killer hard to stop in any given situation. The sprite was killed for her divination skills, making the killer nearly omnipotent if the Sight can be controlled and directed. The killer needs immortality, so he'll have to obtain a true immortal. A vampire heart would be the easiest unless, of course, the killer is already immortal. He'll also need a strong body, his or another's, to get him through the metamorphosis into this new super-creature. And he wants Bahlin's Dragon's Stone in order to obtain immeasurable wisdom and...something. But what?" I paused in the act of picking at my nails, looking up at the god.

"You're on the right track, Maddy," Tyr said. "Does Bahlin pose a threat to the killer?"

"Well, sure. First and foremost is the damned prediction. If it's true, he's going to become the head of the High Council. That's a threat to anyone else interested in power." I harrumphed at the thought, my shoulders hunching at the unbidden memories of what Bahlin had done to secure his power base. I mentally shied away from those intimate memories, instead focusing on the here and now. "Bahlin is also a super strong shape-shifter who can kick nine kinds of ass when he needs to, I'm sure. After all, dragons fight for *fun* of all things..." I froze, looking up and meeting Tyr's eyes. "The killer wants Bahlin's body as his vessel as well as his stone. It's easier if he doesn't have to remove the stone from Bahlin's brain and risk damaging it. Instead, he just absconds with the whole package. That's it, isn't it? And dragons fight with each other over their treasures. So if Bahlin's stone gives the killer the ability to learn the location of all the different lairs he's breached, the killer stands to inherit immeasurable wealth." I put my head in my hands and tried unsuccessfully to contain the trembling of my fine muscles.

"I believe you're right, child. Bahlin's in more danger than he realizes, and the fact that the two of you have broken with each other puts him at greater risk as he's vulnerable right now." Thunder boomed and Tyr hunched his shoulders. "Damnable Odin," he muttered. "Fine. Repeat what I just said to you."

I did.

"Yes," Tyr muttered, eyes glinting in triumph at having worked around the elder god's directive. "That's absolutely correct."

"I've got to get to him," I muttered, standing up and tipping the chair over in my haste to get to my shoes. Then I remembered I was asleep. "Tyr?"

"Yes, Maddy?"

"Is he at the Pemberton?"

"Yes, Maddy."

Thanks, I thought, and Tyr smiled.

I woke with a start, still cocooned under the covers. I flipped them back, breathing in a rush of very cold air-conditioned air. I reached over and grabbed my clothes and my shoes, sitting up and slipping into everything. Picking up the phone, I dialed the operator and asked to be connected to the Pemberton.

"Thank you for calling the Pemberton. How may I direct your call?" came the front desk voice.

"I need to speak to Bahlin. It's an emergency."

"I'm sorry, ma'am. There's no one here by that name," was the cautious reply. The guy was a horrible liar.

"Put Bahlin on the phone. It's Maddy Niteclif." I felt bad but I didn't have time for polite coercion. I need Bahlin five minutes ago.

There was a click and then a beeping.

"Hullo," came the flat greeting on the other end.

"Bahlin?" I asked, not sure I had the right person so despondent was this voice.

"Maddy?" was the cautious reply.

"Yeah. Look, I don't have time to explain but—"

"You had a dream visitor, I assume."

"How'd you know, Bahlin?" I asked, confused.

"Because Aloysius was scared shitless when Tyr visited him the first time, too, and we talked it through. But that doesn't matter. Nothing matters but when I can see you, Maddy. You can't just shut me out." Bahlin's voice was hoarse and choked with emotion. I hardened myself and refused to think about it.

"I need you to come get me at the Hardley on Old Queen Street—"

"I'll be there within fifteen minutes," he said.

"Bring me some clean clothes," I yelled into the phone. But it was useless. He was already gone.

Chapter Sixteen

I grabbed my purse and headed down to the lobby to wait for Bahlin. True to his word, he was there within fifteen minutes. I didn't give him a chance to get out of the car, instead knocking on the passenger window so he unlocked the door. I let myself in and buckled my seatbelt.

"Where to?" he asked quietly. He looked haggard, with circles under his eyes, rumpled clothes and an unshaved face. I hadn't imagined him as suffering with my absence. A small, sick part of me was relieved he was hurting too. Petty, but honest.

"I need to get some things from the hotel—" I began, but he interrupted me. Apparently we'd regressed to that point.

"I brought you a small suitcase of things, including your bathroom stuff. You left in such a rush before that I wasn't sure what you'd need...or want." The double entendre was so clear it rang in the air like a crystal bell—fragile, distinct, breakable.

I shrugged, uncomfortable with this part of a conversation I knew we'd have to have. What did I tell him? That he was my familiar and there was no choice in the matter for him? Did I just ignore that part of things? I was blushing again, damn it. What *was* it about Bahlin?

"Let's head north," I muttered. "I kind of know where Tarrek is."

Bahlin sputtered, wrenching around to look at me, pulling over to the curb roughly and stalling his car. He ignored the honks of irritated drivers and just gaped at me. "Well why didn't you say so? For the love, woman, you're killing me." He cranked the key so hard I thought he'd break it off in the ignition and the little car started up, shooting back into the heavy London traffic.

"I'm..." he and I both said at the same time. "Go ahead," we both said again. He laughed uncomfortably, and I shrugged.

I held up my hand to indicate I was going to speak and said, "First, you need to stop acting like my father, Bahlin. I don't need to be chastised. I need a partner. Second, Tarrek's in Scotland somewhere near Castle Duncan. He came to me in a dream walk and said he was there. He looked bad, so I'm not sure what's been done to him. He said I had until the next full moon to get to him or all was lost." I leaned over and looked up at the sky, the three-quarter-plus moon filling the sky.

"I'm sorry for being overbearing. It's just been...tough since you left."

"Understood."

"Imeena is gone," Bahlin said softly, looking over his shoulder to change lanes.

I whipped my head around to look at Bahlin. "What do you mean the vampire's gone? Gone how? Vacation gone, or disappeared gone?"

"She's gone missing, Maddy. Her kiss called the High Council to request assistance in locating her. They claim she'd been acting strangely since returning from the last Council meeting. When she failed to show up to her kiss's regular meeting, her compatriots called in for help. They fear she may have gone rogue."

I thought about a rogue vampire on the loose in London. The thought wasn't a pretty one. I thought back over my conversation with Tyr, and the idea that a vampire heart would be the easiest means to immortality unless the vampire was the killer. I shared this conversation with Bahlin and he nodded, agreeing that it made sense but equally as lost as I regarding guilt and innocence.

But something didn't set right with me and I said so. "I just don't see her as the killer, Bahlin. She's powerful, she has her gaze available to influence others, she has access to Seers, she's already immortal. True, she's not magical and she doesn't have immeasurable power, but she just didn't seem the type to go nuts."

Shaking his head Bahlin said, "Maddy, she's a master vampire and over a thousand years old. She's lived a long time. Life gets old like that, especially when you've lost your mate. Her partner was killed about a hundred years ago, and she's not been the same since." He swallowed hard and finished the thought. "It broke her heart."

Man, could I relate. And I hadn't had hundreds of years with Bahlin. In reality, I'd had less than even a hundred waking hours as his lover and companion, and his perceived betrayal had crushed me. Tyr's endorsement of Bahlin had been great, but it wasn't his heart on the line. It wasn't his soul he was putting out there to be flayed if it all went badly. It wasn't his reality that would end if I failed somehow. So he'd simply have to understand if I was less than enthusiastic about the thought of immediate reconciliation with Bahlin.

We drove north for three hours, rarely speaking, the tension level so high it made the air feel thick in my chest as I breathed. Bahlin suggested we stop for the night when we reached Manchester. I was exhausted despite my earlier nap and jumped on the idea of getting out of the car both to sleep in a real bed as well as alleviate the uncomfortable intimacy of traveling cocooned in a car.

We pulled up to the Maissonette, a rather tony looking place I wasn't sure I could afford. Bahlin told me to wait in the car and, considering my rumpled state, I thought it was best. He was in and out of the lobby within five minutes and was sporting one room key. Immediately I was indignant.

"Now look here, Bahlin," I began, unbuckling my seatbelt and shifting up on one hip to face him. "You can't seriously think I'm going to share a room with you."

"Maddy, we agreed only three days ago that we were better off sticking together until this was all sorted out. Since then things have gotten, well, hairy. Let's just get to the room and discuss it there." His eyes pleaded with me not to fight with him, and his stiff shoulders told me he expected just that.

"Fine," I whispered, and his shoulders sagged with visible relief.

He parked the car and we got out to retrieve our bags. Bumping shoulders made my stomach clench and my heart contract as we both reached into the boot of the car. I stepped back and Bahlin handed me my bag, clearly as disturbed as I was at the accidental contact.

Taking my bag from him without touching his hand I said, "I don't want you to touch me, Bahlin. I'm not negotiating with you as a dragon, Bay. I'm telling you as the Niteclif to keep your freaking hands

212

to yourself."

His gaze dropped, frustration reading clearly in them before he could school his face. "Fine. Anything else?"

Realizing he'd packed for me I started to get worked up all over again. How had he known he'd need a suitcase? Had he expected me to take him back with open arms? *Arrogant sod*, I thought, using one of my favorite new English words. I turned and stomped off toward the elevator, hoping like hell we were on anything but the first floor.

We rode the elevator in silence to the seventh floor, and Bahlin walked to the end of the hallway. He opened the door to a large suite and I did my best not to gawk. It was a lovers' suite, with a sunken tub in the middle of the floor, bold, rich colors on every surface and a huge bed set to take advantage of the city skyline.

I froze in the doorway, standing on the cusp of a full-blown fit of temper. *Seriously, how arrogant was this guy?* I asked myself incredulously.

"Before you feed my prized possession to the lycanthrope at the front desk, hear me out," Bahlin said. I shot my eyes to him, wondering if he was kidding about the wolf. Apparently not, because he never even paused. "It was this or two rooms on different floors. The sofa is a pullout, so I'll sleep on it. You'll take the bed, and it will keep us close, Maddy. If something happens, there's a balcony I can launch from. It's our best chance for getting away clean. I don't expect anything from you tonight. Just...just accept this, okay? It was the best I could do for you."

If he'd dug his toe around in the carpet and wrung his hands he couldn't have been more sincere...or slightly pathetic. I may have been bitchy for a variety of reasons, but even I didn't kick puppies. It made me feel like an ass for jumping to conclusions.

"It's fine, Bahlin. Thanks for thinking of all those things. Frankly," I said, smiling at him slightly for the first time since he'd picked me up, "I'm exhausted and not thinking entirely clearly. It's nice to have someone cover the details for me."

He glanced up, smiling tentatively, and took our bags into the enormous bathroom. I sat on the edge of the bed and pulled my shoes and socks off. I looked up and found that Bahlin was watching me with hooded eyes, leaned against the doorframe. I froze, then rose stiffly, kicking my shoes out of the way.

"I need a bath," I said, clearing my throat as I tried to speak around the lump forming there, my broken heart aching like a bad tooth. He'd hurt me so badly when I'd wanted so desperately to believe he'd be different than all the other disappointments in my life.

"I'll just grab a shower then hide out in the bathroom while you soak. How's that?" he asked, turning to pull my bag out of the bathroom. He set my bag on the edge of the bed. "Here's your stuff. Call me when you're done. Maybe then we can talk about the elephant in the room." He shut the bathroom door quietly.

It was so symbolic of the trouble between us that I couldn't stop the small sob that escaped me. I was disappointed to find that hate was easier than forgiveness, and even more disappointed in myself for having considered taking the easy way out.

I soaked for nearly a half hour before Tyr's voice interrupted my relaxed state of mind and said, *"Forgive him."* I jerked back to consciousness, splashing water over the edge of the tub.

Bahlin, voice muffled by the door, called out, "Maddy? Everything okay?"

"Yeah," I said more loudly than was necessary. "Give me a minute and I'll be finished."

"Take your time, *mo chr...*" He cleared his throat, clearly uncomfortable. "Just take your time."

I couldn't stand the thought of him in the bathroom any longer, waiting on the other side of the door and listening for my movements. I drained the tub and dressed in the jammies he'd kindly packed, though it wasn't lost on me that he'd picked the nicest satin slip-style nightgown I'd brought to London. I crawled into bed and pulled the covers up around my waist and called out to him that it was okay to come out. Seconds later the door opened and he padded into the room wearing satin lounge pants and nothing else. Bahlin's lower abs flexed as his hips rolled, carrying him across the carpet, and his skin was flushed from the heat of the shower. His hair hung in thick ropes around his shoulders, damp and more wavy than normal. I stared, taking him all in with hungry eyes. My libido had clearly forgiven him. I snorted then shook my head at his confused look.

"Don't ask," I said.

"Okay. Let's start with this. Hi," he said, coming over and sitting on the edge of the bed.

"Hi," I said back. My hands involuntarily fisted the covers.

We stared at each other, neither wanting to be the first to freefall into the chasm between us for fear that the bottom was far enough away to be fatal.

"Maddy, I've got to know. Have you sought out the rest of the prophecy?" he asked, his voice strained as tight as piano wire.

"There's *more*?" I definitely didn't need there to be more. The damage done with the amount I'd heard was bad enough.

"The second part pertains to me now, and is as important as the first. It's why I sent first Brylanna and then Aiden after you. Brylanna didn't find you, and when Aiden came back all he'd say was that you wouldn't forgive me." His brow creased, and he looked up from his lap. "Is that true? You won't forgive me?"

"I don't know if I can, Bahlin."

He turned away but not before I saw the first tear break over his lower lashes. "Fair enough." He stood from the bed and moved to the sofa, pulling up the cushions and setting them neatly on the floor.

"Bahlin?" No response. "Bahlin," I said more firmly.

He stiffened, then turned. "Yes?"

"This isn't a simple yes or no discussion. As much as it kills me to think I might end up worse off, I think we've got to discuss it. I've got twelve years to serve as Niteclif and you're apparently going to end up as the head of the Council." He flinched. "No need to dress it up, Bahlin. I have to know, though, was it worth it?" I couldn't help the bitterness that leaked into the last part.

"Worth it? *Worth it?*" he growled, chucking a cushion to the side as he stalked toward the bed, his fury suddenly a mirror image of mine. "I'd go back and do it entirely differently if I could, even if it meant lettin' the bleedin' faerie bring yeh happiness, Madeleine. And that, *that* thought near kills me, woman." He'd reached the bed and leaned over me, shaking with emotion. "For yeh know the second part of the prophecy, *mo chrid*? For my heart yeh are." He spun away from me, the muscles of his back so tightly ridged they cast shadows upon themselves in the lamplight, the hollow of the length of his spine like a trench between them. "Yeh're to find another, Maddy. It's the most bitter of revenges for yeh, isn't it? And the worst part? I'll be there to watch the whole bleedin' thing. Because I'm yehr fucking *familiar* on top o' bein' yehr lover."

"Bu-but—" I stuttered, realization slamming into me with the weight of a thousand waves. I didn't want another.

Before I could process this new emotion and sincerely consider the last thought that had raced through my mind, he turned on me. Tears had coursed tracks down his cheeks and the raw rage in his face made me truly frightened of him for the first time, his humanity folding in on itself as his eyes flashed to ice blue. "But *what*, Madeleine?"

I didn't bother to correct him. I recollected Tyr's most recent admonition and trembled at the thought. But there was no other option. "I forgive you," I whispered, my voice harsh with emotion.

"Come again?" he said, stunned into immobility.

"I forgive you," I said more strongly. "But I need to know why you never told me about the prophecy and why you went through with it anyway, knowing you'd break my heart."

He sank to his knees at the end of the bed, crossing his arms and laying his forehead on them. His shoulders shook and so did the bed. I threw the covers back and crawled to the end of the bed, reaching out a tentative hand to touch his bare shoulder.

His hand whipped out faster than I could track and he gripped my arm so tightly I knew I'd be bruised later, but it didn't matter. He pressed my hand closer to his shoulder and stilled, the silent, wracking sobs diminishing to heavy breathing.

"I'm so sorry, Maddy," he said, his voice muffled by the bedding and his arms. "I'm so damnably sorry."

"Bay, I forgive you." Every time I said it, it got easier and I believed it a little more. "But that doesn't answer my questions."

He looked up, his eyes still ice blue, the whites reddened, and he said, "For love, Maddy. I did it for the chance at love. Because that's my curse in all of this. I'll truly love yeh, and yeh'll love me back. I could only break your heart if yeh loved me. But I'd hoped that we'd circumvent the bloody cursed part of the prophecy and for once, just once, I'd have a proper chance at happily ever after. I'll settle for whatever time we have together, and when yeh find your heart's desire, I'll wish yeh well, Maddy. I'll bloody sodding hate it, but I'll wish yeh nothing but happiness. Even if it's only friendship between us from now until then, tell me yeh don't hate me, Maddy. I can't bear this loss if I know yeh truly hate me."

With my free hand I pried his fingers from my forearm and laced our fingers together. "I don't hate you, Bay. I don't. You've ripped my heart out a hundred times since I heard that prophecy, but I don't hate you. I never did."

"Please, goddess, tell me I can touch yeh. Because I won't, not if yeh tell me to stay away. But my fingers ache for the feel of yehr hair, and my hands hurt at the remembered curve of yehr hip. My lips burn with the memory of the taste of the salt on yehr skin, and my heart, Maddy, my heart aches for yehrs," he said, burying his face in the covers so I was unsure whether he was waxing poetic or pleading with me. Either way, it didn't matter.

"I love you, Bahlin," I whispered, reaching out to stroke his hair. My stomach felt like it was plummeting into the abyss, and my heart pounded so hard I knew he heard it.

Bahlin froze, even his breath stilling. "What did yeh just say?"

"I said I love you," I whispered again, afraid to say it too loud lest the words somehow break apart, so fragile did they feel.

"Why?" he breathed, still not moving any more than to speak.

"Because you did it for love, not for power. You took a chance at being happy, when I'd decided to do the same. You've cherished me every night together, and respected me every morning after. You didn't use me, Bahlin. You truly didn't. But I expected you to—*oomph!*" I gasped as he threw himself on top of me, wrapping his arms around my waist and burying his face in the bend of my neck.

"Maddy, Maddy, my Maddy," he chanted over and over again. "Tell me again, *mo chrid*, tell me you love me."

I laughed, the relief of love casting aside the burdens of life. "I do, you silly dragon, I *do* love you." I wiggled down under him so that we were face to face. "I have a request, though."

"Anything, *a stór*, anything for you," he murmured, raining kisses all over my face.

I placed my hands gently on the sides of his face and made him look at me. "I want to go slow this time, Bay. You were awfully hard on my morals before, and while I don't regret physically loving you, my heart is still tender. A bruise is a bruise is a bruise, after all."

His eyes were grave when he said, "I will wait for you forever, Madeleine Dylis Niteclif. When the day comes and you leave me, I will continue to wait for you on the hope that one day you'll return. But until then? I'll love you with all that I am. What is mine is yours, from home to hearth to lair."

"What does that mean, exactly?"

"It's a marriage proposal when you're ready for it." I jerked beneath him. "No, Maddy, I'll no' let yeh go." His brogue was again thick with his emotion. "Know that until that day it means I love yeh. And whatever need of me yeh have, it's yehrs."

Shaken to my soul, I couldn't help but try to lighten the moment. "So does that mean I'm rich?"

He grinned wickedly, and his eyes flashed back to dark blue. "Beyond yehr wildest dreams, my love." He rolled me over so I was lying across him, then shifted so I slid down to rest with my head on his chest. "I'll agree to take it slow, but I'll ask that we still sleep together, Maddy."

I stiffened, thinking he hadn't heard anything other than what he wanted to hear and I tried to sit up but he wouldn't let me move. He laughed, and the sound boomed as it echoed through the ear I had pressed to his chest. "No, my heart, *just* sleep. I want yours to be the last face I see at night and the first I see in the morning."

I relaxed, smiling softly and snuggling into the crook of his arm. "Deal."

He reached across me and pulled the covers up over us, flipping the lamp off when we were settled in. "Sweetest of dreams, Maddy. I love you."

I yawned. "I love you, too, Bay." And then sleep claimed me.

Thankfully it was a dreamless night.

I came to consciousness feeling smothered. Then I realized Bahlin was sprawled across me, a rather impressive—if mildly frightening—morning erection pressed into my side.

"Bay," I moaned, elbowing him and trying to get him to move.

He rubbed his hips against me suggestively and grumbled something.

"Bahlin," I hissed, struggling harder.

"What, love?" he mumbled, slowly waking up. "What is it?"

"Get off me," I groused.

"My apologies," he said, rolling over and pulling the covers over his waist. He actually looked bashful having been caught with the horse out of the barn. "I, uh—"

I laughed, reaching out to smooth his hair off his forehead. "It's okay. I just didn't want to let it get too far out of hand." I blushed like mad, and he laughed so hard he wiped tears from his eyes.

"Oh, Maddy. I've missed you so." He leaned over and kissed me good morning. "Let's get put together, round up some breakfast and get back on the road. We've got between five and six hours left, barring any unforeseen trouble."

"Do you expect any? Trouble, that is," I asked, crawling across the gargantuan bed, wondering idly how horrid my ass looked as I crawled away from him. *Ah, vanity, you're dear to my heart.*

Bahlin chuckled and reached over and slapped me on the rump, hard, and I squeaked, launching myself off the bed and landing in a heap on the floor.

"What the hell was that?" I yelled, scrambling to get up.

"Alternate morning entertainment," he said, still chuckling. "Go and have your shower first. I need a moment to, ah, collect myself." He grinned mischievously, and I ran for the bathroom, afraid to ask what he meant.

We were in the lobby when an eloquent voice behind us said, "You should have chosen another name to register under, Bahlin Drago."

Bahlin clamped his arm around my shoulders, stopping me as I began to turn around. He pulled me close to his side. "Fancy running into you here."

I plastered myself even closer to Bahlin's side, and he turned us both slowly so we faced the High Council member.

"Hellion?" I asked, looking up at Bahlin. He nodded, never taking his eyes off the wizard in front of us.

"I've been seeking an audience with you for days, Niteclif. Seems you've been avoiding me." Hellion, rocked back on his heels, head cocked to the side as he considered me and Bahlin. "And since you won't come to me, I decided to come to you. I do hope you'll forgive the delay, though. I have been scrying for you when all along I should have been scrying for Bahlin." He took a step toward me, and I instinctively stepped back. "I seek only to shake your hand."

I shook my head, wrapping my arm tighter around Bahlin's waist. Hellion wouldn't cause a scene here, in public. Too many mundies about.

"If you're so anxious to speak to her, why don't we have a seat in the restaurant and we'll have breakfast. It's where we were headed," Bahlin said, inclining his head in the general direction of the dining room without ever releasing his hold on me.

"Very well, if you're not worried about us being overheard."

"Oh come now, Hellion. A simple auditory occlusion spell and our voices will be muffled and indiscernible. I've not been around you so long without learning a thing or two," Bahlin said, all joviality with an undertone of menace.

This time Hellion inclined his head and he turned to walk ahead of us into the restaurant. It felt like the high noon scene in a spaghetti western. Once again I found myself pinching the bridge of my nose in an effort to keep from losing my cool.

"Hold on to it, Maddy," Bahlin said softly, gripping the back of my neck.

I nodded.

We were seated in a half-circle booth at Hellion's request, forcing either me or Bahlin to sit immediately next to him. Bay took the hot seat and left me on the edge. I was torn whether or not to scoot closer to Bahlin's side or sit on the edge where I had the best chance of getting to my feet if I needed to defend myself. I split the difference and sat in between the two options. Was it a good idea? I suppose that depended on whether I was in a glass-half-full or glass-half-empty kind of mood.

The pleasantly oblivious waitress took one look at the two gorgeous men I was with and nearly lost her ability to speak in coherent sentences. I wanted to offer her Hellion, but that seemed too pimpish. I giggled, fighting panic. Hellion looked at me, his black eyes knocking the inappropriate humor right on its ass. Bahlin grabbed my knee and squeezed, the pain bringing me back to my senses.

The waitress left, and Hellion took out a pen and drew a small symbol on the tablecloth and then pricked his finger with the point of the pen, dropping a fine spot of crimson in the center of the design. Suddenly the background noise of the restaurant died off and we were sitting in near silence despite being surrounded by people.

"Tell me why I shouldn't demand my fair due of a life for a life and kill you right this minute," Hellion asked me.

I stared at him, and Bahlin shifted his position. I assumed he scooted away from Hellion in case he needed to get to his feet, too, but proximity to the bad guy didn't allow me to ask.

Instead, I employed an age-old diversionary tactic used for millennia. When put on the defensive, take the offensive.

"No, you explain to me why I shouldn't believe you ordered Gretta to kill me." I did my best at giving him equally cold eyes with my return verbal volley.

"What nonsense are you spouting?" he demanded. "Gretta may have been manipulative, but she wasn't violent."

"Not violent, huh? That must be why she attempted to poison me first. It's a much cleaner kill. Is that it? Did my unfortunate recovery force her hand, making her act out of *character?*"

Bahlin reached over to lay yet another cautionary hand on my shoulder.

"I'd hate to see what qualifies for you," I nearly shouted, shrugging Bahlin's hand off and turning to him, my eyes blazing. "No, Bahlin. Hellion and I are going to settle this now. I'm tired of running scared and looking over my shoulder every time I leave a building. I'm tired of going to sleep afraid and waking up wondering if he's in the room. Enough is enough."

Bahlin nodded tersely and sat back in the booth. "Tread lightly, wizard."

"Ah, so you got there first, did you? Tell me, Drago, how was she? As passionate in bed as she is right here, right now?" His words were suggestive and offensive, as if he were striving to take what Bahlin and I had and cover it in a layer of filth.

"I won't dignify that with a response, Hellion, and neither will he. But you can answer a question for me."

"I'd love to," he growled, showing his teeth. "Just ask."

"Did you kill Tarrek?"

He physically started, is eyes flashing with shock and he said, "Has the lad turned up dead then? I hadn't heard. Damn this situation." He took a long drink of water and then, with a mocking salute, he settled into his seat with a sense of resignation nowhere near defeat. "It's always the good of the many over the good of the one. I *will* have my vengeance for Gretta's death, Niteclif, but I will agree to wait until the murders are solved." Sitting up straighter, he stiffened every muscle in his body and asked, "For the sake of the Council, how may I help?" He looked like asking to help had physically hurt him.

I sat there stunned into immobility, my face slack, and I shook my head. *What the hell had just happened?* I wondered. *The action at this table was happening faster than a whack-a-mole-with-a-hammer game.*

"While that's generous of you," Bahlin said, "you'll find you've no recourse for retaliation once the Niteclif recounts her chronicle of events."

"Don't you mean her version?" Hellion asked, never taking his eyes off of me though he addressed Bahlin.

"No. I meant exactly what I said." Bahlin's voice dropped low, and his eyes changed color.

The waitress chose that moment to deliver our food, and the moment she broke the plane of the table, the spell dissolved. The sound of the restaurant roared over me like the gut-trembling roll of thunder during a storm. The dining room patrons' voices seemed raucous following our unnaturally silent isolation.

I profusely thanked the waitress for our food, and Hellion smirked. Bahlin dug into his full English plate with gusto, and I picked at my order of egg in the basket. Hellion touched nothing, and it made me uncomfortable. Gee, poisoned once and here I was, paranoid.

Bahlin cleaned his plate and I offered him my breakfast, which he consumed without apology. Breakfast suitably finished, I stood and the men followed suit. We walked to the lobby three abreast and out the front doors. Bahlin acted for all the world as if nothing were wrong while Hellion, and I stood stiffly to either side of him. Bahlin ordered his car from the parking service.

Once the valet was gone, Hellion said, "I demand reparation, Niteclif, and I will have it. But you have my word I'll wait until this is done. Find the boy—"

"Tarrek?" I asked, interrupting him.

"Yes, the fae. Find him, and if you require my assistance we may meet on neutral ground."

"Where is neutral ground?" Having to ask the mage who wanted to kill me for clarification seemed cosmically unbalanced. It was something Tyr could have covered with me and I intended to ask him why in the world he hadn't. Neutral ground could be the best way for me to stay alive.

"Any stone circle will do."

Bahlin smiled snarkily at the other man. "What he's not telling you is that you must be inside the circle and at least seven stones must be standing. Finding the circles isn't hard—getting to and from them alive *can* be."

Hellion sneered at me, his black eyes growing deeper and, impossibly, darker. "Do not think this is over." And he walked away.

Chapter Seventeen

We drove for another five hours with little conversation, both of us reveling in our reestablished whatever-it-was and, equally, contemplating Hellion's promise of help now and threat later. Bahlin held my hand as he drove, not even releasing it to shift gears but working our hands together on the shifter. I smiled.

He couldn't, no he *wouldn't*, stop touching me, albeit very appropriately at all times. He held my hand and when we stopped for fuel he knelt by my open door and caressed my face, leaning in to kiss me gently. He was so profoundly affectionate, murmuring to me in Gaelic, that I wondered how I had doubted his sincerity despite the continued weight of the prophecy hanging in the back of my mind. Words, once spoken, were impossible to take back, including if not especially the three most important words between us. So while I believed he loved me, I was scared. But there would be time for that later.

We pulled into Edinburgh and drove about until we found a hotel. Again Bahlin got a single room, despite Hellion's assurances. We made our way to the seventh floor and Bahlin laid down on the bed while I freshened up and hooked up his laptop to the room's Wi-Fi. When I came out of the bathroom, the computer's screensaver drew random lines across the black screen on the bedside table and Bahlin's eyes were closed, his body relaxed. I tiptoed to the edge of the bed and looked down at him, his hair splayed over the pillow and his hands relaxed across his hard stomach. His eyelashes brushed his cheeks and his lips curved the slightest bit, smiling as if he were already having good dreams.

He spoke and I jumped, not anticipating the deep rumble of his voice in the silence. "Won't you lie with me, *mo chrid?*"

"Bay, we have to get going. I checked and the moon has three nights before it's truly full. That only gives us tonight, tomorrow and the following night until the moon crests to find Tarrek, save him and solve the murders"

"And Imeena?" Bahlin asked, opening his eyes.

Holy crap, I'd forgotten Imeena. "I want to save her as well, Bay. Where should we start do you think? What do we have to work with?"

"Tyr is a great resource and will be more helpful since you're new. But he's still a god, and they're fickle creatures." I snorted, and Bahlin grinned. "I see you agree."

"Understatement made and duly noted. He said I could meditate and reach him." I wandered to the balcony to look out at the new night.

"You've not the natural temperament or training for meditation, so sleep is your best option if you can think of him long enough before dozing off to establish the connection. It's tricky, but you can do it."

"Why does everyone think I'm so angry?" I asked, turning to face him.

Bahlin just arched his brow at me yet again, the physical silence which stretched between us heavily littered with conversations past.

"Okay, okay. I'm not Mother Theresa when it comes to temperament...or anything else. Fine. I'm a raging bitch, but I need help." I stomped back across the room and threw myself on the bed, bouncing Bahlin. He used the momentum to flip over on top of me.

"Calm down, Maddy, and set your pride aside."

"My pride?" I asked, incredulous. *He thought this was about pride?*

"Yes, your pride. You are an incredibly angry young woman, and within the boundaries of your own life you've a right to be...to a point. But you've got to learn to harness the anger and stop letting it control you. Otherwise you'll spend your time as Niteclif looking over your shoulder for all the people you've pissed off who now have the means, and the desire, to kill you." His somber eyes were empathetic, and he smiled just a little trying to soften the kill shot. "Your anger at the universe won't bring your parents back."

I closed my eyes, unshed tears burning brutally. I remembered my dad. He'd taught me to shoot a gun. But I got angry and frustrated at not being as good as he was. He'd admonished me to control my temper and harness my frustration to make me more effective because if I didn't, he'd warned, I'd just end up a victim of my own making. *"Dictate the terms of your anger and the actions you'll allow on its behalf. Don't let it dictate to you what it will and won't do, Madeleine."* Sometimes it felt like he'd only been gone a day, other times it seemed he'd been gone a lifetime.

I rolled into Bahlin's chest, trying to control my breathing lest I burst into tears.

Bahlin rubbed my back, murmuring softly into my hair. I relaxed and gained control of my emotions, slowly drifting to sleep. I tried to steer my thoughts toward Tyr before I ended up a marionette to my emotions. It worked.

"Hello, Maddy," Tyr said. He was dressed in modern jeans, a T-shirt and flip-flops, his hair tied back with a leather thong. He sat on the sofa as if he hadn't a care in the world. Though probably irreverent, it crossed my mind that with his size and the clothes he looked more like a modern day professional wrestler than a deity.

I sat up and looked at Bahlin who had crashed beside me, hogging the bed as usual.

"When I see you like this, am I dreaming or am I having an out-of-body experience? Because everything seems the same except you're here."

Tyr smiled and said, "That's the question, isn't it?"

Divine avoidance. Fabulous. "So I've made it to Edinburgh and I'm only about an hour from where I suspect Tarrek's being held. I need some help, Tyr."

"Ask your questions."

"Imeena is missing. Is she with Tarrek?" I asked, unsure he'd answer such a direct question, but he surprised me.

"Yes."

"Huh. Is she there voluntarily?" I pressed, wrapping my arms around my knees. I was getting a bad feeling.

"I won't answer that. You must use logic to take this last step, Madeleine...*Maddy*," he said with a snort. "You butcher such a beautiful name with a nickname."

I didn't comment, thinking about what he said. The sick feeling was back in the pit of my stomach, and I wasn't sure what to do.

"Is there anything you can tell me?" I reached out and touched Bahlin. He didn't move though I saw him breathing, and the feel of his skin didn't register to my fingertips. It was as if I was nothing more than a dream, and then it dawned on me. I didn't exist. Not in this plane.

Tyr saw the understanding on my face and said, "This is what it is like to have never existed, Maddy. To see and touch and feel, and to be of another dimension. Don't fret," he said as I began to hyperventilate. Apparently breathing was still a necessary function. He stood and walked toward the bed, confidence in motion, reaching me and stroking a hand down my hair and across my cheek and cupping my chin. "Is there anything I can tell you?" he repeated. "There are eons of information at my fingertips." He snapped, and we were standing on the shore of a crystal-clear lake with mountains in the background and a hawk crying out overhead. He snapped again and we stood in the middle of a desert, the night sky filled with an infinite number of stars. He snapped once more, and I was back in my hotel room. "But what you want the most I cannot give you."

"And what is it I want?" I whispered, reeling from the reality of Tyr.

"Reassurance that what you know to be true will not kill you." He bent and kissed my forehead and was gone.

I woke with a start, my heart pounding out a staccato rhythm. I gripped Bahlin's arm, and he rolled toward me in his sleep. I laid down next to him and pulled his trunk of an arm around me and he snugged me up close to his body. I was chilled, and even his body heat didn't feel like it was enough. What did Tyr mean I wanted reassurance? What was it that I was afraid would kill me? *Hellion*, whispered through my mind and I gave an involuntary jerk.

Bahlin grunted and opened his eyes to small slits of midnight blue. "What's the matter, my love?" His sleep-roughened voice was

227

seductive, and my nipples tightened.

I knew he wasn't really awake, but I needed him to be. I twisted around in his arms and tugged his hair, looking up at him. "Bay?" I stage whispered. "Are you awake?"

"No," he muttered, "I'm not awake. Are you?" He arched his neck to look down at me, pulling back slightly so he could see me.

I sighed. "Sorry to wake you."

He propped himself on his free arm and continued to look down at me. "Did you reach Tyr then?"

"Yeah." Skipping the conversation about the alternate realities, I told Bahlin about the statement Tyr had made regarding reassurance.

Bahlin's brow creased in concentration, and he tapped his fingers against my hip. This went on for several minutes before Bahlin finally said, "Let's get a piece of paper and work this out."

He grabbed the notepad the hotel had provided on the telephone desk and we sat at the small table. Putting my name in the middle, he said, "We know you're worried about Hellion." He wrote Hellion's name above mine and drew a short line connecting the two. He did the same for Tarrek and Imeena. "Who else are you worried about?"

I thought about all the monsters I'd met in my short time here. I glanced at Bahlin and immediately looked away. Without a word he wrote his name on the pad of paper.

"It's only fair," he said softly.

"Honesty?" I asked.

"Remember? Always."

"Brylanna."

Bahlin's head snapped up like I'd slapped him, and he looked at me closely. "My sister has nothing to do with the disappearances."

"True, but she's done nothing to help either. Shouldn't a Seer—or would that be Seeress?—be more involved with solving a series of crimes that affect her brother?"

Bahlin dropped the pen and shoved away from the table, nearly sending it over on its side. He stalked to the balcony window and threw it open making the glass vibrate heavily in its frame. "Sodding hell," he yelled to the sunless sky. He spun to face me, his eyes wild. "No," he whispered. But the seed of doubt was cast.

His body shivered and muscles moved beneath his skin as he fought not to shift. He turned away from me and the fabric of the shirt stretched, seeming to strain to contain the twin mounds his wings made as they tried to push through his skin. He was as close to losing it as I'd ever seen him, and it frightened me.

I picked the pen up off the floor where it had landed when Bahlin had shoved away from the table. I wrote Brylanna's name at the bottom of the page and drew a connecting line to me. Bahlin stood there, chest heaving, pleading with his whole being for me to say it wasn't a possibility. But we'd promised each other honesty.

"Come back to the table," I said gently. "We have to discuss this, Bay."

He walked back to the table with jerky movements, nothing like the graceful predator in motion he normally projected. "Give me another name," he said, his voice gravelly.

"There's no one else," I said, reaching over to lay my hand over his clenched fist. He relaxed incrementally, and I squeezed his hand. "The other Seer is dead, the Council all but disbanded in the wake of Imeena's disappearance. Whoever has planned this has done a very thorough job of dismantling the only semblance of organization in the paranormals' society."

We sat staring at the names on the paper. The killer's name was on that sheet. I was sure of it.

"According to Tyr, one of my skills is determining truth when it's in front of me. Let's see if he's right," I said. I tore off the top sheet of paper, setting in the center of the table. Then I wrote each individual's name on a separate sheet of paper and each sheet in a corresponding circle on the table. I picked up Bahlin's sheet first.

"You're serious," he said, his voice flat and emotionless.

"I have to rule you out officially." I reached for his hand again, but he withdrew it before we touched. "Bay, I am about to sentence someone to death. I have to be able to defend my position without prejudice. You taught me that first rule. Tell me why you didn't do it."

"Because I love you," he roared in that gravelly voice. I crossed my arms under my breasts and met his heated gaze with my own cool one. He slapped his hands on the table and the little eddies of air he created sent the paperwork fluttering about. He stood and towered over me. "I love you, and that should be enough."

I held my ground despite my fear that this would create a new, irreparable fissure in our relationship. "It is—for me. But explain it to me as if you were on trial before the High Council." It was too early in our relationship for such slippery conversational ground and I resented it on some level.

Bahlin fell back into his seat, and it groaned at the onslaught of his frame. "You're right. I know you're right." He pushed his hands through is hair, pulling it back from his face harshly and fisting it at the nape of his neck. "The first two murders were committed before you arrived, so you've no point of reference or proof that anything I tell you is other than hearsay. After you arrived, the murder of Meyla occurred while we were together. However I could have tipped the room while you were downstairs with Sarenia. You never did see it, anyway. You just took my word for it. Tarrek disappeared in the sithen. I've no explanation for that beyond Gretta. And Imeena disappeared while we were separated." He paused, sighing and releasing his hair. It fell back around his shoulders and he relaxed slightly. "It looks poorly for me, I know."

I picked up where he left off, not giving him a chance to continue. "You weren't at the sithen when I was shot, but I suppose you could have hired Maddox. Though had you been inclined to shoot me, you could have, and like *would* have, done it when you first came to my rooms to disclose my evolution. You'd no need for a proxy killer when the opportunity to kill me presented itself so simply."

Bahlin's shoulders relaxed even more as he realized I didn't think he was guilty.

I crossed his name off the list and removed his individual sheet of paper, letting it float to the floor.

"That's it?" he asked, shocked.

"You didn't do it, Bay. I know that as deeply as I know that this isn't just a dream."

"Thank you." He reached out to touch the back of my hand, and I flipped it over so our fingers touched, front to front. "I'm sorry, Maddy," Bahlin said quietly. "I don't normally lose it like that. I just saw myself losing you again so soon, and it made me a bit—"

"Crazed? Maniacal? Enraged?" I suggested with a smile.

Bahlin smiled back. "Point made. Who's next?"

Might as well get the hardest one out of the way. "Brylanna."

As expected, Bahlin stiffened again, but he didn't rage at me. Instead, he took a deep calming breath and seemed to collect himself, forcing his eyes back to midnight blue. "Let's trade this one off, because I can't be totally objective about her," he suggested.

"Fair enough. Brylanna hates me. She sees me as interfering between the two of you, which, I might add, is just a little creepy. She knew I was coming and made sure that the prophecy was fulfilled just as she'd predicted. As you've stated, I have no point of reference for the first murders, so let's just say she could have done it."

Bahlin's jaw clenched, his neck muscles cording, but he nodded and gestured for me to go on.

"You got to me so quickly that she didn't have a chance, so she could have hired Maddox to kill me. But it just doesn't ring true. Why would she hire a fae when she has access to the wyvern? And she's already a Seer, so there's no reason for her to kill Meyla. She's not strong enough in her human form to fight Imeena, and there's been no report from Imeena's kiss of a dragon interfering with her. The only claim was that she was behaving strangely. No, Brylanna probably regrets not trying to off me before we got together, but she didn't do it. There are too many negatives in even the column of possibility."

Bahlin got up and walked to the sliding glass doors of the balcony and slid them shut gently. Yet he stood there, looking out over the rooflines and saying nothing.

"Bay?" I got up and walked to him and slid my arms around his waist. "Are you okay?" I rubbed my hands up and down the ridges of his stomach, and they tightened involuntarily. He put his hands over mine to still them, and I laid my cheek against is back.

"A part of me would have died if she'd been sentenced to death." He was so still, so quiet, the rapid beating of his heart the only indicator of strong emotion.

A thought dawned on me. Why I'd never thought of it before was beyond me. "Bahlin, who carries out the death sentences of the Niteclif?"

He looked at me and I could tell he knew I'd finally put it all together. "The High Council member of the offending group."

"So if Brylanna had been guilty..." I couldn't finish the thought.

"Then I'd have had to kill my own sister."

Shakespeare couldn't have done better than this, I thought. I kissed his back through his T-shirt and I squeezed him tight. "I'm sorry I didn't understand that. I would have sorted her out on my own."

"No, don't hold back with me, Maddy. If I have any chance of breaking the prophecy I'm going to need all of you, my love: your trust, your heart, your faith, your confidences and more."

That he would put so much of his blind faith in me was terrifying, but he was asking nothing more of me than he was willing to give himself. I nodded against his back, too choked up to answer him, though what strong emotion was most responsible for my mute condition was open for debate.

I hated myself for asking, but a morbid part of my mind demanded an answer. "Do you think we'd survive your having to kill your own sister if I handed down a death sentence for her?"

Bahlin didn't answer. Instead he twisted out of my grasp and walked to the bathroom, shutting the door behind him. Water ran for several moments before it shut off and, eventually, he came out. He'd rinsed his face and a few of the shorter hairs at his temples curled where they'd been splashed. He stopped ten feet from me and shook his head.

My stomach plummeted, and I involuntarily grabbed it.

Standing straighter and setting his shoulders, Bahlin finally answered the lingering question. "I don't know how I could kill her. She's my baby sister. If you handed down a death sentence for her...if the crime was heinous..." He drew a hand across his lips. "I'd do it, but I don't know how we'd survive it, Maddy. It would be there, between us, forever."

I nodded, swallowed hard and tried to come up with something to say that would offer reassurance to us both. Unfortunately, my mind was nothing but a great, big, cavernous void of white noise.

Bahlin closed the distance between us and reached for my hand.

"Back to our temporary drawing board?"

"Who should we do next?" I asked, releasing him and turning for the table. Before I was fully faced away from Bahlin, he grabbed my arm and spun me back to him so hard that I lost my balance and stumbled into him. His arms crushed me to him, and I grunted at the force of his embrace. He dipped his head to mine, whispering against my lips, "I'll no' take yeh to bed, Maddy, because yeh asked me not to, but I'll make yeh wish I had." And then he closed the distance.

He devoured my mouth with a combination of nibbling kisses that left me straining against him and rough, tongue-delving assaults that left me almost struggling to break free. He was relentless. I pulled my arms free and he let me, snaking them up his chest and grabbing fistfuls of hair and yanking him closer to me. He grunted with pain but continued his onslaught, and I groaned into him mouth. He breathed into me and his breath was searing, lighting me up from the inside and seeming to set my soul ablaze. I wrapped a leg around his and ground my pelvis into his thigh, panting and begging and whimpering all at once. I wanted him flat on his back. I wanted him stretching me to breaking. I wanted... I just wanted.

He broke the kiss and disentangled us despite my best efforts to crawl up his front. "Maddy?" he asked and I opened my eyes to look at him, lust glazing my vision. "You're sending mixed messages, love. I'm about ten seconds from throwing you to the floor and ravaging you, despite your earlier wishes, and I don't think you'd be complaining. Come on now, pet. Tell me what you want with a clear head."

I looked at him, and my mind's haze lingered. I wanted him. I *wanted* him, wanted him. But this wasn't slow. Hell, I'd nearly been screaming, *"Warp speed ahead,"* just seconds ago while looking for Bahlin's thruster with my whole body. It wasn't fair. I stepped back and had to clear my throat, twice, before I could put together an apology.

"I'm sorry, Bahlin. I truly am. I know it's not fair to you, but I've got to ask you to stop. If I don't then we end up right where we left off. Like I said before, my morals, or what's left of them, need to regroup."

"Do you believe I love you?"

I looked at him warily. If he gave me the screw-me-because-I-love-you speech, I was going to break his damned nose. I nodded, not trusting my voice.

"Then you must believe I respect you, yes?"

My fists formed, and my shoulders straightened.

"And if you believe I love and respect you, then you must believe I'll accept your wishes on this matter." He smiled at me, his lips reddened from our kisses, his pants bulging dangerously in the front.

I relaxed my hands and noticed that *he* noticed, then he laughed, rubbing his jaw.

"Besides," he said, "I've no intent of giving you any more reason to punch me, whether I stand before you as a dragon or a man." He tilted his head to the side and chuckled at my blushing cheeks.

"Sorry for that last time." I stumbled through the apology, unsure how sincere it really was.

Bahlin and I gathered up the scattered remnants of our remaining suspects and laid everything back out on the table. We were left with Hellion, Tarrek and Imeena.

"I suggest we start with Imeena since she's the most recent to disappear," I said, running my fingers over her name. I could imagine her with her blue-black hair and Caribbean blue eyes staring at me across the High Council's meeting table. I closed my eyes and took a deep breath, thinking through the events of the last week and a half.

"Maddy, I think it's important to rule out Hellion first," Bahlin said, his voice insistent.

"No. Because I don't believe Imeena did it and if I'm right, she's the most recent disappearance."

He looked at me, his eyebrows shooting precariously close to his hairline. "But she's a vampire," he exclaimed.

"And you're a dragon. It doesn't make either of you guilty." My tone rang sharp. "Harboring a little prejudice?"

Bahlin blushed like mad and I suddenly knew, with alarming clarity and vivid imagination, that he and Imeena were once lovers.

"Bay, you had better come clean about this right now before I pick your damn name up off the floor and reconsider your place in all this," I growled at him. Jealousy made me want to stand on the table and beat my fists on my chest, then throw him to the ground and love him until he begged me for release. Which, of course, I'd deny. Okay, not really, but it sounded good and made me squirm in my seat a little.

"It was about seventy years ago," he said, and my head snapped up as I realized I *still* didn't know how old Bahlin was. "She'd lost her mate and we, well, I'd come out of a bad relationship and the Council had just met and we ended up getting together for a few years, but it wasn't significant. It was a passing entertainment for both of us."

A few years? "How old are you, Bahlin?"

He closed his eyes and let his head drop back.

"Tell me," I said, standing up to loom over his seated form by inches. Pathetic, but it was the best I could do with such a huge man. "Tell me, damn it."

"How about we compromise and I tell you how long dragons live?" he asked, never opening his eyes or picking up his head.

"Both," I said through gritted teeth.

He cracked a single eye.

"Tell me *both*." I had no idea why it was so important to know his age, but he'd been so sketchy about it that now I needed to know...desperately.

"Dragons live to be about ten thousand years old," he said softly. Then he lifted his head up to look at me, slowly pushing himself to standing and never taking his eyes off me as he did it. "And I'm two thousand, four hundred and thirty-seven years old. Are you happy? Does this make you feel *any* better, Maddy?"

I sat and missed the chair completely, catching my hip as I went by it so that it tipped me over. I threw out an arm to keep from face-planting it on the carpet.

"No," I said. "It really doesn't help me much at all."

"Do you understand now why I didn't want to disclose this?" he asked, staring down at me with his dragon's eyes.

"Makes perfect sense," I whispered.

"Should I get the door for you now, or will you wait to run until I've got my back turned?"

"That's pretty low, Bahlin."

"I call it like I see it, love."

We stared at each other, neither willing to give ground. My mind whirred faster than an accountant's adding machine as I worked through a variety of issues but one, *one*, stopped me, tumbling out of my mouth before I could stop it.

"How many women have you loved in your lifetime?" Morbid, but I needed to know how I stacked up against the millennia and the thousands of women he'd likely bedded.

"One," he answered, stepping close to me. "I've waited for you since I was just a lad, Maddy. I've waited since before I was a High Council member. I've waited since Brylanna announced over dinner one night that the first female Niteclif would be mine, and I would break her heart. I've lived with this damnable prophecy hanging over my head for more than nineteen hundred years, Madeleine. It's a long time to wait and know you'll never have what you want, and you'll never love another. I've never been a monk, and I'll always be mythology to most, but I was born to love you. Never forget that."

Bahlin held out his hand to me and I took it, trembling as he helped me to my feet. He stepped toward me very slowly and I looked at him with large eyes, sure that the whites were showing all around the irises. I didn't run. I *wouldn't* run. I'd loved him without knowing and knew there was no valid reason I shouldn't love him now that I did.

He embraced me gently, laying kisses along my temples and down my nose before resting his forehead against mine. "I love you, *a stór*. Not even the ages can change that."

"I love you too."

Chapter Eighteen

Bahlin and I set everything to rights yet again. I kept glancing at him, and he finally sighed. "Is there something else you'd like to know about me, pet?"

It was humiliating, but I wouldn't rest until I knew. "Hwmnywmn?" I muttered, turning away from him.

"Pardon?"

"Oh don't go being all polite. You heard me!"

"What I heard, Maddy, sounded like you need a decongestant and a day in bed, if not a priest to read your Last Rights. Now come clean before I fetch the priest."

"Fine. How many women, Bahlin?"

"Ah. To be fair, that's not fair." He smiled. I didn't. "Okay. I honestly don't know. I spent years trying to prove that I wouldn't be the fool the prophecy foretold."

"Okay."

"Just okay? You berate me, chastise me, dump me and then love me over a prophecy beyond my control, but you just accept the women I've known?"

"Look, you did more than know them, buddy. But it's irrelevant."

"Goddess knows I'm afraid to ask, but why in the world is it irrelevant?"

I looked down, but he grabbed my chin and lifted my face, moving close enough that I could see only him. "Because you've loved only me," I whispered.

"Too true." He moved behind me, took me by the arms and backed me into the chair. Once he had me sitting, he began rubbing my shoulders.

I leaned my head against him, and he sighed before I realized I'd laid the back of my head against his groin. I left it there, as much to torment him as me. Thoughts were swirling all around in my head, and I was getting that sickening feeling in my gut again. I'd been over Hellion's reasons a hundred times, and I'd even spoken to him. But he'd appeared shocked this morning when I spoke to him about Imeena's disappearance. He had displayed none of the physical signs of lying—quickened breathing, dilated pupils, shifty eyes, fidgeting—and had, in fact, done everything to make me think he was sincere, right down to offering to scry for us.

"Bahlin?"

"Hmm?"

"If Hellion were to scry for the killer, and it was him, would he identify himself?" I asked.

"Bloody brilliant," Bahlin yelled, yanking me up and spinning me around in his arms to lay a loud, smacking kiss on my lips. He dropped me to my feet and I stumbled, but I managed to recover and save a little face, sitting back down to watch him. He strode over to his laptop bag and pulled out a cell phone. Dialing a few numbers, he spoke tersely when the recipient answered.

"Meet me at the Glendale on St. George Street. Agreed. How soon can you be here?" Bahlin paced, biting the thumbnail of his left hand. I idly wondered if his dragon claw would be shorter on that hand when he changed. "Fine. Room 1810. Come alone and don't send one of your coven for this." He clicked the phone shut and turned to face me.

"Hellion will be here before the end of the day. We'll have our answer by tonight and, if need be, I'll kill him myself."

I blanched, and Bahlin rushed to my side. "Gads. I'm sorry, Maddy. That was bloody inconsiderate of me. He's going to bring his scrying tools, and we'll ask very specific questions to determine his innocence. But if he's our killer, we won't have the opportunity to issue a death warrant and wait for his coven to carry it out."

"How are dragons killed, Bahlin?" I asked in a small, pained voice. "Because I won't risk losing you over this. Not if we can wait on his coven to carry out the sentence."

"Let's wait and see if he's guilty first, okay?" He smoothed my hair and shifted me out of the chair before pulling me into his lap. The poor piece of furniture groaned, and Bahlin chuckled. He stood and carried me to the bed, laying me down and crawling on top of me, trapping my thighs between his. He leaned in and kissed me tenderly, but I recognized his diversion strategies at this point.

"Bahlin?" I asked into his mouth, refusing to succumb to temptation. "Bay."

"Bloody hell, woman. You make it inconceivably difficult to seduce you."

"Stuff a sock in it. How are dragons killed? And don't kiss me again until you've answered me." I struggled to regain my arms from where he'd pinned them over my head, and I crossed them over my chest in an image of pure defiance.

He sighed, and I knew I'd won.

"Dragons in human form can be killed like any other human. With the exception of our strength, speed and unnatural ability to heal, we're human for all intents and purposes. Of course, you'd never want an autopsy performed on one of us because underneath it we're very different, but you get the point."

"And in dragon form?" I pressed.

"That's a different story. Our bodies are incredibly difficult to kill. There is one small scale missing over our heart that can be pierced by arrow or blade or magic that will kill us. Otherwise our scales are relatively impervious to attack. Our eyes are our weakest point, though in battle we rely on all of our senses to, ah, take down our enemies. To answer your question, we're very hard to kill."

"Do you breathe fire?"

"I do. Not all dragons do, but my weyr is one that is so gifted. Why?" he asked.

"Can you do it now?" I asked, curious. Truth was turning out to be better than fiction.

He smiled and a small stream of smoke snuck out of one nostril and rose through the air. "I could, but we'd not get our deposit back on this fine room."

I laughed, delighted. "Good to know. Can you shift into your dragon-hybrid form and cloak yourself when Hellion gets here? I want to meet with him alone, but I want you near. Cling to the side of the building or something, but give me some time alone with him, okay?"

"No."

"It's not up for debate, Bay. I'll meet with him here or I'll meet with him in the lobby and ask him to do what he can to cloak us there." I sat up, pushing at his chest. "You've got to let me do my job."

"Damn it all to hell, Maddy. Can you not give me something? What if I armed myself prior to his arrival?" he asked, desperation tingeing his words.

"How?" I asked, squinting at him.

He closed his eyes and when they opened they'd shifted. He smiled, and I did what I could to scramble back from him. His mouth was full of razor sharp teeth, and he motioned for me to follow him to the bathroom.

I did, keeping a small distance between us.

He turned on the shower and blew a small fireball into the streaming water. It hissed as it dissolved into smoke. His voice was guttural and he had difficulty talking with his reformed jaw, but I understood him when he said, "I am not without defenses, Niteclif."

Listening to him speak, I realized for the first time that his dragon occupied a different part of his brain than his human form did. It was as if the monster couldn't totally reconcile the man and vice versa. Not comforting.

"Bay?" I whispered, and he nodded his head, never taking his eyes off me. "You can stay. Just don't eat me."

"No promises," he growled, and I didn't know if he was making a joke with sexual overtones or if he was being serious. Scary, that.

The sun had just set, and I was getting antsy when there was a knock at the door. Bahlin went into the bathroom to metamorphose into what I was now calling Scary Bahlin while I went for the door. My dragon had given me a dagger that looked suspiciously like the one I'd used to kill Gretta with. It was taped to the small of my back and the skin was raw where Bahlin had insisted I practice ripping it away from my body and stabbing out with it.

"Good evening. Killed anyone else lately?" Hellion's voice was deceptively light as he brushed passed me and walked into the room. "And where is your lovely companion tonight?" He glanced around the room, and Bahlin chose that moment to open the door.

He'd changed, all right. His jaw was longer than even this afternoon, and his eyes were more almond-shaped in his face. His skin had a very slight blue hue to it, as if the scales of the dragon were peeking out from underneath. His hands had become bonier, and his nails were more pointed than before. Obviously lover boy hadn't been totally forthcoming this afternoon.

"Don't trust me, then?" Hellion asked. "Well, the feeling's mutual." With a rush of wind a circle scorched into the carpet at his feet. "Sorry about your room deposit, mate."

Bahlin walked toward the circle and reached out a hand to touch Hellion. Before he made it to the wizard, the circle sparked and Bahlin gasped, yanking his hand back.

"No one who had any responsibility in Gretta's death may cross this circle." He turned to look at me. "Come ahead, woman. I'm curious to know how far you'll get."

I walked up to him, knowing I was about to get the shit shocked out of me. Bahlin made a grab for me and I jerked away from him, my right elbow reaching the circle accidentally. The shock blew my arm back and made it feel like my shoulder had dislocated. The entire arm went numb, but I knew it was going to hurt like hell when the pins-and-needles phase of Hellion's little spell passed.

"Ah. There's the answer I needed." Hellion sat on the floor and took out a small crystal suspended on what looked like horsehair, then set a map on the floor. He marked the hotel's location and asked us for the room key, explaining that, as a control, he'd put the room key on the opposite side of the map. If he was the guilty party, the crystal would clearly swing back and forth between the two points and he would not be able to hide that.

Bahlin crouched down next to the circle, careful to keep his distance.

Hellion began allowing the crystal to swing freely over the map in an ever-broadening circle. Nothing happened, and he cursed, setting the crystal down.

"Niteclif." His tone demanded absolute obedience, and I couldn't help but wonder if he knew nothing about me at all.

"What?" I said through clenched teeth, my jaw not moving.

"You're going to have to make a small blood donation."

I looked at him, then at Bahlin and Hellion barked out, "Now."

"Look, asshat, I don't open a vein for anybody without a reason, and that includes my doctor. So pony up the excuse, and we'll see."

"I need your blood to break whatever concealment spells are in place. Without your blood? This is a waste of our mutual efforts. I can hate you from afar. I've no need to stand so close to you and your winged mutt."

I held my hand out to Bahlin. "Use your claw and take it from forearm. It hurts less than the hand." More trivia from the Niteclif Evolution. Shaking my head, I silently wished that some of the knowledge that had come to me had been more useful.

My dragon grunted in acquiescence, roughly gripping my wrist and holding it out in front of me. With a small slashing motion, he made a shallow cut. I hissed out a breath as he held my arm close to the circle.

Hellion reached through the circle with a wash of green light and rubbed the crystal across the wound. Drawing the crystal back through the circle seemed to take more concentration.

"Blood makes magic stronger," Bahlin growled, his mouth too full of teeth for normal speech so his enunciation wasn't clear.

The crystal began to spin in a rapidly diminishing circle over the map, moving farther and farther toward what looked like the suburbs and then the countryside of Edinburgh. With vibrating intent, the crystal stopped, the horsehair taut, over a finite point on the map.

Hellion looked up and smiled. "Castle Duncan."

Hellion left after giving his sworn oath that he wouldn't disclose anything he'd learned during the scrying to anyone, not even the Council.

I lay on the bed, miserable. Tyr's voice repeated over and over in my head. "*Reassurance that what you know to be true will not kill you.*" Bahlin had gone deadly still when I told him what I suspected. But he'd insisted I go through the motions after Hellion left, sorting out the how and why of the crime. I had, and now I had my killer—Tarrek. It was what I knew to be true, and I knew from Tyr's warning that Tarrek would try to kill me. I wanted to go to Castle Duncan immediately and demand answers. Bahlin refused to go tonight.

He'd had gone into the bathroom to take a quick shower before we left, claiming he felt out of sorts following his partial shift, healing my arm before closing the bathroom door behind him. I suspected he just wanted to give me some time alone to sort out my mind.

I drifted in and out of consciousness, unaware of the passing of time. Tyr's voice stirred me and I sat up, disoriented.

"Maddy, we must speak." He looked at me with such compassion.

I wanted to beg him to take this burden from me, but I knew that the time was coming when I'd have to issue my findings and condemn Tarrek to death and no one, not even Tyr, could relieve my responsibility.

"Why?" I croaked.

"You know why. Your logic is unassailable. Would it make you feel better to go over it with me? To assure you that you've missed nothing?" he asked, walking over to the bed and sitting next to me.

I scooted over to give him more room. "Please," I choked out, the tears lodged in my throat.

"Tell me what you've discerned, dear girl, and I will do what I can to aid you."

"Tarrek and Bahlin have struggled against each other for hundreds of years, challenging each other for the leadership role on the High Council. Tarrek said to me the first night I met him that neither he nor Bahlin ruled, though they both attempted to lead. It didn't mean much to me at the time." I glanced over at Tyr, my eyes begging for some type of forgiveness that wasn't his to give.

He looked at me tenderly and said, "And why should it have? Go on, Maddy."

"That same night, Tarrek warned me on our way to the sithen that I would find that not all that was beautiful was soft, and not all that was visually unpleasing was harsh. I thought nothing of it. I didn't think it applied to him. But he was warning me, wasn't he?" I asked Tyr.

"He wanted you to know about the prophecy, but he wasn't brave enough to tell you. He counted on Bahlin's sense of honor to do that and more to drive you back to him, thus leaving Bahlin the jilted suitor." Tyr ran his hand down the front of my face, forcing me to close my eyes. With two fingers he began to massage my brow, forcing the muscles to relax. "But what Tarrek never considered was that Bahlin would truly love you, Maddy. The thought of losing you was too much for him to shoulder. So he took the coward's way for the first time in his life, and he waited for someone else to carry the truth to you. It almost cost him the love of his life, though, and I'm willing to place strong odds that he's learned his lesson. We'll not discuss the second part of the prophecy, so don't ask."

"Fine," I bit out. I thought about how to phrase the next part, and I just couldn't come up with a way that didn't make me sound self-important. "Forgive me for sounding arrogant, but..."

"Out with it, kid," Tyr said, sounding for all the world like my father. My eyes squinted shut as I held on to the voice. "Would you like me to manifest as him, Maddy?"

"No," I answered without conscious thought. Seeing my father again, when it wasn't really him, would just be cruel, but I couldn't deny it was a hard draw on the heart. I saw Bahlin throw open the bathroom door. Apparently I'd shouted out in my sleep. Bahlin padded over to me, wearing only a towel, and gently rubbed my head. It was the strangest feeling, nothing like being in the same plane with him.

"I didn't think so, but I wanted to give you the option," Tyr said. "You are a wise woman to love them as they were, Maddy, and not try to hold on to other than their memories."

I cleared my throat before I said softly, "No offense, but you'd never be him."

"As I said, wise. Now please, go on."

I struggled with my heart and mind to let go of the want to see my dad's image again. It was the greatest act of will I'd ever accomplished. "Tarrek instructed Maddox to kill me. This way, if there was no Niteclif, there would be no real punishment. Like Bahlin said, without a

Niteclif, chaos reigned. Jossel was killed not for any special power, but because he overheard the discussion between the fae. That's why his body has never shown up. Maddox just did away with it."

"And the attempted murder of the Niteclif?" Tyr prompted. He continued to rub my forehead, and the thoughts seemed to come easier for the contact.

"Tarrek put up the runes to help ensure Maddox's success. When Maddox failed to kill me, Tarrek was furious. When I was taken to the sithen, he couldn't risk that I would wake up and identify Maddox while Maddox was still alive. So he stayed with me, day and night, and had his lover, Gretta, make a poison draught to kill me. When I awoke and announced the shooter in front of both him and Bahlin, he had to kill Maddox for fear that Maddox would turn him in as the plotter. So he left, ostensibly to go tell his parents of Maddox's treachery, but he was gone too long. He *did* tell his parents of Maddox's sentence, but not before he killed him and ordered someone to dispose of the body. When Gretta took it upon herself to attempt to kill me after the meeting and she was killed, he must have been very angry."

"The heavens shook with his wrath," Tyr said in all seriousness. "He's a powerful member of the Tuatha de Dannan, Maddy. You cannot underestimate him, especially within his own sithen. There he is nearly undefeatable. You must do all you can to prevent him returning there, for I fear his parents will not turn him over to justice."

I nodded, afraid of the same thing though with no justifiable reason other than the fierceness of Tarrek's mother in defending Maddox even after his death sentence.

Tyr motioned for me to continue, saying, "Do not stop again. I believe you have the right of it."

I nodded, just needing movement. I got up and walked around the room, varying my stride and burning off anxiety I could feel even now. In my sleep I twitched, and Bahlin resumed petting my head. It was slightly distracting.

I picked up my last thread. "When Bahlin and I escaped the sithen, we were out of his immediate reach. He went to the hotel, performed simple magic to disguise himself as Hellion, and destroyed my room looking for the Niteclif family tree. It would have saved him time to know where the room was as he'd been there less than five days prior.

"He reached out to me in a dream walk, intent on testing his power to see if he could kill me in my sleep. What better way to dispose of the Niteclif at this point than to have her show up dead in her lover's, his nemesis's, bed? So he came to me, but Bahlin saved me. The ironic thing is, you tried to save me that night, too, didn't you? You were the light in the forest."

Tyr shrugged elegantly, watching me as I paused my pacing about the room. "I told you that I would have saved you some of this heartache if I could, Maddy. I meant it. You are a child of my blood, bone of my bone, and I wish you absolutely no ill will. But some things one cannot be saved from."

I gave a curt nod before continuing, thinking this was sage advice. "Stealing the family tree, Tarrek sent the head to Bahlin's safe house. The only way he could have broken the wards was to have a dragon working with him, so he's at least one partner, though I suspect there are more. A bid for power is never a one-man operation.

"The head gave me my first inkling that Tarrek was a suspect. Tarrek had been wearing a short-sword the day I awoke in the sithen. It would have been an ideal time to behead Maddox, and he had the physical strength to do so. When he left the room he was wearing it. When he returned, he wasn't. He'd also changed clothes. I thought it was for the introduction to his parents, but it was in all probability to discard of bloodied clothes. Tarrek likely had his dragon supporter waiting outside the sithen to dispose of the body. It would have been easy enough to follow Bahlin there and wait for further instructions. Bahlin wasn't paying attention to his surroundings. He was distressed at my having been shot. Following him would have been easy.

"Bahlin and I fled to his lair. Bahlin said himself that dragons are creatures of magic, so Tarrek would not have been able to dream walk against me while I was there. When we left, and I found out about the prophecy, Tarrek had the opening he needed. He set me up to come to him at Castle Duncan, but he couldn't contain his rage when he found out I'd been intimate with Bahlin. It meant he'd never rule the Council as it stood."

"True," said Tyr. "And Meyla actually withheld the second part of the prophecy, so he has no idea that there was another chance for him."

I stumbled to a stop and stared at Tyr. "I don't want it to be true."

"You didn't want Tarrek to be guilty, either. But we must follow behind the choices we make. Have you made all your choices for the future?" he asked.

"No."

"There you have it. Do not ask me more. Finish this, Maddy, for the night progresses and the closer to the full moon we draw, the more violent he will become."

"Okay. The thing I have working most in my favor is that Tarrek won't know that Bahlin and I have reconnected. He will assume that I'll be coming to him alone."

Tyr nodded and patted the bed. I shook my head and stood there a moment longer. He sighed and said, "Tell me quickly, why did Tarrek kill the creatures?"

"That's the strange part." I'd begun to quiver at this point. "He has magic, so it's not for that. He's not immortal though he'll live for thousands of years. The *cù sith* was taken for its nose to discern truth. The *far durrig* was taken so he could generate his own luck. The Seer so that he could discern the future in case luck failed. Imeena was taken so he might become truly immortal." This next was the part that bothered me the most. "And Bahlin? He wants Bahlin so that he'll be more knowledgeable and powerful than any other leader in the world." Fine quivers had developed into shakes, and Tyr again motioned for me to come and lie down next to him. I walked back to the bed and laid down on my stomach, thinking Tyr would have been a wonderful grandfather to have in real life. Tyr began to massage my head with his one free hand, and I slowly relaxed. I smiled sleepily, reassured for the first time since I'd lost my parents that I belonged to someone, that I was someone's beloved. Something in that last sentence haunted me, and I was tense again.

"Ah, so you have it. Tell me, Maddy, what else did the *cù sith's* nose do?" Tyr asked, never relenting in his massage of my scalp.

"It stole the souls of the living," I whispered, my mind feeling sluggish. *Stole the souls of the living, beloved, hands held out in pleading supplication...* I shot off the bed and screamed, Bahlin catching me and throwing me bodily behind him, whipping his towel off and crouching low. He stood naked and vengeful, like a fallen god, between me and an unseen threat.

"Bahlin." My voice was harsh, pleading. "Bahlin."

He spun on his heel and took four huge strides toward me and, reaching me, crushed me to him, seeking to protect me from fear itself. In that moment I knew, without a doubt, that he would die protecting me if that was what the Fates demanded as payment for the opportunity at true love. I screamed and raged at them, cursing them by name.

"Maddy? Maddy," Bahlin said, struggling to keep me subdued without hurting me. Finally he threw me on the bed and dropped on top of me, knocking the breath, and the fight, right out of me. "What is it, *a ghrá gheal?*

I began to cry, great wracking sobs. I was inconsolable.

"Maddy, love, you must tell me what's happened? Did Tarrek come to you in a dream walk? I'll kill the bastard," he hissed, beginning to roll off of me.

But I wrapped my arms and legs around him and refused to let go. "No. You can't."

"Begging your pardon, Maddy, but I *can* and I *will*," he said stiffly.

"No, Bay. Tarrek has taken the *cù sith*." I was sobbing again, unable to speak.

"*A leanbh*, we knew that from the start. Why's it bothering you so?" He stroked my back, going up to his knees so he was kneeling on the bed. Still I clung to him like a barnacle to a whale.

"One of the *cù sith's* abilities is to steal the souls of the living. If Tarrek controls the souls, he'll control the beings. I've seen it, Bahlin. In the dreams I had before I came over here, before the evolution. I just didn't know what I was seeing. There were bodies, and I thought they were dead, but they weren't. They were soulless, and they were holding out there hands to me in a cry for help. Don't you see? They were begging me to save them. He's building a soulless supernatural army, Bahlin."

"Oh, great gods."

"My thoughts exactly."

Bahlin and I sat clinging to each other for a while, darkness pressing against the window.

"I have to call my weyr, Maddy. As put off as I am with my father and my sister, Da's the *Glaaca*, and he'll be able to pull together more members of different clans and get us some help. We can't call the fae to help, though they'd be bloody useful. There are the vampires, and the witches and wizards. I think we can count on them." Bahlin set me gently aside and rose to fetch his cell phone, dialing quickly.

I could hear the rings, one...two...three.

"Da? No, no. Look..." and he told them what was happening. "I don't know," he said, some time later. Turning to me he asked, "Maddy? Can they be killed?"

"I don't know, Bay. Can he just get some of the different clans together and meet us somewhere on the Highlands? We need to meet far enough away from Castle Duncan that Tarrek doesn't suspect us."

He nodded his head and went back to the conversation. "She's not sure, Da. I'm thinking fire, but we're not all so inclined. If we work together, though..." and off they went, strategizing.

Feeling helpless, I curled up on one edge of the bed. If only I could meditate and reach Tyr again I could ask all the things fear had denied me such a short time ago. I closed my eyes and focused on the sounds of the air conditioner, clicking on, clicking off. But after several minutes, I realized it was useless. I opened my eyes and screamed. Bahlin had apparently hung up with his dad and was kneeling on the floor with his face inches from mine.

"Sorry. Sorry," he said, clasping a hand over my mouth as I sucked in another breath to scream. "I thought you were gone to Tyr, and I wanted to be here to make sure nothing interceded in your dreams. No screaming?"

I shook my head and he removed his hand. I smiled weakly, and he returned the gesture. I'd come to a decision while he was on the phone. If we stood a strong chance of dying, and tonight was our last night together, I wanted it to be special.

"Bay?" I said softly.

He looked at me warily. "Yes?"

Denise Tompkins

"Kiss me?"

"Any time, *mo muirnín.*"

He leaned in to me, and I tilted my head to meet his. His large hand grasped the back of my skull and he held me just so, our lips brushing against each other with something akin to trepidation, as if we were new to each other. And in a way we were. Because we'd never come together, truly come together, with intent such as this without something hanging over our heads, whether it was my moral fortitude, his blasted prophecy, or simple fear. For the first time it was just the two of us. Yes, life hung in the balance, but war waited in the wings this one night. Tonight, we were center stage.

Bahlin brushed his tongue over my lower lip and I sighed into his mouth, opening and encouraging him to come inside. He took my offer, gently sweeping inside, then sucking playfully on my lower lip and smiling, releasing it with a *pop.* I smiled back. I looked into his eyes and realized that there was nothing different about Bahlin tonight than there had ever been when he'd taken me to bed. The last tumbler on my heart's lock fell. I was his. Because despite the fear that he'd deceived me with the words "I love you," I saw with crystal clarity that he'd been completely honest with me when he said he'd done things this way for his chance at love. I lifted my head out of his hand as I pressed my lips more firmly to his. He kissed me with renewed passion, and I felt his erection swelling formidably against my thigh. Propped on one elbow, he ran his free hand along my ribs and down my hip, and I sighed.

"Say the word and I'll stop, but say it now," he said softly into my collarbone and he kissed randomly along my neck, across my T-shirt, and scraped at my nipples through my bra. They pebbled without hesitation or apology, and I involuntarily arched into him.

"Bahlin," I sighed, and he froze. "What?"

"It's just, yeh've never been so relaxed, *mo muirnín,* and I'm no' sure what to make o' it," he said gently.

"I want you, and I want tonight to be special in case..." I couldn't say it. "Just in case." Tears burned in the back of my throat, and I knew he saw the fear for what it was.

"I love yeh more than life, Madeleine Dylis Niteclif," he said gruffly, his brogue thick. "But I will no' have yeh, willing or no, due to fear. I'll

250

gladly spend the night with yeh, in the same bed, but I'll no' take my pleasure until this is done." He continued kissing his way down my body, unbuttoning my jeans when he reached my waist.

I pushed up, confused. "I thought you said—"

"I said I'd no' take *my* pleasure." He grinned up at me, the wicked corners of his mouth twitching with suppressed laughter even as his eyelids drooped and hung at half mast. "No, I'll no' take *my* pleasure. I said nothin' aboat yours."

Dawn came and went. Bahlin and I didn't move until around noon. We were both naked, and I'd curled up against his side sometime during the night. He had most of the covers bundled about him and he was snoring softly. I grinned at him, remembering every detail of last night. He'd been true to his word and had not once achieved his own release, though there had been a couple of close calls, poor guy. But he'd made sure in every way but intercourse that I'd found my own pleasure...repeatedly.

I peeled the covers back and scooted under, his warmth a shock to my cool skin. He pulled me toward him in his sleep.

"*Tha gaol agam ort,*" he mumbled and kissed the top of my head.

"I love you, too, Bay."

He opened a sleepy eye and grinned wickedly.

"Oh no you don't, lover boy," I said. "I'm done. Finito. Terminado. Fini."

"I find it incredibly sexy that you can say finished in three different languages."

"You'd find it sexy at this point if I did laundry in a mumu with a cigarette hanging out of my mouth and a glass of bourbon in my hand at nine o'clock on a Tuesday morning. You're out of luck."

"Hmm. A nicotine-addicted, alcoholic of a housewife? I'll take one to go." He dove under the covers and I screeched, scrambling off the bed.

"Damn it, Bahlin, I'm done." I laughed as he emerged from under the covers looking disgruntled. "I'm sore, baby."

"What did you just call me?" he asked, cocking his head to the side.

"Sorry. Do you want me to try something else? Drago? Tesoro? Mi amor?"

"No. Baby, while very American, is the first pet name you've ever called me. I'd like to keep it."

He looked so sweet sitting there rumpled in the bed. I loved him so much. I smiled at him.

"Yes," I said.

"Yes, I can keep it, or yes, something else?" he asked, his browns drawing together with curiosity.

"Yes, something else. If I can still have it."

"Anything, my heart. What is it you want?"

"My marriage proposal," I whispered, butterflies roiling in my stomach.

"Come again?" he asked, stunned.

"Unless you've changed your mind," I said, suddenly feeling like a fool. *Why had I insisted on ruining a perfectly good thing by wanting more?* I wondered, berating myself. I turned away, intent on just dropping it and privately drowning myself in the toilet.

He swept me up in his arms and rained kisses all over my face. "Yes, yes, yes," he shouted, spinning me in a circle like a mad man.

I looked up at him, my head bouncing around like a maraca as he danced about the room performing some naked Scottish version of *Riverdance*. It wasn't pretty.

"I'll have my ma bring the Elder tonight, and we'll be bound in front of all the clans. Oh, Maddy, yeh've made me so happy."

"Shouldn't we wait?" I asked, hating like hell to rain on such a happy moment.

He stopped his maniacal hopping around and set me down. Taking me by the shoulders he said, "No, Maddy. Should the worst happen, I want yeh to have rights to all I own. Yeh'll never have to worry for money again, and the weyr will owe you their allegiance as my spouse. Yeh'll be protected until yehr passing." He cleared his throat and turned away, seeming somehow smaller.

"Bay? What are you not telling me? Please, tell me. Wait." I stalked around to face him, driving a finger into what, on a human, would have been his solar plexus.

He flinched.

"Is there a prophecy about tonight?" He took a deep breath and I screamed, "Tell me."

"No, Maddy. It's just that I'm scared. I've finally found yeh, and I don't want to lose what we have so soon. Forgive me for scarin' yeh."

I physically sagged, and he caught me. "Don't ever do that to me again," I said. "After we shower we're going down to the dining room, and we're going to talk about everything you know, Bay. Prophecies will be our first topic of conversation. Are you clear on this?"

My dragon just smiled.

Chapter Nineteen

We spent the day resting with Bahlin eating every two hours. He explained that this was normal for dragons preparing to go into a fight. "We burn a lot of fuel when we use our magic, Maddy."

"Does shifting constitute magic?" I wondered aloud.

"Ah, now that's a great debate. It's similar to the question about the chicken and the egg, but our version is which came first, the man or the monster?" He laughed out loud at his own hilarity. I just rolled my eyes. I didn't know if I could take a lifetime of bad jokes.

"Hellion called back and his coven will be there, along with three other covens nearly equal in power. He'll not be as powerful for having lost Gretta, but there are several pairs that will be joining us."

"Why are pairs important?" I asked again. *Apparently it was my evening for questions.*

"Ah, because magic is based on the laws of nature. And what is the unarguable fact of nature?"

"In everything there is a male and female?" I responded, posing it as a question just to see if I could.

"Almost. In everything in which there is a male and female, the two are more powerful for their joining. Together a male and female make life, love, happiness, sorrow, anger—all the most powerful emotions. And so when you pair a male to a female you get the tradition of Yin to Yang. One is never complete without the other."

As abstract as the thought was, it made sense. "So are dragons the same way?"

He hesitated only briefly, but I saw it. "They are."

"So I inhibit you by not being a dragon," I said.

"Dragon or not, you're a woman and I count myself lucky to be your *Trékkor.*"

"Is that like a spouse?" I asked...yet again. I had to stop with the questions. I was beginning to annoy myself.

"It is. You'll be my *Trékkar.* But don't fool yourself, Maddy. It's more serious than human wedding vows," he said gravely. "There's no such thing as divorce in the clans. Once you've committed to me, and I to you, we're together until one of us dies. Then there are rules about remarrying. Really you should have a crash course in this, but there's just no time."

"I hate to ask another question, because all my conversation seems to be punctuated with a question mark today, but if that's the case, what about the prophecy?"

Bahlin's eyes hardened. "We'll beat it somehow. I don't know how, exactly, but we'll have to find a way to change the nature of the thread on Clotho's spindle, my love."

All I could think was, *Damn straight.*

We went up to the rooftop deck, Bahlin jamming the door lock with a reverse version of his breaking and entering show from only a week ago. The hotel was one of the tallest buildings in this part of town, minimizing the threat of being seen. He stripped down to his skin and shoved his clothes into the same messenger bag we'd carried days ago. He smiled at me and then ripped through the change, one minute a man and seconds later a full-sized dragon. He took a deep breath and was suddenly cloaked, appearing as nothing more than a vaporous smudge on the night air.

"Feeling frisky tonight?" I laughed before I stepped into him. He scooped me up in his arms, and I was instantly wrapped in the miasma of his cloak. He clutched me tight and shot up into the air without hesitation, the buildings falling away. I realized that, for the first time, he was acting like a dragon with me. No apologies, no coddling, just all animalistic behavior. It was liberating and terrifying.

We flew to the northwest at breakneck speeds, the land and lochs blurring by in the clear light of the nearly full moon. If we failed, the full moon would be upon us and Tarrek's power would be stronger than since this had started. He'd have Imeena's heart, and his own evolution would be complete.

Over the sound of Bahlin's booming breath I heard the flap of other wings. Looking out across the sky I saw nothing in the moonlight, but I knew we weren't alone. And then a figure darted below us, and Bahlin bellowed with rage. He began to swoop toward the offending dragon when he drew up, seeming to remember I was there. He grumbled deep in his chest and I imagined that, for whatever the offense, when he caught the other dragon there'd be hell to pay.

We arrived at the predetermined spot about an hour before we were supposed to be there. Already the clearing was teaming with life despite the remoteness of the location. Men and women in robes stood segregated from the most beautiful creatures I'd ever seen. They seemed to glow in the moonlight, and I knew Imeena's vampire kiss had shown up to either save or avenge her. To the other side of the clearing were groups of dragons. How did I know? Some of them were still in dragon form—the rest were in some state of undress. I knew if I saw Leith or Aiden without clothes I would have to bleach my brain. I couldn't see my in-laws naked and come out unscarred.

"Niteclif," boomed out a disturbing voice.

"Oh good. Hellion's here already," I muttered, schooling my face into polite interest before I turned around. What I failed to remember was that all but the witches and wizards had exceptional hearing and there were some snickers from both crowds.

"Something funny?" he asked frostily.

"Definitely not," I answered. *Honest.* "Glad you made it." *Not as honest.* While I knew we needed him, I didn't feel we could trust him.

Bahlin was speaking to his mother, gesturing in an agitated manner.

"Hold that thought, Hellion," I said, walking toward Bahlin and Adelle. Reaching Bahlin's side I asked, "Problem?"

"The Elder isn't here," Bahlin hissed, staring across the clearing at his father. "Apparently *someone* felt he'd be safer at home."

"Ah, I see," I said, and I did. I pulled off the knives with which Bahlin had been coaching me. He'd improvised harnesses from his own leather belts, boots and duct tape, and I threw them to the ground.

Next I undid my own belt, ejected the clip on the Colt 1911 and dropped it to the ground. Yes, guns were illegal in the UK. But hello? It was owned by a dragon. Obviously the officials weren't asking the *right* questions.

"Maddy," Bahlin said, the warning clear in his voice.

"Sod off, Bahlin," I snapped, storming toward the *Glaaca*. "Leith."

"Niteclif," he answered coolly. "Problem?" he asked, repeating my comment with sarcasm.

I got right up to him and waved him close to me. Being an arrogant ass, he bent at the waist and got close to eye level with me. I gathered myself and, in a perfect single motion, dropped a roundhouse kick on him that would have snapped the spine of a lesser monster. Okay, so he stood perfectly still while I wound up and he didn't know I'd had three years of kickboxing and one year of karate, but really? Talk about arrogance.

My foot would be bruised tomorrow, but it was so worth it to see him trying to determine up from down as he lay sprawled in the heather. He stumbled as he tried to get up and I set up for another kick, but Aiden was in front of me.

"No, Maddy. You get the one, but not another," he said, and I thought I saw approval dancing across his features. Brylanna was at her father's side, helping him up. I backed away from the group of them, watching the blue dragons gathering around their fallen leader.

Leith made it to his feet and spit, discarding a useless tooth. "I imagine you'll pay for that."

"Send me the bill." I turned my back on him and walked back to Bahlin.

We milled about, waiting on the last of the vampires to arrive. Imeena's kiss had called in some favors and we had two other kisses joining us, one from Ireland and one from Galway. It wouldn't be long before our ragtag bunch was together, for better or worse. Leith stayed away from me, and I from him, until it was time to begin tactical planning. He stormed over to our group and announced that he'd have nothing to do with fighting with a human and wouldn't hold his weyr to a war he, himself, intended to avoid.

Bahlin stepped away from the group and said to his father in a low, carrying voice, "Da, what's the meaning of this?"

"Yeh're blinded by yehr cock, boy, and yeh can't see beyond the cunnie standing in front of yeh," he hissed, standing to his full height in a long-practiced move that reeked of intimidation. It was the first time I realized he was slightly taller than Bahlin.

"Yeh've crossed the line, Da. Say such again and I'll knock yeh on yehr ass for the second time in a night, old man," Bahlin said in a conversational voice. "Or I'll let her have at yeh again."

Several of the weyr laughed, but some of the older members looked shocked first, pissed off a second later.

"Speak to me that way again, boy, and yeh're forsaken."

There was an intake of breath, and Bahlin froze. It didn't take much to figure out his dad had just threatened to cut him off.

"So be it," Bahlin said. "When this is over, we'll settle who is *Glaaca* of this wyvern. But tonight, we need every able-bodied warrior we can have to put a stop to the crazed fae."

No one moved. If I'd thought being forsaken was bad, this was far worse. The other clans looked on with great interest, and even the other supernatural groups watched curiously.

"So be it," Leith said. "Let all stand as witness that from this point forward, Bahlin Drago is no longer my son. He is forsaken, and none must offer him aid."

I walked to Bahlin's side and took his hand. "Really?" I asked for the second time tonight. "Over a kick?"

"It's been a long time coming," said Aiden, standing at his brother's side. Adelle was weeping softly behind her husband, and Brylanna was nowhere to be seen in the crowd.

We pulled together quickly after the drama with Leith and Bahlin. Just before we were getting ready to depart for Castle Duncan, Leith announced he was leaving. He offered again to take any of his wyvern that didn't want to fight with him. He ordered Aiden to his side and the young dragon had to go. Bahlin said he wasn't old enough, or strong enough, to do otherwise.

"Brat's the one who did the fly-by on us earlier," Bahlin muttered. "Stupid sod was supposed to stay home," Bahlin said, looking down at me. His hair hung loose around his shoulders and, in the moonlight, cast shadows across his face. A feeling of foreboding skittered down my spine, and I reached up to push his hair from his forehead so I could see his eyes. He looked at me questioningly, and I just smiled.

"It's nothing," I said. "Just nerves."

"It will be over before you know it," he said.

"Did Aloysius ever fight in such a winner-take-all battle?" I asked.

"Truth? No," he said, sighing. "But times were different then."

That didn't give me any hope for the future.

The plan was that Bahlin would fly a shape-shifting wizard and me in to the edge of the castle grounds. The shape-shifter's alternate form was a horse. He'd shift and carry me to the castle on the hoof. Bahlin would follow in the air, watching for any dragon support Tarrek might have. I didn't like it, but all the arguing in the world hadn't changed anyone's mind that this was the best option.

Leith departed with one final offer to take any of his wyvern with him, but other than four members—two males, two females—and Aiden, he left alone. Even Adelle stayed, despite his order that she accompany him. Little Adelle stood her ground, and I was impressed. A few changes were made after Leith departed since we were an odd number now, then we were good to go.

Bahlin packed us up and we were off, the wizard riding behind me on Bahlin's back since it was easier to carry passengers astride than in his arms. He set down in a copse of mature trees just east of the castle. Lights were clearly burning in several of the downstairs windows.

"Take care, *mo chrid*, and I'll be with you again in no time." Bahlin took to the air and the wizard, a spritely little man named Henley, changed in front of my eyes. He was a gorgeous dapple gray, and he knelt to help me up on his back. I'd ridden for years as a child, and it really was like riding a bike. After a couple of false starts and one harsh reintroduction to the ground, we set off at a good pace toward the castle.

I felt it the minute we crossed the magical plane. Someone had set some type of wards around the house, and my wizard friend stumbled.

I leapt to the ground just as he changed back to his human form, his robes strangely intact.

"He's got magical folk inside," Henley said, "though I cannot tell what flavor they are. His wards are strong. Could be fae, could be other witches or wizards, or it could be dragons. I'm just not sure."

"No worries," I said, putting a hand out to stop Henley. "Go back twenty paces and flag down a dragon. Make sure the others know about the wards before they get here. Maybe Hellion's gang can do something to circumvent them."

"Good idea," he said and turned to head back without argument.

I wonder if I can train my dragon to do that. I smiled. *But then he wouldn't be Bahlin.*

I approached the front door of the castle, astounded that they actually had traditional doors. I knocked, and it swung open ominously.

"A little overdone, Tarrek," I called out.

"So you've found me out, little Niteclif," his voice rang out. "Pray tell, what gave it away?"

"Seriously, who else could it have been? Remember, I come from a long line of sleuths. You didn't stand much of a chance." I looked around the barren entry hall, surprised at the detailed woodwork and the beautiful parquet floors. I was going to feel bad about destroying the castle.

"What have you done with Imeena?" I asked, taking a further step into the entry.

A sultry female voice chuckled and I was jerked around only to find her teeth pressed to my throat. "I thought you came from a long line of sleuths, Madeleine," she said, scraping the skin just enough that it stung. Supernatural creatures of every flavor began coming out of the woodwork like roaches in the dark.

My heart thundered in my throat, ironically, just where she wanted it. "I thought you'd be part of the rescue mission, not one of the casualties," I said with bravery I didn't feel.

"Foolish little mortal. What did you think you were walking into?"

"I'll answer that," said Leith.

How many bad guys were *there?* I demanded of Tyr, knowing he could hear me.

"You should be able to," I said, "since you were at the pep rally."

He looked confused and I said, "Forget it. It's an Americanism. *This* you'll understand. How could you turn on your son?"

He strode across the floor, grabbed me from Imeena and slapped me twice in quick succession, my head rocking back. I tasted blood in my mouth and, feeling around with my tongue, felt a couple of loose teeth. I could feel panic beginning to build in the back of my throat and I worked to keep it held in check. If I reacted or screamed before the cavalry arrived, it would be a death-sentence for Bahlin who was circling close by in case of trouble. I was pretty sure this qualified, but I'd wait it out and try to keep Bahlin safe as long as I could.

Leith threw me across the floor, and I crashed head first into the wood paneling I'd admired moments ago. I was less impressed now that it had cracked my skull and left me seeing double. No, make that triple.

I heard a slithering sound and watched in horror as a shambling horde of bodies began coming down the main staircase and making their way into the hall.

"Tarrek," bellowed Leith. "Get in here. Your dead ha' come callin'." And he laughed. He *laughed*. There were all manner of people and supernatural creatures with sightless eyes and slow, uneven gaits. They were like zombies, but worse, they'd never died.

"They aren't exactly zombies, are they?" I asked, my words only slightly slurred.

"No, *Madeleine*, they are not zombies," Tarrek answered, his voice carrying from somewhere in the midst of the mobile bodies. They were like a walking shield. "They are a byproduct of the *cù sith* when it's controlled by a superior creature such as myself.

"You need to understand that this has all been a matter of besting Bahlin, *Madeleine*. I knew of the prophecy from Leith and Meyla, via Hellion. I had hoped you would choose me originally, and then I could rule the High Council without going through this extra effort. But you proved a stupid, sentimental mortal and I was forced to carry on with my original plan of collecting talents. What I couldn't have hoped for was that when you chose Bahlin, he would actually love you so much as he does. Or should I say did since tonight's his last on this plane?" Bodies shifted around the central figure but it was too fast for me to really see him. "I'd hoped for it, but more than anything it's just a bonus. I knew if I could create a competition where he figured himself the winner of your affections and then I destroyed you, he'd be easier to kill. I need his Dragon's Stone to complete the metamorphosis with the vampire's heart. I originally thought I'd need his body, but I've fared well with the change so far, wouldn't you say?"

He emerged from the army of bodies, and I gasped. He *was* transformed, his face part dog, his hair a white-blond like Hellions but with green undertones, and his body infinitely larger.

Nausea was building in my stomach, and I wasn't sure I was going to be able to pull off my part of the changed plans. "I have a question, Tarrek."

Leith looked at me sharply, realizing that this was a departure from my script.

"Go on, *Madeleine*," he said mockingly.

"Why did you need me here so badly? Or am I just bait?"

"Oh, don't flatter yourself," Imeena said sharply.

"Imeena," Tarrek bellowed before regaining control of his temper. "You're looking at my two generals, and this is my army, though everyone needs to remember who their king is." Tarrek called one of the other vampires forward. He came to Tarrek, and Imeena gave a small hiss.

"Not Darrek," she said, the slightest of pleading in her voice.

"It's not your choice, is it?" Tarrek took a deep breath and the man's back arched, something wispy and dark being pulled from his mouth and nose. Tarrek seemed to drink it down. The man stood there, eyes dead, and Tarrek said, "Join the others."

The man walked to the edge of Tarrek's army and stood, one of the mindless masses.

"Bahlin's place as either victim or soldier will be determined by how willing he is to fall into line."

Leith's body stiffened. "You promised me," he snarled, "you promised me I'd take his place in the new order."

Aha. Leith was jealous of Bahlin's political success.

Tarrek shrugged and said, "We'll see when it all comes down. I need the strongest warriors I can find, and so long as I have a Dragon's Stone, *any* Stone, I'll be content." He looked pointedly at Leith, who broke eye contact and glared at me. "Besides, it's so hard to tell who will be the better man for the job. Isn't that right, Jossel?"

A once-beautiful faerie nodded woodenly and my heart broke for him. All these people, all these mythological creatures, and I'd been unable to save them.

Leith trembled with rage, his eyes flashing to icy blue.

Imeena feigned a yawn, walking over to Tarrek and running a manicured hand suggestively across the crotch of his leather pants.

"Nice," I commented. "But I'd save some mystery for the bedroom, Imeena."

She hissed at me, her pupils eating into her eyes until they were a flat black.

A war cry ripped through the sounds of shuffling bodies and the roof four stories up peeled back. Using the diversion I unholstered Bahlin's pistol and shot Tarrek in the chest three times in fast succession. Blood and bone splattered against the faces of the nearest soulless creatures and they turned, watching Tarrek fall. Then they turned back and looked at me, blank faces devoid of any reaction.

"You fool," screamed Imeena. "He was the only thing controlling them." She moved like a flash toward the hole in the roof, scrambling up the stone walls like a spider. The other creatures charged the doors and windows, some flying, some running, but all prepared to fight. Outside the sounds of battle and the flashes of battle—gunfire, magic, fire and more—were already decorating the night.

"Coward," Leith yelled at her retreating form and then he turned on me. "You stupid bitch. You've ruined everything." He launched himself across the hall, shifting mid-leap, his dragon as large as Bahlin's though his scales were more battle-scarred and his eyes slightly milky. I could see several missing teeth in his gaping maw, but it was irrelevant, really. Sort of like saying an orca was ill equipped to catch a seal pup because the orca needed braces to correct its bite.

Bahlin's dragon trumpeted in rage, continuing to rip the roof back. I looked back at the advancing hostile dragon and Tarrek's army and I knew he'd never get here in time. I looked up at Leith and saw a string of Tarrek's soldiers fall onto his back from a break in the upper balcony railing caused by Bahlin's whipping tail as he fought his way into the building. The fallen bodies knocked Leith slightly off balance. He instinctively stuck his forearms out to catch his balance, and I saw the small soft spot over his heart. I squinted, trying to keep him in focus and I squeezed off shots until the gun dry fired. At least one ripped through his flesh, and he screamed in pain just as Bahlin got enough of the roof off to fully pull himself inside the hall. He gripped the back of his father's head in his jaws and ripped, covering me in gore when the body flopped to the floor.

A garbled voice said something indiscernible, and the soldiers turned to me. They fell on me in succession, and I was defenseless. I felt them ripping at my hair and clothes and pulling at my limbs with abandon. I screamed, biting, kicking and scratching to no avail. Suddenly a clawed hand reached through the bodies and Bahlin grabbed me, yanking me to his barrel chest one-handed as he tried to crawl up the walls and reach the night sky. Sounds of fighting could still be heard outside, but it was the voiceless scrabbling across stone and wood that came from behind us that terrified me. I was battered and bleeding, and it felt like my right shoulder had been fully dislocated. My right knee had been violently wrenched and was swollen and hot to the touch. Something was torn.

With a cry of shock laced with pain, Bahlin shuddered as something hit him hard. I struggled to see, but he clutched me closer and I heard a dragon screech at him. He bucked again and I knew we were in trouble. Bahlin set me down roughly on the empty balcony that jutted out from the second floor and looked at me. No one was home in that face but his monster.

"Go," I shouted, as the blue dragon behind him reared back to strike again.

Bahlin launched himself backward and took the other dragon to the floor. I struggled to draw myself to the edge so I could look over, but the stone balustrade was crumbled and piled too high for me to see much without standing, and I could only make it to one knee.

Sounds of intense fighting came from below and I nearly missed the sound of a body being dragged across the floor behind me. I threw myself sideways, away from the sound, and the stone railing I'd been propped against disintegrated into dust. I instinctively reached behind myself to break my fall. The jarring impact shoved my swollen shoulder back into joint, and I screamed.

Tarrek stared at me, blood bubbling from his mouth with every breath.

"I shot you," I rasped, my throat raw. "I know I hit you with cold iron bullets. How..."

"You hit my lungs but missed the heart, bitch," he said, pushing himself up to sitting. "I'll heal," he gasped, blood and spittle raining on the floor around him in a macabre pattern.

I tried to push myself up but it was too much work. I lay there, knowing I was going to die. I reached behind me with my left hand and grasped my last hope. It was the one knife Leith hadn't known about, the one that hadn't been ripped off me by the soulless, grasping hands. I fumbled, trying to get the knife from the tape holster stuck to my skin, but it had been fashioned for my right hand.

"Don't do it, Maddy," Tarrek gasped, beginning to raise a hand toward me. I knew the hand held my death.

I ripped the tape holster from my back, tearing skin away at the same time. Blood ran down my back and seeped between my butt cheeks, pooling under my right hip. That was going to leave a mark. Pulling the knife from the homemade holster, I shoved myself to my feet, my right knee refusing to hold any weight.

"Come on, you jackass," I croaked, weaving like a drunk.

"So eager to die? I should have killed you the first night, at the stones."

"That is *so* canned," I snarked, rolling my eyes. Then I paused, looking at him. "That was *you*?"

"It was."

"Did you put my family tree in the car?"

He cocked his head to one side, considering. "No, I did not." He coughed and some of his discharge splattered me. "Enough."

Tarrek pushed himself to standing, and I knew this was my one chance. I gritted my teeth just as he raised his hands, opening his mouth to begin chanting under his breath, and I pushed off with my good leg. I fell into him and sliced across his face with my knife, splitting his lips horizontally to stop the spell. Blood splattered my face and hands, and I dropped the knife as I fell. I was a dead woman.

Bodies of Tarrek's soldiers rounded the corner at an awkward run. I lay there and accepted death. It had ironically taken me ten days to finally live—to make a wish, to fall in love, and now to die.

A horrible roar came from below as a dragon launched itself over the railing at our little party, shifting into a woman before hitting the balcony.

"Tarrek," screamed Brylanna. "No." She held him to her breast, sobbing. "You must stay with me my love."

That explained a lot. I heard a commotion behind me and Bahlin pulled himself over the ledge. Looking at me he froze and I whispered, "Finit."

With a roar of pain and rage, Bahlin belched out a column of fire that devoured the two lovers, taking them into death's embrace together, but not before Tarrek's final spell was cast. It blew me back into the wall. Bahlin turned to me in slow motion and began to shift back to human. The horror on his face was the last thing I saw before darkness claimed me.

I sat up and was amazed that nothing hurt. I looked around and realized that Tyr was at my side.

"You may have set a record," he said and almost smiled. "Shortest Niteclif service in the history of all Niteclifs. Do I congratulate or console you?"

I thought about that for a minute. "Wait. I can't be dead," I challenged, looking around for proof, but there was none to be had.

"You have a choice, Madeleine Dylis Niteclif," Tyr said. "Do you stay, or do you go?"

"Go where?" I asked skeptically. "Because there are options, apparently."

Tyr tipped his head back and laughed but sobered quickly as something happening over my shoulder caught his eye. I turned to see what he was looking at and I froze, my heart seizing in my chest.

Bahlin was bent over me giving me CPR. Not good. He was

working feverishly, but I obviously wasn't responding.

"Put. Me. Back," I said, my voice and posture uncompromising. "I mean it, Pops."

"Ah, you're shitted. No, wait. That's not right. Hmm. You're pissed. That's it. You're pissed," Tyr said, look pleased with himself for getting the slang right.

"Yes, I'm *pissed*. Put me back or show me how to get back." I turned and looked at Bahlin who continued with chest compressions, a new franticness taking over his earlier smooth efforts. Behind him lay the smoking remains of corpses. They were so charred and mangled, piles of limbs sticking this way and that, it was impossible to tell who had died.

"Do you love him?" Tyr asked.

"I do," I said, pain beginning in my chest. I couldn't breathe. I couldn't...

"Do you believe he loves you?" Tyr asked. I didn't answer for a moment, and Tyr asked again. "I need to know, Maddy."

"He does love me. I have to believe it," I said, turning my back on Bahlin so I could answer Tyr without the distraction Bahlin presented. "I don't want to die, Tyr."

"Then live."

I slammed back into my body with the force of a Mac truck wrestling with a squirrel. I was the squirrel. Everything hurt and Bahlin's chest compressions felt like they may have cracked my sternum. I involuntarily arched my back off the ground, my mouth gaping as I sucked in air, falling back to the floor with a muffled thud.

Bahlin shouted, then grabbed me and pulled me close. "This is goin' teh hurt yeh like the devil, *mo muirnín,*" he murmured, "but there's no choice for it." And then he bit me. Fire breathed through my body, the flames licking at my raw, open wounds the same as wildfire consumes everything, with indiscriminate speed. I swear I saw light flicker behind my eyelids as I clenched them shut, trying to breathe through the pain. But it was too much and I began to struggle, screaming and begging and pleading with him to stop. It was so much worse than the last time...so much worse. My heart stuttered and I thought, *Beat, damn you,* and I focused on its rhythm, willing it into compliance. It was horrible. Bahlin lifted his head and I foolishly thought it was over, but he was just moving on to different wounds. It went on and on, with Bahlin shifting his bite now and again, renewing my screams and pleas. I quit struggling before he made it to my lower body, and passed out somewhere around the bite to my knee. This time Tyr didn't visit me. Smart deity.

I came to lying on the grass outside, Bahlin back in dragon form and crouched over me as a small woman I vaguely recognized from earlier went over my wounds. Bahlin was bleeding all over the grass and the night sky had swallowed the moon so there was no light by which to see his wounds. It must be late. I tried to lift a hand to him, but my arms weren't working yet.

"You know what you've done, dragon," she said in heavily accented English.

He glared at her.

"Do not get testy with me you giant reptile," she barked. I liked her. Noticing I was awake, she smoothed her hand across my head and I relaxed some. "It will take days for you to recover, Niteclif. Your dance card was already full when death came calling, and it took you closer to the edge than a human has a right to go. Rest." She rose and had turned away when a voice rang out through the night.

"Niteclif. I demand my justice. Either stand and face me in front of the coven, or I invoke my right for immediate reparation as per our agreement," Hellion yelled so that everyone heard him.

Seriously? I thought. I could hardly move. He'd kill me all over again, and dying freaking *hurt.* I wasn't going through it twice in one night.

"No," I croaked out, my voice barely above a whisper.

Bahlin hummed low in his chest, and I rolled my head to look at him. He shifted subtly, putting himself closer to me in case I needed him. But he let me have enough space to see Hellion.

"What did you say?" Hellion asked, incredulous.

"I said, no," I croaked again. I tried to roll to my side, but things were still not working right and my whole body ached.

"I *demand* reparation," he shouted.

"I can't, Hellion. Give me a few days and we can talk about what happened to Gretta. But nothing we do tonight will change what's happened."

Bahlin huffed out a sigh, and I realized that my foggy brain hadn't chosen its most diplomatic public voice.

Hellion's head fell back, and he bellowed to the night sky, "You owe me a life."

"But it won't be mine," I said softly. And then I looked at Bahlin. "And it won't be his. I'm not guilty."

Hellion raised his hands as if to strike from a distance, and Bahlin threw himself between us. He grunted when whatever magic Hellion had thrown at him struck his abused back, but he didn't go down. Scooping me up in his arms, Bahlin shot into the night sky, cloaking us with the first flap of his wings. The ground fell away as Bahlin's humming began, and I started to warm up.

Behind me I heard Hellion scream at our retreating forms, "Game on, Niteclif. Game. On."

No doubt.

About the Author

Denise Tompkins lives in the heart of the South where the neighbors still know your name, all food forms are considered fry-able and bugs die only to be reincarnated in aggressive, blood-craving triplicate. Thrilled to finally live somewhere that can boast 3 ½ seasons (winter's only noticeable because the trees are naked), her favorite season is definitely fall. It's the time of year when the gardens are just about to pass into winter's brief silence, and the leaves are out to prove that nature is the most brilliant artist of all.

A life-long voracious reader, Denise has three favorite authors. Why three? Because favorite authors are like chips: a person can't have just one. Her little house was so overrun with books last year that her darling husband bought her an e-reader out of self-preservation. He was (legitimately) afraid she might begin throwing out pots and pans to make room for more books, and he didn't want to starve.

Her debut novel, *Legacy*, is the first book in The Niteclif Evolutions.

You can find out more about Denise by visiting her website, www.denisetompkins.net, or by following her on Twitter, @DeniseJTompkins.

Trust no one...except the one who walks in the dark.

Key of Solomon
© 2011 Cassiel Knight
Relic Defender, Book 1

Anthropology PhD candidate Lexi Harrison never bares it all when she belly dances for a strip club crowd. She doesn't have to—she's that good. Every performance earns money toward her degree, and restores the sense of power that her painful childhood ripped away.

Something is different about tonight. A man whose silver gaze seems to touch her skin beneath her veils. When a rowdy customer crosses the line, he comes to her rescue with the speed of a falcon—complete with wings.

Mikos Tyomni has never seen anyone dance the raqs sharqi like Lexi. Trust his tormentor, Archangel Michael, to put him in close contact with the cause of his downfall: a mortal woman. Particularly this mortal woman. The Defender. He has only thirty days to win her trust before Hell's deadliest demons attempt the mother of all prison breaks.

No matter how sexy the messenger is, Lexi's career plans don't include some crazy idea that she's the last line of defense against the forces of evil. Until her university mentor's murder leaves her holding the key to Hell. And fighting a losing battle against a passion with the unholy power to bring down Heaven...

Warning: This title contains a dark and sexy fallen angel, bad-ass demons, a heroine with kick-assitude tossed together with mythology, archeology and a shape-shifting rock with a fondness for the gangsters of the 1920s.

Available now in ebook and print from Samhain Publishing.

It's all about the story...

Romance

HORROR

www.samhainpublishing.com

CPSIA information can be obtained at www.ICGtesting.com
Printed in the USA
BVOW071416130812

297762BV00001B/6/P